THE CANNAWAYS

THE CANNAWAYS

GRAHAM SHELBY

Doubleday & Company, Inc.
Garden City, New York
1978

Library of Congress Cataloging in Publication Data

Shelby, Graham, 1939–
The Cannaways.

I. Title.
PZ4.S5433Can 1978 [PR6069.H42] 823'.9'14
ISBN: 0-385-09424-8
Library of Congress Catalog Card Number 76–56335

First Edition

For Sallie.

CONTENTS

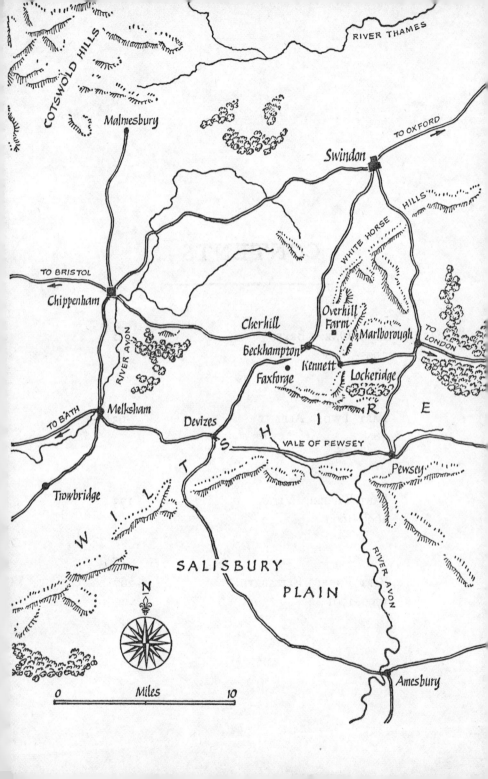

THE CANNAWAYS

PART ONE

BRYDD

1697–1698

ONE

Stripped by the season, the countryside was bleak and desolate. It was evening now. The rain had set in and the light played tricks.

The road that ran westward climbed from a stand of leafless trees and ventured, unpaved and unlighted, across the Wiltshire downs. Alone on a ridge above the trees the young rider had sensed movement below him and thought it the passage of deer. He'd tipped his hat to keep the rain from his face and counted three of them. But by then he had known what they were, who they were: three dark-coated horsemen directing their mounts across the road and into the stand of trees.

He wondered why he had ever taken them for deer. They might have been at first glance, for they'd crossed the road quickly and in silence. But they'd made no attempt to conceal the weapons that looked like post horns—blunderbusses packed tight with moulded shot, the highwayman's loudmouthed friend.

Now that he'd recognised what they were, he could guess their purpose. Robbery, if things went well. If not, then murder.

He thought, I've heard about them often enough, and now I've seen them for myself. And then another, more urgent thought: pray God they've not looked up.

He jerked the reins and urged his horse down from the ridge

and out of sight of the trees. Leaning well back in the saddle, he let the animal slither and scramble to the foot of the grassy slope. He would be safe for the moment, though if the highwaymen had seen him it would not take them long to give chase.

As he reached level ground, the rider gentled his horse, then peered up at the ridge, half expecting to see one of the frock-coated figures levelling at him from the skyline. There was no one as yet, but he knew he must now decide which way to go—eastward along the shallow valley to the lights and warmth of the "Blazing Rag," or west below the ridge and thence on to the downland road in the hopes of warning a traveller that a snare had been set for him. Coach or cart or horseman, someone was approaching from the west, someone the brigands intended to halt and rob, maim or murder.

Thinking himself a fool for having stayed so late on the hills, the lean young man glanced enviously in the direction of the inn, then turned away and spurred along the valley and into the dismal December night.

⁑

The rain drummed against his hat, weighted the hem and buttoned cuffs of his greatcoat and threatened to unfoot the horse. Aware that he must scale the ridge again if he was to find the road and deliver his warning, Brydd Cannaway hammered in with his heels. The trees were half a mile behind him now, and the animal bunched itself for the ascent, slithered on the chalky slope and reared back into the valley. Lurching in the saddle, Brydd stifled his impatience, leaned forward to slap the mount gently on the neck, then took it to the far side of the floor. He'd make a direct run at the hill, counting on the horse to go up straight and on his own ability to control it. There was no time to search out an easier route, for by then the traveller might have gone past and rattled on down to the trees.

He tightened his grip on the reins and sent the animal head on at the slope. It plunged across the valley, raced up the lower incline, slowed and faltered on the steeper pitch. Brydd lay almost flat, growling encouragement as the horse dug and scrabbled its way to the ridge. They went on, reaching the road in a flurry of mud and water, with only the tops of the trees showing to the east and nothing to the west but rain.

It was impossible to tell if a vehicle had passed. New and old alike, the wheel ruts and hoofmarks had been softened and filled with water. If the carriage or rider had not yet come along, well and good. But if it had already descended to the trees, then the highwaymen might even now be pocketing their spoils, or riding up the slope toward him, on the way back to their hideout at Cherhill . . .

Brydd Cannaway removed his hat, squeezed the water from it, then jammed it back on his head. He twisted the sleeves of his coat and squinted westward along the road. "Come if you're coming," he muttered. "I'm not sitting out the night."

He turned sharply in the saddle, imagining he heard the sound of voices and the watery drum of hoofbeats. He saw the treetops as black, high-crowned hats, the gusts of rain reflected from brass-bound pistols and the muzzles of loudmouthed friends. He wondered if the highwaymen would be in range the moment they saw him; and worse, if their weapons would be accurate, even in the fading light.

Why not? he thought. They must have had the practice.

Turning westward again, Brydd let his horse find its way along the rain-washed road. As he did so, the sky darkened perceptibly above the downs.

Then, peering as much to find his way as for signs of the travellers, he saw a faint glimmer ahead. Thinking he'd misjudged his progress and come too close to the village of Cherhill, he reined in sharply. It'd be a poor business to avoid the ambushers, only to ride into their nest. He wiped the rain from his face, looked again and saw that the single light had now divided into two flickering specks. Lanthorns perhaps, the crude oil lamps that shepherds used at night on the hills. And then the lights spread and brightened and became a yellow glow that burned steadily toward him through the drifting curtains of rain. This was why the highwaymen were out. This was their intended victim, carriage or cart or wagon.

As it approached, the glow smudged the edges of the road and revealed four high-stepping horses, the driver perched above them on a wide hammercloth bench. The light spilled from glassed-in lanterns, each suspended from the corner of a stiff tented roof, the polished canopy covering a brilliantly decorated carriage—but then it was time to stop gaping and flag down the coach.

Snatching his hat from his head and praying that the patient horse would hold its ground, Brydd stood in the stirrups and waved the drab grey banner.

❊

There was, as yet, no reason for the driver to stop. The man in the road might be a harmless lunatic—harmless unless he stayed there to collide with the oncoming team. Or he might be a drunkard, lonely for company or in need of direction. Or, more ominously, he might be any of the vermin described on the notices that flanked the Great West Road—Highwaymen, Spoiler, Shooter or Mobster. It might be this one's job to play the innocent and impede the coach, whilst his cronies prepared to surround it. Whoever he was, there was no call to heed him, not in this weather, on this desolate stretch of the way.

Then, almost at the last, the driver changed his mind, for he suddenly recognised the bareheaded young man who barred his path. Cursing fluently, he hauled in, kicking the brake bar and bracing himself against the backboard of the seat. Wooden drag shoes clamped against the wheel rims, skidding as they fought to gain purchase on the hoops. The reins slid back through their series of rings and guiders. The body of the coach dipped forward and down, its springs quivering under the strain. The team lost momentum, the animals barging each other as they swayed and staggered. Mud spewed from the wheels and from the *mêlée* of hooves. The carriage bounced as the weight lifted from the springs, and then the horses broke their rhythm and slowed, blowing, to a halt . . .

The driver lifted his foot cautiously from the brake bar. He spat rain and glared at Brydd Cannaway. The men had been friends for years, but it would put a strain on things if Brydd now produced a pistol.

Instead, he settled back in the saddle, urged his horse alongside the cloth covered bench, then grinned with surprise. "Step Cotter? I thought you'd given up hard work for an easy life at Chippenham."

"And you," Step countered, "is this how you pass your evenings, waylaying a carriage now and then?"

Brydd shook his head and reached up to greet him. But before he could tell Step of the ambushers waiting in the trees, another voice barked, "*Hände hoch!*" And then, correcting itself, "Raise your hands!"

Brydd stared up at the driver, saw him scowl a warning, then glanced along the nearside of the coach. A man was leaning out of the window, couching a heavy-barrelled pistol. His gloved finger was curled around the trigger, his other hand shielding the pan and hammer from the rain.

"*Hände hoch, du verdammter Stehler!* Raise them, you bloody thief!"

Brydd's agreeable surprise at meeting Step soured with the words. He was soaked to the skin, cold and weary and well aware of the picture he presented. But he was no bloody thief. Not in his own language, nor in the foreigner's guttural bark.

Holding the reins high against his chest so the passenger could see he was unarmed, he guided his horse toward the window. As he did so he snatched a sidelong glance at the decoration of the coach. Divided into three panels, like pictures on a wall, the body of the vehicle was painted with pastoral scenes, this one a swing-bridge with barges, this a picnic on some gently sloping lawn, this a hunting trip in the forest, the scene complete with tents and tables and a dead boar turning on a spit.

Not yet opposite the window, Brydd raised his eyes from the panels and gazed impassively at the man. "Time is against us," he said calmly. "You'd do well to take in your pistol. You may need it before long."

A sudden splash and curse behind him told him that Step had jumped from the bench. Slapping at the muddied hem of his cape, the driver ploughed his way to the window. "I know this man," he explained. "He's a lifelong friend and an accomplished wheelwright in the Kennett Vale." In case that was unclear to the foreign traveller, and might be thought suspect, Step added quickly, "He makes carts and wagons, and if he's chosen to come

out in the rain and halt us, it'll be for good reason, you can count
on that." Then he looked up at Brydd and pleaded, "Tell us what
it's about. Tell us why we're stopped."

Hearing him, but with his gaze still fixed on the passenger,
Brydd said, "When the pistol's been taken in, not before."

There was another voice, a woman's voice honed with impatience. "Sit back, Carl-Maria. *Sie hatten uns schön erschossen,
wenn sie wollten!* Do you not think they would have attacked us
by now? Sit back, brother. We have no time for your—displays."

The man stared at Brydd, then suddenly snatched in his pistol
and turned from the window. As he withdrew, Brydd seized the
opportunity to glance at Step, who nodded toward the unseen
woman in the carriage, pressed his fingertips to his lips and
mimed a kiss. That done, he splashed away and clambered back
on the hammercloth bench. So, Brydd acknowledged, the foreign
woman's a beauty, is she? Then I'd better improve my view. He
clicked his tongue and the horse went forward to the window.

✸

The young wheelwright gazed into the coach, his attention
divided between what met his eye and what he had for so long
dreamed of seeing.

A glance at the woman was reward enough for the time spent
thundering along the valley and standing guard on the rain-swept
road. But the greater reward was the coach itself.

It was this that repaid the endless hours Brydd Cannaway had
spent on the hills above the Great West Road. It was why he had
been there on this dank December day; it was why he had been
there throughout every Sunday afternoon for the past weeks and
months and years. It was the time he treasured most, for he could
then watch from the ridge and make use of his chalks and charcoals, sketching the coaches that he one day intended to build.

It was hard to avoid staring at the woman, for she was dressed
to invite attention. Even so, his gaze was diverted, for the interior
of the carriage was illuminated by shielded candles, something he
had never seen in an English coach. But this was a foreign vehicle, the body lined with mahogany panels, the underside of the
roof painted to show the moon and stars, the sun rising behind a

bank of silver clouds. There was glass in the windows, and crimson leather curtains dyed to match the seats.

And there, turning toward him again, was the man he'd heard addressed as Carl-Maria, the pistol clenched on his knee. He was a sullen, box-faced man, and Brydd had already decided they'd never be the best of friends. It was clear that Carl-Maria felt the same.

Beside him sat an older man, pinched in the jaw but with an expression of amused and weary tolerance. He had not yet spoken, but he now inclined his head in a brief, courteous greeting. "As you can see," he murmured, "the pistol has been taken in. Are there further demands, *mein Herr*, or will you tell us why we've come to a halt?"

"For your own safety," Brydd informed him. "I believe there are highwaymen in ambush at the foot of the slope."

Facing the men, and seated alone on the other crimson bench, the woman started in alarm. "Highwaymen? *Die Strassenräuber?*" The older man shrugged, admitting the possibility. Brydd ignored the rain, ignored the glaring Carl-Maria and glanced unabashed at the woman.

Her appearance was far more in keeping with Step Cotter's impudent kiss than the harsh tone she'd used on her brother. Her face was all but free of paint and powder and the black velvet spots that were thought so attractive, though her hair was piled fashionably high and topped with a white lace cap, the material pleated and layered. She protected her shoulders with a stole, leaving the upper curve of her breasts uncovered. This would not have done, of course, in the villages of the Kennett Vale, though it was said that in London and Bristol the ladies were measured—and admired—by the daring of their bosoms and the modesty of their waists. By the nipple, it was said, and by the nip.

No more than a moment or two had elapsed since the coach had splashed to a halt. Brydd looked at the men, again ignoring Carl-Maria in favour of his companion. "I believe I saw three of them take a position in the trees. I'd say they knew of your approach."

The older passenger gazed at him. "So. You were there when they entered the trees?"

"Above them. On a ridge."

"And you chose to ride out here and warn us. Is that it, *mein Herr*?"

Sensing the man's suspicions, Brydd retorted, "No, sir. Not just you. Anyone. It might have been someone I know." Aware that the others were watching him, he held the older man's gaze; no easy thing when the rain was sweeping his face. And then Carl-Maria muttered something. The language was unknown to Brydd, though the message was clear enough, sharp and dismissive. He suddenly lost patience with the man and snapped, "Speak English, if you will, then I'll be better acquainted with your opinions. If I was not out here, sponging up the rain on your behalf, you would now be a mile along the road—and very likely dead. Do you understand the word, sir, dead?"

Answering for his companion, the older man said, "We understand it, *mein Herr*. We have also heard the driver speak well of you, and we accept your warning." He half rose from his seat and with the minimum of fuss said, "My name is Johann von Kreutel; my wife, Annette von Kreutel; my—what do you say?—yes, my brother-in-law, Carl-Maria Schoenholz. We are indebted to you, Master, ah—"

"Cannaway. Brydd Cannaway. But you've incurred no debt. I told you, I'd have stopped anyone."

Johann smiled at the young man's bluntness, then asked, "Is it wise to go on?"

"It's not wise to be on the road at all, this late. But you can't go back, not now. You must have passed through the village of Cherhill with the last of the light, and you'll not get through it again, now the darkness is down. It's where the highwaymen have their nest, at Cherhill."

Annette looked from Brydd to her husband. Carl-Maria shifted the pistol on his knee. Johann pondered the information. "I see. So you'd advise us to go forward?"

"There's not much choice in the matter. However, there's a way it might be done." He waited for Johann's nod, then continued, "The only way we'll get past them is if we take them by surprise, and for that we'll need darkness and silence. As I said before, I think they've been warned of your approach, though they'll be expecting to see the lanterns. We'll have to extinguish them, *and* the candles, then go as quiet as possible down the slope. Step Cotter is one of the best drivers in Wiltshire; you can count on him to handle the team. But we must keep silent." He looked directly at Carl-Maria. "The men I saw were carrying blunderbusses, and I've no doubt their belts are well filled with pistols. If they let fly at us, then by all means return their fire—it might spoil their aim, or make them duck. But on no account shoot first, for it'll mark our position. The plan's to dash past them, not engage in a battle." He turned to Johann again, waiting for the man to accept or reject his advice.

"Very well, Master Cannaway. We will go on. And in silence."

"Are there other pistols, sir, apart from—"

"Herr Schoenholz has another. I, too, have a brace of them." He lifted a flat leather case from the well of the coach and set to, loading and priming the pistols. Brydd asked the passengers to lower the glass in the windows. "It'll be a cold and wet journey from now on, but glass that's shattered by a bullet—" He broke off in deference to Annette, then suggested that the lady keep as low as possible. Finally he said, "With your permission, sir, I'll sit up with Step."

Johann von Kreutel was hard put not to smile. The lean, rain-soaked Master Cannaway had spotted the highwaymen, taken it on himself to warn the travellers, advised them how best to brave the ambush—and now asked permission to share the unprotected driving bench. Johann laid aside his pistols, managed another courteous nod and murmured, "As you will, *mein Herr*. And you may depend on our silence in here."

Tugging gently on the reins, Brydd moved away from the window and blinked up at Step. "Did you hear what was said?"

"That you'd keep me company. Aye, and damn foolish it sounded. Will you douse the rear lanterns whilst I do these?"

One by one the outside lights and interior candles were extinguished, the pool of light growing weaker, smaller in its span. Brydd tethered his horse behind the coach, splashed his way forward and climbed on to the bench. As he did so, Step Cotter raised the final glass orb and blew on the oil-soaked wick.

There was now nothing to see. They were blind coachmen with

blind passengers and a blind team to draw them. Pray God the brigands were similarly afflicted.

❊

Brydd heard his friend catch up the reins and settle his heels against the sloping dashboard of the carriage.

He heard the horses blow and stir.

He heard the water drip from the tented roof and from the traces and from the curled metal stems that held the lanterns.

He heard the rain wash and scuttle across the road, rapping for entry on the decorated doors. He felt it on his neck and face, and the clinging dampness of it on his body and inside his gloves and turn-top boots.

And then he heard himself say, "Take it on, Step. As quiet as you can to the slope."

The carriage creaked and groaned, settling as it moved. The wheels cut their way through the mud, squeezing it out beneath the rims. Totally blind to their progress, the men could only wait for the angle of the bench to steepen, indicating that they'd reached the brow and were now at the head of the slope.

After a while Step whispered, "Is that it? It felt—"

"Not yet. Pass me the whip."

They went on, the horses nervous and uncertain, the wheels sinking and rising, the coach yawing like a mackerel boat at sea. It was Brydd's turn to say, "There, we're dipping." But he, too, was wrong, and the vehicle lifted again, rolling forward through the half-drowned dark.

Then the bench angled steeply and the horses began to trot. Brydd remembered an accident he'd witnessed, a high-set carriage that had descended this very slope and run full tilt into a fallen log. Within the instant, the charging horses had gone down and the carriage had twisted and rolled, reduced to kindling as it crashed to the foot of the slope. If a log had been placed here to-night . . .

Smothering the thought, he judged that the trees were fifty yards ahead, maybe less, and sent the whip snaking above the team. Beside him, Step thrashed with the reins, though the young men stayed silent, aware that the sounds of their approach might yet be covered by the rain. Perhaps forty yards more, or thirty,

and they'd reach the trees . . . Twenty yards more, and the rain
was drumming nicely . . .

The lift of the wheels made them gasp, but they knew they
were now on the level. They'd cleared the slope and could sense
the black, fleshless fingers cupped ahead of them. Not even ten
yards to go . . . The brigands had missed their chance . . .

Brydd opened his mouth to shout success when the nearside of
the carriage seemed to explode with the flash of Carl-Maria's pistol. Even before the bloom of light had faded there were others,
bright enough to show Step Cotter clap a hand to his face,
enough to show the colour of his blood.

Brydd let the whip fall away. He snatched at the reins and held
the stricken driver on the bench. More lights blossomed from the
roadside, each accompanied by the flat bang of a pistol, or the
boom of a blunderbuss. The coach was jarred by the impact of
lead balls and fragments of metal, and there was the double snap
of Johann's pistols as the coach hurtled between the trees.

Carl-Maria Schoenholz, who had fired too early, now fired again
too late. The brigands were behind them, howling their anger and
cheated of their prey. Ahead was the flickering beacon of the
"Blazing Rag," not strong enough to illuminate the road, but a
lighthouse for the mackerel boat.

His left arm around Step, his right dragging back on the reins,
Brydd Cannaway took the horses along the flat and into the
cobbled yard. Someone had seen the flashes, for men were running from the inn, locals and visitors and the landlord, Sam Gilmore. Ignoring their shouts, Brydd wrestled the team to a halt,
abandoned the reins and turned Step's face to the light. A shard
of metal had struck him midway between his left eye and ear,
though, thank God, it had turned on impact, sparing his sight.
Even so, it had cut him to the bone and all but sliced away the
upper half of his ear.

For the moment at least he was deafened and blinded by blood,
and he was thankful that Brydd leaned close to tell him, "We'll
have you washed and filled with brandy, my friend, then stitched
up good as new."

"It's a damn thing," Step managed. "I'd have sworn we were
safely by."

"Yes." Brydd nodded grimly. "So would I."

Willing hands helped the driver from the bench. Brydd glanced at Sam Gilmore, then swung himself to the ground and made his way to the nearside door of the coach. He glimpsed Johann von Kreutel and his wife, apparently unharmed, swung open the door and dragged Carl-Maria bodily from the vehicle. The man stumbled out, caught his balance and went back heavily against the stepping board.

"On no account shoot first," Brydd measured, "for then we'll mark our position. But you *did* shoot first, Herr Show-and-Hold! You poked out your pistol and banged at shadows and told them where we were!"

The man prattled in German; and then, in English, "There is no harm. We have not been struck."

"No, sir, not you! But the driver has been hit, pointed out to them by your flash. It was all set going by you and by your—what the lady said—displays!"

Carl-Maria had been readying himself for a show of indignation, but he now recoiled from the word Brydd had used. It was something Annette had accused him of before, his *Hochstaplerei*, his noisy heroics. He did not like to hear it from his sister, and far less from an ignorant foreigner. "*Sei vorsichtig*," he snarled. "You take care what you say to me."

But by then Brydd's anger had turned to concern for his horse. He left the man to bluster and strode to the rear of the carriage, ashamed of himself for having put the box-faced creature before the well-being of his mount. It broke the habit of a lifetime, for what value was a horseman if he did not first attend to his horse?

He discovered a torn ridge in the animal's flank and found a spent lead ball in its mane. He pocketed the shot and murmured quietly, apologising as to someone he loved. Then he slipped the reins and led the horse across the yard and through the arch to the stables. All the while he patted the beast and talked to it, attempting to re-establish the trust he'd created over the years. He no longer cared a damn for the travellers or their fine painted coach. Johann von Kreutel seemed intelligent and considerate, his wife well worth a stare. But Herr Show-and-Hold was nothing more than a puffed-up coward, just the type to cause injury and distress. To hell with him. What mattered now was that the horse should be gentled, be made to know it was safe. If not, it would never again trust its master, for fear he'd leave it abandoned.

❋

Scowling at what he'd seen, the burly, grey-haired Sam Gilmore emerged from the kitchen and walked through the covered yard that separated the stables from the rear of the inn. He'd left an ostler in charge of the four mud-spattered horses, the travellers installed in a private room at the eastern end of the building and Step Cotter in a chair in the kitchen, a flask of brandy at his side. Hopefully, the driver would drink enough to dull the pain of his wound and not mind the fresh anguish when the skin was sewn together.

He reached the lighted stall, watched Brydd scoop a ration of oats into a trough, then said, "You got up to your neck in things, by the look of it. Was it an ambush in the trees?"

Brydd tossed the shovel in the bin, replaced the wooden lid and came forward, patting the horse. He nodded at Sam's question and asked, "Are they staying?"

"Aye, and they've not yet done with you, it seems. The older one wants to see you when you've finished. What were you doing out there, on the road?"

"What I always do, of a Sunday. I was sketching the vehicles that passed. Then the rain came, and I was about to return when I saw some riders go into the trees. It wasn't hard to guess their purpose."

Sam Gilmore shook his head. "One of these days you'll go a mile too far, or stay an hour too long, in pursuit of your sketches. You've a talent for it, I grant you, but to sit on that forsaken road and let the darkness come down on you—" He matched the first despairing shake with another. He'd a soft spot for the seventeen-year-old wheelwright, though there was much about Brydd Cannaway that gave Sam cause to shake his head. The young Cannaway was ambitious, and made no secret of his desires. He wished to build coaches. Not only build them, but design them, decorate them, drive them, paint his name across the doors. Well, there was nothing wrong with that, so long as he had the sense to come in from the hills before dark, before the Cherhill gang spread their net.

Brydd inquired, "Is Step all right? I'll see *him* before the passengers. My God, Sam, if it hadn't been for that idiot with his pistol—"

"Start from the start," the innkeeper growled. "You were up on the road—"

"Above it. On the ridge near the Cherhill slope. As I said, I was starting back when I saw these three riders enter the trees . . ."

It took him a while to tell the story, and by then Sam had noticed the welt on the horse's flank.

". . . I'm sorry for the disturbance in your yard, but I was damned if I'd let Herr Show-and-Hold stay in ignorance of what he'd done. Maybe you'd have behaved differently, but—"

"Yes," Sam assured him, "I would. I'd have kicked him to Marlborough. Now, you'd best go and see how Step Cotter's faring. And after that, the travellers. I'll find some ointment for the horse." He waved Brydd on his way, waited until he had gone, then grunted, "*All* the way to Marlborough."

❊

Heartened by Sam Gilmore's support, Brydd made his way along the yard and into the kitchen. The wiry Step Cotter was still in his chair, his torn face now swabbed and stitched. Happily, he was lolling drunk, the only sure blanket for pain. He blinked across the room, recognised his friend and beckoned him over. "Come on, Brydd, come and sit with me . . . There's a bench . . . Where is it? . . . There . . . There's a bench . . . Come and sit down . . ."

A dozen spitting candles lit the room, the glow doubled and redoubled by the copper pans and mugs and warmers that festooned the walls. Smoked hams hung from hooks in the ceiling and a crowded soup bubbled on the range. "You should have brought your chalks." Step nodded, pleased with the wisdom of his remark. "Should have brought them and drawn me up, the brave driver . . . You could have called it that, 'The Brave

Driver.' . . . Come and sit down; here's a bench . . ." He watched as Brydd found a place near the range, then waved the half-empty flask. "Don't worry," he permitted, "you can get your chalks later . . ."

Whoever had sewn the gash—a well-meaning shepherd or saddler—had thought it necessary to gouge eight stitches in the driver's face, drawing the skin tight to the wound. Step might well be lopsided in future, his grin turned to a grimace, his expression forever tilted between suspicion and delight. He'd doubtless make a good story of it, enough to bring the girls to tears, though perhaps not into his arms.

"It's a neat job they've done," Brydd lied. "You'll be healed tight in a week."

Step rocked in his seat, fought to balance the brandy flask, then forced his words through the thicket of drink. "Sam told me . . . He said you've been called for . . . Will you do something—will you go hard on them for me, Brydd, and most of all on that Carl —that Carl-Maria . . . ? I've been out of the chair, you see . . . They're as good as mirrors, those pots and pans . . . Good as mirrors . . ."

Before he could stop himself, Brydd glanced at the rows of polished copper, seeing them as Step had seen them, his face reflected twenty times, his dark eyes glaring back from the burnished metal. But not quite as Step had seen them, for although Brydd was tired by the day and the ride, there were no rivulets of blood on his face, as on Step's. There was no ugly threaded scar, no hooded eyelid, no mark of what Herr Show-and-Hold's pistol had caused. Damn the man!

Brydd turned quickly to the driver, reached for the brandy flask and topped the two stone mugs. "Count on it," he said. "I'll go hard on him for you. For both of us. You know I will."

Step nodded dully, sipped and spilled the brandy, then lay back in his chair.

Leaving his out-of-shape hat on a peg beside the range, Brydd walked quietly through the kitchen and along the narrow passage toward the front of the inn. As he approached the room at the eastern end of the building—the room that Sam called The Private, and set aside for gentlefolk—Brydd saw one of the notices that were then being posted along that stretch of the Great West Road.

WARNING

TO ALL THOSE WISHING TO CROSS THE CHERHILL DOWNS.

THESE MILES OF THE WAY ARE SPECIALLY OPEN TO
SUDDEN ATTACK BY FOOTPADS, CUTPURSES,
HIGHWAYMEN, SPOILERS, SHOOTERS, MOBSTERS,
BEGGERS OF DECEIT AND SUNDRY RUFFIANS.

WARNING

CONSIDERABLE SUMS HAVE BEEN STOLEN.
DO NOT PARADE YOUR VALUABLES.
DO NOT BE TAKEN IN.
DO NOT BOAST NOISILY OF YOUR WEALTH.
DO NOT TRAVEL IN BAD CONDITIONS,
OR THE DARK.

GOD SPEED YOUR JOURNEY

Yes, Brydd thought. And do not trust passengers with pistols on their knees, for they'll cause more trouble than most. He stared at the notice for a moment, then slapped the flat of his hand against it, making the wall behind it shake. Then he went along to The Private and rapped on the door and opened it without waiting for a reply.

❄

He'd not thought of it until now, but as he entered the room he realised he had never been there before. He'd often looked in through the windows and seen the hats and wigs and pipes of the gentry, the muffs and tippets of their ladies. But he had never actually set foot in the place. He'd never been invited.

The three travellers were seated on plain, board-backed chairs, each made more comfortable by a flat squab cushion. Carl-Maria was nearest the door, though with his back to it; his sister directly opposite the fire—but not so close as to colour her cheeks—whilst

Johann sat at the far corner of the flag-tiled grate. It was he who first saw Brydd enter, and he rose immediately to his feet.

He was taller than the wheelwright had imagined, his head capped by a campaign wig that fell into three curled tails around his neck and shoulders. His skirted frock coat was unbuttoned to reveal a waistcoat of embroidered silk. The neck of the waistcoat was filled by a matching cravat, though this had been left undecorated, as had his grey, knee-length breeches. He wore darker grey stockings and boots devoid of straps or buckles. Every detail of his dress was correct and uncluttered. Not for Johann von Kreutel the fripperies of lace or velvet.

With the heat of the kitchen still in his clothes, Brydd Cannaway gazed at the traveller, admiring his costume as he had earlier admired his wife's perfect swelling bosom. Then, without any attempt at civility, he said, "Sam Gilmore told me I was wanted here."

"Will you draw closer to the fire, Master Cannaway? And shed your greatcoat, if you'd care to."

But Brydd had no intention of shedding his coat. It was his brother's hand-me-down, and nothing to be proud of, but even this threadbare garment was better than the leather jerkin and woollen vest it concealed. Nor did he intend to stand by the fire and steam for the amusement of foreigners.

"I'm well enough here," he said, aware that Carl-Maria would now have to ignore him or move his chair. Good. Excellent. Anything to inconvenience Herr Show-and-Hold.

Smoothing the way as ever, Johann von Kreutel acknowledged Brydd's decision, filled a wine glass and offered it to his visitor. As he did so he spoke rapidly in his own tongue, and Carl-Maria scraped his chair legs on the tiles. Brydd stepped into the vacant space, from where he could reach the glass and keep each of the travellers in view.

"I believe you find fault with us, Master Cannaway," Johann said quietly. "Do you blame us for what happened on the slope?"

"Yes, sir, I do. Though the blame attaches more to one than the other."

"To me, Master Cannaway?"

"For not controlling your brother-in-law, yes." And then, with his eyes on the slouching Carl-Maria, "But most of all to you, Herr Show-and-Hold, for the reasons you know."

"But I think you're unfair," Johann murmured. "Herr Schoenholz was the first to set eyes on the highwaymen. Or perhaps he only saw one of them. Anyway, he was convinced a weapon was being levelled from the trees, and that's why he fired the shot." He nodded encouragement at his brother-in-law, but the look went unheeded.

If it was possible to think less of Carl-Maria, Brydd thought less of him now. Not enough that the creature had triggered his pistol at shadows, but he'd then given Johann some tale about levelled weapons, and now refused to speak for himself. What a fine example of tarnish the man was.

"I'm not sure why I've been summoned here—"

"Invited, Master Cannaway, invited."

"Maybe, but since I am here, I'm obliged to query your account of things. Herr Show-and-Hold did not see the brigands. He did not see them, or their weapons, or a horse's muzzle. I've viewed that downward stretch of the road more times than I remember, and in every weather, and in every season of the year. It was dark as pitch, sir, and if we could see nothing from the bench, Step and I, then what could you see from your windows, with the rain pouring in? Not even the devil could find a victim on such a night —unless the victim fired a shot."

There was a pause, and then Annette murmured something and Johann said, "Yes, you *are* insistent, Master Cannaway."

Brydd shrugged, not caring how impolite they thought him. Then—and only because Annette disarmed him with a smile—he looked down at Carl-Maria and asked, "*Could* you have seen them in such weather, Herr Show-and-Hold?" It was as far as he was prepared to go, allowing the man to say yes, or no, or admit a reasonable doubt.

But Carl-Maria had his own way of dealing with insolent foreigners. He stretched his feet toward the fire, yawned without restraint, then settled his pale, bleak eyes on Brydd. "*Muss ich wieder sagen? Ja!* Shall I find a priest and swear to it? You are altogether too righteous, Master Cannaway. However, the good must be rewarded. So here. Halve this with the driver." Scarcely troubling to stir, he produced a massive silver coin, its upturned face bearing the heads of Dutch Willy and his double-chinned queen. It was a five-guinea piece, worth more than Brydd Cannaway and Step Cotter could earn in a year. It was six months' money for each of them, if they found someone to give them change for the coin.

Yet Brydd held his glass in one hand and let his other hang flexed at his side. "I'll ask Sam Gilmore to collect it," he said tonelessly, "and pass it on to Step. He's the one who caught the bounce of your bullet, Herr Show-and-Hold. He's the one that should meet Dutch Willy."

"Wonderful," the man affirmed, his lips squeezed in dislike. "Righteous to the end."

There was a longer pause now, a dragging silence, a chill that dampened the fire. And then Annette von Kreutel rose from her chair, kept her glance clear of her husband, well clear of her brother, and extended her hands to the angry young wheelwright. He could do no more than touch them, for he had no idea what was expected of him. However, it seemed satisfactory, for she again smiled disarmingly and said, "I cannot let your help go unrewarded. You refuse my brother's money, and I can clearly see why. When Carl-Maria sets out to be unpleasant—well, no matter. But surely there is something we can do, so that I, at least, shall not feel disgraced."

At seventeen, the ambitious Brydd Cannaway had the power to deal with such as Carl-Maria Schoenholz, but fell victim to the likes of Annette von Kreutel. Easy victim when, in truth, he had never met anyone like her. He could still feel the touch of her fingers and said, "There is something, my lady."

"Ah, *das ist gut*. And what is it, this something?"

"I'd like to know where the coach was made."

"Where the coach—?" Her smile faltered and she looked to her husband for help. "In our home town," he said. "In Vienna."

"And was it made for you, sir, to suit your own requirements?"

Amused and curious, Johann said, "Yes, that's so, to my own requirements."

"And the paintings on it, they're of places around Vienna?"

"Of the Danube River, yes, and the Neuer Markt, and my

lodge at Leopoldstadt. I assure you, Master Cannaway, the coach is mine."

Brydd nodded, once for Johann, once for his wife. "Yes," he said, "I see. Then I wish you a safe journey. To Vienna." He stood his wine glass on a shelf, found his way to the door and left the von Kreutels to exchange a quizzical glance and Carl-Maria to yawn.

As he returned along the passage to the kitchen, he memorised the word—Vienna. He did not know where it was in the world, but he'd be in Marlborough on Saturday, taking his weekly reading lesson from Dr. Barrowcluffe. The doctor would know the whereabouts of Vienna, however far it was from the Kennett Vale.

TWO

Though the road to the west of the "Blazing Rag" was desolate and unpopulated, save by the frightened inhabitants of Cherhill and the brigands who used it as their lair, to the east it was dotted with villages and hamlets.

There was Beckhampton itself, marked only by Sam Gilmore's inn and a loose cluster of dwellings. Three miles away was Kennett, and then Lockeridge and a string of tiny hamlets evenly spaced along the winding Kennett Vale. The name was also shared by a placid river that followed the road to the far end of the valley and the prosperous wool-town of Marlborough.

Brydd Cannaway had been born and raised in Kennett. His parents still lived there, still ran the smithy, and there were few who would dare say that Ezra Cannaway was too old for the work, Amalie too old to help him.

At the age of twelve, Brydd had been apprenticed to the soft-spoken wheelwright Alfred Nott in the neighbouring village of Lockeridge. He had worked and lived there for the past five years, and now knew every twist and tilt of the road, where best to find trout and crayfish in the river, the vantage points from which to sketch the traffic. He had never been further east than Marlborough, nor westward as far as Cherhill. If Alfred could spare him of a Saturday afternoon, Brydd walked or rode to Marlborough to attend his lessons, then idled away an hour or two in the market. Sunday mornings he spent with his parents, then rode alone on the hills, to watch and study and draw. But that was the span of it, as for most of those who made their living in the vale.

❋

At Lockeridge the week creaked by. It rained intermittently, never stopping long enough for the mud to harden underfoot, or the dampness to leave the air. The pace of work deteriorated, and with it the mood of the men.

There were four of them in the yard: Alfred Nott, his lifelong friend John Stallard; a sullen, hulking labourer named Abram Hach, and a restless Brydd Cannaway. Of these, all but Stallard lived on the premises, Alfred and his wife in a cottage by the yard gate, Hach and Brydd in a solidly built hut near the sawpit. The hut was equipped with a wood-burning stove, shutters on the windows and low-walled beds that helped break the draught. The thatched roof was lined with boards, the wooden floor caulked and sealed. Each man had a chest for his clothes and a cupboard for his razor and whetstone.

The centre of the room was occupied by a scarred table and two workaday chairs, though these were never set opposite each other, for Brydd and Hach had nothing in common, save their mutual dislike.

So far as Hach was concerned, the young Cannaway was too cocksure by half. He was forever querying the way things were done, then producing a sketch in support of his fancy ideas. He perched altogether too high, did the impatient young know-it-all, and it was time he was pulled from his branch.

From Brydd's point of view, Abram Hach was a dullard and an oaf, envious of everyone, yet too lazy to cudgel his brains. He had the strength of an ox and was invaluable when it came to dragging timbers across the sawpit or replacing a cartwheel. But his abilities ended with the last grunt and heave, and he went back to being the witless giant he was.

Hach was more than twice Brydd's age, but had been less than two years at the yard. No one knew what he'd done before, or where he had come from beyond his vague assertion that he had been "on some farms to the north." Alfred Nott had needed a labourer at the time and had not questioned him too closely, for fear he'd heave his shoulders and slouch off. So Brydd had been stuck with a roommate, one who stank of drink and rancid sweat.

Winter was the time for building wagons and tipcarts, and the damp December week was spent completing the bed frame of a wagon and its five-foot-high rear wheels. The master craftsman John Stallard took charge of the morticing and assembly of the bodywork, whilst Alfred and Brydd smoothed the curved wheel sections known as felloes, then tapped them into the spokes. When that was done, the wheels were carried across to an elm-wood block and the metal strakes nailed around the rim. The day of the iron hoop had yet to arrive in the Kennett Vale, though it was already there on the sketches that filled Brydd's satchel.

His experience with the foreign coach had left him confused.

Several times he'd been on the brink of telling Alfred, then forced other words to his tongue. Alfred was a good man, much like Stallard, much like Ezra, but he had never shown an interest in fast-running coaches, or wondered if his own vehicles might be improved. He was a fair, honest, hard-working man, but what did he care for pavilion roofs and glassed-in lanterns, panels decorated with landscapes or wheels rimmed with a single band of iron? And what would Alfred know of Vienna when—again like John Stallard or Ezra Cannaway—he'd never left the valley in which he'd been born?

The last days of the week were drenched with rain and the work slowed to a crawl. Stallard had finished his task and gone home, leaving Alfred to check the piles of summer-cut wood and Brydd to settle himself at the table in his hut, sketching yet another aspect of the remembered carriage. There had been no sign of Hach since midday, and Brydd hoped the brute had found enough coins in his greasy jerkin to make it worth the journey to the "Blazing Rag." If so, he'd be gone for hours, until he blundered in with the darkness and sprawled on his bed, to snore and dribble through the night.

But the young Cannaway had set his hopes too high. It was still afternoon when Hach shouldered the door and stumbled into the room. His voice never more attractive than stone on stone, he grated, "Here's a lift for you, chalker. Real gin in a good glass jar. Only the best for my friend."

In fact he was bearing two jars, one unopened, the other empty to the waist. Widening his step to keep his balance, he loomed over the table and set the jars down side by side with exaggerated care. Then he sank into his chair and blinked vapidly at his room-mate. "My, but don't you nurse your chalks."

There was an unspoken question in what he said, the demand for an answer. Aware that Hach was not only drunk but danger-ous, Brydd continued working and murmured, "So I do, Abram, so I do." He filled in the panels of the coach, sketched the swing-bridge and its barges, exchanged a brown chalk for crimson, a yel-low for grey. Hach was nodding, planning his response.

"Why don't you ever show them? Sketches, isn't that what they're called?"

"It is, and I do. Alfred's seen them, you know that, those that apply."

Hach reached for the half-empty jar. Squeezing the cork almost flat between finger and thumb, he plucked it from the neck and swigged the raw gin. He was less careful this time in setting down the jar, and it rattled the coloured chalks. "Ah, yes," he said heav-ily, "*he's* seen them, but who else has, eh? *I've* never seen them, unless I catch you by surprise, like now. Is that 'cause they don't apply to me? Is that it, chalker? 'Cause you don't think I'm clever enough for them?"

Brydd coughed and used the outburst to ease his chair from the table. Hach was out for trouble. Another swig from the jar and he'd convince himself he had a right to look at the drawings, then smudge them with his dirty fingers and the gin.

"Very well, Abram. Which would you like to see, cart or carri-age, harrow or wagon, a completed picture or detailed sketches, which do you want?"

Taken aback by the offer and even more so by the choice, the man's aggression leaked away. "I don't care. Anything. Something you showed Alfred. Whatever applies." He watched as Brydd pulled a sheet from the satchel. Then he suddenly stretched his mouth in a triumphant grin and pounded down on the table. The jars clinked and almost went over.

"I know who sees them! I know who you show them to! They're done for that girl who moons over you, that Elizabeth Darle. You chalk 'em for her, yes you do!" He used the table as a pulpit, leaning forward on it, his foetid breath blowing across. "I'd wager she sees the best of your work. The very best of it, eh, my friend?" He meant it to sound unpleasant and it did. "Come Saturday, and you'll be meeting her at market. And then you'll be off somewhere together. Oh, I bet you'll apply your chalk to Mistress Elizabeth, so you will!" He wagged a finger and was reaching for the uncorked jar when Brydd came to his feet and swept it from the table.

"Now, you listen to me! That girl you malign is fourteen years old! Fourteen, you canting bastard, and not to be smeared by you!" His voice was as rough as Hach's, his lean face corded with fury. "Not ever, is that clear? *Not—on your life!*"

It was a bold performance, but after that things went against him. As incensed by the loss of his gin as by Brydd's attack, Abram Hach rammed out an arm like a cart shaft and sent the young man staggering. Then he moved after him, fit to kill.

The fight was overdue; they both knew it. It had been the substance of too many dreams, the ingredients of a pot left to simmer too long. It was time it boiled up and spilled over.

At best, Hach was slow on his feet, and slower yet with drink. But his first blow had been hard and telling and Brydd had gone down, entangled in his chair. He was still on his knees as the labourer padded clear of the table and came toward him. "Who's the one smeared now, eh, chalker? Who's in a nice trap now?" He lashed out with his boot, catching Brydd under the ribs. There was no crack of bone, but he gasped with pain and scrambled out of range. It took Hach a moment to steady himself. By then Brydd was on his feet, his chest numbed by the blows.

He was tempted to keep the wall at his back, but he'd no wish to be cornered and wrapped in Hach's massive embrace. One good squeeze and the man would crush him like a wicker basket. So he made himself move, first to the side, then quickly forward, punching left and right at the face. He heard the labourer grunt and saw blood trickle from his nose. They were both strong men, the one younger and more agile, the other solid and seemingly impervious to pain.

Brydd landed another ringing punch and was rewarded with a blow to the head, Hach's knuckles as hard as agate. "You're done for, my friend. Maybe I'll see Mistress Elizabeth in your place." He lumbered forward again, his arms curved to enwrap his victim. He was slowed by another well-aimed fist, but he had Brydd cornered now. The stink of his breath preceded him and there was no longer room to manoeuvre. He grinned with the blood on his mouth. The chalker was as good as snapped.

Then the bang of wood against stone, the rattle of a loose-hung catch. And after it a snapped-out command from the doorway— "Stand back, both of you! Hach, get over here! Cannaway, stay where you are!"

It was necessary for the labourer to turn, but Brydd could already see Alfred Nott silhouetted against the dull light of the yard. And thank God for your intrusion, he thought. Thank God you're not always soft-spoken, Master Nott. He stayed obediently still, massaging his chest and feeling blood ooze from a cut above his eye.

"Now follow me out."

It was an intelligent move, for it brought the protagonists into a chill drizzle. Alfred directed them either side of the doorway, then gazed up at them, not at all surprised that the pot had come to the boil. "Well, am I to hear about it?" He waited, hearing nothing, then said, "I shall, if it concerns the yard."

Hach ignored him, cupping a hand around his nose and sniffing back the blood. Brydd shook his head, winced with pain and muttered, "No, Master Alfred, it does not. It's a private thing."

"And finished with, I trust. Is it finished?"

Again Hach said nothing, but turned his dangerous eyes on Brydd, letting the young man know how close he had come to being crushed. Hach was the victor, Brydd Cannaway merely wickerwork, or chalk.

"For a while," Brydd replied. "It's over for a while."

"And a long while at that," Alfred warned, "if you're to be em-

ployed in my yard. You're of some value to me, Brydd Cannaway,
as are you, Abram Hach. But you're not beyond price. Don't
think you are." He turned on his heel and, skirting the sawpit,
crossed the muddy yard to his cottage. Hach blew his nose with
his fingers, spraying blood, then shouldered his way into the hut.
Brydd stood for a moment, inhaling the damp air and waiting for
the pain to lessen in his chest. Then, concerned for his drawings,
he followed the labourer inside.

Hach had collected the second jar and taken it with him to his
bed. Brydd watched as the man plucked out the hammered cork,
like a splinter from skin.

❃

There was reason enough to leave the yard this Saturday and ride
the three miles from Lockeridge to Marlborough. As always,
Brydd was up with the light, though less willingly than usual for
he had stayed awake until he'd heard Hach snore and dribble into
his pillow. If this counts as fear, he told himself, then I'll admit it,
I'm afraid. But I'll not risk being strangled or smothered by that
gin-filled monster—a murder he'd have forgotten by morning.

However, he'd survived the night, then awakened with the feeling that he'd been roped to the bed, his head throbbing, his arms
and chest leaden from the fight. Hach had bruised him severely,
and he winced as he eased himself into his breeches, dragged on
his boots and looped his arms into the work-stained jerkin and
hand-me-down coat.

It was normal practice for Brydd and Hach to make their way
to the cottage, where Mary Nott would serve them a breakfast of
warm bread and a mug of steaming chocolate. Alfred had invariably eaten by then, though he was sometimes willing to take a second mug with an early riser—in other words, with Brydd. Hach
would stamp in later, to gobble his bread and slurp his drink, his
face still stubbled, his brain awash with gin or cider. Mary had
never once remarked on his appearance, though the loaf and chocolate pot vanished at the stroke of seven. After that the late-
comers could wait until noon and a lunch of beef and cheese and
ale.

Today, however, Brydd hesitated before knocking on the kitchen door. He'd defended Elizabeth Darle and was glad of it, but he'd lost the fight with Abram Hach—yes, and almost his life, the way the monster's arms were curved—and he'd then been marched out of the hut and dressed down by a man he respected. It was bad enough that he'd let Hach kick and all but crush him to death, but even more shaming that Alfred Nott had discovered him trapped in a corner, a common brawler who'd been downed in a brawl. That was not how he'd presented himself over the years, but what would Alfred think now of the ambitious designer, the self-styled critic who found fault with the width of a wheel and the angle of a brake bar? How seriously would he take the next suggestion, the next improving sketch?

But he knocked anyway, eager to get out of the cold. It was too dark to judge the content of the sky, but the drizzle had been blown away by a stiff westerly wind, a likely harbinger of snow. Mary Nott opened the door and beckoned him inside. "Your politeness'll freeze you one of these days," she chided, fussing him toward the fire. "There's no need to wait like a stranger." She noticed the cut above his eye, but said nothing, and Brydd realised she'd been told about the fight.

As he found his seat at the scrubbed oak table Alfred emerged from the next room, a cramped cubicle that served as his office. His fingers were stained with ink and he was muttering under his breath, ". . . damned ledger, what's the point to it? I can *remember* what's been bought and spent . . ." He caught Mary's eye, showed her his hands in a vain bid for sympathy, then stamped out to the pump. The stains and grumbling and mute appeal were all part of the ritual. Twice a month the master wheelwright wrestled with the accounts, and twice a month he splashed rust-coloured ink on the ledger or upset the blue glass well. Careful and precise when it came to making wagons or barrows or toys for a neighbour's child, he never failed to spill and spread the ink. The ledger was already short of twenty pages, the desk and the floor beneath it spotted and veined.

Mary placed fresh-cut slices of bread on the table, a dish of butter and a bellied jug of chocolate. She exchanged a conspiratorial smile with Brydd and said, "If I didn't make him do it, I don't know where we'd be. He says he can remember, but—" She clicked her tongue, then nodded to him. "Help yourself now, Brydd, while it's warm."

He thanked her and poured chocolate for Alfred and himself. Mary had already taken half a mug, her ration for the day. As he buttered the bread, he discovered that his knuckles had been skinned and wondered how Hach would behave when he arrived. With any luck the man would snore on and miss breakfast. They'd have to meet sometime in the next hour and work together, at least until midday. But if there was to be further acrimony, it could take place outside, not in Mary's kitchen.

A gust of wind accompanied Alfred in from the pump. Closing the door, he hazarded, "There's snow on the way, I wouldn't be surprised." Brydd nodded, waiting to see if he'd settle at the table, or collect his mug and take it with him to the office. Alfred, too, seemed undecided, standing for a moment between the table end and the fire. Then he settled himself in his wing chair, reached for his chocolate and cupped his hands around the thick warm clay. "Will you be taking your lesson today from Dr. Barrowcluffe?"

"If I may." He saw Alfred give his permission with a shallow nod, then blurted, "Master Nott, I apologise for—"

"A fine man, the doctor. He'll teach you all you can learn."

"Yes, he's a clever man." He cleared his throat for courage and again said, "I wish to apol—"

"Latin, Greek, French, *and* something of German, so I've heard. He knows them all. Now I can't tell you where they speak those things, but it must take a brilliant mind to hold all the words." He glanced pointedly at his wife and added, "It's all I can do to remember what's been ordered and how much it cost." Mary smiled at him and tutted—lord, but he was stubborn—then came forward to top the mugs with the thick, unsweetened liquid.

So, Brydd thought, I've been let off the hook. Alfred doesn't want an apology, or at least not one spelled out. I've made the effort, twice, and he's recognised it and decided to let it lie.

He relaxed in time to hear the man say, "And another thing Dr. Barrowcluffe could teach you: to bridle your temper. You and Hach were bound to collide, but it's a long valley and there's room enough on the hills. You do your tusking there in future, not in the hut I've provided for you, nor anywhere else that's

mine. You were right in the way you behaved with the foreign
coach, but you were not right to trade blows in my house, and
that hut's part of it, as you know full well. Be a little more
choosy, Brydd Cannaway, else you'll be regarded as a common
buncher, sniffing for a brawl." He gazed implacably from his
chair, while Brydd scowled in confusion.

This was not what he'd expected, this dressing-down. He knew
Alfred tolerated Abram Hach because he had to, because he
needed a strong labourer in the yard. And he acknowledged, too,
that the master wheelwright must treat them alike, avoiding
favouritism and jealousy. But to embarrass him like this— And in
front of Mary— It was the kind of treatment one reserved for a
hotheaded member of the family— Or for one who had accepted
the kindness of a couple denied their own.

Understanding Alfred's intentions, Brydd found it easier to
take. The old man had been harsh with him, but he hadn't raged
or waved his arms or left his views unleavened. He'd mentioned
the coach, and even commended him for his behaviour, allowing
the good in with the bad. And he'd finished with a warning,
where it would have been easy to slam the lid down with a threat.

But a grim warning it was, the ambitious and talented Brydd
Cannaway regarded as a common buncher, sniffing out a brawl.

"I'll not be that," he said, "though neither will I let an insult
go by."

"I'm sure you won't," Alfred murmured. "Why? Did Abram
Hach insult you?"

"No."

"But he scorns someone you know."

Brydd chewed his breakfast, aware that Alfred had made a comment of the question, knowing there'd be no answer . . .

Stiff and aching, the young man worked out the morning in the
yard. Hach appeared with the daylight, too late for bread and
chocolate, his memory of the fight lost in the fumes of gin. He ac-
corded Brydd his usual blank greeting, then shuffled off to stack
timber as though nothing exceptional had occurred. There were
no marks on his face, no vestige of a swelling around his nose, no
abrasions on his massive, fire-tong hands. Brydd stared after him
with a mixture of horror and disbelief, then shook his head and

made his way stiffly across the yard to help John Stallard hang a wheel.

"What's this?" the craftsman asked him innocently, pointing at the mark of Hach's knuckles. "Did you fall out of bed?"

"Close to it," Brydd muttered, busying himself with the work.

By late morning the wind had dropped and, as the workers at Lockeridge had suspected, the air was thickened with snow. The flakes descended gently, tentatively, as though feeling their way into the valley. It was the first fall of winter, but the ground was already cold enough to receive it and the snow settled on the thatch and tiles of the roofs, capped the walls and eddied down into the sawpit. Blowing on his hands, Brydd turned the newly fixed wheel and the two men knocked the wedges from beneath the axletree. The cart settled, an inch at a time, still creaking after the last block had been tapped free. A further inspection would be made of the hub- and lynchpins, further measurements taken to ensure that the "dish" was seated right. But this was Stallard's job, and he said, "You'd best be off for your lesson. If it's not hung right we'll lift it first thing Monday."

Brydd nodded and crossed the snow-blind yard to ask Alfred's permission to leave. "I'll ride quiet," he promised. "I'll not bunch anyone on the way."

Alfred might have smiled at that, it was hard to tell, but he said, "You'll not see them well enough to do it, in this weather. Away you go then, and take my regards to your parents. And, Brydd?"

"Master Nott?"

"You be most careful when Hach is swinging timbers."

So that was the story he'd be allowed to tell Ezra and Amalie when he returned from Marlborough, that he'd been clouted by a plank. It was a lie, but a harmless one, and better than having to admit he'd almost been snapped in two.

Released from the yard until Monday, he took a washed handkerchief to Mary Nott, who wrapped it around a hand-thick slice of beef, a wedge of cheese and bread half the height of a shoe heel. She also filled a leather pouch with ale and told him to find room for a bittersweet apple. He was already encumbered with a scribbling tablet, the reading primer he kept well hidden from

Abram Hach and a bundle of pure white chalks. He took none of his sketches with him, and gave no thought to the girl he'd defended, the young Elizabeth Darle. After all, she *was* only fourteen, and if she mooned over him it was her affair, not his.

❊

Dr. Barrowcliffe had been farsighted enough to select a wig that would last. Fashions changed with the years, and several of his friends had been forced to discard their high-piled perukes and buy something less flamboyant. Others refused to admit their age and looked faintly silly, their natural grey hair peeping from beneath black-dyed ringlets. One of the recent magistrates of Marlborough had favoured a bagwig, complete with a three-foot-long pigtail bound around with ribbon. He'd worn it stubbornly for a year, catching the tail in closing doors and the backs of chairs, and all but inviting mischievous children to tug it like a bell rope. It had been as much off his head as on, and he'd eventually returned to his wigmaker to demand "something as plain as, well, have you occasioned to meet my lady wife?"

The doctor's headpiece was of goat's hair, one of the cheapest materials available, and its grizzled colouring was a perfect match with what remained of his own sparse growth. As a result, he looked dignified and at ease, no younger than his sixty years, but neither a ruin refurbished.

He had dismissed the class and was wiping the blackboard with a rag, erasing the words COOPER, FARRIER, VINTNER and SMITH. His pupils would be expected to employ those words in simple sentences and present them at the next lesson. Not hard, since all the trades were evident in the town.

He heard a movement behind him and turned to see Brydd Cannaway, still at his desk. "Do you want the words left up? You can wash them off when you've finished."

"No, sir, I've copied them on to the slate."

"Then what's to do, Brydd?" He cleaned his board, laid aside the rag and slapped industriously at his waistcoat. "Your sister, Sophia, used to say I taught too slow. Perhaps I do, but there are the youngsters to consider. It wouldn't be fair to outpace them."

"No, sir, it would not. I think your teaching has—great clarity."

"Well, I thank you," the doctor smiled, "and we're in agreement, for so do I. However, if you've no complaints, what keeps you from the market?"

Aware that he should not be sitting whilst his tutor stood, Brydd came to his feet and said, "I'd ask your advice. Do you know the whereabouts of a city called Vienna? I can't say how it's spelt, but—"

"Like this, I think." And he scratched chalk across the board. VIENNA. "It's on the continent of—I'll spell it for you— EUROPE. And it straddles a river, yes—THE DANUBE. And that passes through what the inhabitants of the country call— AUSTRIA. Why on earth do you want to know?"

Brydd told the story as he'd already told it to Sam Gilmore and Alfred Nott. "I was up on the hills last Sunday afternoon, near a group of trees by the Cherhill slope, and I'd just started back toward the 'Blazing Rag' at Beckhampton when I glimpsed these riders, three of them, trotting across the road . . ." He described his meeting with the foreigners and the vain attempt to escape the ambush and his assault on Carl-Maria. Indignation coursed through him again as he saw Step Cotter's stitched face and the glint of the offered coin.

"This is most exciting," Dr. Barrowcluffe enthused. "That mark on your head, that'd be from a bullet, I suppose."

Brydd gave a noncommittal grunt, then completed the story with Johann's mention of Vienna, home of the von Kreutels and their extraordinary coach. The doctor plied him with questions, and it was a while before Brydd could repeat, "The whereabouts of Vienna, is it far from here?"

"Aye, it is, and far beyond your imagination. At a guess I'd say eight hundred miles and more." He fussed with the goat's hair wig and continued, "I think I know where it's stacked. If not, Mistress Cable will know."

Brydd waited in silence, shivering as the snow clung to the mullioned windows. Eight hundred miles and more? And he'd not spanned more than twenty in his life. Of course he could not imagine such a distance, though his respect for the von Kreutels, and even for Carl-Maria Show-and-Hold, increased at the thought. But his real admiration was reserved for the coach that had brought them. How perfectly it had survived the journey, its lights still burning, its paintings clear and unfaded, its springs intact, with no sign of brace or rivet. They knew what they were about, all right, the coachmakers of Vienna-on-the-Danube.

"I remember now, it's under the medicine cabinet. Come along, I'll show it you on a map." He strode out of the schoolroom, leaving Brydd to push his chalks and slate and primer into a bag.

The young Cannaway had never seen a map, though he'd once been shown a crudely drawn plan of Marlborough. It had been hard enough for the artist to squeeze a dozen streets into the confines of the paper, so what size would one need for the whole of Vienna, or Austria, or Europe?

❊

They were met in the hallway by the elderly Mistress Cable. She nodded politely at Brydd, then reminded the doctor that he was expected in one of the nearby villages. "You said you'd make the visit today. It's the husband, he's got a swelling behind the knee. I've washed your needles. *And* dried them in a candle flame, though I'm sure I don't know why they can't just be wiped on a towel. Nobody ever said I couldn't bring towels up clean before this. Study them all you like, you'll not find a speck of dirt on the towels I wash." She marched off, leaving the doctor to shake his head and sigh. "She's convinced I think her slapdash. She cannot accept that disease can be transmitted on a cloth, however well it's been scrubbed. Never mind, come along, I've time to show you your city."

He led the way into his office, stooped beside the cabinet and dragged out a thick, leather-bound book. It was heavy enough to make him groan and threatened to collapse the gate-leg table on which he laid it.

The spine of the massive tome was ribbed and decorated, the hammered gold lettering identifying it as *Itinerarium Europae*. The doctor turned to the title page and said, "D'you see what it says here? 'A Complete Admeasurement of the Principal States of Europe.' And here, below it? 'Giving the most Considerable Cities, Towns, Rivers and Natural Geography.' Now then, let's find—ah, yes, here we are. 'The Entire Continent of Europe.' "

The map itself was coloured pink and brown and blue, the margin of the pages filled with descriptive notes. Brydd stared at it, not knowing which part of it was England. He assumed correctly that blue was reserved for water, but supposed that his own country was situated squarely in the centre of the map. He looked in vain for Kennett and Marlborough, and waited for the doctor to point them out.

Instead, Dr. Barrowcluffe tapped a blunt fingernail against the left-hand page. "That's where we live," he indicated. "The islands of Britain."

Brydd glanced at him, searching for the humour. Then, as he realised he'd been told the truth, he said, "They can't be so small. The kingdom is not as small as that."

"It is, you know, in comparison with the rest. There's France, for example. And the Netherlands. And the Spanish peninsula. And that coaching boot, that's Italy. And this—follow my finger —this is Austria. The Danube there, and where it says 'Wien,' that's your Vienna." Without altering his tone he asked, "It's where you intend to go, is it not?" and Brydd gazed at the far-off speck and said yes.

It was the first time he had ever voiced his dream, and the word startled him, as though he'd betrayed a trust. But Dr. Barrowcluffe merely hummed and nodded, his head down over the page. "I was not far off in my guess, eight hundred miles. You've some travelling before you, when you go. Down to the coast, that's the route, then find yourself a fishing boat to take you along to Dover, and go by packet across to Calais. From there you can ride to Paris and—well, you'll choose the way that suits you best."

Brydd nodded at the sense of it, then said, "It isn't known that I want to go. I've not told my father, or Alfred Nott. In truth, sir, no one's been made aware of it—"

"And why should they be, before you knew it yourself? It took the map to bring it out of you, and there's no need to falter now. There it is, your distant Vienna. Study it all you want." He laid a workmanlike hand on Brydd's shoulder, collected his bag and started for the door. "When you've finished with it, put it back under the cabinet. It damn near pulled out my arms." He heard the young man hurry his thanks, then went along the hallway,

praying he'd avoid Mistress Cable. She was loyal and efficient and
he treasured her, but if she caught him now she'd wrap a scarf
around his neck and force him to don his gauntlets and pull down
his hat and button his coat and . . .

Left alone in the office, Brydd travelled to Vienna. Not trusting
his ability to read the tiny scripted names, he kept a finger on the
city whilst he roamed the Channel coasts. Along to Dover by
fishing craft . . . then across on the packet to Calais . . . then
somehow to Paris, by horse or cart or on foot, it wouldn't matter
. . . and then further, much further, moving eastward through the
pinks and around the browns and between the blues until he
reached Wien—Vienna—where they made coaches that ran as
gracefully as deer upon the downs.

❋

The snow was drifting all along the High Street, the dry, delicate
flakes settling on market stalls and saddlecloths, in the animal
pens and on the spokes of stationary wheels. The wind that had
brought it had left it to find its own way down, the snow twisting
and spiralling on to the tiles, then clinging there, not yet ready to
slide.

There had been no thatched roofs in Marlborough since the
fire.

Less than ten years ago it had swept through the wool-town,
the flames dancing from house to house and devouring them, fed
by the thatch. A few buildings had survived, among them the doctor's residence, saved by its grey peg-tiles. But much of the town
had been destroyed, and a prohibition placed on all straw-topped
dwellings. Bad news for the local thatchers, though it had brought
the slatters from miles around. Their wagons had inched along
the roads from Kent and Cornwall and Wales, the ten-team vehicles bowed beneath the weight of mottled Penrhyn slates, of grey-
and-green Prescelly, of split sandstone from the eastern counties
and the thicker Rough Rim from the north. By the time the slatters had finished, the roofs of Marlborough were a study in colour
and style.

The tilted High Street had remained unchanged, and Brydd
walked along it now, the snow stealing a ride on his hat. He

watched critically as a gig skidded and almost overturned—*they'd be better balanced than that in Vienna*—then snorted to himself as two farm carts locked wheels in passing. He ran forward to help separate them, but the thought was still there—*the wagons would run more smoothly in Vienna.*

Dissatisfied though he was with the clumsy vehicles, he was nevertheless pleased to see his friends. He knew most of the farmers and stall-holders by name, and spent the next hour chatting his way through town. Word of the ambush had spread, and Brydd was expected to tell the story on both sides of the street. He did so without embellishment, making sure the listeners understood the part Step Cotter had played in getting the carriage through. From time to time he was told, "I saw him during the week. If I'd been in your place I'd have killed that Show-and-Hold for what he did."

"Don't worry, somebody will. He appeals for it."

Halfway along the street he reached a stall he favoured and treated himself to a slice of imbal, a shortcake biscuit baked with fruit and almonds. It cost him a farthing, the smallest coin of the realm, and he thought it good value, making it last until he reached the Market Hall.

He had turned back and was sucking the sweetness from his fingers when he saw a high, ladder-framed wagon rumble toward him from the western end of town. He recognised its occupants, the stocky sheep farmer George Darle, flanked on the bench by his raucous son, Jedediah, and the young, shy-eyed Elizabeth. Brydd watched as the farmer reined in, then backed his wagon into the narrow space it had occupied every Saturday for the past thirty years. After such a time, the wagon itself seemed to know the way.

Jed was the first from the bench, grinning and hallooing. He was the same age as Brydd—a month older, but a month spread thin over seventeen years—and in many ways more the brother than William Cannaway, businessman of Melksham. They collided in a noisy greeting, spraying snow as they wrestled, then stood apart, the vapour on their breath, two young men of an age and height and build, not ever thinking that they might one day be less similar than this.

"Don't you shoot me now," Jed pleaded. "It wasn't me in the trees. Hey, tell me about it. Is that where you got the scar?"

"In a while," Brydd said, going forward to greet George and his daughter.

The Darles and Cannaways had been close-knit for years. As there had always been Cannaways at the smithy, so there had always been Darles at Overhill, a low-roofed farmstead that hunched down in a shallow valley two miles north of Kennett. It was an earlier Cannaway who had made the ploughs and harrows for Overhill, and been repaid with lamb and mutton from the farm.

George Darle's wife had borne him Jed and Elizabeth, but had died of pneumonia when the boy was twelve and his sister only nine. From that day on Elizabeth Darle had been expected to cope. Scarcely strong enough to lift the pans and cauldrons, she'd prepared the slaughtered livestock and cooked the meals and pounded the clothes in a wash trough in the yard. Amalie had helped, teaching the girl the myriad skills of the country housewife, and now, at the age of fourteen, Elizabeth deserved her place on the wagon bench, the accomplished mistress of Overhill.

She smiled down at Brydd, who merely nodded and chatted with George.

"I hear you were busy last Sunday," the farmer told him. "Quite a thing, that, to take an ambush by surprise."

"We'd the weather on our side, else we'd never have tried it." He jerked his head, sending snow billowing from his hat. "May I help with the pen?" He went to the rear of the wagon, where Jed was already erecting the split-wood hurdles. They tied the sections together, whilst George assisted his daughter from the bench, then prepared to lower the tail gate and herd down the sheep.

When the men had finished they shared a jar of cider, their ritual reward. They did not offer the jar to Elizabeth, nor include her in their talk of highwaymen and prices and the early winter snow. There was no discourtesy in their behaviour; she'd been brought to market and was now free to find her way. She had her own friends among the women, her own topics of conversation, and she would not be interrupted by her father or brother or Brydd.

Shaking the snow from her hooded crimson-cloth mantle, Elizabeth edged past the carts and market stalls, her gaze divided between the busy High Street and the cluttered shop windows. She was greeted by another young girl, the daughter of a local saddler, and they walked on together arm in arm, never tiring of the sights they knew so well. Suddenly, mindless of the snow, Elizabeth tossed back her hood, to reveal her fine blond hair. Unwilling to compete, her friend pulled her own hood tighter, and sniffed as though the victim of a chill.

They were met by other young women, one of whom insisted that they visit a Man of Magic who had set up his table at one end of the market. Chattering and laughing, the girls made their way along the street. Some of them had bought scraps of lace and lengths of coloured ribbon, inexpensive decoration for a simple country dress. These fripperies were passed from hand to hand and dutifully admired. The animated conversation turned to the next village dance, the next heavy-booted suitor. No one asked Elizabeth Darle whom she hoped would lead her in a jig or jaunter. They knew already.

Brushing at the snowflakes, the girls joined the half-circle of onlookers who were already assembled and awaiting the appearance of the magician. He had halted his brilliantly painted caravan near the edge of the street, set up a low, tapestry-covered table and retired to dress for the occasion.

The onlookers were treated to a drum roll from inside the caravan and then, swirling a magnificent silk cloak, the Man of Magic appeared on the shallow wooden steps. His features were dark and sinister, his left eye covered by a black velvet patch, his head crowned with a turban, resplendent as his cloak. He did not so much study his audience as glare at them, seeming critical of their workaday dress. When he spoke, it was in a language they could not understand, but it earned him their fullest attention, and Elizabeth found herself clutching hands with her friends.

Pausing for effect, the man then descended the steps to the table.

Once again he made the onlookers wait, then snapped in English, "There are few as blessed as I. Few with the gift of alchemy or transmutation. Few who can change earth to water as I have done in the dry parts of the world. Iron to gold I have changed, and birds into animals, and clay into marble. But such accomplishments have left me weary, and my physicians advise me to rest. Were it not for the force that drives me on I would have passed through this town in silence. I shall make no golden palaces today, nor line your street with marble. But my inner force insists that I give you the merest glimpse of my powers, and you shall see me change mice into cats, and cats into mice. It is a cruel goad that drives the true magician."

The onlookers were already sympathetic. The man looked as weary as his word, and they felt privileged to be offered an expression of his powers. Elizabeth Darle was as anxious as any to see how the mice that gnawed through the grain sacks at Overhill could be turned into cats. It would be a well-spent morning if she could pass on the secret to George and Jedediah.

The Man of Magic raised the near edge of the tapestry, muttered a strange incantation, then drew it forward to reveal five pale grey mice. No matter that the girls had been born and raised in the country, a few of them shivered and drew back.

Elizabeth watched, fascinated.

The magician again raised the tapestry, smoothing it across the table. A few more words and he repeated his performance, drawing a gasp from his audience as they saw two black kittens stalk and scratch the table.

"Mice to cats," he said triumphantly. "And to show there's been no mealtime, the cats shall return to mice."

Elizabeth stared, not yet knowing how it had been done.

Glaring all the harder, and making a fine show with his cloak, the Man of Magic again smoothed the tapestry and again, with the necessary incantations, withdrew it to reveal the mice.

There were cries of appreciation from the audience and the clatter of applause.

Exhausted perhaps by his turning of iron to gold and clay to marble, the man drank too deep of his triumph. Whatever his condition, he did not return the mice to their secret box beneath the table in time. One by one they scampered to the edge, tumbled to the ground, then ran riot among the crowd. The girls shrieked in alarm, whilst the men who had been watching stamped wildly with their boot heels.

Abandoning his glare, his turban and his accent, the magician scrambled in pursuit. Elizabeth saw him jab a thumb against his eye patch and push it upward, the better to chase his quarry. Laughing at his embarrassment and at the way she herself had been taken in, she told her friends, "We're not to learn his secret, so it seems. Perhaps we'd best reclaim our families."

They walked back together along the street, reached the saddler's shop and kissed farewell. Still smiling at the performance and its disastrous conclusion, Elizabeth continued on alone. Passing stall and cart, wagon and table, she returned to find that George and Jed and Brydd were still in conversation, the cider jar now empty.

Waiting for a lull in the talk, she then glanced at Brydd and said, "May I speak with you for a moment?"

Her brother started to grin, and would have jabbed Brydd with his elbow if George had not intervened. "It'd pay us to check the hurdles, Jedediah." He escorted his son to the far side of the pen, leaving Brydd and Elizabeth alone.

"What is it?" Brydd asked. And borrowing Dr. Barrowcluffe's phrase, "What's to do?"

"I heard about the ambush," she told him. "It was courageous of you to help those people. I'm sorry Step Cotter was injured, but at least you were only struck a glancing blow. It won't show at all when it's healed."

"What blow—? Oh, this. No, this wasn't caused by the ambush." He explained that he'd been grazed by a plank, preferring his lie to the one she'd have welcomed. It did not occur to him to impress her, and he glanced back to see if Jed had finished checking the hurdles.

The girl held out a hand to catch the snow. "Do you realise, it's less than a fortnight until Christmas?"

"Yes, I suppose it is."

"Well, don't be so dulled by the thought! You'll see your sister, Sophia, and her husband, and William will ride over from Melksham." She smiled up at him, although he was now gazing impatiently in the direction of the pen. "Or is it the thought of having *us* that leaves you indifferent? The Cannaways invaded by the Darles!"

"What? No, of course it isn't, that's a foolish thing to say." His impatience infected his tone and the girl's smile weakened. She too looked away, blaming herself for her inability to hold him. Brydd would welcome Christmas when it came, though in common with most men, he'd leave the anticipation of it to the women. Jed was the same, shrugging off the thought, yet happy enough to sample the pies and sweetmeats as they were taken from the oven.

Not quite knowing where the next remark would lead, Elizabeth said, "It was a strange coach those travellers were in, so I heard." Then with inspired invention she added, "With its six wheels."

"In God's name, who told you that? It would have been strange, indeed, but it would not have been the vehicle I helped drive. Four wheels were enough for that fine carriage, and the side panels painted with scenes. It had lights inside and out; ah, yes, sheltered candles on the inside and weatherproof lanterns at the corners. And springs, the like of which I've never seen on any—"

I should have taken more interest in this before, Elizabeth acknowledged. It's what most interests him.

"And did you sketch it?"

"I've been doing so ever since. It's been drawn to perfection," he said immodestly. "If I'd the materials and the time I could build another to match it. Do you know—?" He stopped as Jed gripped him on the shoulder. "Father'll look after things here. Let's go down by the river. And you've your shopping to do, sister. The stalls will be empty if you don't get on." He saw Elizabeth glare at him and grinned, delighted to have rescued his friend from her aimless chatter. Brydd said, "I'd not finished telling about the coach," but Jed waved that away and strode off toward the Market Hall.

"Will you tell me later?" Elizabeth ventured.

"If you like."

"Yes," she said, and he nodded and tapped snow from the

forebrim of his hat. It was no sweeping gesture, though it might
have been a salute, of a kind.

❄

The young men skidded their way down a cobbled alley to the
river. Flailing his arms for balance, Jed crashed against the door of
a terraced cottage, then yelled joyfully at Brydd to flee. The pair
of them ran headlong, jackknifing over a low riverside rail and
twisting around to see the irate cottager lean from his doorway
and show them what he'd do to them with his good right fist.
Gasping and grinning, they nodded up at him—yes, we bet you
would, oh, yes, old man, if only you catch us, yes.

They used to rattle door knockers and run like that, years ago
. . .

When they had regained their composure they walked in silence for a while beside the river. The snow had given a false
width to the Kennett, for the flakes had already formed a crust
above the roots and grasses that fringed the banks, enticing the
unwary to step too near the edge. Brydd sprang the trap by tapping his foot on the ground and watching his boot sink through.
He swayed upright and angled away from the bank, rejoining Jed
on the path. They went on at an easy pace, the young Cannaway
recognisable by the leanness of his features, the young Darle by
his thick, flattened nose and more credulous expression. But from
behind one would have to know that it was Brydd who wore the
misshapen grey hat and hand-me-down coat, Jed who was dressed
in sheepskin, from hat to coat to boots. A closer inspection might
show that Brydd's hair was darker, and that Jed was broader in
the shoulders by an inch. But they gave each other nothing in
height, nor in the length of their stride.

"Damn me, I'd like to have seen it, that rattle through the
trees."

"We could have done with you." And then because there was
no one else to hear, "By the devil we could."

"Where were they from, did you discover? I heard they were
foreign, but it wasn't said from what parts."

"Yes, they were foreign, as foreign as you can get without

starting back here again." He had already decided to confide in Jed, and now pulled him close as they walked and told him the travellers hailed from Vienna, in the state of Austria, and that the city was eight hundred miles from Marlborough and the vale of Kennett.

"You'll be scraped out for a liar, you will," Jed warned him. "Eight hundred miles in a painted feather of a coach? Am I the fool I look?"

Brydd's next pace was enough and he stopped abruptly, rounding on his friend. "Strike me or believe me, that's your choice."

"You'll be in the river if I do," Jed grinned. "I've the very hell of a punch."

"Then use it, or take what I say for the truth. It was Dr. Barrowcluffe who told me— Aha, I see that impresses you. And so will this, for he showed me Vienna on a map. *Showed* me, Jed; showed me the ports of England and France, and the states that make up the Continent of Europe, and—"

"The what?"

"No matter. Listen. He showed me where they're from, the travellers and their coach, and *he's* the one who told me it was eight hundred miles. Now, will you put Dr. Barrowcluffe in the river?"

Jed frowned at him, swung aside and shook his head, scuffed snow with his boot cap, then returned for another inquisitive look. "If you're having me for a fool, Brydd Cannaway—"

"That I'm not, Jed Darle, and you're the first I've told of it. The doctor knows, of course, because he told me, showed me where it was. 'Wien,' they call it, but it's still Vienna."

The snow drifted around them, whitening the ground and filling the river, a flake and a thousand flakes at a time. The young men gazed at each other, their breath leaking like pale smoke in the air. Jed knew by now what Brydd would tell him if he asked.

"So that's where they're from. I see."

"That's it."

"And you'll be going there, will you, to learn about, well, coaches and the like?"

"That's it."

"Well, damn me," he said quietly, "there's a thing. But I do wonder what I'll do on Saturdays and such, I'm beginning to wonder that." He nodded at the problem, then walked off along the path, the spirit gone from his stride.

Brydd tracked him and drew level, and they continued on in silence, though no longer walking so close. They covered the better part of a mile before Brydd said, "That coach will never come through again, you know, nor anything to resemble it."

"Then you'd best chase after it, hadn't you?"

"Yes, and return with what I've learned."

"Oh, and set up here in the valley, is that the scheme? The famous Brydd Cannaway, come back from Vienna, the great coachmaker of the Kennett Vale."

"Just so, Jed, but a coachmaker for all Wiltshire, and why not?"

They both knew they were salting their sorrow, and waited for the bitterness to pass. In unspoken agreement they turned and walked back along the path, aware that they'd climb the cobbled alley and regain the market and go their ways from there.

This time it was Jed who spoke. "When will you leave? You'll let me know—"

"Every step, my dear friend. I've yet to tell my parents, and Alfred Nott; then there's Sophia and William, your own father and Elizabeth—"

"—who will squall the roof down. She'll strap tethering-weights to your feet. She'll dig holes in the road to impede you. She already thinks you're famous, so she does."

"She's a child, Jed, a determined and delightful child."

"How she'd love to hear that! You'd best be packed and in the saddle before you tell Elizabeth where you're bound, else she'll hamstring every horse in the valley."

They grinned at the thought. Then Jed queried, "Where will you raise the money for this journey of yours? From Sophia, or rather her husband, the merchant, Joseph Biss? He's wealthy enough, and amiable toward you."

"Yes, he'd help if I asked him, but first I'll visit my brother, William. He has always encouraged me to—how does he put it?— enact the dream."

"When were you last over there, at Melksham?"

"Well, the truth is, I, uh—"

"You have never been? *You've never been to Melksham?*" He bellowed with laughter, startling the snow. "Oh, I should put you in the river and shock some sense into you, damn me I should! It's not sixteen miles from Kennett, and you've been shown eight hundred on a map!"

Brydd avoided his friend's instructive fist. "They don't make fine coaches," he retorted, "not at Melksham. I'll go where they do."

THREE

He still thought of Kennett as his home, for his parents were there, the sixty-year-old Ezra weakened by age, Amalie by the chills and damp of winter. But the ring of hammer on glowing metal was Ezra's doing, for it was his smithy and he who mended the barrows and barrel hoops, he who squeezed the bellows and forged the nails from thin iron rods. He paused more often these days and took longer to catch his breath. But he still began work with the light and let the glow of the furnace settle with the sun.

And Amalie continued to make candles, well practised at it after forty years. Forty years of rendering mutton fat and dipping rushes or twisted cotton; leaving them to harden, dipping them again, then once more setting them out to dry. Slowly the coating of tallow would build around the stalks until they were thick enough to be weighed—and sold for fourpence a pound. She too stopped more often, turning away from the smell of the grease, her eyes watering with the smoke. But she still demanded firm orders for her candles and worked on until they were met.

There was no need for Ezra and Amalie to slave as they did, for although Brydd could not yet support them, they had other children, further advanced in success.

The eldest was William, a shambling bear of a man, not yet

twenty-five, but one who would pass for forty. He was taller than Ezra and seemed taller even than Brydd, though back to back the brothers were equal in height. In most other ways they were dissimilar, the massive William calm and easygoing, his patience all but inexhaustible, his humour hesitant and shy. He could not draw a circular wheel on paper, let alone a detailed wagon, but he could add columns of figures in his head and balance the cost of a job against the time it would take, then gauge his profit to within a few pence, more or less.

Like Brydd, William Cannaway had been apprenticed at twelve, not to a local blacksmith or wheelwright, but to a stonemason at Melksham, another burgeoning wool-town a few miles south of Chippenham. Twelve years on, and he was now set to inherit the yard from its present owner, a childless widower named Andrew Cobbin. Not that Andrew was dying, pray God he wasn't, but eventually, when his time came, he would leave the yard to William and had already told him so. As Cobbin saw it, the fair-minded William was a Cannaway in name but had long ago become the son he'd never sired. He had even painted it on a board to see how it would look, how it might have been. He'd done it in secret, when the yard was empty, then hidden the board beneath a pile of sacking in a loft. "Andrew Cobbin and Son—Stone Masons."

Lacking Brydd's imagination, William was content to absorb Cobbin's teachings and employ the traditional methods of dressing and shaping the stones. He brought nothing new to the work, for his real strength lay in his ability to organise and administer, to keep proper records and so ensure a profit for the yard. He knew that his brilliant young brother would have questioned and improved the design of things, and he admired and envied his talents. Brydd was the bright one in the family, no question of that. But would he have found time to add the columns and balance the costs? It was not likely, William thought, not unless someone closed the road between London and Bristol.

In the twelve years he had worked with Andrew Cobbin, William had risen from apprentice to quarryman, then from mason to a full-fledged partner. He did not pretend to know as much as the craftsmen twice and three times his age; but they, themselves, had been quick to acknowledge that, as they put it, "Young William could find a way to bag and sell the dust."

If it would have turned a profit, he'd have done so. Yet even without it, William Cannaway was well enough off to support his parents. But that was the thing they refused . . .

Almost midway in age between William and Brydd was the lively, dark-eyed Sophia. Born a Cannaway, she was now Sophia Biss, the wife of Joseph Biss, merchant of Bristol. She was the only member of the family who could read and write with ease, and the only one who could choose what she'd wear from a dozen changes of dress and more than twenty pairs of shoes.

She was also the only Cannaway who had ever travelled the thirty-five miles from Kennett to Bristol.

If Brydd was proud of William's progress as a stonemason, and William filled with admiration for his brother's talents with charcoal and chalk, they were both in awe of their sister. They remembered how, at the age of nine, Sophia had contributed a penny a week to the family purse by cleaning house for those villagers who were too infirm to do so, and by collecting berries from the hedgerows and tufts of wool from the briars on the downs.

William had already served two years of his apprenticeship and was in Melksham on the day Dr. Barrowcluffe called at the smithy. But Brydd was there, a youngster of eight, and remembered how the doctor had treated Ezra for a severe burn on his arm—the price of a moment's inattention near the furnace. He had stayed on to talk with the Cannaways and had learned that Sophia, then eleven years old, was unlettered and unread. A little more talk whilst he mulled things over, and then he'd offered to enrol the girl in his Saturday-morning class. Brydd had seen his father glance at Amalie, then shift with discomfort as he asked how much the lessons would cost.

The doctor had smiled at Sophia. "I'd in mind some vigorous scrubbing of the steps and floor tiles. Would that be agreeable to you, Mistress Sophia? An hour of your time for an hour of mine?" The girl had nodded immediately, eagerly. Oh, yes, she'd indicated, it would be quite agreeable to her.

"Ezra? Mistress Cannaway? No taint of scandal will attach to your daughter, I assure you of that. My housekeeper has been with me since my wife died, and she is known throughout the district as a fine and commonsensed woman. Mistress Cable; from this very valley, I believe."

Amalie had blinked approval, and Ezra said, "But for two hours' cleaning. And before she takes her lessons. Your time is worth more than the girl's, though she'll bring a shine to the tiles."

And so she had gone to Marlborough to clean and scrub and learn her letters and string them into words. There was always a family bound for market who were willing to find room in their cart for Sophia Cannaway, even though she asked ten questions to the mile.

By the time she was fifteen she had made the transition from pupil to teacher, helping the younger children with their lessons and taking over from the doctor in his absence. He also called upon her to assist in the office, at first entrusting her to treat simple cuts and abrasions, then encouraging her to watch as he worked with probe and scalpel. She fainted once at the spurt of blood, but never again, and some while later he made a special journey to Kennett to ask Ezra and Amalie if they would allow their daughter to join his household.

"She is as near the perfect helper as I'm likely to find, and I admit it, I've come to rely on her. She'll be paid out of my own pocket, so I fear it won't be much—"

"However much it is," Amalie told him, "it will do her very well. You are paying her out of your head, are you not, and that's the better wage."

Loving her for her faith, he said, "It's a head that's thinning with hair, Mistress Cannaway, though there might still be an idea or two in there, under the dust." She nodded, almost sternly, unwilling to accept his self-mockery, then offered him a jar of cider, cold from the barrel. Ezra did not drink unless the occasion warranted it—the birth of a neighbour's child, or a wedding, or when the harvest was in—but now he took the mug his wife handed him. With William successfully apprenticed to Andrew Cobbin and Sophia about to enter the doctor's household, it only remained for the twelve-year-old Brydd to be taken on by Alfred Nott and prove himself worthy.

But Sophia was to progress still further.

A few months after she had moved to Marlborough, and a week short of her sixteenth birthday, she had been walking along the tilted High Street when she noticed that a young man who had passed her earlier was about to pass her again. Taught never to stare, and at best to disguise her glances, she gave no more thought to it until she reached the imposing new Market Hall, situated in the middle of the street. There were few towns that could have found room for such a building in their main thoroughfare, but Marlborough prided itself on possessing one of the widest in England. And it was then that the young man reappeared in her path.

He did not rush past her this time, but stopped, as good as barring her way. Removing his tricorn hat, he bowed hurriedly and gasped, "You'll go on—and I shall miss you—and that'll be that. I pray you, don't go by—just let me—let me catch my breath."

He'd be presentable enough, she supposed, once the colour had drained from his face. And once he'd learned to link more than three or four words together without sucking in like bellows. She allowed him an instant in which to compose himself, then stepped aside, as though he was too coarse to give way to a lady.

"No, please don't go by. My name is Joseph Biss and I'll declare the truth. I saw you when you were back there along the street and I've been circling you since, you didn't notice, why should you, but I'm here from Bristol on my father's business, family business I might say, and when I set eyes on you, well, I had to effect a meeting—" Another heave on the bellows and a repeated, "Joseph Biss."

"So you said."

"Did I? Oh." He drew breath again and persevered. "My family's in the wool trade. Though not just wool. Fabrics, lace, even hemp and cord; we sell all kinds of rope to the chandlers in the port. You know Bristol of course, yes, well, we sell sailcloth too. And oilskins, and canvas, sheets of the stuff. Not much we don't sell in that line, the truth be told."

"I'd continue on, Master Biss."

"What? Oh, I see yes, certainly Mistress—?" He raised well-drawn eyebrows, though they failed to earn him an answer.

Sophia waited for him to move fully into the street, then walked on. She did not acknowledge that he had fallen into step with her, not quite at her side, but a pace behind, at her shoulder.

"You live in Marlborough's my guess, you've the grace for it. Town bred, that's clear enough, it's in the poise." Satisfied that he was right, he adopted the ridiculous clipped style that was in vogue with the fashionable young. "On your way home, eh? Pretty place, Marlborough. Only been here a week or two, m'self. Quite like to see what's doing. If there's aught to do, that is!" He tried a laugh, then let it die, unwanted. He was not at all sure of himself, and it showed.

The girl suddenly felt sympathy for him. He was so clumsy, so —what was the word Dr. Barrowcluffe had taught her?—so mala-droit. Yes, that would do nicely. Needing to pass her twice before finding the courage to speak . . . And his affectations . . . And his inventory of the family business . . . Oh, dear.

But he was harmless enough, and perhaps not quite the fool he seemed. And he had his looks, even and unblemished, and that was something. Naturally, she could not permit him to approach her like this, without being formally introduced. However, if he cared to present himself in the correct manner, and at the proper time . . .

She stopped abruptly. "The sun is bright enough for me to cast my own shadow. I've no need of yours. Anyway, I do not care to be followed by strangers."

"I've explained who I am," he protested lamely. "Joseph—"

"—Biss, yes, you hawk the name around. Well, announce it somewhere else, Joseph Biss. The doctor would not enjoy hearing that I had been accosted in this way. With your permission, sir?" She walked on again, leaving him hat in hand.

He was on the doorstep next day. Dr. Barrowcluffe happily took it upon himself to play the guardian and inquisitor, and when Sophia was summoned to his office she found Joseph pale and nervous. The formalities were duly observed, the housekeeper brought in as chaperone and the young couple allowed to sit op-posite each other and make of things what they would.

Fourteen months later they were married, and Sophia Canna-way, now Biss, went to live in Bristol, in a house that overlooked the estuary of the Severn. Joseph's parents had given him the ten-room house as a wedding present, along with a banking certificate for a thousand pounds and various other securities that assured his status in the mercantile district of the city. They opened an account for their daughter-in-law to the amount of two hundred pounds, with a further two hundred in company bonds. Joseph's mother took her shopping and a new cabinet was ordered to accommodate the clothes.

Far more wealthy than her brother William, Sophia could well afford to support Ezra and Amalie, and had implored them to let her do so. But that was the thing they refused . . .

To the best of Ezra's knowledge, there had always been a Cannaway in the smithy at Kennett. As a child, he'd heard his grandfather tell of how *his* grandfather had once shoed a horse for Queen Elizabeth's favourite, the arrogant Earl of Leicester, though the glory of the occasion had been marred by the earl's point-blank refusal to pay. Since then there had been judges and sheriffs, peers of the realm and members of the aristocracy, famous men reduced to walking their horses or waiting in the village whilst a cleat or coach bolt was repaired. It was expected that son would follow father into the business in unbroken line, and that there always would be a Cannaway at Kennett.

But it was Ezra himself who had chosen to break the line. Bound by the promise he had made his parents, he had spent all his working life in the yard, assisting travellers on their way, yet never leaving the confines of the valley. More inquisitive perhaps than his forebears, he had nevertheless accepted that his own curiosity must go unsatisfied. The world would know where to find Ezra Cannaway, even though he knew so little of the world.

But he'd determined that things would be different for his children; he'd forge no chains for them. They would be free to ride their own paths and encouraged to do so, and only when all three had left the valley would he accept their support and allow the fire to die in the furnace.

Thus he had seen William established as a stonemason at Melksham, and Sophia married to the likeable Joseph Biss. As for Brydd, it would not be long before he too found his path. Alfred knew he would soon move on, and had said as much to Ezra. But it was for Brydd himself to decide which path he'd take from the valley, and when. Until then, Ezra Cannaway was content to pound the anvil at Kennett, whilst Amalie dipped and cooled the candles.

❉

Brydd spent that night with his parents, eating their food and sharing the warmth of their fire, then excused himself with talk of a full day's sketching tomorrow. He retired to the low-beamed bedroom he had once shared with Sophia and William and stood for a long time at the window, watching the snow build against the panes and letting the sense of his own deceit chill him from within.

There'd be no sketches chalked tomorrow, for it was then that he'd be riding across the downs in search of the stoneyard and his shambling, good-natured brother. He would tell William about the von Kreutels and Carl-Maria and the ambush, but most of all about the coach. And William would understand. He'd see why it was impossible for Brydd to work on as a common wheelwright, wasting his life and squandering his talent on the construction of clumsy wagons and hay sleds and crude two-wheeled dung carts. If anyone understood it would be William, for he too was enacting his dream.

Shivering in the window alcove, Brydd was not to know that his parents already understood. They had kept their secret too well for that, leaving their younger son to decide for himself on the path he'd take from the valley. He would tell them when he was ready, when he felt the time was right. Meanwhile, there were candles to be made and barrels to be strengthened—no shortage of work for for the elderly Cannaways, not when they worked so well.

❉

True at least to his story, he was up at dawn, saddling his horse and tying on the satchel that contained his paper and chalks. The snow must have stopped for a time during the night, for there was no depth to it in the yard. Fresh flakes were tumbling from the overcast, but he heard a distant post-horn blare from the direction of Beckhampton—a coach about to set out from the "Blazing Rag"—and he took it as an indication that the roads and hills were passable.

Amalie gave him breakfast and asked pointedly what he hoped to sketch in a snowstorm—"Unless it's the storm itself. It would do you no harm to attend church with us. And the snow might have abated by the blessing."

Brydd glanced at his father and said, "I will next week, I promise, but I need the day to—I need the day, that's all."

"Next week then," Amalie affirmed, tossing the words over her shoulder like a pinch of spilt salt. "I've made a mark of it."

Brydd nodded dutifully and devoured the cheese and roasted ham, the crusty bread and the measure of warm, dark ale.

"Where will you look for your perch today?" Ezra asked. "Toward Cherhill, or in the valley?"

"Toward Cherhill, most likely," Brydd lied. "It offers a better vantage of the road."

"Then make sure you don't tangle with the brigands again."

"I didn't seek them out," he protested. "I'm armed with chalks, not pistols."

"It's well known what you carry," Ezra reminded him, "I'm saying take care, that's all. You may not be looking for *them,* but you denied them their prize and who's to say they'll not be sniffing for you?"

No coward, but no fool, Brydd Cannaway decided to stay well south of the coaching road on his sixteen-mile journey to Melksham. It would be senseless to catch a bullet so soon along his path.

He knew the first downland miles as well as anyone, keeping to the ridges where necessary, then letting his horse canter across the crisp white snowfields, their surface unbroken save by the tracks of fox and hare and deer. He did not see another horseman all the way, and revelled in the loneliness of the bleak rolling downs. He shouted things he had never dared say in the yard at Lockeridge, lifting his face to the snow and yelling in the knowledge that there was no one to hear him. The hills around were empty, desolate and bare. They offered a natural privacy that needed neither lock, nor shutter, nor bar.

He reached the first country road for miles and reined in, his mind swept clear. "God," he said fervently, "I hope there are grounds like this around Vienna. I shall miss them if there are not."

He turned south and followed the road to a crossing. Then he nudged his horse against a tall, snow-caked signpost and balanced in the stirrups whilst he wiped the lettered boards. That way to Calne—3 Miles. That way to Devizes—3 Miles. This way to Melksham—6 Miles. He patted the horse for its obedience, then set it at a trot. He did not think of it then, but realised later that somewhere along that stretch of curtained road he had passed the perimeter of his world and gone unwittingly beyond his ten-mile span. At last, he would grin—the traveller.

※

It had taken a day and a night for William Cannaway to regain his hearing, though even now his ears still dinned from the effects of the blast. He had twice opened the door to imagined callers, admitting gusts of snow into the small flagged room that formed the lower half of his bachelor dwelling. The flakes had melted from the heat of a bellied stove, then trickled across the uneven floor to be absorbed by the drab plaster walls.

In all the years he had been with Andrew Cobbin, first as an apprentice and later as a full-fledged partner, William had visited dozens of quarries and witnessed scores of firings. Occasionally one of the workers would curse as a splinter of stone flew from the rock face, tearing his leather jerkin or drawing blood from his face or forearm. Accidents happened when gunpowder was being used, though for the most part the quarry-masters were cautious and reliable, taking care to safeguard their men. A whistle would be blown as a warning to clear the area, then blown again in a series of short, shrill blasts before the fuse trains were ignited. By then the workers would have taken cover, huddled behind a wagon or a shed, their folded work gloves pressed to their ears.

Yesterday, however, there had been a mistake.

It was the first time William had visited that particular quarry, drawn there by the promise of some "English marble." No true marble existed in the southern counties, but the term was used for a type of hard, reddish-grey limestone. It was a handsome piece, without cracks or fissures, but also without a cleaving grain. Denied this natural guideline into which his workmen could hammer their heavy conical wedges, the quarrymaster had decided to split it with a measured quantity of gunpowder.

Whilst the holes were being bored and the powder inserted and the fuse trains laid, the man had prattled on in an attempt to sell more of his stock. He had already heard of William Cannaway—the twenty-five-year-old who looked forty and would one day inherit the yard at Melksham—and he was eager to impress him. "I can get you whatever you want, sir, granites or sandstone, Bathstone or Rigate, ragstone, freestone, you put a name to it and I'll have it dug out and delivered to you. I keep a row of samples, you'll find them over there, just brush the snow off them and give them a look. You count on me, sir, they say I've a nose for stone!" He smiled a salesman's smile and left William to inspect the propped-up slabs.

Maybe it was the wind that snatched the sound, or the snow that muffled it, but whatever the cause, the first warning blast of the whistle went unheard.

A few moments later came the final shrill series. William heard those clear enough, turned in disbelief, then started running flat-footed for cover. But his size robbed him of speed and he was still lumbering toward shelter when the powder caught and exploded.

The sound banged out to club him around the head and send him sprawling to the ground. The fall was softened by the snow, but he was nevertheless shocked and winded, and convinced his hearing was gone. The pain roared inside his skull, then turned and padded away, leaving its echoes to settle and fade. Yet it left something behind, less a sound than a feeling, or perhaps just the memory of noise.

He pushed himself to his knees in time to see a workman stagger past, blood running from his ear. Then the quarrymaster appeared, ignoring the man in favour of the purchaser from Melksham. He mouthed something at William, who waved him away and pointed at the workman. The quarrymaster nodded, mouthing again, but made no effort to go after him. It was Cobbin's young partner that mattered and would need a generous measure of gin. "Come along to the hut, sir. I've something there to quell the shock." He mimed uncorking a jar and dispensing its contents. Then he smiled and reached forward to help.

It was all William needed to bring him to his feet, shoulder the quarrymaster aside and make his way up the long curving path from the pit. To hell with a man who ignored his workers and his responsibility. He'd sell nothing to the yard at Melksham, not even if he priced it at a farthing a ton.

The ride home had been slow and painful, and William had slept the night by the stove, his ears muffled with a scarf, his body wrapped in a blanket, his hat still on his head, his feet in his boots. This morning, when he'd awakened, he had inspected the scarf for traces of blood, but found nothing on the wool. Encouraged, he had rapped his desk with a walking stick and heard the wood strike wood. An indistinct sound, to be sure, but better than silence.

Apart from the desk, the room contained the box-backed chair in which he'd slept, a cheap scarred table and bench, a free-standing shelf misshapen with books and ledgers, and a stairway that tangled up steep as a ladder to the attic—his bedroom if he cared to brave the cold. Beneath the stairs was a clothes rack from which were suspended his two greatcoats—the one for summer, the other for winter—two pairs of breeches, a patched assortment of shirts, his one cravat and, below them, his good pair of shoes and his bad.

The shabby furniture and threadbare garments were not much to show for thirteen years' work in the stoneyard, and the house itself was a poor advertisement for an established young partner. But William Cannaway had never sought to display his wealth. Why should he, he reasoned, and for whom?

He heard another rap on the door—thought he heard it—and disbelieved his ears. He had already imagined two morning callers and felt foolish, answering the weather. The rapping stopped after a while, then started again, this time as a sharper tap in the direction of the window. He turned from his desk and saw a figure beyond the glass. It was too tall to be Andrew Cobbin, though it might be someone looking for the stonemason. At least it *was* someone, proof that his hearing was on the mend.

He opened the door and said, "Can I be of help to you?" and did not recognise his own hand-me-down coat or his brother's shadowed face.

"You can let me in, William, that'd be a start."

"Brydd?" He peered under the snow-rimmed brim. "By God, it is! Yes, Brydd, yes, in with you, in you come. Are you alone?" His brother said yes he was, removed his hat and slapped it against the outer wall. Then, feeling strangely unsettled, he edged past William and stood like any common caller, waiting to speak his piece.

The time for a renewed greeting came and went, and then it would have seemed foolish to embrace. So the brothers merely looked at each other, Brydd nodding to reassure William that all was well at Kennett.

But William asked anyway. "This is the first time you've ever— Are you here with bad news?"

"Far from it, I hope. Our parents are in good health, though of course Ezra—"

"What of Ezra?"

"Nothing. Don't alarm yourself. I was only going to say that of course Ezra works too hard."

"They both do."

"Yes."

"Yes, Amalie the same."

They lapsed into silence, and Brydd waited for his brother to ask the reason for this first-ever vist to Melksham.

Ask me something, William, anything, or I'll think you're about to wish me Godspeed. Am I to regard you as an uncle these days, and myself as your nephew?

"There's some ale about somewhere. Shed your coat and pull that bench to the stove. I'll search out some mugs." He turned away, then swung back again, awkward in his attempts to be at ease. "I'm glad to see you, Brydd, that I am. It's not often enough we meet, and I know this is the farthest you've ever travelled from the valley."

"Don't shame me," Brydd told him. "I've come for your support in a venture that will take me a world away from here. In truth, William, I've come to ask you for money."

"Put your coat on that peg there." He located an earthenware jar and two stone mugs, filled the mugs and set them on the table. Then he fitted his broad frame into the box-backed chair and asked Brydd how he'd earned the cut above his eye.

From then on it was better between them. Brydd described the fight with Hach, admitting that the monster had damn near crushed him. William smiled and recounted the incident in the quarry, and the brothers agreed that they'd both been thrown about. They talked of Ezra and Amalie, of Dr. Barrowcluffe and the Darles, of the innkeeper Sam Gilmore and the wheelwright Alfred Nott and the stonemason Andrew Cobbin. And later, leaning forward on the bench, Byrdd said, "I was up on the hills, a week ago today . . ." and went on to tell William about the coach and the ambush and his venture.

"Eight hundred miles? *Eight hundred?*"

"Or more, so the doctor said."

"And you'll cross between England and France?"

"According to the map."

"And go to—what is it?—Paris, then on to Vienna?"

"That's the intention. It may lack sense to you, but I'm bound to try it. After all," he grinned, "I came sixteen miles today."

William gazed at him, nodded ponderously, then behaved quite out of character, reaching forward to cup his brother around the neck and hug him close. "Sixteen miles and you'd be well on your way, well along to Vienna. I'd say you're bound to try it!"

❋

He kept the money well hidden, as did most of those who lived beyond the protection of a bank. They were fine institutions, and no doubt to be trusted, but they were for the convenience of city folk, their tiled floors laid to take the clip of a polished boot heel and the rap of a gold-tipped cane. It was said that in some banks the counters were draped with velvet, to stifle the vulgar chink of coins, and that a clerk would be dismissed on the spot if he failed to remember the name and title of a client. True or not, these edifices with their marble columns and frescoed walls were a long way from Melksham, and of no use to William Cannaway.

He had discussed the situation with Brydd, who'd insisted from the outset that he would borrow whatever William cared to lend, and write out a receipt for it, dated and signed by them both. William would, of course, retain the paper.

"I know nothing of interest rates, nor how they're arrived at, so I'll repay whatever seems correct."

"Well, let's see now," William teased. "I must balance risk against the probability of reclamation, then take into account the length of time the money's afloat—that's the term the bankers use for dispersed coinage—and the underscore that with what's called foreign departure."

"I don't follow a word," Brydd surrendered. "I'll repay whatever seems right."

He did not think he'd heard his brother laugh so uproariously in years, and William accounted it his best laugh ever. To tease the tough, ambitious Brydd and get away with it? It'd be a memory to treasure.

"You'll repay me nothing," he said, "at least, not in coins. But there's something I *shall* require from you, something you should be delighted to supply. When you return—if you return, that is, and have not already been employed as coachmaker to the courts of Vienna—you can fashion me a gig, a good one mind, one that'll hold the road. How much does a gig cost these days?"

"It depends," Brydd demurred, the challenge not yet sunk in. "If you want one that's—"

"Don't warm to your subject, or you'll have the room full of shafts and wheels. Just quote a figure."

Loth to generalise, Brydd retorted, "Why not ask the price of a house? I don't know, it varies. Five pounds. Ten. Twenty. A thousand if it's to be hooped and hammered with gold! I don't *know*, William. I don't make gigs. I wish to God I did."

"Well, I'll tell you this," his brother gasped, pulling the misshapen bookshelf from the wall. "You'd better make it for twenty. It's all I can let you have."

Brydd stared at him, at the same time seeing the hovel in which he lived; the damp plaster walls and torn clothes, the stub ends of candles, the worm-ridden desk and torturer's chair. "Twenty pounds? You're willing to lend me that?"

William lifted a flagstone from the floor, blue with the exertion, then looked across at his brilliant young brother. "It had better set off, even without the horses. Perhaps you'll learn to make one that runs on air. Anyway, I shall want all Wiltshire staring as I go by." He grinned at his own mild humour and lifted a drawstring bag from the recess in the floor.

❋

They talked through the morning. They found it easy to talk now, though behind their discussions and exchange of views they questioned themselves as to why it had become so easy. Surely not because Brydd had asked for money and William had supplied it? Surely the Cannaways did not need to pay and be paid for their words, least of all with each other?

And yet the money was a part of it, they acknowledged, a spark for the fuse train, a chalk with which to sketch. Brydd had set out from Kennett in the hopes of borrowing money, then ridden beyond the former bounds of his travels and drawn closer to his brother and been challenged to make a gig. True, he was twenty pounds richer than when he'd arrived, but the money itself had been a token of faith, to be repaid with his skills. And, in a way, the gold and silver coins had been proof of William's skills, reflecting his thrift and sense of business. Who else at twenty-five was a partner in a profitable yard and able to advance such a sum?

There was Sophia's husband, of course, and the thought prompted William to remark, "You'd have raised more if you'd gone to Bristol. Joseph Biss would have let you have fifty pounds, or a hundred."

"Very likely," Brydd agreed, "and I'd have approached him if you'd turned me down. But I knew you would not."

"Oh, you knew I would not? I see. You knew I'd hand you half my savings. Good old William."

"No," Brydd grinned, "I didn't count on half. I'd have been happy with less, though I was sure you'd help me. And I promise you this, good old William, you'll get the best-made gig for your money."

"That I will, brother, that I will. What else, when it's a Cannaway coach?"

They both liked the sound of it, and sat quiet for a moment, thinking of the day when Brydd would deliver it and William ride it out.

The first Cannaway carriage . . .

Then William said, "You'll need something to wear on this journey of yours, a thornproof coat and breeches. Finish your ale and we'll disturb a friend of mine and get you measured up."

"Very well." Brydd nodded. "But before we go—I've told Dr. Barrowcluffe of my plans, and Jed, and now you. But I've kept things from our parents, and from Alfred Nott. Alfred knows I'm disgruntled, but how will Ezra and Amalie take it? How deep will it cut with them when I tell them I've leaving? Sophia has gone to Bristol, and you're here in Melksham, and I'm the only one remaining in the valley. What will they think when they hear that I, too, wish to leave? The family will be so—dispersed."

Shifting within the confines of his chair, William then settled himself and gazed at his brother. "It may upset you to hear it, Brydd, but it won't cut them at all. You know they've refused Sophia's support and mine—"

"I know they're prideful, I know that for a fact."

"They are, but it's not just pride that's made them reject our help. They are waiting for you. They could not tell you so, for fear you'd give you life to the smithy. So they worked on there in the knowledge that one day you would find your path or, as I say, enact the dream. They love you, Brydd, but I'm the one to tell you—they'd love it more to see the three of us dispersed. You tell them about Vienna and how far it is and why you must go there, and with any luck you'll get Ezra to dare a jar of cider. They'll applaud what you tell them, my dear brother, and it'll be all through the valley in a day. 'You know our daughter married that fine young merchant from Bristol, and the hefty William's established in the stoneyard at Melksham? Well, now it seems that young Brydd has stuck his nose toward Vienna, someplace in Europe, I forget where he said.' That's what Ezra will tell them, and it'll be all through the valley in a week."

"And Alfred Nott? When do I give notice to him?"

"As soon as you like; I'm sure it won't surprise him. Tell everyone, brother, they've waited long enough, and it's time you put the Kennett valley at its ease." He smiled, then knuckled the table—the sound coming back to him clear and full—and said, "Let's get you measured up for your travels and, what's her name, Annette?"

❋

The news did indeed go through the valley in a week. Ezra took it calmly, satisfied that Dr. Barrowcluffe had approved of the venture. "Nevertheless," Ezra cautioned, "travellers tell all kinds of tales. I've heard of countries where there's only gravel and sand, no grass or forests anywhere, just gravel and sand. I didn't dispute it with the man who told me, but that doesn't mean I believed it. Oh, yes, and the horses stood eight feet high and had humps." He chuckled at the traveller's flight of fancy.

"I'd not believe that either," Brydd agreed. "But it's different with Vienna, I saw the paintings on the coach. There's a river called the Danube, and hunting grounds and markets and suchlike. They'll speak a different language, but they'll otherwise be the same, near enough."

Amalie was satisfied because her husband and William and the doctor were satisfied—and because Brydd would not be setting out until the spring. She listened to what he had to say about the fishing boat and the Channel ferry and the ride to Paris and beyond, but she offered no advice, this gentle woman who had not been to Marlborough in fifteen years, nor ever to Chippenham or Melksham or the towns that ringed the valley. As a girl she had splashed across the Kennett River and, stripped to her shift, waded in a spill pool near Lockeridge. Ezra had enticed her in, and she could still recollect the guilt and pleasure of their escapade. But she not could imagine the breadth of water that divided England from France. The Kennett was quite wide enough, and the spill pool was supposedly twenty feet deep in the middle . . .

At Lockeridge, Alfred Nott and his wife listened and nodded with equanimity, careful to avoid each other's glance.

"So I'm to be rid of you at last, come the spring. I'll not have to put up with your complaints and suggestions? I'll be free to make the cart and wagons the way I've always done, without you to shout improvement?" He shook his head, as though bemused by his good fortune. Then he said, "I'm not a cursing man—and you'll forgive me, Mary, when I tell him—but I shall be as sorry as the devil to see you go. Aye, I shall, Brydd Cannaway, sorry as the devil."

"I, too," Mary said. "I'll be sorry as—can be. And as for the complaints, you go on voicing them. There's been room for improvement here, and I daresay there'll be call for it in Vienna." She pursed her lips, a staunch warning to the foreigners.

At Overhill Farm, George Darle and his daughter had already heard the news, for Jedediah regarded secrets as something to be told. Brydd visited them in the week before Christmas, to find Elizabeth offhand and unpleasant, one moment scorning the venture as an impracticable dream, the next accusing Brydd of deserting the wheelwright who had taught and employed him.

"How *can* you run off and leave Alfred after all he's done for you? You've been five years at the yard, and now's the time to repay him for his teachings. Instead, you nurse some wild scheme —"

"It's not wild at all. I know where I want to go, and why, and Alfred understands it perfectly well."

"You're running off," she insisted, "though if you ask me you'll not get far."

"*If* I ask you," he snapped, "*then* you can tell me."

The retort brought tears and Elizabeth fled from the room, leaving George to explain what Brydd should have known for himself. The girl was heartbroken because he was leaving *her*. "She's not concerned for Alfred or Mary. But are you so blinkered that you can't see she's drawn to you?"

"She's a delightful—"

"—child? Yes, Jedediah told me it's how you regard her, and no one but Elizabeth can alter that. But she's a sight more than a child, my friend, and if you cannot respond to her feelings, I'd ask you to respect them. Now you'd better ride on home. We will see you at Kennett for the Christmas meal." He nodded brusquely— the firmest dismissal Brydd had ever received from him—and the young Cannaway left the house, trailed by Jed.

Outside in the yard the friends shrugged at the ways of women.

"You know what?" Brydd said. "It makes me all the more determined to be gone. You'd think a marriage had been arranged, the way she acts."

"It probably has," Jed grinned, "inside her head. And then we'd be brothers, or the next thing to!" He thought it worth a punch, and Brydd's shoulder ached all the way across the downs to Kennett.

FOUR

Bowls and platters had been borrowed for the occasion. The log shed had been filled and the kindling brought indoors. The covered stables had been swept and cleared, making room for William's horse and Joseph's curricle and George Darle's cart. Sherry and cider and ale had been purchased. A new bench had been pegged together, and one of the kitchen chairs repaired. Squat yellow candles had been set in their dishes. Rye and wheat had been mixed to make maslin flour and the loaves baked and wrapped in sacking. Sugar, starch, egg white and rose water had been beaten into a paste, the prime ingredients of marchpane. When the paste had stiffened it would be sprinkled with ground almonds or pistachio nuts, then served before the cheese. The goose dish had been entrusted to the baker, the only man with an oven large enough to accommodate it. He would keep the oven alight throughout the Christmas morning—his present to the villagers of Kennett.

A warped door had been shaved to fit. Beds and pallets had been made up. Amalie, Sophia and Elizabeth would sleep in one room; Ezra and George, William and Joseph in the other; Brydd and Jed in the hayloft. Downstairs, the beams and windows had been decorated with sprigs of holly and painted wooden stars.

Amalie had found time to make a batch of minced beef tarts and biscuits and take them as her offering to the church. Other villagers would deliver pies and cakes and sugared fruits which the parish priest would then distribute among the poorest members of the community. The Reverend Swayle had never yet sampled the offerings, though he'd come close to it—God knew how close. It was a severe temptation, especially when his wife was such a splash-and-spatter cook.

Other problems had been solved or circumvented, tempers calmed, neighbours visited, errands run. It was not the time to get under Amalie's feet, nor allow the draught into the kitchen, nor let the heat of the stove die down. It was a serious business, the preparation of the festive meal, and woe betide anyone caught idling. Amalie Cannaway would have things done her way, the correct way, and neither Ezra nor Brydd was foolish enough to argue. She had, after all, made the Christmas dinner forty times to date.

❋

Sophia and Joseph Biss arrived, the worse for their journey. They had travelled from Bristol to Chippenham in safety, but when they had reached the wool-town they'd been advised to change their route.

"It's the Cherhill gang up to their bloody tricks. They waylaid a westbound coach this morning and interfered with the women, and there's a stage wagon long overdue. Someone's bound to get his throat cut in the next day or two, or a ball through his head. You take your lady by the lower road, sir, and you'll come to no harm."

It had added hours to the journey, and Joseph had several times dismounted from the light, hooded curricle in order to guide the horse through the snowdrifts. However, they reached Kennett before nightfall and turned shivering into the yard. It was Christmas Eve, and Ezra and Amalie and Brydd were out to greet them.

There was a deal of embracing between parents and daughter and her exhausted husband, and then Sophia went forward to where Brydd was sweet-talking the horse.

"You're taller yet, you know. And thinner, are you thinner?"

"Very likely," he said. "Mother keeps me alive on crusts."

"Oh, I'm sure she does. Once you've eaten everything else."

"And you, you look very fine, Sophia."

"I'm chilled to the bone; *through* the bone, if it's possible."

"Even so." He nodded approval, praise indeed from a brother and a man who had set eyes on Annette von Kreutel.

She asked if William had arrived and he said no, then looked past her and said yes, seeing his benefactor ride into the yard. There were more shouts of greeting, more hugs and handclasps, another mount to be fed and curried. Joseph unloaded a travelling bag and a large something-or-other wrapped in a blanket, but refused to say what it was. Amalie led her daughter into the house, whilst the men unsaddled William's horse and unhitched the curricle, then wheeled it into the stables. It was the first time the family had been together since the harvest festival, and the brothers nudged each other like children as Ezra said, "Let's get the animals settled, and we'll froth some cider."

❄

The talk was of Bristol, which Joseph maintained was now the second city in the kingdom. Speaking with the assurance that marriage to Sophia had given him, he said, "It's long been the port to follow London, but these days it's more populous than either York or Norwich. At the last count there were more than twenty thousand souls in Bristol, though I've heard estimates run as high as forty or fifty thousand. We're taking the sea trade even from the capital, particularly on those routes to Virginia and the Carolinas. We're building sugar houses at the rate of three and four a year, and extending the quays and laying out new streets and I don't know what else." With a smile that was too disarming to be smug he boasted, "There's a new Biss warehouse just completed, and another under construction. And, since we paid for most of the wharf that fronts them, we've called it The Biss. I tell you, Bristol's the place to be."

"Perhaps," William murmured, "though I doubt if Brydd would agree with you." Then he nodded at his brother and waited for him to tell Sophia and Joseph about the von Kreutels and their coach and the ambush, about Vienna-on-the-Danube and the dream he intended to enact.

The news was greeted with delight—and a further measure of

cider—and the talk was then of distances and methods of travel, of the cheats and cozeners who preyed on the unwary, of the need to keep one's baggage at hand and one's money in a thick buttoned pocket.

"You look capable enough," Joseph told him, "and it'd be a fool who came at you face to face. But there are other ways of misleading a man, and—" He broke off and glanced at Amalie. "With your permission, Mistress Cannaway?"

"You tell him what he should hear, Joseph. Better a warning than a wounding."

"That's true enough," he agreed, returning to Brydd to continue, "There's the child who appears to be lost, and pleads with you to see it home. It'll snivel and clutch at your sleeve, and you'll feel sorry for it and soon forget that the child is leading *you*. A turning here and an alleyway there, and then *you'll* be the one who's lost. At which point the urchin will dart away, leaving you to the mercy of cutthroats, crouched in the shadows. Children are an attractive lure, Brydd. It's their very harmlessness that misleads."

Ever courteous, he paused in case the others wished to speak. But the Cannaways were content to listen, wondering at a world in which children could be so abused. It didn't happen in the Kennett Vale, nor in Marlborough or Melksham. Robbery there was still the province of the footpad and highwayman.

"And then, of course, there are the young ladies and the stories they've been rehearsed to tell. You'll be seated at some coffeehouse table and an attractive woman will catch your eye, and the next thing you know she'll be outpouring a tragic tale of eviction or an illness in the family. Or maybe she'll wish to redeem some heirloom or other, pawned from necessity. And the complications that can arise from that . . .

"Accompany her and she, too, may lead you to the cutthroats. Advance her the money and you will never see her or your coins again. Demand some security and you'll discover that whatever she leaves has been stolen, and you'll be pleading your case from a foreign gaol. Again, *you'll* be the one who's lost."

Brydd grinned wryly, grateful for the advice, but convinced that Joseph was, well, the merchant he was, given to counting his

fingers after every handshake with a stranger. "You're saying that
the men might be cheats and cozeners and must be watched?
That a lost child is in reality a lure and must never be assisted?
That an attractive woman is all of those and must be made to occupy a separate table? Hell, Joseph, can you not find some deceit
in a horse?"

Unabashed, his brother-in-law replied, "You'll be sold such an
animal, and an hour later it'll unseat you and trot back to its former master, taking with it your saddle and baggage and I don't
know what else. Never trust a market-bought horse, or think it's
yours just because you're astride it. They're called prodigals in
Bristol, for they always return home, and there is no limit to the
number of times a prodigal can be sold. So you see, there can well
be deceit in a horse." He watched straight-faced as Brydd stared
at him, then saw the young Cannaway throw back his head and
laugh to stir the holly. "It's done, Joseph, I'm converted! I'll be
wary of them all, I promise you! I'll button my pockets and use
my satchels for a pillow; you've my word on it, I will!" He turned
to his father and found that Ezra had already lifted the cider jar
by its neck.

❅

All week it had snowed and stopped and snowed again, scattering
a few more flakes before drifting westward to whiten Bristol, or
sweeping east to turn the muddy streets of London into a chill
and dripping morass. It was said to be the heat of the cities that
made conditions worse, the snow melting before it ever reached
the ground. True or not, there was little to be said for the drifts
that blocked the country roads, or buried the sheep, or stranded
travellers on the downs. Snow was pretty from the other side of a
window, but it had never yet helped a shopkeeper sell his merchandise, nor made a farm cart run faster. The children loved it
because they could make snowmen and castles and show off their
aim. But for their parents it was something that brought down a
roof or weakened a wall or doused the kitchen fire. Better the
wind and the rain than the swirling lace of snow, for it came in silence and settled in silence and leaked its destruction without a
whistle or a drum. A coverlet of snow was attractive, but who'd

wish to sleep beneath such a blanket when it might melt and drown the sleeper in his bed?

There was the danger of too much snow on Christmas morning in the Kennett Vale. It was blowing along the valley from the east and sticking to the cloaks and capes of those who made their way to church; to Amalie's hood and Sophia's; to Ezra's hat, now beyond age; to Joseph's smart grey cape and William's serviceable *surtout* and Brydd's hand-me-down with its frayed collar and cuffs. It was what the villagers referred to as sidesmen's weather, for it hustled the congregation to their pews.

They were met at the door by the Reverend Swayle, the skeletal victim of his wife's splash-and-spatter meals. He thanked Amalie for her offerings and seemed to shrink as he did so, not wishing to dwell on the subject of minced beef pies and sweetmeats. It was right that the poor should receive them, but where was the justice when the man who dispensed them was visibly wasting away?

Amalie could see no justice in it at all. Swayle was down to the bone this winter, and if his wife wouldn't fill his belly, then others would. There'd be pies in the porch from now on, and thick wheaten biscuits. God would see to it that he ate them and, hopefully, keep Mistress Swayle on the far side of the lych-gate.

The service was as boisterous as a country fair. There were those who roared the responses, or insisted on talking through the prayers; those who changed places, edging along one pew and stumbling into another; those who had brought their dogs with them, or puffed at their pipes; those too enfeebled to stand in the jostling throng, or too drunk to try. Some arrived when the service was half over, passing others who'd decided to leave. Hats were waved in salute, children cuffed, invitations extended and acknowledged. The local squire arrived with a dozen booted friends, growled something about an overloaded ark and stamped out again, his duty done.

The Reverend Swayle led the congregation as best he could, then intoned the blessing and dismissed them. He would rather they'd left their dogs at the gate and extinguished their pipes, but at least this raucous flock had none of the white-gloved sanctimony of those who visited their churches only at Easter and Christmastide. The inhabitants of Kennett and the district were regular in their attendance, and could be forgiven their impiety.

They'd be more subdued next Sunday, no doubt of that, when the gallons of ale and cider that turned to vinegar in their blood . . .

Outside, the snow was thinning in the air. Brydd caught sight of Alfred Nott and his wife and strode across to bid them the season's greetings. They, in turn, introduced him to a group of Mary's relatives who had ridden up from Devizes. Then the relatives themselves were hailed by others, and Brydd felt the sting of Jed's fist on his arm. So it went, the ripples of recognition spreading out from the church and across the common ground.

The young men chatted with their own friends and neighbours, then walked over to where George Darle and his daughter were talking with the Cannaways. Brydd remembered how, earlier in the week, Elizabeth had scorned his venture and run weeping from the kitchen at Overhill. He recalled George's words on the subject—"If you cannot respond to her feelings, I'd ask you to respect them"—and decided to do just that. If the girl was in love with him, and both George and Jed seemed to think she was, then he must avoid distressing her. She was a delightful—well, yes, more than a child, a delightful friend. He *liked* Elizabeth. He'd always liked her. But that was not the same as love, surely it wasn't?

The Darles had come down from Overhill by cart, and the farmer offered Amalie and Sophia a lift to the smithy. Elizabeth chose to walk with the men, and the two families made their way through the village. Amid a flurry of farewells the other members of the congregation were dispersing from the common. The Reverend Swayle watched them go, then left the door open to rid his church of pipe smoke.

※

No one knew when the song would come, only that it would. No mention was ever made of it at the Christmas table for fear William would shy off. He'd sing when he was ready, and only then would the talk die away.

It would be the same song he had rendered each Christmas for the past ten years, a sentimental piece that sounded well in his deep, comfortable voice. It never failed to make Amalie sniff at the sadness of it all, though she would not have missed hearing it for the world.

But it was not yet time. Elizabeth was in earnest conversation with Sophia, William discussing business stratagems with Joseph Biss. George and Ezra were arranging when best to repair one of George's grille harrows, Brydd and Jed passing their plates to Amalie for a further helping of goose pie, turnips and cabbage. Above the table, the painted wooden stars revolved on their strings, stirred by the heat of the fire. Candles glowed and spluttered. More food was offered and heaped on the platters. More drink was poured, more conversations started and interrupted, one topic entwined with another. Jokes they had heard before were told again and treated as new. The Cherhill gang was mentioned, and opinions aired as to how the brigands might be defeated. Plans ranged from an all-out attack on their hideout to petitioning Dutch Willy. Perhaps the king would dispatch a troop of fusiliers, or lend the villagers a cannon with which to blow the bastards to hell. Jed was sure he could operate a fieldpiece and banged the table, a willing artilleryman.

They ate cakes and cheese and leaned back in their chairs or against the dry, whitewashed walls. The talk was more desultory now, the mood relaxed and reflective. They had earned their meal with a year's hard work, a year in which warehouses had been erected, stone quarried and dressed, candles dipped, wagons constructed, sheep farmed on the downs, horseshoes forged in the smithy. They deserved this respite, the Cannaways and the Bisses and the Darles, and they were in no hurry to move.

And then, without intrusion, William began to sing. He sang only for himself at first, his deep voice catching the melancholy of the tune. What little talk there was faded away and the listeners gazed unseeing or closed their eyes, losing themselves in the song.

"Ne'er shall I see her, ne'er again, the maid that
        once I saw.
    Her hair was like the wind-tossed wheat, gold-woven
        on that sunlit morn,
    Her eyes were gentle as the dawn, yet held me they
        in awe.
    Ne'er shall I hear her, ne'er again, the maid that
        once I heard.

Her voice was like the zephyr's sigh, clear as the
    songbird's melody,
And all she said enchanted me, each mystic, magic word."

Only now did he rise to his feet, lifting the chair and setting it
back with the merest tap on the flagstones.

"Ne'er shall I hold her, ne'er again, the maid that
    once I held.
Her mouth was soft and scented sweet; ah, fashioned
    were her lips for love,
And all the world I vowed to move, so deep was I
    enspelled."

His voice was stronger and he was singing for all of them, the
shy William Cannaway turned eloquent. He had no woman of his
own, but who would have guessed it when he made the loss so
real?

"Ne'er will she free me from her spell, the maid
    that chained my heart.
The vision came but once and now I'm left to weep,
    my strength to wane,
Never the maid to meet again, forbidden though to part."

A pause, and then the melody changed, the final refrain sung
low and wistful.

"Beware the maid with wind-tossed hair and eyes as
    gentle as the dawn,
For you may come at morn to love, then live alone to
    mourn . . ."

He stood for a moment, sharing the silence. Then he dragged
his chair forward and sank into it, refreshing himself from his
mug. Elizabeth led the applause and the families clamoured to
tell him he had never sung it better. They doubted if it could be
sung better than that. They decided it could not.

❄

Sophia and Joseph had promised a different kind of entertain-
ment, and when the table had been cleared and scrubbed the mer-

chant produced the wrapped something-or-other he'd brought from Bristol. He detailed Brydd and Jed to move the table against the wall, then arrange the chairs and benches in front of it, facing the far side of the room. He did not remove the blanket until everyone was settled, with their backs to the table.

"It'll lessen the enjoyment if you turn around," he warned them. "Just look ahead of you and you'll be amazed and astonished. Ezra? George? Would you snuff the candles?" The men reached out obediently and pinched the wicks, plunging the room into darkness. Sophia had seated herself next to her mother, and now she took her hand and murmured, "Don't be afraid."

The watchers heard the rasp of flint and a weak yellow glow spread past their shoulders. Then a beam of light leapt across the room and formed a perfect square on the opposite wall.

In his best theatrical manner Joseph intoned, "Ladies and gentlemen—come with me now to uncharted places, to the lair of strange creatures." There was the click of glass and metal, and Amalie's involuntary gasp was chorused along the row.

The monster raised its long upper jaw, showing rows of saw-edged teeth. Its ridged tail curled forward, the beast silhouetted beneath the arched roof of a cave. Then the tail whipped back and the jaws closed . . .

"The Crocodile is to be found in the lakes and rivers of the region, and devours the luckless natives with a single swallow."

Jed put a hand to his face and squinted through the vizor of his fingers. Elizabeth caught Brydd by the arm.

The monster vanished, its place taken by a serpent that twisted and undulated, then reared up, its forked tongue flicking out and back; out and back . . .

"The Python is to be found in the swamps and rivers of the region, and is upward of one hundred feet in length. It devours cattle and pigs with a single swallow, and crushes the luckless natives in its coils."

George stared, hypnotised. Brydd watched the tongue, lest it flicked too close. Sophia comforted her mother.

The serpent was gone, and now a giant bird descended, its talons curved and ready to snatch the unwary, its wings flapping as it swooped . . .

"The Condor is to be found in the mountain fastnesses of the region, and will carry off livestock and the luckless natives. The spread of its wings is sufficient to darken the sun." For special effect he passed his hand through the beam of light, grinning as the watchers flinched and ducked.

Amalie could take no more of it. Her voice trembled as she said, "That's quite enough, Joseph Biss. I'll not sleep at all to-night. Ezra, light the candles again, if you please. They're the most horrible things I've ever seen. I shall be awake till dawn, I know it."

"Nonsense," Sophia chided, "you loved the excitement." As the candles were lit she led her mother gently toward the table. "See how it's done—no, don't hang back, you've nothing to fear—it's a most remarkable machine, the magic lantern. It's all the rage in Bristol." She smiled at Joseph whilst the others crowded around the table, anxious to learn how the monsters had been brought so unnervingly to life.

The lantern was simple enough in construction. A large mahogany box contained an oil lamp topped by a cowl, a lens to condense the light and channel it forward and, at the front of the box, a long brass nozzle inside which was a second, enlarging lens.

"And here," Joseph announced, "here is your Crocodile. Now, show me the terror in that." He held up a thick, double-glass slide, the wood-rimmed panes enclosing a stiff paper silhouette. The monster, less than four inches long, was cleverly jointed at the base of the jaw and the tail, the joints worked by a thread. He inserted the slide in the machine and nodded at the wall. "Mind your fingers, or it'll snap 'em off!"

They turned and watched the jaws open, the tail arch forward. Amalie frowned, her fears not yet assuaged, but George Darle shook his head, amused that he'd been so gullible. "Once you know," he chuckled. "Half the fears in the world are cut from card, once you know."

They insisted on seeing the Python again, and the Condor, and whatever else lurked within the slides, and the wall crawled with creatures until well into the evening. Amalie busied herself at the fire, warming biscuits and stirring chocolate in a pan. But she, too, glanced across the room from time to time, shuddering at the bat that sucked blood from luckless natives . . .

※

Two days later the reunion was over. The Darles had stayed only one night at the smithy, returning next morning to their isolated farmstead. Before she left, Elizabeth asked Brydd to walk with her, and they went along the narrow street and beyond the village, the snow crunching beneath their thick-soled shoes. The sky lightened in the east above Marlborough, roofing the countryside with a pale grey slate. They climbed Roman Hill, the girl hoping that Brydd would take her hand, or offer his arm. He did, but only where the slope was steep, releasing her again as they neared the top.

They could see Beckhampton from there, and smoke rising from the chimneys at Lockeridge. But otherwise there were only the snow-covered hills and valleys, a vast stretch of the downs, yet a tiny portion of the whole.

"I enjoyed the day," she said. "I always enjoy Christmas, when we're together." Then, aware that he might misunderstand her, she added hastily, "I mean your family and mine and the Bisses."

"I, too," he agreed, "though it seems the shortest day of the year." He wished Jed was there in her place, for they could then relive the moment when the Crocodile had snapped its jaws and accuse each other of having cringed in their seats. It would probably have ended with a wrestle in the snow and talk of Annette von Kreutel and her smooth, half-naked breasts.

But there'd be no such talk with Elizabeth. She was altogether too serious, too intent on playing the woman.

"Is there any reason why you asked me—?"

"There is," she said. "I'd hoped to tell you yesterday, but the opportunity never arose. Do you remember when you came to Overhill last week and announced your venture?"

"And was accused of deserting Alfred Nott? You said I was running off, but wouldn't get far."

"Oh, you *do* remember it clearly. Yes, I said all that because— well, no matter why I said it—the fact is I regret it and I'm sorry."

"There's no need—"

"There is," she repeated, gazing southward across the white, treeless downs. "I was wrong to say what I did, wrong to say it and wrong because it was false. You'll get to Vienna. You wouldn't be stopped by a regiment of—what are they called, fusiliers? You'll get there, Brydd, and become a master coach-maker, and when you return you'll have all Wiltshire clamouring for your skills. Next Christmas you can lecture to us on the subject of—"

"I'll not be back by then."

"—coaches and the variety of—Yes, you will." She blinked at him, unable to keep the urgency from her voice. "Of course you will."

"Not if I'm offered a position abroad. Hell, I might be in Vienna or Paris or anywhere in Europe. This is not a shopping trip to Marlborough! I'm going eight hundred miles, and that's just to reach the place! This is my chance, don't you see, and I shan't be scurrying home at the first fall of snow—God forbid!"

Elizabeth stared at him, her dreams dissolving as his own hard-ened and took shape. She managed to say, "Who's to know what will happen?" but the phrase was as empty as the winter hills. She turned and floundered down the slope, appalled that she had misled herself so utterly and for so long. He'd never cared for her, other than as a childhood companion, a friend of the family, though in her dreams he cared. He'd never confided in her, not in the latter years, though in her dreams they had no secrets for they'd shared them all. But her dreams were unreal, not at all like his. They were blind to the truth, vaulting any obstacle, however high it loomed. She'd supposed he would stay because he was al-ways there in her dreams. And then, when she'd accepted his need to travel, she'd supposed he would return. Why not, for he did so in the dreams. In the hollow, mocking dreams.

She went on alone, pulling the edges of her hood across her face; not for the warmth it afforded, but for the privacy she needed for her tears . . .

Next morning, Sophia and Joseph set off for Bristol by the lower road, having promised to visit the smithy before the middle of March, when Brydd planned to leave. William stayed until the

afternoon, assured his brother that he'd deliver the thornproof
coat and breeches in time for his departure, then rode across country to Melksham.

Brydd knew his parents would welcome the chance to talk together and doze in front of the fire—little enough reward for the
efforts they'd made—so he walked the three miles to the "Blazing
Rag" to join Sam Gilmore for a jar of ale. Tomorrow he would be
back at work with Alfred and John Stallard and the hulking
Abram Hach. But tomorrow would be one day closer to spring.

❋

He had long since learned that idleness slowed the clock. Alfred
helped by herding him from one job to another, though both
Mary Nott and Amalie Cannaway were concerned that he was
thinning to a shadow.

Each Saturday he attended his lessons at Marlborough, request-
ing that Dr. Barrowcluffe give him more difficult words to read and
letter on the slate. He read children's books and mastered them.
Then a weekly broadsheet. Then the simpler passages from Shake-
speare and Jonson, and the poems of Robert Herrick and John
Donne. He deciphered the timetables that were posted outside
the coach houses, and was only too pleased to assist those to
whom the hours of arrival and departure were just marks on
paper.

Abram Hach stirred trouble again. Gin-drunk as usual, he
scorned the books his roommate had borrowed from the doctor
and demanded to know if Brydd found the work in the yard too
strenuous.

"No," Brydd retorted, "I do not. Why do you ask?"

"Well," Hach grinned unpleasantly, "clerks have to read, don't
they? I thought you might have found yourself a clerk's job, somewhere soft and warm."

The young Cannaway gazed at him for a moment, then went
back to his studies. The labourer flopped on his bed, sharing it
with the gin.

❋

Brydd continued sketching the traffic, but saw nothing to compare with the Viennese coach. Nor did he see any highwaymen

crossing between the trees at the foot of the Cherhill slope. Nevertheless, during the month of January they waylaid three carriages and shot dead a solitary traveller. It was impossible to tell if the man had resisted them or put spurs to his horse in an attempt to flee. In truth, there was no way of knowing if he'd been on horseback or on foot, for his corpse had been stripped to the skin. Unclaimed, the body was buried at Kennett.

Appeals were made to the district magistrates, who promised to investigate. "If their promises were bricks," Sam Gilmore commented sourly, "those bewigged gentlemen could have built themselves a house by now. The coach owners have appealed to them, and so have the drivers, and so has every village around. I've added my mark to the list of innkeepers who want something done, but all we've had is promises. It's clear to me that our magistrates never cross the Cherhill Downs, for they'd think different once they'd had a pistol levelled at their heads."

In the second week of February, William rode over from Melksham and presented Brydd with the made-to-measure clothes. Along with the coat and breeches was a collared cape and a linen cravat, the outfit a splendid array of pleats and buttons, cuffs and deep flapped pockets. The thornproof material was a mixture of mauve and grey and Brydd paraded in it, feeling quite the dog.

However, he was less cheerful when he said good-bye to his gentle, shambling brother.

"You should find yourself a woman, you know, William. What are you now, twenty-five?"

"And looking twice that."

"Damn rot. You're a fine, tall man, but it's time you stamped on your shyness and married up. There must be scores of young women at Melksham who'd look with favour—"

"Aye, I daresay. But you know what I need, if I'm to make a show?"

"More strut and swagger, for a start."

"Yes, that might help. But what I really need is the gig you promised. So you come back one day and hammer it out for me. Before too long, eh, my dear brother?"

"Before too long." Brydd nodded, then clasped and was clasped by William.

✻

The rest of February was awash with rain. All work ceased in the wheelwright's yard, though there was plenty to be done on the roofs at Lockeridge and Kennett and Beckhampton. The December snows had compressed the thatch and shifted the roof beams, and Brydd worked alongside the carpenters and thatchers, raising the oak frames and reseating them on the walls.

Sophia and Joseph arrived—minus their magic lantern—but with a magnificent silk shirt and a pair of jackboots. Brydd paid his sister the perfect compliment when he said, "I'll bet there are no shops in Vienna that'd stock shirts like this."

"Nor in Bristol either," she smiled. "I made it at home. Now, don't spoil things by looking so askance. I'm not entirely helpless when confronted by a needle and thread."

"By God, you're not. But it'll make me the target for every ruffian that claps eyes on it."

"It's not for the street. It's for when you're invited to dine, or to a musical soirée." Seeing him grimace, she added, "Anyway, you'll need it when you visit the von Kreutels."

"Oh, I don't think I'll be—"

"But you must, Brydd, most certainly you must. I don't say they'll befriend you, but you as good as saved their lives and they're honour-bound to receive you. Johann, is that his name, the more intelligent of the men? Well, I'm sure he'll assist you with introductions to the coachmakers." She nodded decisively. "You present yourself to the von Kreutels when you get there. You've the right."

Joseph told him to try on the boots, then laughed as Brydd acclaimed them a perfect fit. "So they should be. I went into the hayloft on Christmas night and borrowed your old pair whilst you slept! But I warn you, don't be so trusting abroad. The ruffians you mentioned will prise them off your feet if they think they can get away with it."

To a young countryman who had worn castoffs and hand-me-downs all his life, the new outfit was something to be marvelled at. Amalie insisted on storing the clothes in a dry, linen-lined chest, but that did not prevent Brydd from lifting them out to admire them, to feel the softness of the silk and the strength of the thornproof weave.

He accompanied his sister and her husband on the first few miles of their journey back to Bristol. They turned south at the Beckhampton crossing and then Brydd reined in his horse and Joseph halted the curricle. The brothers-in-law shook hands and Brydd rode around the vehicle to embrace Sophia. "I'll write to you," he said. "It'll be a labour, forming the letters, and I'm no hand at spelling. But I'll put something down. You'll know where I am and what I'm about."

"I already know this," she told him. "You're a brave and ambitious man, and you will succeed because you deserve to. As I said before, you've the right."

Joseph had been nodding agreement and now he raised a hand in farewell and clicked the horse. The curricle rolled forward, taking them through the February drizzle toward their world of merchandise and warehouses and the wharf known as The Biss. How far would it stretch, Brydd wondered, by the time he returned? Would it be Bristol at all by then, or Bisstol?

❋

The pace quickened and there were only two more weeks, ten days, a week to go.

He roamed the hut that had sheltered him for the past five years, collecting his razor and whetstone and emptying the chest that held his work clothes. There was no sign of Abram Hach, and his absence allowed Brydd to stand for a moment, remembering the twelve-year-old boy who'd been apprenticed to the wheelwright and had shivered with fear throughout that first long night. There had been no Hach in those days, and thank God, for he'd have made the boy's life a misery. But the young Brydd had been miserable enough at first, alone in the strange room, listening to the unseasoned timbers creak and settle in the yard.

He made his way around the edge of the sawpit and knocked on the cottage door. Then, to show Mary that her scolding had finally brought results, he went in without waiting to be admitted. The Notts saw the bundle of clothes under his arm and Alfred said, "So it wasn't a fancy tale? Vienna really exists, does it?"

"I shall be writing to Dr. Barrowcluffe and my sister, Sophia. They'll pass on the news to Ezra and Amalie, so if you want to know what scrapes I've got myself into—"

"We will," Mary assured him, "though don't put it like that. You keep your wits about you and there won't be any scrapes."

Reaching under his chair, Alfred amended, "You keep *this* about you, Brydd Cannaway. Then, if your wits won't save you, you can lay on with something more sturdy." He handed him a polished-oak walking stick, at which Mary shook her head with disapproval. The base of the stick was unmarked, and it was clear that Alfred had made it as a gift. "Grip it with both hands. Further apart, that's it. Now twist it, as you'd wring out a cloth."

Brydd did so and nearly cut himself on the foot-long blade that was concealed in the hollowed lower section. He realised now why it had earned Mary's disapproval, though he had no qualms about accepting it. "I'd need a magnifier to see where the sections join. And it'd make a damn good cudgel besides. Thank you, Alfred. Now I've been dressed and armed."

They talked of the years they had worked together, of the serviceable wagons they'd made and of the day Abram Hach had returned drunk from somewhere or other and stepped straight into the sawpit. He'd been too heavy to move, so the disgusted wheelwright had finally thrown a sheepskin over him and left him where he lay.

During the night he'd awakened from his stupor and imagined himself in a freshly dug grave, about to be buried alive. His howls of terror had been heard throughout Lockeridge, and several of the villagers had later voiced their regrets that it had not been a grave, with them in attendance, wielding shovels.

"By the way," Brydd asked, "where *does* he get his gin? He says he has friends who keep him supplied, but I've never seen him with anyone. He's either here or in the 'Blazing Rag,' and no one approaches him there."

Alfred shrugged. "I've thought about it, but I've no conclusions. Perhaps he's more wealthy than he admits. Or perhaps he does have a friend, who just happens to market gin."

"Well," Brydd pondered, "I know you'll not allow me to speak against a fellow worker—"

"That's right."

"—but I want you to beware of him, Alfred. There's more to him than just the drunken oaf. He does *something* to earn that gin, and I've the suspicion—"

"That's right," the master wheelwright repeated evenly, "I'll not allow talk against a fellow worker. Now, let *us* have a drink, and you can describe the route you plan to take to Vienna. Lord knows, if I was your age, I'd snap at the chance."

"I hope you would not," Mary said ominously. "You were married to me before you were seventeen, if you care to remember. Or do you still say you'd snap at the chance?"

Brydd watched them and saw their slow, easy smiles. They were an enviable couple, the Notts.

✳

On the final Saturday, and with Amalie's blessing, he donned the thornproof suit and set out on a circuit that would take him to Marlborough, Overhill Farm and the "Blazing Rag."

The doctor's class was over by the time Brydd reached the house, but the front door was open and he discovered Mistress Cable in the schoolroom, sweeping crushed chalk from beneath the benches. When she saw him she instinctively wiped the chalk from her hands and smoothed her apron. "Well, now, Master Cannaway, you're a bold sight and no mistake." Not sure if she should know about it, she said, "The doctor did mention something about a foreign journey; just in passing, as it were."

"It's no secret, Mistress Cable. I'm leaving on Monday for the coast, and thence to Dover and across to Paris and Vienna. This outfit was purchased for me by my brother, William, and the boots by Sophia's husband." He wondered what else he could say that would secure her the advantage when she chatted and gossiped with her friends. But she seemed satisfied with what he'd given her and told him the doctor was in his study. "You go ahead, Master Cannaway, there's no one with him."

He was seated at his desk, reading a copy of the local broadsheet. His goat's hair wig was pushed back on his head and he grabbed at it as Brydd entered. "Blast the thing, it never did fit. I was so taken by the colour, I quite forgot to have it shrunk. My, but you're the gentleman this morning. Shall I jump up and clear those papers off the chair?"

"Not on my account, sir," Brydd grinned. "And that wig would hold perfectly well if you were not to fiddle with it." He transferred the papers to the gate-leg table, then sat as he supposed a gentleman would sit, his back stiff, his arms steepled across his chest.

"When do you leave?" Dr. Barrowcluffe asked, and nodded as Brydd told him. "Then I'd better alert you to the dangers of pox."

Brydd swallowed, knowing what was meant but not daring to show it.

"It's an unpleasant disease, the pox, and most forms of it are incurable. In time, no doubt, someone will brew the correct medicine, but it won't avail you or me or any man foolish enough to consort with whores and harlots. Not that I condemn them as such, mind you. They exist because men wish them to exist, and the initial weakness is ours, not theirs. More shameful than that, a man with the pox can infect a woman, be she a virgin, his wife, his mistress or the most raddled harridan in town. It's a contagious disease, the pox. And, I repeat, incurable in all but its mildest forms."

Brydd thought it safe to nod.

"Now," the doctor continued, sparing the young man's embarrassment by crossing to the window, "you understand *how* it's contracted. Just so, by intercourse of the most intimate nature. Well, I for one shall be surprised if you don't seek such pleasures and take them, from time to time. It's in us to do so. The woman with whom you consort may or may not be diseased; for obvious reasons it's not so easy to tell." He chuckled to himself. "I should say, for less than obvious reasons." Then he turned and glanced at Brydd. "However, if the disease is incurable, it may at least be minimised, or even prevented. And the way to do it is with this."

Unwilling to look for fear that Dr. Barrowcluffe would produce some ghastly instrument from his bag, Brydd squinted, then caught what was tossed at him—a block of castille soap.

"Wash yourself every day if possible, but unfailingly after intercourse." With supreme arrogance he remarked, "I imagine one can purchase soaps of a kind in France and Austria."

Some while later Mistress Cable brought sherry and biscuits on a tray. The doctor had reclaimed his seat and agreed to convey Brydd's letters to Kennett and read them to Ezra and Amalie. He had also dipped into the side drawer of his desk and come up with a parcel wrapped in yellowing newspaper. Now he fussed with his wig, raised his glass and said, "There's much I'd wish you, Brydd Cannaway. You've considerable gifts, though I've heard that you become violent when crossed. I would suggest you curb your temper, for even if they don't have soap abroad, they're bound to have prisons. Oh, I looked this out for you. It might help to clarify their more obscure behaviour." He manoeuvred the parcel across his littered desk.

It was a copy of the 1680 edition of Charles Colherne's *Observations on Foreign Travel and Attendant Customs*, a small, leather-bound volume complete with a folded map of Europe. Not wishing to write in the book itself, Dr. Barrowcluffe had inserted a piece of grey card on which he had penned the Latin phrase *Abiit, Excessit, Evasit, Erupit*.

"It's by the Roman, Cicero. 'He is gone, He is off, He has escaped, He has broken free.' It seemed appropriate. You can use the paper to wrap up the soap."

❄

He had always enjoyed the solitude of the downs, and he let his horse set its own pace on the journey from Marlborough to Overhill Farm. He chose the bleak countryside in preference to the coaching road, for this would be his last chance to ride the hills and valleys that fringed the Kennett Vale. He might be a year or ten years older when he crossed them again; it all depended on how things went in Europe.

He knew nothing about Vienna, save what he'd gleaned from the paintings on the coach, but he had recently heard some colourful stories about Paris. The women there were uniformly attractive, and all but free of inhibitions. They had a passion for Englishmen and there was no need to learn their language since they were all fluent in the Anglo-Saxon tongue. They wore pretty gowns and satin shoes, and drank sparkling water from fountains situated in all quarters of the city, the effect being to make them more amorous and affectionate.

Brydd frowned in an effort to remember who had told him those stories. Then, when he did remember, he smiled ruefully, acknowledging that Jed Darle was no real authority on the matter.

The ground ahead was sewn with massive upright stones, hundreds of them in a line, and more in a series of corridors and circles. From a distance they resembled sheep, and were thus known as grey wethers. But is was not known who had placed them there, or what function they'd performed. They were of no value to the farmers or shepherds and, whenever the real sheep got amongst them, it was the devil's job to separate the livestock from the stones.

Brydd didn't like the way the wind keened around them. They were less like sheep today and more in the image of hunched grey sentinels sent to guard the downs, then abandoned at their posts. For the first time he spurred his horse, sending it along one of the corridors and up the slope. From there he followed a ridge of hills eastward until he found the track that angled down, steep and rocky, to the farm.

Jed was in the yard, splitting logs for kindling. He stared at the rider, recognised Brydd and buried the axe blade in the chopping block. He would normally have yelled a greeting, but he knew why his friend was dressed in such finery and the knowledge depressed him. He stood silent as Brydd entered the yard, then went forward to hold the bridle. "You're well fitted out, by the looks of it."

"It's William's doing." He noticed Jed's dulled expression and wanted to tell him that he, too, was sorry they'd be apart. But for the moment he said, "Is George about?"

"He's in the feedstore. Or he was."

They were both surprised that they found it awkward to converse—the least of their problems in the past. Brydd dismounted and reached forward to take charge of the horse.

"Leave it," Jed told him. "I'll see it's tethered. It's not worth unsaddling it, I suppose."

"Well, I've only called by to—"

"Then leave it. Go and see George."

"And Elizabeth, is she—?"

"In the house. I must finish these logs. I'll catch up with you in a while." He walked away, leading the horse and leaving Brydd to choose between the feedstore and the kitchen.

Since Christmas, when the girl had floundered away in tears, he had seen her at the Saturday markets in Marlborough, but always in the presence of her family. They had never been together, just the two of them, nor exchanged more than the time of day. Elizabeth seemed frightened of him, not daring to ask a question in case his answer tore the remnants of her dreams. He had hurt her twice, first with the news that he was leaving the valley, leaving England, and then with the disclosure that he'd be away for an unspecified length of time, somewhere in Europe. Twice was enough, and she did not want to be hurt again.

Nor did Brydd Cannaway wish to be held responsible for another squall of tears. So he avoided the kitchen and made his way past the end of the house to the feedstore. As he reached the long tiled shed George Darle emerged, his arms around a hay bale. He gazed at Brydd for a moment, then said, "You mind you don't get your clothes muddied. I'd keep on the path, if I were you." There was no mockery in his voice, but Brydd realised he was too well dressed to help the farmer, too well shod to move freely about the yard. The gap was widening all the time.

He waited for George to break the bale and scatter it in a sheep trough, then walked back with him to the house. Jed came toward them, wheeling a barrow piled with kindling, and Brydd found himself stepping aside to let his friend tip the load into the woodbox. Then George had opened the kitchen door and was gesturing Brydd inside.

Elizabeth had seen him ride down the track and had brushed her hair and hung her apron behind the door. She told herself she'd have done as much for any visiting neighbour. There was nothing so special about Brydd Cannaway. Not any more.

They made conversation and used it to bridge the silences. The Darles showed a polite interest in whatever Brydd told them, taking it in turns to ask questions about the journey. Elizabeth served slices of rabbit pie and Brydd complimented her on her cooking. George drew cider from a barrel and the family wished the young wheelwright well in his venture. They rephrased questions they'd already asked, to which Brydd refashioned the replies.

Jed fidgeted, then crossed to a cupboard and returned with

a sheepskin jerkin. He'd prepared a speech, but it now came out flat and unnatural. "It's a present from all of us at Overhill. My father skinned it, and I had it cured, and my sister stitched the borders. We hope you'll think of us when you're— Anyway, here it is."

They waited and tried not to watch as Brydd unhooked the clasp of his cape, slipped the eighteen buttons of his coat, then tried on the jerkin. It looked odd with the thornproof breeches, but they nodded and admired him in it and he was effusive in his thanks.

After a decent interval he said, "I'd better start back. I must see Sam Gilmore on the way."

"Give him our regards," George requested, "and tell your parents we will be down to see them soon." Then he pushed himself to his feet and Jed unlatched the door. Brydd wanted to shout at them, "Don't usher me in and out! I'm no different from what I was yesterday! Why do you regard me as such? *Why?*" But he held Elizabeth in a light embrace, shook hands with George and Jed, collected the sheepskin and ducked under the lintel.

They came as far as the doorstep, then stood there while he crossed the yard to his horse. He could not believe that the easy relationship had evaporated, or that his intended journey had set him apart from such lifelong friends. What did they fear? That they were beneath him now? That he would no longer acknowledge them? Or did they think he'd worn the suit to intimidate them, to show that he was better dressed in preparation for better company than theirs? He shook his head at the thought. It was not true. He was what he had always been. He was one of them, and the only difference—

The only difference was that he would not remain one of them, not once he'd crossed the Channel and tasted the delights of Paris and travelled to Vienna-on-the-Danube. The Darles knew it, and so in his heart did he . . .

He tied the sheepskin behind the saddle and mounted up. The family were still in the doorway. Jed took a step forward, then stopped. George raised a hand in farewell. Elizabeth looked at him, then murmured something to her father.

Byrdd attempted a smile and called, "The ship'll probably run

aground and I'll be back within the month!" They returned the
smile or nodded, yes, very likely. He guided his horse toward the
gate.

Then Elizabeth ran across the yard. "Brydd! Wait!"

He reined in and she stopped beside him, her blond hair in
disarray. As she pushed it from her face he glanced back to see
that George and Jed had disappeared into the house.

"Elizabeth?"

She held something out to him and said, "These might be use-
ful to you. You'll need them if you're to stop the coaches in their
tracks."

The words intrigued him, but it was not until he looked down
and saw the bundle of charcoal sticks that he realised how well
she had phrased the gift. "Yes," he nodded slowly, "that's just
what I'll use them for—to stop the coaches in their tracks."

The girl waited until he had ridden through the gate and up
the slope and across the brow of the hill. Then she waited a while
longer, as though something might happen—to bring him back.

※

That evening he sold his horse to Sam Gilmore. It upset him to
do so, but William had convinced him that he would have to sell
it sooner or later, either in the valley or when he reached the
coast.

No money passed hands, for Brydd still needed a horse to take
him southward. He chose one from the stables behind the inn,
transferred his saddlery, then accepted the flask of brandy Sam
offered, to make up the value.

"That's that then." The innkeeper nodded. "You watch out
for yourself, young Brydd. I'd hate to think I'd lost a customer for
good and all."

"You haven't, Sam. I'll be back when I've a thirst for your terrible ale."

"Aye, and no doubt demanding to be served in The Private."

Brydd's smile faded for an instant. Was this really what Sam
expected of him, just like the Darles? "No, I won't," he said, and
the words sounded more indignant than he'd intended. God, he
thought, am I already protesting too much?

❀

There were two more gifts to come: a serviceable leather hat from Amalie and a bulky valise from Ezra. Brydd would not risk ruining his thornproof suit on the rough-and-tumble journey to Calais, so the garments were folded and packed in the holdall. With them went the silk shirt, various workaday shifts and stockings, Charles Colhere's *Observations*, the block of castille soap, the razor and whetstone, the boots Joseph had borrowed from the hayloft, the box of chalks and charcoals, including the bundle Elizabeth had given him, and his satchel of sketches. In too went the flask of brandy, its cork hammered tight.

Balancing the valise was a blanket and the stained leather jerkin he'd worn in Alfred's yard. He would travel in his new boots, old breeches, a woollen undershirt and the Darles' sheepskin. He'd wear Amalie's hat, of course, and a belt into which he had carefully sliced four pockets, each deep enough to take five pounds' worth of coins. He would strap the belt under his shirt and hope no one had occasion to clutch him around the waist.

He talked away Sunday evening with his parents. They knew he would leave before dawn and prolonged their final embrace. He stayed on for a while in front of the fire, then they heard him bolt the doors and shutter the downstairs windows. They listened as he climbed to his room.

A few hours later they heard him get up and dress and fasten the straps of the valise. The latch rose and the door hinges creaked. They heard his bootheels on the stairs, the scrape of the bolt, the clatter of the horse in the yard. Amalie moved and Ezra murmured gently, "No, my dear. He'll not want to be delayed. Not this time." The hoofbeats were muffled as the cobbles gave way to mud, and then there were hills and cottages between.

Life could be easier now for the elderly Cannaways. Ezra had kept the promise he'd made, working on at the smithy until all of his children had chosen their paths. He might now accept help from William and Sophia, and his wife need only make candles if it pleased her to do so.

Knowing Amalie, he was sure it would.

PART TWO

ALBANY

1698

FIVE

Humming softly to himself, the white-haired gentleman stepped out into the street and almost under the horse. With a violent wrench Brydd turned the animal aside, then glared down at the man, amazed by his stupidity. Not twenty yards into Portsmouth, he fumed, and I'm the prey of damned old fools.

"It'd pay you to look where you're going, sir! A speedier animal would have trodden you under."

The pedestrian turned toward him and Brydd frowned at the circles of black glass that covered his eyes. "Quite correct, young man. You *are* a young man by your voice, and you use it well to admonish me. However, looking is not the thing for me, sir; I should have been listening. There's no excuse for such carelessness. I'm obliged to you."

Brydd gazed down the narrow, winding street. "You startled me, that's all. I did not realise you were—"

"Oh, yes, my sight's been gone these ten years or more. But I'm not deaf, and that's where the fault lies. You've spared me, sir, and I'm obliged— Did I just say that?"

A cart lumbered past, almost filling the street and driving the pedestrians to the wall. "Are you going on down?" Brydd asked. The old man's face was a picture of contrition, and it seemed only fair to walk with him and keep him clear of the traffic.

"I am." He nodded. "I have a sister who lives in Harbour Crescent, and it's the pattern of my day to visit her and drink one of her herbal teas. I then try to identify the leaf, though I'm not much good at it. Why? Am I to have company I don't deserve?"

By now Brydd had dismounted and, holding the reins in one hand and the old man's arm with the other, he set an easy pace down the street. Signboards squeaked overhead and he glanced up, then left and right, not wishing to miss a thing. He had travelled the seventy miles to Portsmouth in a day and a half, and was eager to see how the town compared with Marlborough.

As though aware that Brydd was sponging up the scene, the old man said, "You must stop me if you think I'm prying, but you are not from around here, are you?"

"No, sir. I'm from the Kennett Vale in Wiltshire."

"Ah, yes, the beautiful Kennett Vale." He smiled and nodded.

"You know of it?"

"*Knew* of it, to be precise. Such a pretty place, with its groves and forests."

"There are no forests in the district; anyway, not west of Marlborough."

"My, my, that *is* the voice of youth! There are none now, perhaps, but I'm speaking of, oh, forty years back. You'll see an opening somewhere on our left. The passageway connects with the Crescent. It's narrow, but you'll get your horse through with no trouble. Now, what were we discussing? Ah, yes, the dearth of trees."

"There's a pointing finger chiselled on a board," Brydd told him. "Is that the way?"

"That's it. You have a good nature, young man. There are not many who'd keep company with a sightless old wreck. It's the eyeglasses that frighten them off. They remind people that the human body is a fragile vessel." He chuckled and added, "I must say, though, you've a good healthy grip."

The shortcut to the Crescent was empty but for the two workmen who were chipping lazily at the base of a fire-gutted building. The old man seemed set to walk into them and, aware that they'd probably curse him and push him away, Brydd guided him alongside the opposite wall. As they drew level with the derelict building the man turned to the pair and said, "Strike hard on him, boys, he's strong, our country rat!" Then he pulled loose, snatched the glasses from his face and watched as the pair went forward to deal with their victim.

The shock should have numbed him, that was the intention. But there had been too many small mistakes.

A blind man would not forget to listen when he was crossing a busy street; his ears *were* his eyes, sharp and alert. Nor would he be so certain that an unseen horse would navigate the passageway, for the animal might have been laden with panniers or sacks. And as for the old man's talk of the Kennett Vale—"such a pretty place, with its groves and forests"—that was just guesswork, the only thing about him that was truly blind.

Brydd stepped back, reached behind the saddle and drew Alfred's cudgel from the blanket roll. The white-haired Judas snarled encouragement at his men and they advanced, crouched forward, confident that they could batter the country rat, walking stick and all. They were both armed with pick hammers, one favouring the squared-off head, the other preferring the spike. Either would be sufficient with which to fell their victim, once they got in close.

But Brydd was in no mood for such intimacies. He held the stick across his body, twisted the shaft and lunged at them with the foot-long blade. They reared back and the old man snapped, "Rush him, blast you! Get your weight on him!" An instant later they'd have done so, but Brydd had already taken the initiative, closing the gap and stabbing the nearer man in the side of the neck. He yelped and caught blood in his hand, and then his companion was shouting and backing away along the passage. Brydd jabbed forward again for good measure, but his assailants had lost their nerve. They ran off, shouldering aside the old man as they went. He hurried after them, whining that he could not have known, how *could* he have known without searching the rat's belongings?

Brydd leaned against the burned-out building and felt the sweat of fear on his body. His arms hung heavy at his sides and he gave a spasmodic jerk, the strength draining from his legs. He forced himself upright, stared in disgust at the streak of wetness on the blade, then wiped it on a tuft of grass near where his attackers had been chipping. It took him several attempts before he could fit together the sections of the stick, by which time people were shouting at him to move the horse, it was still a public way unless the law had been changed overnight.

※

He saw the sea for the first time, and the vessels that crowded the harbour. He did not know which were the galleons or barkentines, which the sloops or frigates, which the brigs or schooners, the pinnaces or yawls or wherries. But he knew they made a fine sight and was content to watch them slide or splash across the water, or swing at anchor, or rock gently at their moorings. He saw soldiers drilling on the quay, and workmen hammering strands of pitch-soaked oakum between the deck planks of a three-masted warship. A cannon was swung ashore, its barrel split and twisted, and there were roars of fury as it slipped from its cradle and crashed through the bed of a waiting wagon. Mariners swarmed over the rigging and edged along the crosstrees. Various sails were unfurled, some of them scorched and shot through, others torn by the wind. There was a constant traffic of small boats and, even as Brydd watched, one overladen craft began shipping water and sank to the gunwhales. The oarsmen were rescued and a line was attached to the boat, but whatever had been in the sacks and barrels they'd been transporting was lost. There were more shouts of recrimination and someone aboard the rescue craft went among the bedraggled oarsmen with a belaying pin. No doubt they could expect worse when they reached the shore.

His imagination fired by the scene, Brydd took out his satchel and chalks and began sketching. He knew immediately that he could capture the likeness of the vessels, though the intricate detail of the rigging defeated him. No matter, these were only impressions—this of a high, decorated stern, this of the port buildings, this of the flags that rippled like coloured sails and were mirrored in the water. He covered the first sheet of paper, then a second. A platoon of soldiers marched past and stopped somewhere behind him and a voice said, "Best show me the authority, lad."

Brydd turned and looked up at the grizzled, uniformed speaker. "Authority? What authority?"

"I admit, it'd be spying in an open fashion, but it might be the way you choose." The soldier peered at the sketches, grunted a compliment, then said, "On your feet, lad. Maybe there's things there as shouldn't be." Making sure he was within his rights, he queried, "You don't have a permit from the naval office, do you? No? Then I'll thank you for that satchel. You walk with me. Your horse'll be brought along."

Brydd closed the flaps of the satchel, tied the strings and surrendered it to the soldier. "Take care of it," he said. "It's mostly full of coaches and wagons, and I don't want them lost."

The soldier stared hard at him, then nodded slowly, almost amused. "Oh, I'll take care of them, don't you worry." The young man was either as innocent as a babe or as brazen as a brass carronade. *I don't want them lost?* The very evidence that could send him to the gallows? What a card.

He was interrogated by an army officer, two naval representatives, a customs official and a man dressed like himself in a sheepskin jerkin and well-worn breeches. This man did his best to befriend him and talked earnestly of "coming clean" and "pointing the finger at the real culprits" and "naming the master spies, there'll probably be a reward in it for you, you're young enough to claim you'd been misled." Throughout all this Brydd repeated that he'd been sketching the vessels because it had pleased him to do so. He knew nothing about permits or ships or the ways of spies, though he'd be damned glad to leave Portsmouth to its garrison and the white-haired Judas. "When I'm not being attacked, I'm being arrested. Is it an offence to chew on a bread crust here, or has the wheat been poisoned?"

It was late in the afternoon before they released him. He insisted on checking the contents of the satchel and discovered that his sketches of the harbour and its vessels had been confiscated. He'd expected as much, though he thought it wonderfully impudent when the soldier who'd arrested him confided, "They took a sheet each, the naval officers. They're going to frame them like proper pictures and hang them in their cabins. Well, don't look so truculent, lad, they're not hanging you."

Nevertheless, he was escorted to a section of the harbour reserved for the fishing fleet, and the platoon kept an eye on him whilst he sought passage to Dover. Eventually he found a ketch that was leaving with the next tide and struck a bargain with the skipper. It was a one-sided bargain to be sure, for the skipper insisted on the horse as payment for the fare and the saddlery in exchange for a meal of cold meat and ale and the loan of an oilskin.

"I could get the best quarters aboard the largest ship in the harbour for that!"

"Aye, you could, but you wouldn't like it," the skipper assured him. "The largest ship's the *Battledore*, and she's slipping for the Indies tomorrow. Now, collect your belongings and keep out of the way." He sent a man to take charge of the horse, and Brydd found himself a place amidships from which he could study the town that had tried to kill him with pick hammers and the port that had hoped to hang him as a spy. Joseph Biss had been right when he'd warned of cheats and cozeners, but he might also have mentioned imitation blind men and naval officers and the skippers of foul-smelling ketches.

A deckhand tossed an oilskin at him and said, "If you have to vomit, use the leeward rail. There's a bucket down below for your other needs. And if you go overboard, you're lost, remember that. We don't trawl for passengers."

Brydd said nothing, but looked at the man until he had broken his gaze. "I'm just warning you, that's all," the deckhand grumbled. "There's no need to measure me for murder."

And why not? Brydd thought. It seems the popular pastime.

❈

An hour later he was as sick as a poisoned dog, though he had the sense to remain on deck and sip the brandy Sam Gilmore had given him. The ketch yawed and pitched its way along the coast, and Brydd clung to the nearest available rope or stanchion, a grim, tented figure in his sleeveless oilskin. He had stowed his belongings in a rope locker and was glad he'd done so, for the decks ran with water, swirling into the scuppers and founting against the base of the masts. The skipper decided to take pity on him and bellowed at him to come aft into the wheelhouse. Brydd returned the favour by offering him a good gulp of brandy, and after that they were yelling stories at each other, a tale of smuggling repaid with an account of highway robbery. Lanterns were strung from the port and starboard trees, and all hands were told to watch for the lights on Beachy Head. It was beginner's luck that allowed Brydd to spot the distant smudge, but it earned him a thick slice of beef and a hunk of bread that would have served as a mounting block. He swallowed ale on top of the brandy and forked onions from a cask, and he grinned into the weather because he no longer felt ill and was matching the skipper, fork and mug. Not bad, he told himself, for a country rat.

The storm abated and a following wind drove them past the smugglers' paradise of the Romney marshes, a desolate stretch webbed with channels and inlets and dotted by officialdom's favourite warning signs, sturdy oak gibbets. The vessel kept a respectful distance, though the skipper took the opportunity to spit over the rail.

"They dangled my brother from one of those. We went ashore at night and cut him down, then buried him decent, at sea. You couldn't have found a better man. Good as they come, he was, and better than any they sent against him."

"Was he unfairly dealt with? A victim of circumstance?"

"I've no doubt he thought so at the last," the skipper smiled wryly. "But he'd not wish me to sell him short. He was one of the most successful smugglers that ever rolled a barrel. Fifteen years in the business, and he never wanted for a coin or a woman or a drink to slake his thirst. They called him the Shadow of the Moon, and when they did catch him he was in bed with two wenches—two, mind you—and the floor stacked high with bolts of silk and brocade. Was he unfairly dealt with? Not in this life, he wasn't."

The ketch ploughed on toward Dover. Brydd had not slept at all, yet felt wide awake and was eager to make the crossing. The skipper said, "You'll be travelling outside on the packet, so you'd better keep the oilskin. And guard your belongings. I wouldn't trust those ferry crews with a blunt nail." He went on to warn his passenger that not even a churchman could hope to board the

packet without a passport, a bill of health and a customs seal on
his baggage. "It's a strict formality, if an empty one, and it's
prison for those as get caught without the papers. Now offer me
another swig of your brandy, then go up for'ard and watch for the
castle at Dover. I'll show you the agent's office when we're
docked."

They drank each other's health, and then Brydd clambered
along the deck to the bows. Waves slapped the hull like heels
against a horse, urging the clumsy vessel along the coast. Spray exploded in his face, freshening him for the next part of his journey.
I'll be in France today, he told himself, unless I fall foul of blind
men or footpads or the navy or the customs or the ferry crew or
lost children or . . .

※

They asked him where he was going and why, charged him half a
crown and issued him with a pass to Calais.

They inspected his face and arms for any boils or putrescence,
satisfied themselves that he was free of disease and charged him a
shilling for a bill of health.

They demanded to know if he was carrying any jewellery, plate,
gold coins or weapons, then searched his valise and sealed it with
a loop of wire. If he opened it during the voyage he'd be in trouble with the customs officers at Calais—a rough breed at the best
of times.

The seal cost him a crown, and he was halfway to the packet
before he realised he had contravened the law. The customs
officials had asked him to declare any weapons, and what was the
walking stick if not a weapon? He'd already *used* it as a weapon,
and it was only Alfred's excellent workmanship and his own innocence that had got it through. If the authorities had discovered it,
with its wicked secret blade, they'd have roasted him for days. A
gentleman was allowed his sword and his case of duelling pistols,
but what penalty would the officials have exacted from a country
rat if they'd twisted the polished-oak shaft?

The thought filled him with guilt and a perverse sense of excitement. The skipper of the ketch would have smiled at what he'd

done, and the Shadow of the Moon would have approved of it,
God rest his soul.

He bought an outside ticket at the gangway and was herded on
to the forward deck. Inside tickets were for gentlefolk and wealthy
merchants, allowing them one of the cramped cabins that ran like
a spine along the midship section. They could pay extra for food
and drink and a palliative to calm their stomachs, but no such
luxuries were available to the outside passengers. They'd be ferried
across the Channel, and that was that; what more did they expect
for ten shillings?

There was a long wait for the ebb of the tide, and then the
gangplank was hauled aboard and the ropes cast off and there was
water between the packet and the quay. Brydd grinned at his
fellow passengers. He banged the rail with his fist. He looked up
at the castle and at the town that clung to its hem. He laughed
once, aloud, and felt no need to apologise. They could think what
they liked, his apprehensive shipmates. Too bad if the crossing
upset them. *He* would enjoy it, every dip and roll of it. After all,
he'd been the one to spot the light on Beachy Head. *He'd* been
the one to fool the customs and *he* was the one who had come
from the Kennett Vale and was on his way to Vienna.

He remembered to guard his belongings and took an occasional
sip from the brandy flask. The ship nosed its way toward a dark
horizon . . .

One moment they were flecked with spray, and the next
drenched by a downpour of rain. They had seen it coming but
misjudged the distance and were in it before they had time to
huddle against the bulwarks. Brydd murmured his thanks for the
oilskin, then spared some pity for those who were unprotected. He
saw a young woman and her infant son clinging together near the
forward hatch. The mother draped a rain-soaked shawl around the
child's shoulders, but she might as well have doused him with a
bucket for all the good it did. The boy shivered and hugged his
knees.

Brydd waited, but there was no sign of a husband or anyone
who could aid them, so he collected his belongings and stumbled
toward the hatch. Kneeling on the deck, he removed his leather

hat, pulled the oilskin over his head and said, "Drape this around you, mistress. And wear the hat, the brim's wide enough to protect the child."

The woman was too sensible to dither, and Brydd nodded approval as she donned the waxed cape and broad leather hat. The boy recovered his spirits and poked his head through the oilskin, grinning in triumph at the less fortunate voyagers.

Young though she was, the woman looked drawn and exhausted. Her movements were listless, her ungloved fingers thin and clenched, as though in defence against the times. She might once have been attractive, but misfortune had hollowed her cheeks and frightened her eyes into their dark-rimmed sockets. "I can't pay you," she said. "You should have asked first if I could pay you."

"I don't want payment, why should I?"

"It would be the custom," she responded with a faint, worldly smile. "Isn't it always?"

"Are you alone on board, mistress, you and the boy? Is there no one—?"

"My man is around somewhere." It was an effort for her to add, "He's busy, else he'd have seen to it we were dry."

Brydd nodded, disbelieving her. Where was he, then? What business was so urgent that he preferred it to protecting his wife, his woman, whatever she was? And what did a child care about business if it meant he died of cold?

He said, "If there's anything left after the skipper's been at it—" then produced the brandy flask, shook it and offered it to the woman. Again she made no pretence at refusal, but let the boy wet his lips, then took the merest sip herself. "What *do* you want," she insisted, "when there's no money and my looks went years ago? A hat and coat and brandy? You should have auctioned them. They'd have got you a good price in this weather."

Brydd shook his head. "Where *is* your man?"

The woman must have glimpsed him, for she hurried, "He's had some success in the past, but he's been dogged by bad luck; don't let him anger you, sir, his temper runs away with him, it's not his fault."

"What's this, then? Am I billed for an outfit? Is this how the pedlars get rich?"

The man was as sorry a sight as the woman, but where her face had been hollowed by fatigue and fear, his was etched with bitterness, his expression sly and put upon, the blameless victim of an unfair world. "You'll make no sale on this trip, so take back your outfit and hawk it elsewhere."

"Your woman and the child seemed abandoned," Brydd told him, climbing to his feet. "They've been lent those garments and that's the sum of it. There is no price attached."

"But isn't that the patter?" the man said knowingly. "There's never a price at first. Then there's talk of a penny, and then the pitch is made, and by the time we're in sight of Calais—"

"I'm not a parrot bird that's been taught to repeat what's said. But for you, sir, it seems necessary. There is no price attached. I have lent those clothes until the rain lifts or we disembark at Calais. You already possess a coat, I see. A pity you weren't here to share it."

"Well," the man said, "so long as there's no charge." He sank down beside his family, mumbled something about business coming before all else, then let the rainwater wash around him. Brydd collected his holdall and the blanket that held his leather jerkin and walking stick and went to lean on the rail. When next he looked back the man had spread the oilskin so that it protected him from the downpour.

The tide and disposition of the sandbars prevented the vessel from entering the port. It anchored a few hundred yards offshore, and the outside passengers were left to mill about whilst rowboats took off the more important inside travellers. Brydd watched the gentlefolk in their tricorns and dry velvet capes, then smiled at the woman as she returned his oilskin and rain-blackened hat.

"I'm glad you were not too harsh with him," she said. "We had a shop in the north of England, a cutler's—he knows every kind of steel—but he wanted to expand and borrowed the money and there wasn't the trade, not what he hoped there'd be—"

"We should get into the boats, mistress."

"Yes. But I wanted you to know. I felt I owed it to you. I have a cousin in Italy—she married a sailor—so we're going there. There's bound to be work for a cutler in Italy, wouldn't you say?" "Bound to be." Brydd nodded. "I've heard they all carry swords and daggers in Italy, so there should be plenty of work." He made a hasty joke to cheer her—"You keep him sharp, mistress, and he'll come to the point"—and she managed the spectre of a smile. Then she went off with her man and the child, and Brydd folded the oilskin and jammed the hat on his head. He could not for the life of him remember where Italy lay in Europe, but was confident that somebody there would need swords and daggers.

The cutler and his family were rowed ashore with a dozen others. Brydd followed in the next boat and was in time to see the man remonstrating with the oarsman. The young Cannaway was about to do the same, for he had just been told that the journey between ship and shore would cost him a guinea, twice the price of the Channel crossing, but he hesitated when he saw the fate of the cutler. The furious oarsman was howling and waving his arms and a moment later a group of soldiers descended the beach, knocked the cutler to the sand then dragged him off, cuffing him as they went. The woman and child trailed after them, and Brydd handed over his guinea.

The French, it seemed, were every bit as heavy-handed as the English.

※

Porters intercepted him as he came clear of the surf. They were quick, wiry men in stocking caps and loose woollen shirts and they jabbed viciously at each other with their elbows, vying for trade. One of them snatched at Brydd's valise, then gabbled something as the traveller pushed him away. "I carry my own belongings. I don't require assistance."

Armed with a smattering of English—all he needed for the job —the porter recovered his balance and said, "Yes, I assist you. I take you to the Douane, to the Customs. Is necessary I take you, m'sieur. Donnez-moi vôtre valise. I am your man for Calais." He made another grab at the holdall and Brydd watched a second group of soldiers start down the beach. They had not yet singled him out, but he saw them surround another unwilling traveller and lean in close, poking him on the chest. The man surrendered his baggage, and Brydd thought it wise to follow his example. "Your soldiers have a convincing way with them," he commented, releasing his grip on the case. "Do they shoot those who prefer to be left alone?"

"Yes," the porter said, "I assist you, sir. *Je suis à vôtre service pendant le séjour. Vous voulez me suivre, m'sieur?* You will follow with me?" He extended his free hand for the blanket roll, then nodded as Brydd reclaimed his walking stick. The English liked their *bâtons*; it helped them to strut.

Accompanied by the porters and fenced in by the guards, the travellers were escorted up the gently sloping beach then along to a tiled, open-fronted building above which billowed the flags of France and Calais.

Those passengers who had purchased cabins on the ferryboat were already assembling in front of a trestle table manned by a group of shabbily dressed officials. The less wealthy travellers, instantly recognisable by their rain-sodden clothes, were herded against a side wall of the building and told to wait. The porters stood apart from them, still retaining their baggage.

Brydd looked around for the cutler and his family, but they were nowhere to be seen. He remembered what Dr. Barrowcluffe had said—"Even if they don't have soap abroad, they're bound to have prisons"—and wondered how far the embittered cutler would get on his journey to Italy.

A handbell was rung and the officials reached for the first dry cases. Brydd watched, at first with passing interest, then with a growing sense of indignation. He was a world away from the rich merchants and embroidered gentlefolk, but it appalled him to see the way the customs men went about their work. Trunks were opened and their contents pulled out and dumped on the table. If a folded shirt fell to the greasy floor, too bad. If a vial of perfume was cracked or broken, too bad. If the pages of a book were torn through careless handling, that was just too bad. But it did not end there, for the passengers themselves were searched, the men raising their arms whilst the officials patted their waistcoats, pinched the folds of their breeches, ran inquisitive fingers along the hems of their cloaks and greatcoats. Their hats were inspected and in some cases the hatbands ripped off. They were required to raise their feet, like a horse at the anvil, and an official tapped the soles and heels of their boots with a small black hammer. Brydd wondered what they were doing, then learned immediately as an inspector gave a triumphant yell and all but dragged down the wearer in his eagerness to remove the offending boot. Helped by his colleagues, he wrenched at the heel until it came loose, scattering the gold coins and rings concealed inside it. *"Je vous l'ai dit!"* he crowed. *"Je vous l'ai dit!"* The other officials nodded. Yes, he'd said he'd find something. And he always did.

The discovery made matters worse, for the customs men seemed to take it as a personal affront. The gentleman smuggler was bundled away, hobbling on his one good heel, and the search continued with brutal thoroughness. Even so, Brydd's sympathy for the passengers was fading by the minute. Why did they allow themselves to be manhandled? Sheep fared better than this on the Wiltshire downs.

Had the line consisted only of men, he'd have remained where he was and let them make the best of it. But there were several women, and he stared in disbelief as the officials plundered purses and vanity cases, broke the ribbons of hatboxes and opened parasols so clumsily that they snapped the thin cane struts. And then came the worst of it—a search of their persons.

He saw an elderly lady recoil as one of the *douaniers* patted her waist, then deliberately thrust a hand inside her bodice. Brydd waited for the passengers to remonstrate but nothing happened, and he broke away from his own rain-soaked group. By God, this was too much! He'd tell the shabby official what he thought of his behaviour and let the whole room hear it! He'd shame the lot of them, or have a damn good try!

The arm that barred his way was bony, even in its black velvet sleeve. The gloved hand was skeletal and the creature that turned him from his path resembled a heron with a hat on. That was Brydd's first impression, and he never sought to better it. He'd been deflected by a heron in a hat.

"It would be a gallant gesture, but a costly one. They'd take everything you have, you know, clothes and money and a year or more of your freedom. Oh, they'd love it, those fellows. They'd knock you senseless and swear most piously that it was all in self-defence. And you'd get no support from us, not a bit of it. Why should we join you on the floor, and then in the dungeons of Calais?"

"I've not asked you to. And have done with my arm, sir." Still incensed by what he'd seen, he was unwilling to accept that the heron had steered him clear of trouble. "We are already on the floor, wouldn't you say, if we let them behave like that?" Standing back, he gazed challengingly at the man, at his black velvet suit, black boots, black kidskin gloves, voluminous black cape and tricorn hat, black with a black feather trim. In contrast, his cadaverous face was pale, his wig a bluish white. He was half a foot taller than Brydd and perhaps three or four years older. His movements were not clumsy—he'd intercepted the wheelwright with the minimum of fuss—but it seemed that his limbs were an inch or so too long for comfort. One could imagine that he'd been stretched and starved as a child, until his bones were formed and his appetite lost forever. All he needs, Brydd thought, is a long yellow bill.

"That was nicely turned around," the young man told him, "about being on the floor. Maybe we are, for the moment, but I'm sure even the ladies would rather suffer the brief indignity of a search than a lengthy delay in the commissaire's office. Where is your destination, may I ask?"

"It's Paris, but—"

"Mine, too. Well, I hope you get there, my dear chap. That's the place for gallant gestures, not this leaky shed. They are like playing cards, gestures. It's not always enough to have the right card; one must know when to play it. You, I fear, would be throwing away an honest hand if you tried gaming with these unpleasant fellows. Paris, eh? Have you been there before?"

"No, sir. Nor anywhere in France."

"Wonderful city. Be as gallant as you like in Paris, it'll be properly appreciated." He smiled easily and gangled back along the line. The elderly lady had already left the building and the other well-to-do passengers voiced no complaints as they and their belongings were searched.

Brydd rejoined the poorer group against the wall. Now that his indignation had drained away he realised how close he had come to disaster. He'd held the right card—in the suit of Honourable Intent?—but he'd damn near jeopardised his entire venture. Yes, the officials would have loved to see him rant and rave. Then they'd have attacked him, as the soldiers had dealt with the cutler, and how far would he have got toward Vienna without clothes or money, and with a year's prison pallor on his skin?

Dr. Barrowcluffe had been right when he'd warned him to curb his temper. And the heron had been right when he'd talked of costly gestures that Brydd could not afford. It was time he learned discretion, or he'd never get far enough to learn much else.

❊

Zealous though they were, the *douaniers* reserved their suspicions for those passengers who had arrived in dry clothes. The outside travellers were left until last, but the search was rough and cursory and Brydd emerged from the building with his money belt intact, his sword stick undiscovered. He had been charged sixty sols, or rather more than five shillings for the right to import his thornproof suit. Fortunately, he had already transferred a few coins from his belt and used them to pay the duty. The officials had confiscated the brandy flask for no better reason than that it still contained some brandy and had broken a few of his chalks. He had made no move to check their clumsiness and had forced himself to nod obediently as they'd hustled him on his way.

As he walked from the building he estimated his expenditure so far. There had been the night's lodging on his way down to Portsmouth, a meal and a bed for himself, feed and shelter for his animal. There had been the value of the horse and saddle, payment for his trip to Dover. There had been half a crown for the passport, a shilling for the bill of health, five shillings for the English customs seal. There had been half a guinea for the cross-Channel packet and a full guinea for the rowboat that had brought him ashore. And now he'd just parted with another five shillings, whilst the porter who lurked outside had yet to be paid.

The long journey was catching up with him. He was tired and hungry and he swayed uncertainly as the damp air blew in from the sea. The porter sidled up and reminded him, "*Je suis à vôtre service, m'sieur.* Do you wish for a bed? I know an inn, is not far, is not expensive. My own cousin, *il est le patron. C'est par ici.*" He no longer snatched at the case, but seemed happy in his new role as the unencumbered guide. Dulled by fatigue, Brydd followed him into town.

In layout, Calais consisted of little more than a marketplace and eight narrow streets. The light was fading as the men crossed the deserted square, and Brydd was intrigued to see that it was fringed with lanterns, forty of them in all. The effect was pleasing, a simple welcome that helped dispel the atmosphere of the customs shed.

The porter led the way to a corner of the *place*, then stopped beneath an inn sign depicting a crudely painted wild boar. "*Voilà, m'sieur, l'auberge de mon cousin. 'Le Sanglier Sauvage.'* You will pay me ten sols? A shilling English?"

If I don't, Brydd reasoned, he'll enlist the help of his cousin or the militia, and I'll yet see the inside of a local dungeon. Or perhaps there is a wild boar and they unleash it when the need arises.

He paid the man what he asked, grunted a good-night and pushed open the heavy, studded door. He was too tired to eat, handed over another shilling to a man behind a board-and-barrel counter and was directed by the jerk of a thumb toward a room that contained six worm-eaten cots. All but one of the cots was occupied, and the room stank of garlic and stale sweat, enough to blunt the last of his appetite. He used his valise as a pillow, covered himself with the blanket and kept the walking stick at his side. It made him feel more secure, but it would have availed him nothing, for he'd have slept on whilst robbers stripped him to the skin . . .

※

It was dawn when he went to meet Calais. He had left the room as he'd found it, the other five cots still occupied, the air still thick enough to grasp. He had ventured out into the yard behind the inn, discovered a pump and a soot-smeared lantern, and washed and shaved with the help of Dr. Barrowcluffe's castille soap. His appetite had returned and, dressed in a clean woollen shirt and the workaday leather jerkin, he collected his belongings and headed in the direction of the square.

He was inordinately pleased with himself; pleased that he'd reached Calais, pleased that he'd kept silent when the *douaniers* had appropriated the brandy flask and snapped the chalks, pleased that he was now feeling refreshed and ready for the day. He'd change a portion of his money into French coins, then buy something to eat and find the cheapest way of getting to Paris. Most likely it would be by stage wagon, one of the lumbering vehicles that contained four canopied benches and, for those who could not afford protection from the weather, massive wickerwork baskets slung at the front and rear of the wagon. They were like ferryboats, catering for insiders and outsiders. They *were* ferryboats the way they dipped and rolled.

But for the moment he was content to idle around the square, watching and listening as Calais came awake.

He saw fishmongers wheel their barrows up from the quay and bakers set out their first batch of *baguettes* and *couronnes*. He heard the creak of farm carts and watched vegetables spill into the street. A butcher's dray rumbled past, its carcasses dripping on to the cobbles. Beggars appeared from the doorways and snatched up the leavings, be they fish or fruit or offal. They stalked any ill-laden cart, not daring to snatch the produce from it, but pouncing on anything that fell. A man went from lantern to lantern, extinguishing them with practised ease, then refilling the bowls. Dogs licked at the viscous sheen in the wake of the butcher's dray and Brydd saw a beggar compete with the dogs for possession of some blackened entrails.

Stalls were slotted together in the marketplace, then piled with foodstuffs, earthenware pots, shoes and fabrics, iron cauldrons, straps and harnesses, tubs of nails, all the provisions of a working community. Different only in detail, the objects would have sold as well in Marlborough, and Brydd found himself nodding approval of some well-made piece, or frowning at whatever he deemed inferior. They certainly knew how to display their wares, the stall-holders of Calais, and he was impressed by the array of saws and chisels, each coated with a grey protective grease. Ezra and Amalie would have enjoyed a walk around this square, for it would not have seemed foreign to them at all. He'd write to them, he decided, and tell them about it.

He reached the far side of the marketplace and marvelled at a four-storey building resplendent with painted shutters and a flight of tiled steps leading up to an ornate entrance. Curved above the open double doors were the words "Hôtel de la Trompette," the title bedecked with pennants and chained baskets of flowers. It was a far cry from "Le Sanglier Sauvage," and Brydd told himself, I'll put up there on my way back to England. I'll arrive in my own carriage and demand the best room in the place. I won't even ask what it costs—why should I?—for I'll be too well heeled by then.

Amused by his own presumption, he started past the hotel, glancing back as a voice said, "My dear chap! So they didn't throw you in prison, those objectionable types. Got yourself fixed up for Paris, have you? How will you travel there, do you know?" It was the heron, gangling out on to the tiled steps and making the entranceway seem cramped and modest.

He had changed his plumage from black to bottle green, with a paler shade for his cravat and cuffs and the lining of his greatcoat. The outfit was heavy with silver buttons, the crown of his hat half buried beneath a cockade of virescent feathers. He carried a malacca cane and now used it to point at the sky. "There'll be better weather today," he forecast. "We should get to Boulogne with no trouble."

"How far is it—?" Brydd asked. Then he stopped, aware that the gaunt young man was not alone. A woman joined him on the steps, linked her arm in his and said, "Where is it, Albany? You said you'd have it brought round. I don't want the smell of fish in my clothes. Oh, look there, d'you see, they're selling wooden shoes!" She trilled at the sight, then remembering her earlier complaint, arranged her lips in a pout. "Where *is* the carriage?"

She was a pretty young woman, and Brydd guessed her to be about seventeen, painted to pass for twenty. With a total disregard for her companion's colouring, she wore a full-length velvet mantle, the mass of it vermilion, the collar of pink satin edged

with white. Her blond hair was all but hidden by a feather-
trimmed tricorn. Her lips had been reddened and she sported a
black velvet beauty patch high on the cheek. Brydd decided she
would be tiresome if things did not go her way.

He stepped back, but as he did so Albany levelled his cane. "It's
twenty-seven miles. Was that your question; how far from here to
Boulogne?"

"It was, sir."

"Good. And let's see, it's a hundred and eighty or thereabouts
to Paris. What's your name, may I ask? Mine's Albany Jevington."

"Brydd Cannaway."

"Well, the young lady is Mistress Georgina Warneford. She's
eloping with me. Don't tell a soul, there's a good chap." He
smiled and Brydd shook his head and Georgina Warneford tried
to scowl without lining her brow. "You say don't tell a soul, but
you've just told a perfect stranger! It won't do, Albany! He might
go straight to the authorities."

"Oh, I don't think he would."

"No, sir," Brydd said evenly, "I would not." He gazed at the
woman. "I've better things to do, my lady. Your secret is as safe
with me as—I'm sure it is with you."

The remark puzzled her. She again implored Albany to find
them a carriage. "Something comfortable. I don't want to be
bruised all the way to Paris."

He nodded patiently, unlinked her arm and strode down the
steps. "Better things to do?" he asked. "And what'd they be,
Master Cannaway? You've cleverly wormed out our little secret,
so you're bound to tell us yours." He grinned and made his boot
buckle ring with a tap of his cane.

"I'm a wheelwright," Brydd told him, "though it's my aim to
make coaches. I'm simply going to where they're made best."

Albany nodded, looked across at the square, then glanced back
at Brydd. A thought had occurred to him. "Then you must already have some experience of them, wouldn't you say?"

"Some," he agreed, "but less than of carts and wagons."

Albany nodded again, the feathers stirring in his hat. Almost
diffidently he said, "This carriage I'm supposed to have ordered

up. Since we're all bound for Paris, I wonder if you'd care to drive the thing?"

"Yes, sir, I would," Brydd responded, "though it's only fair to tell you, I know nothing of the roads."

"Nor do you need to, my dear chap, for they're clearly marked all the way. I'd be happy to settle for the meals and shelter. And then, when we get to the Île de la Cité—"

"Where's that?"

"In the centre of Paris. It's an island on the Seine. When we get there I'll pay you three guineas, or its equivalent. A wheel-wright, eh? Then you can help me choose a vehicle. There's all types in the yard behind the hotel." He extended his bony hands, gloved in green, and said, "I knew I was right to save you from the *douaniers*."

And I may yet return the favour, Brydd told himself, for I can see the brigands of France stampeding at the chance to pluck the heron. His buttons alone must be worth a fortune, and they wink like beacons.

"I want something comfortable," the young lady repeated. "Meanwhile, I shall wait inside. I'm sure the fish they're selling down there have been a week out of water." She turned prettily, swirling the velvet mantle, and Brydd made a point of avoiding Albany's gaze. If it was me, he thought grimly, I wouldn't be elop-ing with her; I'd be escaping from her.

❊

They chose a two-horse berline and, whilst Albany settled the bill, Brydd exchanged some English money for French, bought himself a bag of crusty sugared cakes, then drove the vehicle cautiously around the square. He was confident he could handle it, but it was not until he returned to the hotel that he realised why Al-bany had insisted on a four-seater, with a wide rear platform. There were no other passengers, but the extra space was needed for the eleven separate trunks and cases, hatboxes, shoe bags, pic-nic baskets and medicine chests. "It was a well-planned elope-ment," Brydd murmured, a remark that earned him a sharp glance from the lady.

He helped stow the luggage on the forward seat, roped the

larger trunks to the platform, then climbed aboard the driving bench. Albany assisted Georgina into the enclosed, bowl-shaped body of the carriage, then came forward beside the bench.

"It may not matter, but I forgot to ask— Can you read?"

"I can"—Brydd nodded—"if the words are not too long."

"Excellent. It's just that France is better signposted than England. We'll go south from here to Haut Buisson, then Marquise, then Boulogne. Knuckle the roof if you're concerned about anything, though I'm leaving the judgement of the roads to you." He glanced around, tapped the head of his cane in a cheerful tattoo against the bench and said, "Shall we be off then? You'll be enchanted by Paris. We'll be there in a week." Stooping and twisting, he clambered through the small side door. Brydd gave him time to get settled, then snaked the reins and took the berline through Calais and along the flat sandy road to the south. *It's a good start*, he thought. *The first full day abroad and I'm already coaching.*

He was tempted to whip up the horses and see how the vehicle would behave, but he guessed it would only bring squawks of protest from Mistress Warneford. She was pretty enough, he allowed, in a dollish sort of way, but she was too spoiled by a mile. He couldn't imagine what Albany saw in her, though it doubtless had to do with her performance in a bed. He told himself it was none of his business, then grinned and tried to visualise her, sprawled out naked, her blond hair in disarray. *So long as she made no comment about the dampness of the pillows, or the market smells that blew in through the window . . .*

The berline rolled southward to Haut Buisson. There was no village, no hamlet, nothing more than a ramshackle posthouse, a barn that leaned in obedience to the prevailing wind and a smithy that would have had Ezra muttering with disgust. Brydd urged the horses onward, settling himself for the run to Marquise.

The sand and scrub gave way to grass-covered hills and stands of elm and poplar. The going was steep in places, and Brydd let the horses rest when they reached the top of the long inclines. During one of these brief halts Albany and his lady descended from the carriage to enjoy the view eastward into Picardy, westward across the sunlit Channel. Then Georgina ran her tongue around her lips, spat indelicately and exclaimed, "It's salt! I can taste salt!" She insisted on returning to the sanctuary of the coach and Brydd heard Albany explaining that the air was always a trifle salty when the wind gusted in from the sea.

"Can't we turn inland?" she implored. "Salt makes eruptions on the skin, everybody says so. Please, Albany. There must be other ways to Paris."

Hoping the heron would understand—he might even silently applaud—Brydd took the carriage onward again and down the slope to Marquise. If Mistress Warneford started plotting the route they'd be half the summer in Picardy.

The posthouse at Marquise was a distinct improvement on the one at Haut Buisson, and they stopped there for a midday meal. The passengers ate at a proper table in the tavern, Brydd in the yard outside. This was how it would be throughout the journey and it suited him. He was their servant, not their companion, and he was content to drive the berline and keep his distance and earn the valuable three guineas. If Albany chose to address him, that was fine, but he would not give the petulant Georgina cause for complaint, though God knows she was doing well enough without it.

They reached Boulogne before the town gates were closed, and Brydd spent the last hour of daylight sketching the various coaches housed behind the inn. Other drivers wandered over to study his handiwork, though their comments were lost on him. It was enough that they nodded or tapped their eyes.

Since Albany Jevington was footing the bill, it was up to him to decide what the young Cannaway would eat and drink. Brydd had expected nothing more than stew and ale, but chewed his way in delighted silence through a dish of whitings and a bowl of spiced hare. He drank something called Vin de Bourgogne and was forced to admit that it was far superior to the hedgerow wines of the Kennett Vale.

Next day they reached Montreuil, a fortified town some ten miles from the sea. On the way they passed a stage wagon, its axle blazing as the result of a friction fire. And small wonder, Brydd thought, as he counted the eighteen passengers and two jack-booted drivers who'd scrambled from the overweight machine.

The coastal journey had done little to pacify Georgina. It seemed that she was always the direct victim of the wind, or prey to flying sand. It was always her side of the berline that hit the hardest stones, hers that lurched deeper in the ruts. If her mood was rebellious during the journey the self-centred young woman was in open revolt when the vehicle finally arrived in the town.

Aware that Mistress Warneford had suffered—and done so noisily all day—Brydd was nevertheless appalled at the way she then behaved.

He had delivered his passengers to the tavern door, looped the reins around the brake bar, then jumped down to help Georgina from the coach. For reasons best known to herself, she refused his bracing hand, and stumbled as she reached the ground. He'd afforded the woman a common courtesy, but she now turned on him, then shouted past him at Albany. "Not only an ill-made carriage, but the clumsiest driver you could find."

Striding forward in an outfit of sky-and-river blue, Albany took her by the arm and marched her with an easy firmness toward the inn. Brydd heard him say, "Worse than a clumsy coachman, my dear Georgina, is a lady who'd shout as though to sell things from a barrow. Besides which, I saw you choose to avoid his hand."

There was more—Georgina whimpering and the innkeeper bowing them in—but Brydd had had enough of it for the time. He slammed the door of the berline, stormed aboard the bench and took the vehicle through the nearby arch. He could get along well with Albany Jevington, and was pleased to have taken the job. But Mistress Warneford did nothing to brighten the landscape, pretty and powdered though she was. It'd take a man like Albany to handle her, he thought sourly, but only a man like Albany would care to do so.

The following day's drive brought them to Abbeville, centre of the local wool trade. Situated in flat, marshy country and bordering the river Somme, the city was too damp for Georgina's throat. She coughed like a kitten and affected a strangled voice, though she rallied remarkably well under the influence of a cognac syrup. She prattled drunkenly for an hour, then said, "I feel a little overcome, a little faint, I—" and promptly fell asleep. His expression impassive, Albany lifted her from her chair and carried her to their room.

As a precaution against disease, the more knowledgeable travellers came equipped with their own bedclothes. The mattresses were often stained and damp, so Albany had included silk sheets, a linen coverlet and a large dressed deerskin in his luggage. The deerskin was laid directly over the mattress in the belief that the treated hide would prevent the passage of infection. He placed Georgina on the bed, spread the coverlet over her, then sat in front of the tall, twelve-paned window, his feet on the sill, tapping his boots with the malacca cane. But tonight the rhythm of the stick on leather was less a cheerful tattoo than the dull drumbeat of a funeral march. Mistress Warneford had changed for the worse, and it had nothing to do with the cognac.

She had seemed so amusing in London, so willing to attend the theatres and parade on his arm and bundle into bed. He'd taken her to the races and the gaming houses, to his estate in Lincolnshire and on a week-long tour of Kent. She had never complained then about the salt in the air, or the dampness, or the smell of fish on a barrow. But there had always been other women in the offing, eager to supplant her in Albany's affections, to take her place on his arm or the pillow. It was only now that she wrinkled her nose, drenched herself in cologne, retired to bed without him. It was an ominous sign, and he wondered if he should tell her about the women he knew in Paris, bored wives and flirtatious mistresses, more compliant than complaining.

In the morning she bemoaned a headache and laid the blame on the marsh gases that bubbled from the fields around Abbeville and the mud flats of the Somme. "It's a miracle I'm alive," she whimpered. "Those effusions can poison a person whilst they sleep, everybody says so."

"I doubt it," Albany yawned. "The citizens look healthy enough."

"Oh, they're used to it. They're hardened to it, I'm not." She begged him to search the medicine chest for a special powder, moaning encouragement as he checked the jars and pots. "There's also a bottle with some rust-coloured liquid in it. Pour half the contents into a glass, then add a pinch of the powder, yes, that's the one." He did as she asked, stirred the mixture and watched her down it in a single swallow. "What was in it?" he queried. "It smelled absolutely vile."

"Just crushed ivy berries, colewort and mustard seed. The juice is radish and vinegar. It drives the gases from the head."

"And rots the innards, I wouldn't be surprised. How can you wince at the smell of fish, then start the day with that concoction? You were mildy drunk on the syrup last night and—"

"Nonsense. I've been inhaling poison all night, and this is the antidote. Everybody says so."

He sat beside the bed and waited for her to writhe in agony. She lay still for a while, then said, "There, I told you it would work," and reached for her face powders, patch glue and mirror. "Well, go along, I'll join you soon. Have them prepare some chocolate. It settles the stomach, a bowl of chocolate."

Albany stared at her, shook his head in wonderment, then made his way from the room. She was either in possession of a miracle cure or had the constitution of an ox.

They crossed the Somme and continued south to Poix, a hundred miles from Calais and only eighty short of Paris. It was one of the smallest posthouses on the route, but it offered soup and turkey, a dry bed for the passengers, a dry cot for the driver. It was there, in the coach house, that Brydd discovered a strange, three-wheeled cart. He made a sketch of it, started to his feet as the owner accused him of mocking the vehicle, then managed to convince the man that he had a genuine interest in carriages, however outlandish their design. The owner insisted on seeing the contents of his satchel, grunted with satisfaction and conveyed the desire for another sketch of the three-wheeler, for which he'd pay ten sols.

Without hesitation, Brydd extended his hands and uncurled his fingers; once, then twice. Twenty sols, or it wasn't worth putting chalk to paper. The man nodded immediately, twenty sols it was, and Brydd realised for the first time that he could make his way as an artist. He had never before sold a drawing, or set a definite price on his skills. It was not so much, twenty sols, but it would buy him a bed or a meal or progress toward Vienna. He took time over the sketch, and the man handled it with care and was gone before Brydd realised he'd been given two twelve-sol pieces, his asking price and a tip.

He'd remember Poix for its dark roast turkey and the three-wheeled cart and the first sale he'd made from the page. He knew now that he would not need to starve or turn back from his goal. He could mend wagons and drive coaches and stop either of them in their tracks, and by doing so pay his way across the map.

The fifth evening brought them to Beauvais. The northern approach was drab and forbidding, but once inside the town, they entered a market square bustling with activity and draped with flags and fabrics. Stalls sagged beneath the weight of pottery, the product of the area, and iron bars were bowed by the carcasses of deer and mutton. Brydd found it necessary to show the whip, cracking it in the air in order to clear a path around the *place*. He was greeted by a few clenched fists, but there was no real threat in the gestures and no one sought to tangle with him. The coach was obviously the property of a gentleman, and a gentleman could make trouble for those who got in his way. Besides, it was better to let him pull up at the inn, so he could start spending his money.

Georgina denounced Beauvais as the noisiest town she'd ever visited, on either side of the Channel, and slept with a shawl around her ears.

In the morning they rode on toward Tillard. The posthouse there was like the one at Haut Buisson, a ramshackle building that seemed happier to be left alone than visited by strangers. Once again Brydd slapped the reins, urging the horses onward, and the berline rattled along the wide, tree-lined track that descended to Beaumont and the final run to Paris.

A few miles short of Beaumont he saw a light coach on its side in the ditch. The horses had been freed and a man was standing beside the vehicle, flagging one arm in a plea for help. Brydd slowed the berline, rose from the driving bench and peered at the upset coach. Alerted by the change in pace, Albany leaned out of the window. "What is it, Brydd? Is the road blocked?"

"There's a carriage gone over ahead of us. I'm debating what to do."

"Perhaps we can help. If we put our shoulders to it—"

"Not yet," Brydd muttered. "I don't see anyone trapped beneath it."

"Well, we could at least get the coach turned upright."

"For what purpose? The spokes will be smashed and the axle driven up by the impact." He peered ahead and thought, But that's just the thing . . . the wheels are not broken at all . . . and the traces are intact . . . and the wood's not splintered, there are no shattered lanterns, none of the debris of a spill . . . and the luggage, it's all been opened by the lid, nice and gentle . . .

He watched and waited, seeing if the man would come forward from his vehicle and make an urgent appeal for help. It was what the victim of an upset coach would have done in the Kennett Vale. So why not here? Why should an accident make things different in France?

He let the man gesture for another moment. Then he made his decision and called back urgently to the passengers. "Keep inside! It's a damned arrangement! It's all been dressed up!"

He pulled at the reins, flicked out with the whip and sent the berline racing along the road. The victim stayed where he was, though Brydd noticed that he was now only waving with his left hand, the right fallen to his side. There was reason enough perhaps, for his right arm was bandaged and might have been injured in the spill. But the young Cannaway had made his decision and was acting on it, and it came as no surprise to him when the man pulled a pistol from his belt. He'd have done it anyway, the vermin, had the berline rolled to a halt.

With no more thought for the passengers, Brydd drove directly at the man. As he did so he again half rose from the bench, and it was this that caused the brigand to hesitate, balance the risk, then scramble wildly aside.

Only now did Brydd take the coach on to the verge, judging the distance and passing within inches of the upset carriage. He heard the report of the pistol, but there was no jar of the berline, no howl from the passengers, no stumbling of the team. However close the leaden ball might have come, it had failed to hit its target.

Georgina squealed, suffering the roughest ride so far. The

berline bounced and rattled along the verge, then thudded back
on to the road. But Brydd would not slow it until he felt he'd put
sufficient distance between the coaches. Then and only then did
he rein in.

He twisted on the seat and looked back above the black-tarred
canopy. The bandaged man had been joined by three others, all
of them gesticulating, each with a pistol in his hand. They were
not at all like passengers who'd been shocked and dazed in an accident, but very much like brigands who'd seen their miserable
plan go awry.

Albany Jevington leaned from the berline. He studied the scene
for himself, then said, "And I suggested we should stop. Damned
lucky you were up there, old chap, even though you've given us a
jolt. If you'd care to take us on to Beaumont, I'll order the best
wine in the place." He paused and then murmured, "And to
think I would have halted. Good God, it drains the blood." He
sank back and comforted Georgina. Terrified though she'd been
by the hectic ride, she was now more concerned that her hatboxes
had fallen from the seat and that in the excitement she'd broken
the buckle of a shoe . . .

❄

The next few miles were uneventful, though there was more
traffic on the road, none of it willing to give way until a collision
was imminent. Forked lightning stalked the countryside to the
east and, with the approach of evening, a chill wind blew across
the meadows above Beaumont. It turned the sails of a dozen
black-painted mills, rocked the berline and clouded the road with
dust. A group of horsemen rode past, one of them shouting,
"*Allez-y, allez-y! C'est tout près, l'orage!*" Brydd shrugged and the
man indicated the lightning, then pretended to shelter behind his
arm. The message was clear enough: take cover from the storm.

They were cuffed into Beaumont by the wind. As usual, Brydd
followed the road as far as the market square, then skirted it until
Albany called a halt. The passengers alighted and hurried into the
tavern, leaving Brydd to take the berline through a wide, ivy-
fringed archway and across the cobbled coachyard.

An hour later, when he'd seen the horses stabled and fed,

helped unload the luggage and checked that the carriage was still properly balanced, its axles greased, its hub-pins in place, he slapped the dust from his clothes and washed in the communal trough.

He was retying his travel-stained scarf when Albany Jevington came across the yard. "I found it. It's as black as ink and the man says he's had it in store longer than he can remember."

"Found what, sir?"

"The wine, young Cannaway, the wine! Get your coat on and—" He stopped as Brydd collected his satchel and valise. "There's no need to bring those."

"I always do. I was advised to keep them by me, and I can't afford the loss."

"What's in that thing, that satchel affair?"

"Sketches. Drawings."

"Indeed? Did you do them? The most I can draw is a cork from a bottle. I'd like to see them sometime—with your permission." He led the way to the front of the building, then past it to a small, tree-lined yard. The trees brushed together in the wind, but once inside that yard the air was still. There was no sign of Mistress Warneford, and only two crimson cut-glass goblets on the table.

"I fear the journey is taking its toll of the young lady," Albany commented. "She seems only now to have gathered the full import of what happened on the road. Or what didn't happen, thank God." He waved Brydd to a seat, an all-weather piece carved from a substantial oak log, then poured the wine and nodded to him to take a glass. "Here's to your suspicious nature and damn good eyesight. Well, do you like the stuff?"

"Yes, sir, it's excellent."

Albany grinned and admitted, "I've a lively curiosity, Brydd Cannaway, so let me ask what set you to coachmaking, and where you come from, and—oh, I'll not run short of questions!"

A while later he asked, "Is that true, that the officers intended to frame the sketches for their cabins?"

When the bottle was almost empty he announced, "I've a few friends in Vienna. They might help get you a post with a coachmaker."

Sharing the last of the fine black vintage, he remarked, "I shall need a driver, even in Paris. Would you consider it, if it did not interfere with your studies? You'd be free to leave whenever you wanted. By God, I can't get over that fellow with his bandage and his pistol."

He had ordered up again by the time he asked if he might see the sketches—"With your permission, of course. Particularly the von Kreutels' coach and the three-wheeled cart you drew at Poix." Then he fell silent for a while, leafing through the pages, the vehicles seemingly startled into motion by the occasional flicker of lightning. When he had finished he folded the leather flaps, tied the strings and returned the satchel, as tidy as before. "You've quite a few talents about you. I think we might enjoy ourselves in Paris. You have the abilities, and I'm surely one of the wealthiest drones in Europe. What's your answer, Brydd? Will you sponge off me for a while?"

"You deal with the *douaniers*, and I'll watch for the cutthroats, how's that?"

Even when he laughed, Albany Jevington made the sound one would expect from a heron.

No matter what route they might have taken, they would have found their approach to Paris barred by iron gates. It was a civic precaution, and it meant another search by the Customs, another display of passports and bills of health. There were none of the indignities of Calais, but it was a frustrating delay, for the towers and steeples were visible, as were the carriages that ran along the levelled ramparts that had once encircled the capital.

And then, thanks to Albany's charm and Georgina's décolleté and the curb Brydd had placed on his temper, they were through the gates and rolling past farms and fields, the patchwork fringe of Paris. One moment they were in the country, the next in the long tunnel that led under the ramparts, the next in the city itself, with the horses shying from the din.

SIX

There were an estimated 21,714 dwellings within the statistical area of the city, though the precise figure was changing even as the clerks recorded it. New houses were being constructed, old ones collapsing, fires consuming a single edifice or half a street.

It was further estimated that each house contained some twenty or twenty-one inhabitants, and that the resident population was therefore approaching the half-million mark. Of these, fifty thousand were said to be beggars, and at least eight thousand abandoned or orphaned children. The authorities might as well have combined the figures, for the majority of the children survived by begging.

Larger than London or Vienna, the city covered an area of more than four thousand acres, extending to the west beyond the mediaeval ramparts and crossing the swamps to the south. It boasted upward of seven hundred streets, ten thousand street lanterns—though these were easily stolen or extinguished—scores of new pumps and fountains, dozens of public gardens. It contained an observatory, five academies, a hundred and twenty monasteries and theological colleges, thirty hospitals, an opera house, theatres, libraries and the finest collections of paintings in the world, assembled in the Louvre, the Tuileries, the Palais Royal and the Palace of Luxembourg.

A visitor with the wind in his face could smell the stink of the city when he was still five miles from the walls. Sewage flowed along open drains into the river, or seeped under the foundations of the low-lying houses. The mud that filled the streets was sufficiently corrosive to rot boot leather, and those who could afford to would hire a *cabriolet* or *fiacre* and be driven a hundred yards rather than risk stumbling in the thick black slime.

The wide bridges that spanned the Seine were popular with those who wished to parade in their finery—to see and be seen. But they were also the stamping grounds for snatchers and cutpurses, trimmers and sharps. Most of them still favoured the traditional weapons of knife and bludgeon, though a few preferred to blind their victims with pepper or acid. It was easy enough to escape across the bridge and disappear into the warren of alleyways, leaving the victim with his hands to his eyes.

Paris was a splendid, decorated garment, its hem caked with filth. Poverty scuffed at the steps of the palaces, whilst violence lurked in the shadows beyond the boulevards, clawing at the fabric.

Only a dullard would spurn the chance to stroll along the tree-lined Champs-Élysées, or visit the grounds and gardens of the Tuileries, the mills of Montmartre. Only the narrow-minded would refuse to enter the cathedral of Nôtre-Dame, and only the lazy or enfeebled would not attempt the three hundred and eighty-nine steps that led up to its linked towers and an unparalleled view of the city.

But only a fool would stray far from the main streets by day, only a madman venture out by night, alone. If Paris was a magnificent garment, it was one that could be used as both a cloak and a shroud.

❅

The city brought Brydd Cannaway to a halt, then enticed him, dared him, challenged him to roam.

He was out of his country and out of his depth. He knew neither the streets nor the language, but he was determined to learn something of both. One of many, Brydd Cannaway stood in awe of the fine French capital; one of few, he decided to master his fears. He'd come a long way, after all.

⁂

Albany and Georgina installed themselves in one of the best ho-
tels on the Île de la Cité. True to its name, the walls of the "Silver Blade" were hung with rapiers and broadswords, Italian sti-
lettos and an artilleryman's dagger, its blade calibrated for
measuring powder. The main doors were inset with glass panels,
protected by ironwork in the shape of crossed sabres. The floor
was patterned with red and white tiles, the entranceway flanked
by leather chairs and cushioned settles.

The four-storey building contained a number of individual
rooms and, on the uppermost level, two large apartments. Albany
had rented the one that faced west, toward the prow of the island
and the twelve-arched span of the Pont Neuf.

The apartment had been designed so that its occupants might
be attended by their servants, yet also enjoy complete privacy. Immediately inside the suite was a square antechamber, again
furnished with solid leather chairs. To the left and right were
small, single doors, giving access to the cubicles that were the servants' quarters. There was no maid, though Georgina was already
pleading for one, so Brydd was free to choose whichever room he
liked. He took the one that overlooked the river, rather than the
courtyard.

Facing the entrance were a pair of larger doors, their panels decorated with the virtues of Grace and Generosity. "And that," Albany had remarked, "is someone's way of saying they expect a
good tip, but no complaints." The doors led through to a short,
tiled hallway, at the far end of which was a second pair of doors,
these illustrating Conviviality and Relaxation. "By which they
mean order up the most exotic foods and wines, but don't make a
study of the bill." The two sets of doors ensured that the servants
would be out of earshot, unless summoned; the uncarpeted hallway an extra hazard for those who tried to creep up on their
masters.

Beyond was the *salon*, a well-proportioned room that ran the
entire width of the apartment, with three tall windows at either
end. Beyond that again, past doors that depicted Love and
Repose, was the bedchamber, though Brydd Cannaway had kept a

respectful distance from it. Georgina's squeals of delight had indicated that the room was prettily furnished and as flouncy as a
draper's display.

They had settled in, the heron and his lady and their driver. In
the mornings Brydd was free to explore the city and sketch the elegant, pair-drawn *cabriolets* and the box-bodied *fiacres*. He gazed
at the fashionable crowds that thronged the Pont Neuf, shouldered aside the beggars, allowed himself a breakfast of bread and
bitter coffee. He cast sidelong glances at the women, then stared
openly, since they seemed to have no shame. He watched them
hitch their skirts to their knees, adjust their stockings, then laugh
with pleasure at some passing comment. He saw their companions
fondle them in broad daylight and be kissed for their impudence,
and he once saw a man accost a girl on the bridge, lift the hem of
her gown with his walking stick, then assist her into a carriage.
He'd have had his nose bloodied for that in Marlborough . . .

In the afternoons Brydd drove Albany and Georgina about
Paris, on one occasion to the foot of Montmartre, on another to
the gardens of the Tuileries, on another to the shops near the
Place Royale. Whilst he waited for them to complete their walk
or purchase whatever it was they were after, he sketched the windmills, the street scenes, the flamboyant couples who paraded
around the squares and dodged the splattered mud. He sold five
of his charcoal drawings, not only from the page, but from the
driving bench of the berline, and he learned that it was best to
look grim and unapproachable, no hard task when he was concen-
trating on a sketch. Strangely enough, a winning smile made customers hesitate, thinking perhaps that he was too eager to sell.
But a scratch of the charcoals and an angry glare as they interrupted him and it was *they* who wished to please, *they* who first
mentioned money.

He made the most of his situation, looking and learning, and
was in no hurry for it to change. It would, he acknowledged, if Albany married the lady, though the more Brydd saw of them together, the less likely it seemed. Meanwhile, he did what was
asked of him, driving them on their excursions and keeping the
berline polished and in good repair.

※

He went out at dawn to explore the island. From the vaulted embankment of the Quai des Orfèvres he gazed down at the rag-wrapped scavengers who'd emerged from their hovels to rake the narrow beaches of the Seine. They were like creatures risen from the grave, their faces caked with grey sand, their clothes as rotten as any they found beside the river. Each armed with a sack and pole, they floundered along the water's edge, striking out at anyone who trespassed on their particular stretch. Whatever they unearthed was either hurled aside as worthless or thrust into the sacks to be inspected later, when the tide had driven them from the beach.

Keeping to the north bank, he reached the Pont St. Michel and stopped to admire it, regretting that he had not brought his satchel and chalks. Where the Pont Neuf was wide and open, the Pont St. Michel was lined with houses, literally a street that spanned the Seine. The risk to ferrymen and bargees was obvious, for the occupants of the houses must have found it all too convenient to empty their scraps and ordure straight into the river.

Further along from the bridge was New Market, a broad cobbled area with its own quay and warehouses. Brydd wondered if there was any similarity between these weather-boarded buildings and the ones his brother-in-law owned in Bristol. Knowing Joseph, he'd bet the warehouses on The Biss were probably larger and better provisioned.

He approached the cathedral of Nôtre-Dame, peering at it until a wagon driver yelled at him to get out of the way. He retreated to the far side of the square, but at that hour of the morning the sun was behind the great twin towers, shadowing the west front and the Place du Parvis. Even so, he could see the three arched portals, the frieze of statues ranged above the doorways, the central rose window and the delicate columns that supported the balustrade. He imagined he saw birds perched high up on the façade, then realised they were hideous gargoyles, a malevolent reminder of how the godless would look in Hell.

Albany had told him it was possible to climb the towers and, dodging the *fiacres* that rattled around the square, Brydd made

his way into the shadows. He was surprised that the inner doors of
the cathedral were locked, though he could hear the chant of
choristers from somewhere deep within the building. Inside the
portico he found the entrance to the left-hand tower, hesitated for
an instant, then began to climb the unlit steps.

Fifty . . . Eighty . . . A hundred . . . How many had Albany
said there were, three hundred and something? He fumbled his
way in the dark, the walls smoothed by the shoulders of those
who had climbed before. One hundred and fifty , . . Two hundred . . . And thirty, and sixty . . . It was not the place to freeze
with fear. Three hundred, his footsteps echoing above and below.
Another sixty, seventy, eighty-nine and he emerged on the platform and was unsteadied by the wind.

He looked down at Paris, seeing the shape of the Île de la Cité
and the other islands in the river. He saw the windmills on Montmartre, and the northern ramparts, and beyond them the farms
and fields and a web of narrow, raised cart tracks. To the east the
view was obstructed by the spire of the cathedral and the deep
pitch of the roof, but it was possible to glimpse sailing barges far
away on the river, a child's boat on the Kennett.

He leaned over the balustrade and saw the toy-box carriages in
the Place du Parvis and inching along the quays. The New
Market was now a patchwork of canopies, each covering a stall,
the road in front of it congested with delivery carts and drays.
Smoke rose from a thousand chimneys, pillaring the air until the
wind broke the columns and scattered the fragments.

He had never climbed so high, nor seen so many vehicles; more
now than had come by in a year along the Great West Road. It
had been worth the climb for many reasons. Worth it to see the
city. Worth it to know that he could later say he'd surmounted
Paris. But here, alone on this clear-cut morning, the greater value,
the greater worth, was the traffic that moved below him. It was
visible proof that carts and coaches were needed wherever a city
cared to stand. Paris would not be Paris without such a jostle of
vehicles, and Brydd was pleased to see them run around.

He saluted the city with a nod, and hoped that the heron
would stay on his nest—the longer the better.

When he returned to the hotel he wrote his first letter home, trumpeting his success as a traveller and an artist. It took him the best part of the morning to choose his words and loop the letters, and he made no mention of the white-haired Judas who'd lured him aside in Portsmouth, or the upset coach near Beaumont, or the women of Paris who raised their skirts and enjoyed being fondled. Nor did he admit that he was sharing an apartment with a pair of runaway lovers, preferring to describe Albany as "a companyon I mette on the way."

He sent greetings to Sophia and Joseph, to William and the Darles, to the Notts and Sam Gilmore. Then he wrapped the letter in a sketch of the Pont Neuf, asking that it be given to Ezra and Amalie. He addressed the missive to "Doctor Barrowcluffe, His House in Marlborough, The Countee of Wiltshire, England." He took it to one of the post inns, from which the stage wagons would leave for Calais, and winced at the charge—twenty sols, as much as he was getting for a sketch.

In the afternoon of his fourth day in Paris, he brought the berline to the steps of the "Silver Blade," collected Albany and Georgina and drove them around the levelled ramparts that encircled the northern half of the city.

It was clear from the start that his passengers were in an ill humour; there was an edge to Georgina's whine, and Albany was altogether too polite. Brydd had learned by now that whenever the heron was displeased he was at his most courteous—cool and formal and damned brittle company. If he'd been happy he'd have made jokes against himself, teased Georgina, bantered with the driver, expressed the most outrageous opinions about Paris and its inhabitants. He could tell an indecent story with style and wit, identify most of the statues they passed and supply a brief biography of the monarch or statesman in question. When he was relaxed—with his feet on the seat, as Brydd termed it—he was amusing and knowledgeable company, far removed from the chilly diplomat who now infuriated Georgina with his faultless good manners.

"You think you won't be goaded," she howled, "but we'll see! I can't help it if I'm prey to the stench and jostling—"

"There's an ample supply of that in London."

"I don't care! I don't like Paris. I don't like anything I've seen of this country. You must take me somewhere else. Where's Germany?"

"To the east, and just as muddy."

"Switzerland, then. I've heard it's very picturesque in Switzerland."

"It is. But didn't you tell me you had an aversion to snow? It freezes the breath and turns to ice in the throat, wasn't that it?"

"So it does. Everybody says so."

Brydd returned them to the hotel, stabled the horses, then joined the other valets and drivers and servants in the kitchen. When he had eaten, he made his way to the fourth floor and his cubicle. He was sorting through his sketches—which to keep and which to sell—when he heard the distant bang of Love and Repose, the closer slam of Conviviality, the more immediate crash of Grace. Then his own unpainted door was knuckled and he opened it to find Albany, pale and a little drunk.

"D'you have anything to wear in that case of yours?"

"I've a suit my brother, William—"

"Put it on then. It's bound to do. They're not fussy."

"Who are they?"

"You'll find out. It's a place I know. A gaming house. We'll pay them a visit. Why not?"

"I don't gamble. I don't have the money for it. Anyway, I'm ignorant of cards and dice, or whatever games they play."

"Oh, they play most games," Albany grinned. "Come along, get into your suit. You can drive me there and see I'm not sprung on by night birds."

"Is Mistress Warneford—?"

"Mistress Warneford is staying in tonight. I advised her that the air would be thick with tobacco smoke and that charged glasses would doubtless get spilt. You might say that Mistress Warneford has been warned off." He lowered himself into one of the chairs in the antechamber and hummed tunelessly whilst Brydd donned the shirt Sophia had made for him and the thornproof suit. He remembered to take his sword stick, for use against the night birds.

❉

They drove to the prow of the island, turned south across the Pont Neuf, then followed the Rue Dauphine as far as the Rue des Fosses. Obedient to Albany's directions, Brydd took the berline along the curving Rue de Bussi, past the entrance to the St. Germain market and into a narrow side street.

"You'll see an archway on the right; turn in there. Stop when you come to the gates."

He did so, and a man appeared beside the carriage. He looked capable of lifting the berline with his bare hands, but his voice was quiet and husky and he chuckled at something Albany said. He opened the extravagant iron gates, indicated that Brydd was to take the carriage through to the yard, then closed the gates behind them. Following the visitors along the cobbled entranceway, the massive gatekeeper waited for them to descend, then beckoned an ostler to take charge of the horses. That done, he escorted the young men as far as a small side door, nodded equably at the tip Albany gave him and bowed the visitors inside. They climbed a rickety wooden staircase, pushed open another nondescript door and entered the warmth and haze of Madame de Boncoeur's gaming and recreation parlour.

Brydd learned the lady's name when she came forward, gave a squeal of welcome and clasped Albany in a wrestler's embrace. "*Attend, attend!* Wait, I never forget! *C'est Monsieur Yevingson.* No? Jevingson? *Ah, oui, bien sûr,* I remember. It is Jevington, ton-ton-ton!"

"My dear Madame de Boncoeur. Are you still adding to your fortune?"

"Of course. Why else would I stay open? When the government needs to borrow money—" She gave an expressive shrug, then gazed with innocent curiosity at Brydd. He was aware that she had already valued him—none too highly, it seemed—and taken note of the heavy polished cudgel. Testing him further, she spoke in rapid French to Albany, satisfying herself that Brydd had not followed a word.

"The ageless Madame de Boncoeur is rather nervous of that stick of yours. You won't need it here, so it might be sensible to let her take custody of it." Turning to his florid, lace-frilled hostess, Albany said, "May I present my travelling companion, Monsieur Cannaway? He's an artist of some considerable skill, and a valuable chap to have around on the road."

Brydd bowed to Madame de Boncoeur, who returned the courtesy, took the walking stick and smoothly twisted it apart. "*Il est aussi l'escrimeur, par hasard?* You are also a swordsman, M'sieur Cannaway?" She tutted fiercely, shook her head and relocked the sections. "Well, there's a thing," Albany murmured. "I'm in safer hands than I thought."

Yellow around the lanterns and merging to grey in the spaces between, the pall of pipe smoke was evidence that the gaming house had been open since midday, if it ever closed at all. It was possible to make out the dim figures that ringed the card tables or crouched above the dice pits, and Brydd noticed several young women, a number of whom were actually participating in the games. None were seated at the card tables—was that a rule of the house, or a condition imposed by the players?—but he could see at least ten elegantly gowned spectators, fanning away the smoke and leaning forward to whisper affection or advice.

Of greater interest were those women who threw the dice, perched as they were on the circular leather benches. He peered through the haze at their low-cut bodices and trembling breasts, and found himself excited by the way they snapped their fingers and swore at an errant throw.

There was still the ingenuous puritan in Brydd Cannaway, and he was shocked to hear a woman curse in English, preferring that it be done in silky, spiteful French.

There were other women in the room, though he could not decide if they were serving girls or guests. They wandered about, sat with a man for a whispered exchange, then left him, often to be followed a moment later into the haze. Whoever they were, they seemed quite at home in Madame de Boncoeur's establishment.

"I'm off to the dice," Albany announced, and Brydd realised their hostess had left and that the heron was holding two glasses of wine. "We never did decide what you were worth, eh, young Cannaway? I owe you three guineas for the journey from Calais,

and lord knows what else for driving me around. D'you want five
to play with? It won't get you far, but it'll give you the taste of a
game."

"Five guineas? No, sir. That's a year's money."

"Is it, indeed?" He managed to nod and click his tongue and
look pensive, all at once. "Then you'd best keep clear of the
tables, for you'll not like seeing what's wagered. Still, there's a
game you can play later, and it's one I'm sure you'll enjoy."

"How, when I'm not bidding on it?"

"You'll see. But first I have to separate Madame de Boncoeur
from her fortune. Isn't that the most perfect name, Boncoeur? In
English it means Good-heart, but say it quick and what is it—
Banker. It's the only reason I come back to this place, the name's
so damned appropriate. Here, take your glass. Drink's free, but
don't get awash with it, it'll spoil your game." He grinned and
gangled away, the feather in his hat brushing against the beams.

Well out of his depth, Brydd Cannaway made a circuit of the
room. He hovered near a card table, glanced at the amount the
players were bidding, then blinked and stepped closer, frowning at
the piles of gold and silver coins. He knew that a louis d'or was
worth much the same as a guinea, and that five guineas was a
good year's wage in the Kennett Vale, and that each player had at
least three hundred guineas worth of coins in front of him on the
black velvet cloth. It was a lifetime's money, on the trip of a card.
Ezra's lifetime certainly, or George Darles', or Sam Gilmore's, or
Alfred Nott's; all they might earn at risk on a single hand.

He watched the game progress and saw a treble-chinned man
scoop the money and quiver with laughter, shaking the powder
from his wig. The winner said something that sounded self-
congratulatory, tapped his chest and beamed around the table.
The other players sniffed, or drew on their long clay pipes, or
beckoned for a drink. Brydd estimated that the man had won
more than fifteen hundred guineas, treating it as casually as a
penny prize at a fair.

He investigated the other tables and found that the players
there were as fleshy, the coins piled as high. One game went to
four thousand guineas and beyond, the losers merely shrugging or
digging deeper into the silk bags they kept between their feet.

A serving girl replenished his glass, glanced furtively at Madame de Boncoeur, then murmured something he didn't understand. He smiled awkwardly and thanked her for the wine, then wandered across to a long side chamber where the less extravagant gamblers were playing skittles or throwing duck-feathered darts at a board. That's perfect, Brydd told himself, once you've lost your fortune at the tables, you can lose your farthings in the alley.

"We have nothing to please you, M'sieur Cannaway?" It was Madame de Boncoeur, concerned for the well-being of her guest. "You must not, how do you say, count your pennies. *Au contraire.* You must enjoy yourself. An artist and swordsman by day, but now you play like the children. *Il faut jouer, mon cher! Amusez vous!* You are in my home, where it is all for pleasure, *n'est ce pas?*" She squeezed his arm and winked up at him—her last warning before she had him ejected as a parasite.

He played skittles and won consistently, a few sols a game. He had an eye for it, and the steadiness of hand. Madame de Boncoeur glanced in from time to time, satisfied that the lean young Englishman was away from the tables. He'd looked altogether too sour, no doubt disapproving of the way the gentlemen spent their money. She would tolerate him, of course, so long as he stayed in the alley and Monsieur Jevington rolled the dice, ton-ton-ton.

❋

The game was known as *Locataires*—Tenants—and was the rage of Paris. Albany had played most variations of dice, but he stood for a while beside the pit, occasionally smiling at the women, missing nothing that happened on the cloth.

There were six large ivory dice, their faces engraved in black. Each dice was identical in that it bore the image of a Palace, a musket for the Soldier, a mitre for the Bishop, a wig for the Chancellor, a coronet for the Queen, a bejewelled crown for the King.

The object of the game was to people the Palace with as many different tenants as possible, thus the cynical *Locataires.* If one could not obtain a Palace, the tenants were valueless and the game moved on.

The Soldier was the least important, but it was essential to

house him in the Palace before one could include a Bishop. Both
were needed if a Chancellor was to count, all three before a
Queen could be installed, all four if a King was to be accommo-
dated and the player call *Locataires!*"

In keeping with the spirit of Madame de Boncoeur's gaming
and recreation parlour, where it was all for pleasure, there was no
limit to the amount that could be wagered. Even before the first
dice were thrown, the players tossed money into a square metal
dish known as the vault, and Albany accepted that the opening
bets were never less than twenty guineas in golden louis. Twenty
from each player, of whom there were usually seven or eight on
the curved leather seats.

The first player then cupped his hands, rattled the dice and
sent them bouncing across the pit. A Palace, a soldier, three
Chancellors and a King.

The Palace and the Soldier were left on the cloth, a new bet
laid and matched by the others, the Chancellors and the King
rethrown.

This time a Bishop, two Palaces, a King. The player had already
gained his Palace and his Soldier, so the Bishop could be added as
the next most important tenant. But the other three dice were
useless. Without much enthusiasm he called, *"Évêque!"* and
passed on the heavy ivory cubes.

The next player threw, nodding as the dice showed a Palace, a
Soldier, a Bishop, a Chancellor and two Kings. He wagered fifty
guineas and was matched by all those who had yet to play. Then
he rolled the Kings and earned the Queen he was after. He did
not win back his King, but he'd come close to *Locataires* and was
happy to call, *"Reine!"*

And so it went, each player betting whatever he wished after
his first throw, then attempting to improve his situation with a
second and final roll. The vault was soon full, the winnings fluc-
tuating between several hundred louis and upward of two thousand. If the stakes were somewhat lower than at cards, the game
was faster, and the tenants did not stay long in their palace.

Albany Jevington waited for a player to clap his hands as a sig-
nal that he was through—either bored or broke—then perched his
gaunt frame on the bench. He grinned at the ladies who flanked

him, produced a bulky purse from inside his frock coat and waited for the dice to come around.

Within half an hour he had lost four hundred and fifty guineas, and was enjoying himself no end.

✻

Brydd, on the other hand, was winning, but driving away the competition. He knocked down the last of the bottle-shaped skittles, collected the few sols that had been wagered, then watched his adversary stump off to the far end of the alley. They were all there, the men he'd defeated, clustered around the dart board, and they wanted no more of him. He was an excellent player, they wouldn't deny it, but he should have had the sense to lose once in a while. Instead, he'd won a dozen games in succession, and showed no sign of missing his aim. Well, they all knew how good he was now, but preferred to make their money last the evening.

A thin, pale-haired girl appeared beside him. She was carrying a pitcher of wine and held out her hand for his glass. Denied his small victories in the alley, he passed it to her, then frowned as she moved away, nodding at something or someone across the room.

"What is it?"

"Please. You come."

Albany's ready to leave, he thought, and wants me to get the berline. Or else it's Madame de Boncoeur, eager for half my winnings. There was nothing to keep him in the alley, so he followed the girl past the tables and toward a door at the rear of the parlour. On the way he glimpsed Albany perched between the ladies. He was sure the heron had seen him, but there was no indication of it and Brydd guessed he was preoccupied with the dice.

The girl led him through to a narrow staircase and again said, "You come."

"Where are we going? Madame de Boncoeur's counting room?"

"Please?"

"Even if she does take half, it'll be a damn sight less than a guinea."

"*Viens-toi.* There is nothing to frighten. *Je m'appelle Mariette.*"

"That's your name? Mariette?"

The girl smiled. Then, with her thumb hooked through the handle of the pitcher and her palm curled around the glass she climbed the stairs, as steep and insecure as a ladder. Well, Brydd thought, she's worth following, and I seem to have exhausted the possibilities in the parlour. They reached the head of the stairs, where Mariette opened another door and was instantly bathed in a deep crimson light. More curious than apprehensive, Brydd followed her along a passageway walled with grogram and hung with lanterns, their sides painted to give the hue. They passed several curtained doors and then the girl stopped outside one with its curtains drawn back. "You come inside now," she said. "I serve you the wine now. And we love."

❋

Below, in the smoke-filled gaming room, Albany Jevington had lost six hundred guineas. Undeterred, he was on first-name terms with the ladies who flanked him on the bench. "D'you know what?" he said, grinning left and right. "I feel the tide's turning. Another hour and I'll have recouped the lot."

He called, *"Chancelier!"* then lost to a player who snapped, *"Reine!"*

❋

It was achieved with gentleness. The girl was eighteen, the same age as Brydd, and had been a member of Madame de Boncoeur's establishment for almost five years. Five years of serving drinks and being with men in the gaming room, five years of taking them to bed. She'd retained her looks, and only once in a while did a customer—a guest—become violent, blaming her for his physical inabilities, refusing to admit that he'd lost more than he could afford at the tables and that this governed his failings in the bed. But these attacks were infrequent, for most gamblers preferred to spend the last of their money on a hand of cards rather than a whore.

She gave Brydd his wine, made a show of closing the curtains and bolting the door, then came close to him and held him and murmured to make him less nervous.

She sensed that although he might have fondled women in the

past he had never made love to them. She was pleased that he
didn't strut or boast, for that would only have magnified the lies.
His innocence encouraged her, and she traced the tips of her
fingers along his jawline, then across the flatness of his chest and
stomach, then the hardness of his thighs. The years with men had
taught her that the young were serious and intense, and that only
with the worldly could one enjoy the act as a *divertissement*, a
pastime as individual as the men themselves. The old, of course,
were as nervous as the young, fearing they'd lost their powers.

The room was crimson with lamplight, its corners softened by
curtains, the bed discreetly dark. Mariette made no attempt to
disrobe him, nor did she ask if he would like to see her undress.
He would, naturally he would, but if she asked him he might feel
beholden to attempt it, fumbling with the buttons, a man preparing his woman, though not yet accomplished with buttonhook
and eye. His embarrassment would make him more clumsy and
he'd wonder if she was laughing at him, scorning him for his
unschooled ways. It was better to lead him this time, this first important time.

She stepped away from him, pulled a comb from her hair and
bowed to shake her head. It was fine hair and she'd kept it
washed. He grinned awkwardly, not daring to say he liked it, the
way she'd released it, the way she'd kept it clean. But the grin said
it for him, and she straightened up and shook her hair again,
framing her thin, unblemished face.

"Mariette?"

"Yes," she murmured. "*Que tu es beau, cheri.*"

He returned no expression, but watched her use the metal hook
to unbutton her corset. Then she tossed the hook aside and removed the corset to reveal a simple linen shift, pink in the
lamplight.

He wanted to ask her why she was doing this for him.
Shouldn't she be paid? Wasn't that the way of it? But he had the
sense to keep silent, and encouraged by her smile, he put his wine
glass on a table, shed the thornproof greatcoat and unbuttoned
the matching waistcoat.

Mariette stooped to unlace her boots, rolled down her stockings, then released the drawstring of her long, frilled skirt. Now

she stood before him in the plain sleeveless shift, as she'd stood before a hundred other men, five hundred, in this or another of Madame de Boncoeur's profitable rooms.

Dressed only in his breeches and visibly aroused, Brydd Cannaway faced her and watched her raise the shift above her head.

"Mariette?"

"*Oui?*"

"You are very pretty."

"*Tu viens, mon beau. C'est pour toi.*"

❊

At a rough count he was seven hundred and thirty guineas down, and loving every minute of it. He was convinced that the tide was on the turn, though the women had edged away from him and the dice were obviously deaf.

Then he won the sixteenth game, and the eighteenth, and four of the five that followed. There were more sharp claps as players absconded, but the women were back, soft against his hipbones, whispering unnecessarily so that he might enjoy the heady scent of their perfume.

He won the twenty-fifth game on his first throw, the dice rolling and bouncing and clattering together, then stopping dead on the cloth. There, beautifully engraved, was the Palace, the Soldier's musket, the Bishop's mitre, the Chancellor's wig, the Queen's coronet, the King's baubled crown. He'd been the last to throw in a high-stakes game and had gained *Locataires*, and with it fifteen hundred guineas.

This, added to his earlier wins, brought him something approaching three thousand guineas. Not only did the coins fill his purse, but the flip pockets of his greatcoat, the pockets of his breeches, the four small pockets of his waistcoat—and both his gloves.

Madame de Boncoeur jabbed her way to his side, congratulating him in a voice with which a road mender could have shaved. "You're a fine pair, Monsieur Jevington, you and that forbidding young driver. The skittle alley is empty since he played, and now you would do the same for the dice. If I'd known how greedy you would be—"

Chilling her with his charm, Albany said, "My dear Madame de Boncoeur, your visits are always a pleasure, though akin to those of a farmer who ignores his scrawny geese, yet ogles the plump. You surely knew when I was down, when my purse was as scrawny as my arms. But you were not beside me then. Seven hundred golden louis, madame, seven hundred and more. And now time has passed and the dice have rolled and I've put on a little weight, put a few *Locataires* in the Palace. As for young Brydd, he always had a damn sharp eye."

"You play cards," she snapped. "The cloth here needs brushing. The pit is closed." She scooped up the dice and moved away, regretting that she'd ever let foreigners into the place, even though they lost more often than they won.

※

There were no regrets in the room upstairs. Mariette had let her shift fall to the floor, then turned and made her way toward the bed. She knew the young man would be pleased by the smoothness of her shoulders, her long shadowed spine, the curve of her buttocks, the trimness of her legs. She took her time, climbed slowly on to the bed, then lay back and drew the coverlet across her breasts.

He removed his breeches, not wanting her to look at him, then not minding at all. He stretched out beside her on the mattress, trembling at her touch. "*Doucement, doucement,*" she whispered. "Now come to me. *Ah, oui, comme ça.* We have love gently, like this, yes, like this." They moved together, his heart drumming, his lips on hers, then more daringly on her neck and breasts and the shallowed gulf between. And then he was being guided and the pleasure raked through him and he stormed above her, hearing himself moan and thrilled because she too was moaning and not at all unhappy. And then he came to manhood within her, his moan guttural and uncontrolled, his eyes bleared by the crimson light . . .

A while later they lay side by side, the girl's head on his shoulder, her arm langourous on his chest. It did not seem right to spoil the moment with words, and there were none he could think of that would convey the sense of giving and taking, of what he'd shared with Mariette in the room above the gaming house, in the side street of Paris. He leaned over and kissed her and said, "My name's Brydd Cannaway."

"I know. Monsieur Jevington—*il m'a dit*. He told me."

❄

They shared the driving bench on the way back to the hotel. Brydd had reclaimed his sword stick from an unsmiling Madame de Boncoeur, but it was not until Albany had collected something from the interior of the coach then climbed up beside him that he realised why Mistress Good-heart had turned so sour.

"You're chinking, do you know that? You're swollen!"

"Just get me home safely, young Brydd. I'm the most precious cargo you'll ever carry." He sat quiet until the massive gatekeeper had let them out, then unfolded an empty book-bag. For all the ten thousand street lanterns in the city, the Rue de Bussi and the Rue des Fosses were dark, enabling Albany to transfer his winnings from his gloves and pockets and stow them in the bag.

"You seem to have done well," Brydd observed, then looked straight ahead as the heron amended, "We both did well, wouldn't you say?"

They crossed the Pont Neuf to the island and rattled along the embankment toward the "Silver Blade." Perhaps to celebrate his victory at the dice pit, or by way of marking his friend's initiation, Albany produced a flask of brandy and insisted they pass it back and forth. Brydd contented himself with small measures, for there was nothing but a low railing between the embankment and the river, but Albany drank generously of the amber liquid. And so would I, Brydd thought, if I had Mistress Warneford waiting for me when I got back.

He stabled the berline, unharnessed the horses, then grunted as Albany thrust the book-bag at him. "You take care of it, my dear chap. Keep it in your room. I'll reclaim it tomorrow."

"How much is in here?"

"I don't know. Three thousand or so, less Madame de Boncoeur's expenses."

"And you'd trust me with it? I could be out of the apartment and ten miles away before you ever—"

"Here, have a nip. You're not the stealing type; you wouldn't filch a coin of it. Would you?"

"No, but what other answer would I give?"

"Very true," Albany grinned. "I'll be tormented by doubts all night long." Finishing the last of the brandy, he pocketed the flask and led the way upstairs. He told himself he'd done well to deflect the wheelwright in that greasy shed at Calais. They got along splendidly together, and he hoped the young Cannaway wouldn't set off for Vienna too soon, with or without the money.

He reached the topmost floor, opened the door to the apartment and gangled in, followed by Brydd with stick and bag.

The two men who were waiting for them in the antechamber were both armed, one with a riding crop, the other with a snaphaunce pistol. For a moment Albany imagined he'd been waylaid by a poor loser, a player who'd hired a bodyguard, trailed the berline from the gaming house, then sneaked ahead of him up the stairs. But they didn't launch themselves at him, or show any interest in the state of his pockets.

The one with the pistol wore a drab, military-style uniform, the dark grey material enlivened by epaulettes and a polished black belt, from which hung the pistol holster, a steel powder flask and a wallet for his flints and shot. The badge on his stiff leather hat proclaimed him to be a city constable. Albany noticed that the man had cocked the pistol and uncovered the flashpan. All he had to do now was pull the trigger.

His companion was dressed in a serviceable travelling coat, a no-nonsense tricorn and a wig that was ten years out of style. A businessman, Albany decided, and one who pinches pennies flatter than the mint. An Englishman by the breadth of his lapels and the knot of his cravat. An eruptive volcano by the way the blood suffuses his face.

"So you're the one! I've had you described to me, sir, and you're the one, damn your easy smile!"

"An affliction of birth," Albany dismissed. "But can you say the same for your manners? Who are you, sir? Paris is surely not so short of rooms."

"I?" That seemed to upset him more than the retort, and he shouted, "Shouldn't you have guessed it by now? I am Samuel

Warneford, and come a long way to reclaim the daughter you stole from me!"

"Now that's a statement that needs correcting. But first things first. I see you've enlisted the support of a city constable—"

"I have."

"Is it with the consent of the authorities, or have you hired him in his out-of-work hours? I ask, sir, because he's bound to blow a hole in someone if he's not disarmed, and you'd be on firmer ground if the injury was official."

"My methods are my own. But you take care, sir, for it'll be you that gets hit! You're a damned abductor, a seducer of—"

"Where *is* your daughter?"

"Ah, no. You'll not learn her whereabouts from me. She's safe now, well hidden. Search all you like, but you won't clap eyes on her again. You've seen the last of the unhappy Georgina."

There was no way of telling how things would have gone. Samuel Warneford might have ranted on for a while, then stormed from the apartment, taking his bodyguard with him. He might have challenged Albany to a duel, or demanded financial restitution—"You cannot restore her good name, but you can at least assure her a modicum of comfort in the lonely days ahead." He might even have calmed down, become wistful and acknowledged that he, too, had once been young and hotheaded—"I trifled with a young lady's affections, when was it, oh, a great while ago, when I was callow and selfish."

Unfortunately, the heron lost patience and said, "I assure you, sir, if you were to hide your capricious daughter behind that chair in the corner, it would defeat my utmost attempts at finding her."

"What?" Warneford rocked. "*What!* By God, I'll beat you down for that!" His face the colour of boiled plums, he raised the riding crop and prepared to carry out his threat. Brydd barged his way into the antechamber, shouldering his friend aside and parrying the blow with his sword stick. The constable panicked and levelled the snaphaunce, then doubled over with Albany's bony knee in his midriff. The spark of flint on steel seemed instantaneous with the flash of ignited powder, the deafening bang of the report, the plaster that gouted from the wall. Warneford lashed out again, striping Brydd across the face. Albany snatched the book-bag, found time to shrug at the consequences of his action, then cheerfully clubbed the constable with the sack of coins. The man's stiff leather hat proved insufficient to save him and he sprawled senseless in the plaster dust.

Grunting as Warneford lashed him again, this time on the neck, Brydd twisted the sword stick, slid the sections apart and put the point of the blade at his adversary's throat. "That's enough, you bloody menace. Stand still!" The welts on his face and neck had split and were seeping blood. He was in pain, and his mood was not improved by the knowledge that it was *he* who'd been horsewhipped, not the culprit. However, the constable had levelled the snaphaunce at him, and it was quite possible that Albany had saved him from a ball in the brain. Better the welts then, though they hurt like the devil.

Keeping the point of his blade against Warneford's throat, he glanced at the prostrate figure on the carpet. "Christ," he murmured. "I hope he's not done for."

"Nothing of the kind," Albany told him. "D'you see the dust stirring as he breathes? We, on the other hand, are most assuredly done for, at least in Paris. They're a notorious lot, the constables, and it's a bad business to knock them cold." He hefted the book-bag and said, "I suggest we put the monstrous Warneford and his hireling in one of the small rooms—the one the maidservant would have used—then collect our belongings and be off. Keep that blade up nice and high, there's a good chap. I'll find something to truss 'em with." He strode along the tiled hallway to the salon.

Brydd felt the blood trickle under his shirt collar, the shirt Sophia had stitched and embroidered, and it gave him reason enough to make Warneford raise his chin.

"Tell me, sir. How did you learn they were in Paris, Albany and your daughter?"

"And who are you to ask?"

"I'm the man who'll stick you if you don't reply. How did you learn of it?" He inched the blade and watched Warneford's hat tip askew against the wall.

"My daughter's chambermaid!" The man hurried. "Georgina confided in her."

"And you whipped the story out of her, I suppose."

"I gave her a good lesson, one she deserved. She was keeping it secret from me! She knew all the time and was making a secret of it!"

Then I was right. Brydd nodded wearily. When Albany first said they were eloping, on the steps of the hotel at Calais, and Georgina complained that he'd told a perfect stranger—I said then that her secret was as safe as she'd cared to keep it. Of course she told her chambermaid! She wouldn't be Georgina Warneford unless she boasted to the servants. And now, because of that and her father's ready whip, I'm forced out of Paris and striped into the bargain. Still, it could have been worse. Samuel Warneford might have arrived yesterday, and then there'd have been no visit to the gaming house, and no Mariette.

Albany returned with some lengths of cord and secured the constable, hand and foot. They marched the irate Warneford through to the small side room, trussed and gagged him, then collected the constable and laid him on the bed. Brydd locked the door, though the fugitives were aware that it would not take Warneford long to free himself and yell for help from the window.

Georgina's belongings had already been removed, and Albany abandoned several of his cases. "Speed is of the essence, my dear chap. The city gates are closed, though I'm sure I can purchase an exit for us—until the constable alerts his colleagues. After that it may not be so easy."

They locked the main door of the apartment, stumbled down the back stairs—the province of servants and lovers—and emerged near the coaching yard. Albany proved himself an efficient porter, stacking the cases on the floor of the berline, then stowing their most precious possessions, Brydd's satchel and his own book-bag under the driving bench. A sleepy ostler came forward to help, yawned as Albany gave him some coins and a piteous story about a dying aunt and his desire to be with her at the last, then roused himself sufficiently to help hitch up the animals. Meaning well, he said, "I hope you reach her, sir, before she dies."

The berline rattled the length of the island, across the Seine and eastward through the city. Albany knew his Paris, and when they'd gone some way he said, "I'd better sit inside till we're clear.

The gates are at the far end of the street. Ignore the *gardiens* if they speak to you. And muffle yourself, there's a good chap, you look like a whipped dog." He clambered from the bench, crawled inside the body of the coach and rapped on the canopy.

His story—and the coins that chinked accompaniment—persuaded the *gardiens* to slip the bolts, and Brydd took the carriage through the gap in the ramparts and out on to the pitch-black road. He stopped so that Albany could rejoin him on the bench, then let the horses go carefully in the dark.

The young men were silent for a while. Brydd did not repeat what Samuel Warneford had told him about Georgina and her maidservant. Albany might well be harbouring his own suspicions on the matter. Nor did he ask the heron if he'd procured and paid for Mariette; doubtless he had, but it was not something they need ever discuss.

Then Albany said, "D'you know what? If we were to keep going east for the next seven hundred miles, we could scarcely fail to miss Vienna."

"Is that what you want?"

"It's on the same latitude as Paris, near enough."

"But is it what you want? It's been my destination from the start, but it was never yours."

"Wonderful place," Albany Jevington grinned. "We'll be properly appreciated in Vienna."

SEVEN

It was a good spring for some of the inhabitants of the Kennett Vale, a bad time for others. The weather was mild, the hedgerows and riverbanks crowded with hart's-tongue and foxglove, primrose and wild saffron. The apothecaries and herbalists rode out from the wool-towns, tethered their horses, then plunged up to their knees in the river, scouring the banks for vetch and lady smock.

It was a good spring at Overhill Farm. The lambing had gone well, with only a few, unavoidable losses, and the grass on the downlands was a deep rich green. Too dry a summer and the hills would be brown and balding, for the water drained easily from the chalky slopes. But for the present the Wiltshire countryside was colourful and alive, and even the cautious farmers like George Darle were prepared to admit that things were not too bad, all in all.

Elizabeth made regular visits to the Cannaways at Kennett, invariably taking with her a jar of preserves, a batch of biscuits or a handkerchief she had edged and embroidered. Ezra told her she should keep the foodstuffs for George and Jed, but Amalie accepted the gifts, knowing full well why Elizabeth had brought them. The young mistress of Overhill was proud of her achievements and each small gift was a reminder, woman to woman, that

Elizabeth Darle would make a good housewife, a daughter-in-law of whom the Cannaways could be proud.

And I wish it were so, Amalie told herself. I never met a more enchanting young lady, nor one so destined to be a beauty. But then she was forced to say, "We expect a letter from him any time, my dear, though it's not come yet."

"Well," Elizabeth smiled, "next week."

"Aye, very likely we'll hear something of him next week."

❋

It was a bad spring for the wheelwright Alfred Nott. His customers continued to bring their gigs and wagons for repair, but with Brydd gone from the yard it became increasingly difficult to complete the work on time. Alfred was helped by his friend, the master craftsman John Stallard, though they were annoyed and hindered by the hulking Abram Hach. He worked when he chose —when he was sober enough to choose—and only then could the great timbers be hauled about the yard, the farm carts set up on blocks, the stripped tree trunks rolled lengthways across the sawpit.

Within a few weeks of Brydd's departure a wagon slipped from its wedges, knocking Alfred to the ground and severely injuring his leg. The fault was Hach's, and his alone, for he had failed to tighten the mooring chains that should have held the wagon immobile. He glowered and rejected the blame, then shambled off to his hut and his fathomless supply of gin.

Quietly, almost casually, the wheelwright's friends throughout the valley called at the yard, chatted for a while with Mary and the bedridden Alfred, then left the cottage and asked John Stallard what they could do to help. They were not skilled in the construction of carts and farm implements, but there were sawyers and coopers among them, and Ezra Cannaway was there each afternoon to fit new bolts or take away springs and hinges for repair. Under Stallard's guidance, the villagers cut and stacked the timbers, put two gigs back on the road and strengthened a number of ploughs and harrows. They made Hach work until his body glistened with exuded gin, then told him the day had only just begun.

Meanwhile, Mary implored her husband to take on a new apprentice. "He'll not be as inventive as Brydd Cannaway, nor as strong as Abram Hach, but he'll offer another pair of shoulders, another pair of hands. I've never told you your business, Alfred, but you must allow me to say this—Brydd is in some distant part of the world by now, and he'll never come back to the yard. It's time we had a new man."

It was a while before Alfred replied. His wife was right, of course; Brydd Cannaway would not be back. Oh, he might return to England, and even to Wiltshire and the Kennett Vale. But he wouldn't be content to work in the yard at Lockeridge, not once he'd seen how things were in Vienna-on-the-Danube. Mary was right and he knew it. It was time for a new man, and, God willing, one who was eager to learn.

"But can we afford it? Wages are going up all the time. He'll want more than we paid Brydd."

"Then we'll pay him more. I'll forgo my dream of solid gold shoes, and you won't get any fur-lined cloaks. That'll be a saving right there."

"Indeed it will," he grinned, "if only on embarrassment."

❊

It was a troublesome spring for Sam Gilmore, landlord of the "Blazing Rag." His was still the best-run inn in the district, but trade had fallen off, and he could only count on the local inhabitants, with their pennies for beer.

The trouble stemmed from the Cherhill gang. Emboldened by their past successes, they now ventured almost as far as the Beckhampton crossing, and word of their activities had spread. The stage wagons that had once made their overnight halt at the "Blazing Rag" were now stopping several miles to the east, denying Sam the custom he'd relied on in the past. If a private coach stopped short, or rattled by, it was no great loss. But a lumbering stage wagon carried between ten and twenty passengers, and it was these who provided a valuable source of income. Two wagons a week from London, and two a week from Bristol, and the loss was not something to be shrugged aside.

He shaved carefully, donned his best clothes and again appealed to the district magistrates. Their sympathy bordered on tears, and then they clenched their jaws and issued stern assurances that the brigands would be smoked from their lair, struck from the register of humanity, sniffed out and hunted down until even the memory of them grew faulty. Sam Gilmore thought the men wonderfully determined, shielded as they were by their desks and refreshed with goblets of sherry.

"And who, my lords, will accomplish the task? Will you send soldiers, or raise volunteers from the region? Will we have your permission to arm ourselves, or will you provide us with what's necessary?"

"We will crush them, Master Gilmore, have no fear of that. We'll rid the county of them and air all Wiltshire of their stench. You'll not lose your livelihood because of the depredations of a few damned brigands."

"You give me fresh heart," Sam said tonelessly. "But how will you achieve it? How, my lords, will you smoke them, strike them, sniff them, crush them and perfume the air around Cherhill? Will you, yourselves, lead the band as an example to the rest of us?"

"We'll see them off, Master Gilmore. Be content with that. Who's the next appellant?"

On his way out he thought, if their promises were bricks they could spurn a house and build themselves a palace. With towers. And turrets. And a vaulted cellar for their bottles.

❄

It was a businesslike spring for William Cannaway. He worked alongside the stonemason Andrew Cobbin, keeping the accounts and ensuring that the yard at Melksham turned a profit.

Fully recovered from the deafness that had come with the explosion in the quarry, William had continued his search for a reliable supplier of Rigate and limestone. He'd visited a score of veins and workings, discussed the manufacture of bricks, cored out samples of clay, chipped and hammered at a dozen types of mortar.

He was in the yard at dawn, revelling that the days were longer and dusk farther off. He ate his lunch in the yard, dined with Andrew Cobbin or alone in the local inn, then returned to his bachelor dwelling to tot up columns of figures and balance them and inspect samples of rock in the lamplight. This one was too brittle, this too contradictory in its grain. This one was sticky and would need another ten years to dry, whilst this one crumbled at a touch; the Romans might have found a use for it, but it was no good now.

He stopped occasionally, steepled his fingers and wondered how his brother was faring abroad. Young Brydd was the gifted one, all right, with his ability to design and draw. He'd do well, would Brydd, for he'd not allow himself to do badly. Had he reached Paris yet, or got beyond the city? Was he sketching what he saw, then sliding the satchel under his mattress for safekeeping—and a woman on top of it? He'd be popular with women, a lean young artist; a sight more popular than if he totted columns of figures and wiped the mud from samples of rock.

William shrugged good-naturedly and took a piece of ragstone from the box on his desk. He'd meet someone, someday, who would listen to him prattle about cleaving lines and compass bricks, pavers and pilasters. She might not see any special artistry in what he did, but it would be enough that she respected him as a man who knew his job. It was what he most respected about himself.

✻

It was a sunny and more rewarding spring for Ezra and Amalie.

In the last week of April they were visited by Dr. Barrowcluffe, his goat's hair wig pushed back on his head, his fingers stained with the juice of sorrel and celandine. "It's my herbalist," he apologised. "He's had me mixing all kinds of concoctions. And tasting them. He says he thinks he's found a cure-all, though all it did was numb my mouth for an hour. He confides in me as a friend, but I know he won't rest until he's poisoned both of us. You're looking well, Mistress Cannaway. And you too, Ezra."

"Can you taste things now?" Ezra asked. "Homemade cider, for example?"

"Oh, I'll get the flavour of it somehow." He took the seat that was offered, then dug a thick, square package from his pocket. Tapping the envelope with his stained knuckles, he said, "I was asked to deliver this and read it over to you. It's from a fellow named Brydd, in Paris."

Amalie hummed with delight, whilst Ezra filled the doctor's mug to the brim.

He unwrapped the package, smoothed the outer cover and handed them Brydd's drawing of the Pont Neuf. They gazed at it until Amalie said, "If you please, Dr. Barrowcluffe, the letter?"

He smiled and nodded. "Let's see now. He's marked the date, so we can assume the letter's been three weeks coming. No doubt you'll want to memorise it, so I'll read it slowly."

Amalie sat upright in her chair, frowning with concentration. Throughout the reading, her lips moved a word or two behind his. Ezra was also silent, then grunted at the description of the market stalls in Calais, perhaps approving of his son's eye for detail, perhaps because the French had the sense to grease their saws and chisels.

Personally, Dr. Barrowcluffe thought Brydd's account of his journey flat and out of character. His stay in Portsmouth had been "of greate interest to me," the coastal passage aboard the ketch "as gentil an introduct'n to the sea as I could have wished," the Channel crossing "remark'd upon by everyone for the smoothness of it." Apparently, he had found the customs men "civil, tho' too busy to accord us a personal welcome," and the tavern at Calais "of suficent comfort for one as weary as I."

I don't believe a word of it, the doctor told himself. There's more excitement on the road between Kennett and Marlborough than in young Brydd's laundered version. He's left the best bits out.

Even so, he read it with warmth and a nice emphasis, and the Cannaways heard Albany Jevington described as "a companyon I mette on the way. He resembles a heron in a hat, and is the most spirited company."

Brydd's account of Paris and its variety of coaches, of Montmartre and Nôtre-Dame, all this was more colourful, and there was an understandable note of triumph in his report of the sketches and drawings he'd sold—"for which I am being payed a good sum." This gave Ezra and Amalie the chance to take a second look at his charcoal sketch of the Pont Neuf. Convinced that his son would not have misrepresented the bridge, Ezra nevertheless glanced at the doctor and asked, "Is this accurate, would you say? I can see three carriages running abreast. Is that how it'd be, the bridge as wide as a coaching road?"

"I've never known Brydd to add a spoke or harness strap that wasn't there. If he depicts three carriages going abreast, then that's how they must cross the Pont Neuf." Referring to the letter again, he said, "He sends greetings to, well just about everyone. He promises to write again, when he's further along with his journey."

"We're grateful to you, Dr. Barrowcluffe," Amalie said. "Not only for reading the letter, but for teaching him how to write it. I don't suppose he too can be addressed?"

"He's probably on the move," the doctor said kindly. "He still has quite a way to go." Then he finished his cider and left the elderly Cannaways to pore over the sketch and correct each other as to what precisely Brydd had said about Portsmouth and the ferryboat and the windmills on Montmartre.

✻

It was, finally, to be a heartening spring for Elizabeth. She paid her weekly visit to Kennett, this time armed with a fresh-snared rabbit—compliments of Jedediah Darle—and learned that the Cannaways had heard from Brydd. She insisted that Amalie recite the letter and encouraged Ezra to interrupt if he thought his wife had misquoted as much as a word.

They showed her the drawing and she said, "They were just like that, the charcoals I gave him! To stop the coaches in their tracks, that's what I told him, and it's what he's done, do you see?" She was trembling with excitement, and Amalie looked directly at Ezra, held his gaze and murmured, "It *was* done with the charcoals, my dear. He said as much in his letter. And he asked that it be given to you. The bridge is called—"

"The Pont Neuf," Ezra supplied, aware that Amalie was a deal more sensitive than he.

"Yes, that's it, the Pont Neuf. You've a birthday soon, haven't you Elizabeth? Well, this'll be his present to you, I'd say."

Tongue-tied, the mistress of Overhill nodded and looked at the coaches. They were not really stopped at all, but racing across the bridge, whilst the pedestrians jumped aside, or stared after them, or continued on their way. There was enough detail in the picture for her never to tire of it, never to grow weary of the arched span and its milling population, of the river that swirled beneath, or the trees and houses that shrank to infinity on the left-hand bank. The picture would last as long as was necessary—until the artist returned.

❈

Several hundred miles to the southeast the artist was hefting his sword stick and glancing at his companion in the hope that Albany Jevington could explain why the world had grown so still . . .

A full month had elapsed since their nocturnal flight from Paris. Albany had sold the berline as soon as possible, not that he'd expected the city constables to carry their pursuit through France, but simply because he had no more need of the coach. The fretful Georgina had gone, most of his luggage had been abandoned in the hotel and it was easier to continue on horseback, riding alongside Brydd Cannaway.

They had passed through the cities of Strasbourg and Stuttgart, enjoying the sights and the Rhine wines and the women. The marks on Brydd's face and neck had healed and, although he would never entirely forget the crimson-lit room above the gaming house, or the practised Mariette, there had been other rooms and other women since then. Unnerved perhaps by his experience with Georgina, Albany had spent his time at the tables. He'd been delighted to find that the dice game *Locataires* was played in all the major cities, though his beginner's luck deserted him and he lost as much as he won.

From Stuttgart they had ridden due east and were now approaching a small village called Essenbach—and frowning because its streets were empty, its shutters closed, a rusted pump dripping water on to the cobbles.

Holding his sword stick ready beside the saddle, Brydd asked, "Why is the place locked up like this? Are they plague-ridden, do you think, and we've missed the warning signs?"

"It's odd," Albany granted, "but they'd have been fenced off if they were victims of disease. Let's just trot through and see what happens."

There were chickens pecking in their enclosures, horses in their stables, clothes and hopsacks hung out to dry. A vegetable seller had left the produce on his stall, though his shop door was closed, its windows shuttered. Mown grass lay in the street, an indication that a cart had passed by not long before. Albany's horse stopped to chew the grass and Brydd reined in, laying his stick across the saddle horn. The stillness was disconcerting, for it was late afternoon, long past the rest period. Even then there'd have been somebody about, a few doors left open, the murmur of families at a meal table. And now, an hour before dusk, the village of Essenbach should have been bustling with life.

Throughout the journey from Paris, Brydd had allowed the heron to set the tone of their relationship. It was Albany who paid the bills—"for which we may thank Madame de Boncoeur's patrons"—and Brydd who saw to the welfare of the horses. But the young men ate together and shared whatever accommodation they could find on the way. Unalike though they were, the country wheelwright and the gentleman traveller, each would now say the other was his friend. Albany was at his best in the cities, Brydd the one who could read the sky and gauge when a downpour would make the road impassable. It was Albany who spoke the language, Brydd who knew how to use his stick as a cudgel or a sword.

But, for the moment, there was no one to address, no attack to be parried. The village had been given over to its livestock and the occasional snarling dog, to the rapid drip of pump water and the shadows that lengthened across the cobbled street.

The riders went forward again, glancing left and right between the houses. They heard a child squall and Albany said, "They're all inside, don't you sense it?"

"Aye, I've been pricked by their stares since we arrived. If you see the glint of metal, ignore it. I don't know why they're in hiding, but we don't want to set a finger twitching on its trigger."

They made their way slowly along the street, then were suddenly clear of the village and climbing a long treeless slope. "If I was going to shoot strange travellers," Albany murmured, "now's the time I'd do it. We're showing them a nice pair of backs."

The thought had already occurred to the wheelwright, and he could feel the sweat on his spine. "Just go on," he said. "We'll speed up at the ridge."

But the chance was denied them, for when they reached the top of the slope they saw that the road ahead divided and that a number of men were busy at the fork. They also saw a sturdy ten-foot gibbet, from which was suspended an iron cage on a chain. The grille was equipped with a hinged door, now hanging open, its weight tilting the cage toward the gibbet post. A little way off lay a bloated, bird-pecked corpse—the late occupant of the airy cell.

Several of the men were armed with muskets or pistols, and it was these who mounted guard over the corpse. Others were digging a trench in the road, exactly where it divided, whilst a third group unloaded a length of heavy chain from a farm cart.

The elements of the scene were clear enough. The body of a hanged man had been lifted from its cage and was to be buried in the trench. But why at the fork, and why the armed guards, and why the thick-linked chain? As a felon, the man could not be buried in consecrated ground, but what was so terrible about him that even his body had to be interred under the shadow of the gun? And what was the purpose of the chain—to stop him rising from the dead?

"Put the stick away," Albany said, "or we *will* set more fingers twitching. They're nervous enough as it is, those fellows. God knows what they're doing, but we might as well go on until we're stopped."

"I'd rather wait and let them finish," Brydd told him. "There's something evil about it." Nevertheless, he forced himself to keep pace with Albany, praying that someone would soon cry halt. There was a gibbet at Beckhampton and three of them at Marlborough, and the young Cannaway had often seen hanged men spin in the wind. But they'd never been buried in the road, or wrapped in chains as was happening here. This was something different, something more than the laying away of a common criminal.

The riders were told to stop, and four men approached them. They were all armed, their expressions drawn and suspicious. *"Woher kommen Sie, meine Herren? Warum sind Sie hier?"*

Answering them in their own language, Albany said, "We are English travellers, on our way to Vienna. Our purpose here is simply to further our route." Then, almost casually, he asked, "*Was ist los?*"

Satisfied that the foreigners were no threat to them, the men of Essenbach seemed almost relieved to talk. Whilst Albany nodded at what they said, Brydd watched their gaze slide toward the horizon, then toward the bloated corpse, now swaddled in its chains. He noticed that the gravediggers were stabbing frantically at the ground in their attempts to deepen the trench. *They* could sense the evil. It was rising from the body, and darkening the air.

"What is it, Albany? What's occurred?"

"Well, my dear, chap, if I tell you I shall expect you to stay your ground."

"Just tell me, and we'll see."

Albany nodded, accepting the retort, then said, "I can only tell you what *they* recount, what *they* believe. Personally, I think the devil makes pretty women tiresome and weights the dice in my disfavour and sours expensive wine. But you may think different; you're a countryman, after all."

"What's the devil's part in this? Am I to know or not?" He was staring angrily at his friend, both of them aware that his belligerence was a threadbare cover for his fears. Brigands and cozeners he could deal with, but the devil and its minions posed a different threat. He'd seen them on the Wiltshire downs, the spiny phantoms that scuttled from rock to rock, or flew low across the moon. They killed animals in the night, sparked fire with their fingernails, brought down the rain to drown livestock and led travellers into the marshes, to be swallowed and lost. He'd seen them at work, the Satanic forces, and now he snapped, "Are you ever to tell me?"

"That corpse there," Albany indicated, "was once the property of a murderer. No foreigner to Essenbach, but a man of forty or so who'd lived in the village all his life. He wasn't especially popular, it seems, but he was known throughout the district. A family man; a fence maker, and good at his work. They made a point of that, of how ordinary he was."

"And yet he committed murder. Who did he kill?"

"Well, that's what unsettles them. He murdered his wife and

all four of his children, then went out on to the street and cut down a man he'd not spoken to in ten years. He tried to kill someone else, apparently, but by then he'd been surrounded."

"Dear God," Brydd murmured. "To murder one's own family."

"Yes," Albany agreed, "but it's not that alone that terrifies them. It's what followed, when they tried to arrest him."

"What are you saying, that he could do worse than slay his wife and children?"

"I'm saying, *they* are saying that it took twenty blows of an iron bar to subdue him. That's what frightens them, that he had to be thrashed with iron before he could be stilled. And the reason, my dear Brydd, again so they say, is because he'd been collecting fence wood in the nearby forest and was bitten by a werewolf. Do you know what a—?"

"I know." His body was rigid, his lips and knuckles pinched white. "I know what a werewolf is. There was one that roamed near Chippenham. I never saw it, but it was described to me. Aye, and what it did. There were five deaths in a month, and a woman who set fire to her house, and another who attacked a priest with a scythe, cutting off his arm." He was breathing hard, and peering past Albany at the horizon. "So that's why they've chained the body and put it where the carts can run over it, to stop it being dug up and possessed. Well, they won't succeed. The rest of the pack will be here after dark and they'll tear the chains like paper and savage anyone they find! Christ, Albany, let's get on! We'll be done for if they sniff us!"

The fear's contagious, Albany acknowledged. Another few minutes and I too shall be listening for the howl of werewolves. "Yes," he said, "we'll go on, we're not needed here." He edged his horse wide of the grave, bade good-fortune to the burial party, then rode past the vacant rusted cage.

It took the young men all their courage to hold the animals at a trot, for the temptation was to flee pell-mell across the shadowed plain.

❁

Three days later they reached the city of Passau, from where they would be rowed two hundred and fifty miles down the Danube River to Vienna.

The boat trip was Albany's idea, something he'd wanted to experience on his previous journeys to the Austrian capital. However, he had invariably been in the company of young ladies who flinched from raindrops and from gentlemen who dusted their wigs. The overland route was arduous enough, they'd insisted, with its potholed roads and pigsty taverns. But at least there were no cataracts or whirlpools, no waves to wash a man from the deck, no currents to dash him against the rocks or drag him down to be strangled by the weeds.

It had amused Albany to hear his companions wax so eloquent on the subject of danger and discomfort. One day, someone would lay a flat, featureless road across Europe, from east to west, from north to south. The porcelain travellers could then ride in a carriage that was sealed as tight as a fruit jar, marking their progress by the signs that fringed the road. "We're in Denmark, it says so . . . Look, the board reads SPAIN, we've come a long way south . . ."

But there were no such problems with Brydd Cannaway. The werewolves of Essenbach were forgotten, and he seized the opportunity to descend the Danube.

"It'll be a rough ride," Albany told him. "The spring floods will have swollen the river. Still, the vessels are designed for the work and we'll get to Vienna a damn sight quicker than by coach or horse. They can make fifty miles a day, so I've heard, and sometimes more."

The young men rode through Passau, climbing the steep outcrop that held the city, then pausing to look down on the river. The base of the outcrop was smoothed by two smaller rivers that bubbled into the Danube. The waters of one were a light brown, the other black as coal, the colours mingling with the pale grey of the mainstream. They could see barges being hauled upriver, fishermen trawling from a line of small, brightly painted boats, a sailing craft tacking unsuccessfully against the current. But none of this was worth a second glance, for their attention was devoted to the extraordinary vessel that would carry them to Vienna.

It was not a boat at all, but a raft; a vast mosaic of logs, some set lengthways, others sideways, then bound together to form a platform more than eighty feet long and twenty or thirty across. Two notched fences ran the width of the deck, one at either end, with a number of poles and broad-bladed oars propped against them. In the centre of the raft were two log cabins, each sprouting a chimney stack. But there were no protective walls around the vessel, not even so much as a guard rail, nothing to stop the water swirling across the platform and into the isolated huts.

Brydd glanced quizzically at his friend. "So the vessels are designed for the work, eh?"

"It's an unusual sort of craft, I agree, but perhaps it's more suitable than it looks."

"It'd have to be, would it not, when it looks like a door tossed in?"

They rode down the zigzag path to the landing, where they learned that the vessel was indeed bound for Vienna and would be poled off within the next few minutes. They exchanged their horses for a redemption ticket, allowing them to collect fresh mounts when they reached the capital, paid their fares, then lugged their saddles and belongings across the great roped logs.

They discovered that one of the huts was for the passengers, the other for the oarsmen, and edged their way into the dormitory.

It was already crowded, and it took them a while to locate the last two empty bunks. There were a dozen in all, set in tiers of three around the walls, with space between for the door, a pot-bellied stove, a small window and a storage box that held kindling, wine bottles and a variety of luggage. The two vacant beds were on the upper level, the other high perches occupied by a misshapen man who serenaded the occupants with a reed pipe, and a boy of ten—the man's son, perhaps—who trembled involuntarily, yet seemed to derive pleasure from the melancholy tune. The newcomers tossed their saddles into the storage box, then lifted their few belongings on to the beds. Brydd grinned at the boy, who immediately hooked his fingers in his mouth and stretched it in a lopsided smile. The piper blinked his gratitude and continued with his haunting tune.

The middle level was occupied by a burly drover, his badge of rank the ox whip looped around his shoulders, a cherubic merchant and two peasant farmers, their clothes held together with patch and twine. Below them, on the lowest tier, were their wives, along with a slender young woman and another, twice her age, who might have been her mother, her aunt, her sharp-eyed chaperone. The young woman watched Albany and earned herself an admonishing murmur from her companion.

Each of the twelve berths was now occupied or claimed, so the passengers were surprised when the door banged open, admitting two more men to the hut.

It was hard to tell the one from the other, the haughty from the arrogant. They were soldiers, resplendent in jackboots, loden greatcoats with scarlet cuffs, sand-coloured breeches, wide belts and sword hangers, holstered pistols, starched cravats and black tricorns piped with white. They muttered something to each other and Albany said quietly, "They're Russians. Severians or Cossacks, I don't know which. Unpleasant fellows, as a rule."

The soldiers let their gaze rest on him, included Brydd in their assessment, then studied the other occupants of the cabin. It was clear what they were about—deciding whom to evict, whose beds they would usurp for the journey downriver.

They chose the piper and his retarded son, lifted their chins the merest fraction and indicated that the man should collect his offspring and find a place on the open deck. Or get off the raft altogether and wait two days for the next. They didn't care which.

As though unaware of what was happening, Albany turned his back on the newcomers, nodded cheerfully at the musician and said, "You may not have the breath for it, *mein Herr*, but it would be a privilege to hear the tune again. From the start, if you will?" He addressed the man in German, but the soldiers understood the gist of it—and did not like what they heard. One of them stepped forward, determined to make the bony foreigner answer for his interference. It was only at the last instant, as he was reaching for Albany's shoulder to pull him around, that he was recalled by his companion. Then, ignoring the women on the lower berths, they let their gaze slide past the drover and the merchant and settle on the patched and mended farmers. Another, more insistent lift of the chin and the farmers climbed resignedly from their bunks, explaining to their wives that they'd seek shelter with the rowers in the other cabin.

Dear God, Brydd grated to himself, I'm back in the shed at Calais. The customs officials are now called Severians or Cossacks, but the bullies are at work again.

Aware that he could do nothing to help, he snatched his satchel from the bed and went on deck to watch the raft being poled from the bank. Albany stayed until the piper had finished his tune, then thanked the man and gangled from the cabin. The soldiers gazed after him, wishing that it could have all have happened in their own country. They'd not have been so tolerant with him there . . .

❄

No sooner had the great platform begun to move than Brydd Cannaway acknowledged the wisdom of design. Roped this way and that, the logs formed a flexible carpet on the water, undulating as the current churned beneath. The fence at the stern was now manned by a dozen oarsmen, some poling the raft from the landing, others steering it parallel with the bank.

The ungainly vessel moved away from the outcrop, its squared-off bows butting the water, wrinkling the pale grey skin. A moment earlier it had been tied firmly to the landing and now it was pushing its way down the Danube, the first small bow waves spilling on to the logs. Another moment and few coaches could have matched its speed, and only then on a short, flat run. A horse could have kept level at a canter, then at a gallop, and then the animal would have lagged behind as the river narrowed and the water fought for space between the banks. The oarsmen were already straining to keep the raft in line. It no longer seemed extensive, but was merely a box lid, to be splashed and buffeted and swept on as far as it would go.

Braced against the rear wall of the cabin, Brydd sketched his departure from Passau. He captured an impression of the outcrop, used his thumb to smudge the colours of the river, drew the traffic that plied it and the oxteams that plodded along its banks. He used one of the charcoal sticks Elizabeth Darle had given him, pleased that it didn't crumble with the urgency of his work. She must have gone to the printer's shop in Marlborough and asked for the best in stock.

And then, long before he finished the drawing, the raft curved with the current and slid between hunched grey cliffs, a monastery visible on the right bank, a village crouched on the left. Passau was out of sight, another name to be added to those of Portsmouth and Dover, Calais and Paris, Stuttgart and Essenbach. A few days more and he could add the name that had so often held the centre of his thoughts, so often been the object of his dreams.

❄

The raft emerged from the narrows, made its sedate way past the imperial city of Linz, then crashed into the first of the rapids. Time and again it was turned full circle, its edges splintered by the rocks, its ropes loosened so that a thick fir log would spring up from the deck like a stepped-in snare. The water boiled alongside the clumsy mosaic, then flooded across it, bursting into the cabins to run inches deep below the bunks.

The cherubic merchant was the first to vacate his bed, helping the slender young woman into the dry. The drover surrendered his berth to the mother-aunt-chaperone—no one knew which for sure —whilst Brydd and Albany assisted the farmers' wives on to the topmost level. The soldiers stayed where they were, clear of the water, unwilling to ruin their uniforms or rust their massive wheel-lock pistols. They had brought their own rations with them, black bread and salted fish and a colourless brandy, but they shared none of it with the civilians and ignored anyone who spoke to them. A day of that and they too were ignored.

The mood of the river dictated where the passengers would spend the night. As dusk approached, one of the oarsmen went forward to the bows, scanning the banks for a likely mooring, then shouting back at the rowers to steer the platform this way or that.

The first night was spent alongside a wide, pebbled beach, the next in a stretch of marshland, the air alive with insects.

The third day brought them to another series of jarring rapids.

During the first hours of the descent an oar snapped without warning, felling one of the rowers and gouging another in the chest. The man who'd been hit recovered to take his place at the fence, though the one who'd been stabbed by the broken stem was carried moaning to the rowers' log-lined cabin. Such injuries were all too common on this downward run, and it was understood that the able-bodied passengers would be called upon if the need arose.

It was now such a time, and an oarsman fought his way along the deck to bang on the door of the passengers' cabin. His phrase was the one he'd used a hundred times before—"The weather's playing up, *meine Herren*, and we'd be grateful for your help. There is no call, of course. It's merely an appeal."

Nodding from his bunk, the drover wrapped his whip inside his shirt and made his cumbersome way to the door. Brydd followed him, as did Albany, though the soldiers stretched further on their beds, ignoring the plea. Brydd called across to them, "I've no doubt we could do with every set of shoulders," then waited in vain for their gaze to flicker or turn. Even as he spoke the deck lifted and threw him against the wall. The soldiers blinked, then stared again at the boarded roof, and Albany said, "It's stones down a well, my dear chap. Those fellows won't ever grant your wish."

Accepting his friend's advice, Brydd followed the drover from the cabin, and the three willing passengers staggered in the wake of the oarsman. They were joined on deck by the two evicted farmers, and they took their places at the oars.

It was a long descent, and the raft was not yet halfway down.

The logs were already springing in three or four places, the water piling across the deck. The volunteers slithered about as they found their positions, and Brydd found himself grinning as the heron remarked, "Not the place for Georgina Warneford, would you say?"

"I'd say snatch at an oar," Brydd told him, "and no, it's not."

Assisting the oarsmen, the five volunteers were then joined by the Austrian merchant, who clung manfully to one of the long, scalloped poles. "I'm not much practised at this," he admitted, "though I'm willing to try." No sooner had he spoken than the raft was lifted like a trapdoor in a floor. It was immediately slammed back on to the water, but it broke the merchant's grip and sent him skidding across the logs. He yelped with surprise, and the drover leaned down to catch him. But the tilt of the raft and the sluice of water had taken the man out of reach. He yelped again, thinking himself lost, and then the last man in line fell back to grab him and caught him by the front of his spoiled silk waistcoat. The material tore apart, buttons flying, though the seams of the garment held long enough for Brydd Cannaway to hold the man on deck and roll him clear of the surf. "Just as I said," the merchant gabbled "I'm not really practised. I can't swim an inch."

The raft lifted again, and Brydd held his grip and said, "Then you'd best hang tight to the oar, sir. That's what I've been doing, for I'd swim no better than you." He helped the merchant to his feet, to his place at the springy pole, then snatched at his own position near the fence.

The raft banged and twisted its way through the rapids. The motion of the water was uneven, lifting the platform and then, when one felt it might drop, lifting it again. There was no rhythm to the movement. One would not know how to brace one's feet, and all the time the oars whipped and quivered, now straining against the current, now thrown high in the air. The oarsmen themselves were taken off balance, the passengers shaken like a ferret on a stick. They were swung against each other, their chests and arms bruised by the snap of the poles, their feet drummed against the deck.

The platform crashed and lifted, spun and fell, and it seemed as if the Danube wished to shake them defenceless, before it pulled them down.

And then it suddenly ejected them into a long, tranquil lagoon. The ruined platform slid eastward. The oarsmen draped themselves across the fence. The volunteers sprawled in the puddles, grinning weakly at each other, though far too weak to shake hands. The farmers' wives merged from their cabin, and then the other women, finding their way between the sprung logs to nurse those who'd been most damaged by the oars.

The darkness pursued them, but there was sufficient light to show that the forward fence was broken in a number of places, the deck spiked at random by the logs. Even so, it seemed a fair reward for their labours when the current guided the raft to the far end of the lagoon and set it against a shallow gravel bank.

❋

When the crew had rested, they worked through the night to repair the platform. The women had roamed the bank in search of twigs and driftwood, which had been stacked at intervals along the beach. As a result, the scene was soon bathed in the flicker of firelight and the glow of lanterns. The volunteer passengers helped the crew secure the great elm logs, their work serenaded by the crippled piper. His son slept against his knee, waking now and again to search for Brydd, then pull his lips in a smile. Brydd found time to nod at the boy and pat him briefly on the shoulder.

There was no sign of the soldiers, who seemed content to stay in the warmth of their bunks. No one dared challenge them, though the farmers who'd been evicted took a sly delight in swinging one of the logs against the cabin wall. With luck, it would knock the bullies clean out of bed.

The work continued until dawn. As the river mist was slowly burned away the crew carried out a final inspection, stamping the deck and testing the fences. They decided that the platform would hold, and the raft was once again poled downriver.

The fourth day passed without incident. On the fifth and final morning the travellers lost sight of the banks, so wide was the approach to Vienna. One by one, the passengers emerged to cluster against the forward rail, beckoned on by the spires and watchtowers—the fingers of Church and State.

But for Brydd the welcome was different. It was only when he saw his first Viennese carriage, a canopied vehicle running high up on a hillside, that he acknowledged his destination.

This was why he'd left the security of the Kennett Vale, why he had left his parents and family and friends. There, rattling ahead of him, was the challenge, and it pleased him to imagine that the foreign coach had issued forth this morning on purpose, daring him to do better.

PART THREE

VITAR

1698 – 1699

EIGHT

He was on his own now, wanting it so.

He and Albany would meet from time to time in the fashionable thoroughfare of the Graben, or near the heron's apartment in the Am Hof square. But the common interest that had brought them across Europe was at an end. They were no longer just young travellers, well met abroad, but an ambitious wheelwright in need of employment and a gentleman in pursuit of distraction and the dice.

They'd remain friends—they both wanted that—though their paths would diverge within the city. Albany Jevington already knew people in Vienna and the *Vorstädte*, the wooded suburbs beyond the walls, and the paths he would travel were across private estates. Brydd's route was more commonplace, plunging him into the alleyways of the Old Quarter in search of a stable for the horse he'd redeemed and a cheap room for himself.

Armed with a few dozen words of the language, most of them learned from Albany, he made his way along the wool merchants' street of Wollzeile and into the bakers' street, the Bäckerstrasse. There were some who ignored his questions, others who nodded at the words, then shrugged with regret. A few had dingy hovels to let; damp cellars, or rooms that overlooked an abattoir or a fish-

gutting yard, and one man offered him a wooden shed that
bridged a wide, open sewer.

He continued his search and was eventually shown a raftered
room above an archway. The accommodation was narrow and ro-
mantic, draughty and ill furnished and cheap. He took it immediately, stabled his horse in the nearby yard, then again climbed the
spiral steps that led up beside the arch. Alone now, he re-entered
the room and noticed that the door swung shut of its own accord.
The floor creaked underfoot. He reached up and slapped one of
the roof beams. It shivered, and dust tumbled from the rafters.

The sky was visible where the tiles had slipped or cracked. The
bed was large enough for a family, the single chair brittle and
eaten away. There were windows on each side of the room,
opaque with grime and shadowed by the eaves. The door was
equipped with a massive lock and key. The room was his, if he'd
understood correctly, for as long as he paid his rent.

His.

He stood and grinned around at it, letting the street sounds
come up to him, watching the particles of dust swirl and drift in
the air. It was his to make habitable, to clean and paint and nail
firm, to decorate as he wanted, to furnish as he liked. The view of
the Bäckerstrasse was his and, God, yes, from the other window,
the view of the Danube.

For the first time in his life he had a place of his own, no matter that it was draughty, or would be cold in winter, stifling in
summer, a colander when it rained. Before this it had always been
the room in his father's smithy, the hut in Alfred's yard, the servants' quarters in Paris, taverns and lodging houses and the cabin
on the raft. But now the place he was in was his—so long as he
settled the rent.

❊

He allowed himself four days in which to put the room in order
and explore the city. After that he would look for work.

He borrowed a ladder from one of the neighbouring bakers and
edged precariously along the roof, closing the gaps in the tiles. He
cleaned the windows, scoured the beams and rafters, nailed down
the errant floorboards, whitewashed the walls.

He visited the local market and staggered back with chairs and a table, then made a second foray, this time returning with a straw-filled mattress, candles and holders, a pair of thick glass goblets, some bread and wine, and *Rohwurst* caged with string. He'd forgotten to buy a knife, grinned at the omission and cut slices of bread and sausage with the blade of his sword stick.

Then, as the sky darkened, he lit an extravagant number of candles, leafed through the book Dr. Barrowcluffe had given him and read what Charles Colherne had to say about the city of Vienna-on-the-Danube . . .

During the next few days he studied the coaches that rattled along the Graben, the wagons that delivered foodstuffs and poultry to the Neuer Markt, the carriages that crossed from island-to-island-to-island before they reached the far bank of the river. He found time to sketch them, sometimes in detail, often as an impression, with the vehicles clattering past an equally splendid building, or backed by the curve of the Danube, or set against the distant outline of the Kahlenberg hills.

He found time to eavesdrop on conversations, learning a new word here, a simple phrase there.

He roamed the city by night and thought it far less menacing then Paris—or than Portsmouth had been by day.

He tasted *Apfelstrudel* and goulash, wild boar and—a flavour of the Kennett River—trout and crayfish.

He thought of stretching the four days to a week or more, so pleased was he with his newfound city . . .

But his brother, William, had not advanced him the money to live a life of indolence in Vienna. He was there to make coaches, and it was time he toured the yards.

And then the harsher realities intruded.

The coachbuilders of Vienna were jealous of their skills, secretive in their methods, suspicious of foreigners. They were polite enough to the young Englishman and genuinely impressed by the quality of his drawings. But they were not prepared to admit him to their workshops, least of all when he'd shown them his obvious abilities as a spy. Whatever promises he might make, whatever oaths he might swear on the cross or the Bible, there was nothing to stop him memorising what he saw, then transcribing it to paper for the greater benefit of the English. Ah, no. Vienna was famous for its coaches because it guarded its skills, not because it invited young foreigners to take note of its secrets.

We regret, *mein Herr*. But you will be welcome again. Next year.

It was the same in every yard he visited. We regret, *mein Herr*, though we compliment you on your sketches. You are a most talented artist. Again, *leider nicht*, we regret.

❊

He sat with Albany at a coffeehouse table in the Am Hof square.

Almost three weeks had elapsed since their arrival in the city, time enough for Brydd to have earned a score of regrets. He'd managed to sell a few of his drawings, but each day he was taking a coin or two from his money belt, exchanging the crowns and shillings for kreutzers and florins. One more withdrawal, he'd decided, and then, if the yards remained closed to him he would take whatever job he could get—anything that would allow him to stay in Vienna.

Albany had found time for more leisurely pursuits, among them a visit to the tailor. As a result, he was dressed from hat to heel in crimson, a sight that made pedestrians falter in their stride. Gone was the tricorn, its place taken by a velvet stove-pipe, the brim as wide as an umbrella. The stitching on his frock coat matched the embroidered hatband, whilst his dark-dyed gloves were of the same scraped leather as his shoes. Lace fluttered at his throat, billowed around his wrists and escaped from a side pocket in the form of an artfully draped handkerchief. His buttons and buckles were of silver, his attitude relaxed, his confidence unshakeable.

"It's envy, my dear chap, stark, staring envy. They, themselves, would love to be outfitted like this, but their wives wouldn't have it, don't you see. Nor would their business associates. Still, it's just as well, I suppose; crimson's not the colour for the plump." He glanced at Brydd, wondered why his friend was in such low spirits, then added, "I'm having the same thing prepared in mauve. Though with more warmth to the buttons, of course. Gold snail shells, I think, with the mauve, don't you?"

Brydd nodded dully, and the heron observed, "You're very far down today. Why's that?"

"I'm sorry. I'm witless company."

"Indeed you are. But why?"

Brydd told him, then listened as Albany explained the error of his approach. "You might as well have gone around the yards with a pistol in your hand. You've displayed your sketches, shown them your ability to capture aspect and detail and given them a damn good fright. How would *you* react if you'd perfected a vehicle and someone—worse, a foreigner—knocked at the gate, armed with drawings and a pen? Would *you* admit him? I assure you I wouldn't."

"Very well," Brydd accepted, "I can see the mistake. But how else am I to present myself and convince them—?"

"You won't. But I know who will. I've already met them. Johann von Kreutel and his wife . . ."

I should have expected it, Brydd thought. Albany Jevington must be the catch of the season. Every high-flown family in Vienna will be eager to entertain him, the von Kreutels no less than the others.

"Where did you—?"

"Oh, at some gathering in the Vorstädte."

"And you mentioned me to them?"

"I did more than that, my dear chap. I told them how you'd evaded the ambush on the way to Paris, and how you'd stuck by me when that dreadful Warneford fellow attacked us in the hotel. I had you brimming over, don't you worry."

"That was good of you, Albany. I'd not have had the temerity to approach them. It was a long time ago, that business on the Cherhill slope. Did they remember it?"

"Johann did. Oh, yes, and his brother-in-law, Carl-Maria Schoenholz. He referred to you as the righteous Master Cannaway. Do you know what he meant?"

Thinking back to the ambush and the confrontation in the private room of the "Blazing Rag," Brydd knew exactly what he meant. He remembered accusing the box-faced Carl-Maria of banging off at shadows and causing the innocent coachman to take a bullet in the face. He remembered the rain, and the way Step Cotter's wound had been stitched, and how Carl-Maria had yawned and offered the silver five-guinea piece. Half a year had passed since then, but he could clearly remember Herr Show-and-Hold.

He nodded, and Albany said, "Thank God his sister is more charming. She's much as you described her, the voluptuous Annette, and with her breasts still in conflict with her bodice. One watches and waits . . . watches and waits . . ."

"And Johann? What little faith I have in that family resides in him."

"As it should. He seems a fair man, Johann von Kreutel. He says I'm to bring you with me on my next visit. They live on the island of Leopoldstadt. I'm intending to go on Sunday. Does that suit?"

"You had no need to mention me."

"None at all," Albany agreed, "but the conversation was flagging."

"I'll need a lesson in the language," Brydd told him, "and then I can order a wine to match your clothes."

And it's true, he thought, he does crake like a heron when he laughs.

※

Brydd Cannaway stood in the entrance hall of the von Kreutels' house in Leopoldstadt. He was nervous enough, God knew, surrounded by mirrored gilt and marble, his boots drab on the tiles, his thornproof suit turned to sacking alongside Albany's crimson velvet, crimson doeskin, cream-catch-crimson lace.

He had no card to present, but stood dutifully silent whilst Albany took a pen from the hall table and added Brydd's name to his own deckled card. The butler received it on a tray, tapped politely on a door fringed with plaster vine leaves, then bore the identification to his master.

He reappeared a moment later, inclined his head and preceded the visitors through the doorway.

They stopped short of the *salon* and, for the first time since the night of the ambush, Brydd gazed at the tall and uncluttered

Johann von Kreutel, at his beautiful wife, still happily devoid of patches or paint, and at the sullen Carl-Maria, his boxlike face padded out with too much flesh.

And then the butler announced them—Brydd first because his name had been written across the top of the card—and, as a special courtesy, in English.

"Master Brydd Cannaway . . ."

Johann was rising from his chair, Annette smiling, Carl-Maria finding more interest in the condition of his fingernails.

". . . and Lord Albany d'Enville-Zurrant-Jevington."

Byrdd blinked and said nothing, his gaze fixed on a distant porcelain vase. He wanted the man to repeat the announcement, for the words and title had taken him by surprise, washing around him and becoming confused in his mind. *Lord* Jevington?

The heron?

"Passed down to me," Albany murmured. "Worth having for the income, but a millstone most of the time. In we go." He gangled forward, executing a splendid bow for Annette, then stretched out a bony hand to draw Brydd into the circle.

"My lord Jevington," Johann greeted. "And Master Cannaway. It's a pleasure to see you again." He bowed correctly, with none of Albany's flourish, and Brydd responded in kind.

"I hear you saved Lord Jevington from an ambush, Master Cannaway, much as you did for us."

"Herr von Kreutel. My lady. Herr Show-and . . . Herr Schoenholz. Not saved, sir. More led around."

"Well, however it was done, you're a valuable talisman on the roads."

"And his value doesn't stop there," Albany commended. "He's looking for work as a coachbuilder, designer, that sort of thing."

There was the briefest pause, during which the favour was acknowledged, weighed and granted. Lord Jevington had spoken well of his friend and, by doing so, accepted responsibility for his behaviour. Furthermore, he had involved the von Kreutels, for it was Johann who would assist the young Cannaway with his career. If he shirked the hard work that would be expected of him, or in any way took advantage of his position, it would show Albany as a poor judge of character and Johann as a gullible host.

But there was no hesitation beyond the pause, no words of warning, no conditions imposed. Johann looked directly at Brydd and said, "You might care to visit my own yard."

"I would, sir."

"Good. You'll need a letter of introduction. I recollect the interest you showed in that coach of ours, the night you brought us down the hill to, ah, Beckhampton, was it?"

Brydd nodded. "That's well remembered, Herr von Kreutel."

"Yes, it is rather, isn't it?" he smiled. "And the inn was the Burning Rag. No—the 'Blazing Rag.'" He waited for Brydd to verify the name, then said, "Well, now, gentlemen, will you take a glass of wine? I suggest we try the Kahlenberg."

❋

They stayed an hour, Annette grinning with delight when she discovered that the von Kreutels and Lord Albany d'Enville-Zurrant-Jevington had friends in common, some in Vienna, others in London. She made no secret of her liking for the heron, and Johann too derived wry amusement from his tale of the Warnefords, *père et fille*.

Carl-Maria was, as always, Carl-Maria. He was bored and sullen, his remarks unleavened by humour, his pleasure restricted to the wine bottle. He again referred to Brydd as "the righteous Master Cannaway," and seemed disappointed when the provocation was ignored.

Brydd contributed little to what was said, though he recounted the incident at Essenbach, readily admitting that he believed in werewolves and had come close to panic on the gloomy, shadowed plain. It gave Carl-Maria the chance to mutter something in German, something that went well with a smirk.

Six months ago, even three, and Brydd would have asked that the words be repeated, clear and cold, in English. But Albany had taught him otherwise, and now he said, "You must give me time, Herr Schoenholz. I'm not well up in your language, not just yet. The remark defeats me."

It was beyond Carl-Maria to translate, and Johann took the conversation smoothly toward Passau, asking what it was like to come downriver on a raft.

"Well," Brydd assured him, "it's all the encouragement I need to make coaches."

"I'll put it in the letter." Johann nodded. "They love to hear that kind of thing in the yard."

There was talk of hunting, of the theatres to be visited, of the Turkish invasions, the last of which had been led by the Grand Vizier Kara Mustafa, with an army of three hundred thousand men. He had besieged the city for two months, failed to overwhelm a garrison that was outnumbered twelve to one, then fled before a relief force of less than eighty thousand. It had been a glorious day for Vienna, with the Turkish pennants streaming in flight.

"No formal peace has yet been signed," Johann said, "though it's expected in the near future. Even so, it pays to be watchful. The Grand Vizier recruited a number of mercenaries, and there are still disbanded groups at large to the east. We think ourselves safe enough here on the island, but I'd advise you to go armed if you ever cross the river."

"There was a saying," Annette remarked. "When the Turks had been driven off, our soldiers found pyramids of sacks in their encampment. The sacks contained green beans, unlike any we'd seen before, and then one of our spies, I forget his name—"

"Kolschitsky," her husband murmured.

"Yes, well, whoever he was, he said we should roast the beans and brew them. And that's how the saying came about, that the Turks had left us two flavours—*Sieg und Kaffee*—victory and coffee."

There was talk of forthcoming banquets, of the attractions of the Wiener Wald, the Vienna Woods to the west of the city, and of the zoo that would one day house every species of animal in the world, from dragon to unicorn.

"And," Annette added mischievously, "we'll have a werewolf from Essenbach."

There was talk to fill the hour. Johann moved away, returning a few moments later with a stiff linen envelope, its flap sealed with wax. He handed it to Brydd, indicated the address and said, "Take it along when it suits you, Master Cannaway, and they'll have you working within the hour."

Brydd came to his feet, thanked him and bowed as he'd seen it done, stiff and correct. No one seemed to find the gesture amusing save Carl-Maria, who thought it wonderfully righteous and smirked above his glass.

The visitors took their leave. It was a fine June day and the young men were in high spirits, urging their horses along the forest tracks that linked the mansions and lodges of Leopoldstadt. Albany rode with a hand to his hat, Brydd with the letter jammed inside his waistcoat. They raced for a while, then let the animals slow to a trot, and Brydd said, "So it's *Lord* Jevington, is it? Should I drop back a few paces, from respect? By the way, where are they, Enville and Zurrant?"

"The one's in the north of France, the other in Holland. And if you do drop back, my dear chap, I'll give you a thick ear for your pains. You dealt with Carl-Maria very well. I expected to see you both rolling on the hearth. Though he will be anyway, I'd say, if he stays with the Kahlenberg." They rode on for a while and then the heron asked, "What do you think of the enchanting Annette?"

"What most men would think."

"Yes," Albany cemented. "Quite."

❊

The inhabitants of the Bäckerstrasse came to accept Herr Cannaway as no better or worse than themselves. He was a foreigner, yes, but who wasn't in the Old Quarter, with its Greeks and Spaniards, Hungarians and Slavs, and those whose homelands had been overrun and absorbed and lost? There was nothing special about an Englishman.

On the day Brydd had presented himself at the coachmaking establishment, he'd shown the *Kutschemeister* the letter from Johann and the contents of his satchel. He'd left the bad drawings in with the good, the unfinished sketches shuffled amongst those that were complete. It had been his dowry, his declaration, there for the *Kutschemeister* to see. What was it Albany had said —"You might as well have gone around with a pistol"? Well, that had been his pistol, and with it the bullets and flints. It was up to the coachmaster to decide if the risk was too great, the foreigner

too sharp-eyed to be let loose in the workshops. Johann had recommended the young Cannaway, but it was for the *Kutschemeister*
to say yes or no.

Cautiously, and in his own good time, he'd said yes.

And from then on there'd been a routine, six days a week from
dawn till dusk, and longer if need be. Brydd washed and shaved in
the stable yard, stumbled blearily through the archway to the
street and gulped down coffee or chocolate at a stall. Then he set
off along the Bäckerstrasse with his chalks and satchel, chewing a
seeded roll as he went. He could never count on it, but occasionally there would be a slice of meat in the roll, or a smear of
honey, and nothing extra to pay. Those were the best mornings,
and he'd steal a few moments to stop and gaze down at the river,
the spiced beef sharp on his tongue, or the honey sweet and thick.
Then he'd stride on along the street and down the swayback steps
and in through the unmarked gateway, allowed in without question because he, too, was a member of the finest yard in Vienna.

He had an address now and a job, and he wrote to his parents, via
Dr. Barrowcluffe, and to his sister, Sophia, in Bristol, and to
William in the stonemason's yard at Melksham. It would take the
better part of two months for the letters to reach their destina-
tions, a further two months before he received a reply. But it was
something to look forward to, news that would brighten his evenings as winter encroached on the city . . .

He learned new methods of springing, absorbed the language, saw
the way pastes and varnishes were mixed as a protective coating
for the bodywork. He made a few hesitant suggestions, all of them
rejected.

He sketched one of the finished coaches, offered the drawing to
the *Kutschemeister* and was told to pin it on the workshop wall.
No one remarked on the exactness of detail, but it was reward
enough that he'd been allowed to decorate the room. The paper
curled and discoloured, becoming as much a part of the workshop

as the scrubbed-down benches or sharpened tools. A few days later
he offered another drawing and was reminded that he was in a
coachmakers' yard, not a gallery.

❊

In the middle of August he was sent to collect a gig from a house
in the Wiener Wald. It was unusual for the yard to carry out
repairs, but this particular vehicle had been made there, and the
craftsmen were anxious to learn why the elm-wood shafts had
twisted. Brydd was told to find out exactly where the gig had been
kept, in the damp or the dry.

The cause of the warping was obvious, and the owner admitted
his mistake. The vehicle had been kept in a shed, but always in
the same position, with the shafts below a broken run of tiles. He
shrugged apologetically and agreed that, yes, if the rain dripped
long enough—

"So you absolve the yard of all responsibility?"

"Certainly I do."

"And you'll have the roof mended by the time the vehicle's returned to you?"

"As you say."

"Good." No mercy from Brydd Cannaway for those who mis-
treated the best-made gigs in Vienna.

He'd come out to the Wiener Wald on horseback and now
steered his own mount between the shafts. Then he guided it
back in a loosened harness, enjoying the ride that led through valleys of beech and poplar—very different from the bald Wiltshire
downs. He drove slowly, gentling the horse whenever the twisted
shafts touched its sides. It was the animal he'd redeemed in
Vienna, but he'd taught it English and murmured, "Easy boy,
that's the way, easy we go."

He reached a clearing and saw two tethered horses. A crimson
velvet stovepipe had been hung from a saddle pommel, as from a
hat rack. The other horse carried a sidesaddle, with a lady's travelling cloak draped across it. There was no sign of the heron—it
had to be the heron—or his companion.

"Easy we go," Brydd said, and took the gig gently on through
the woods.

✳

He spent the September days in the yard or on errands in the district, the evenings in his room. He'd long been dissatisfied with the clumsy drag-shoe method of slowing a coach, and he devoted his free time to what he called pinch-braking. Instead of the downward pressure of a single wooden block, the Cannaway method offered two pinching blocks, squeezed together against the sides of the wheel. It involved a complicated series of hinges, a specially fashioned spring and a sheaf of explanatory drawings.

Two weeks of it, and he abandoned the project as insoluble.

Then he went back to it again, his eyes bloodshot from the sting of candle smoke, his face drawn from lack of sleep. He got it wrong, and wrong again, and was too tired to recognise the moment in which he got it right. But he'd sketched something that night, something that made sense the next day, and from then on it was all downhill—and safely so, with the pinch-brakes.

He presented his work to the *Kutschemeister* and was made to stand for two hours in the workshop, explaining why this was done this way, that done that. It was a matter of weights and pressures, angles and bearings, strains and tensions. There was no doubt that the *Kutschemeister* knew his job, and the questions he asked were direct and unremitting. It was only when he came to the tenth measured drawing that he said, "You've done some work on this device, Herr Cannaway. There is a bottle and a mug in the drawer; pour out enough for the two of us. So, if this is depressed, and the arms clamp inward here . . ."

And then, at the end of it, he nodded. "It is worth a try. You've nothing else, I suppose?"

It took Brydd longer than usual to see the joke, for the *Kutschemeister* was not renowned for his humour, and the young designer was anyway half asleep on his feet.

"No, sir, nothing else."

"Then get on home, Herr Cannaway. And stay home for a day." He accompanied Brydd to the gate, and repeated, "It is worth a try." Then he nodded Brydd out with a gentle, almost caring, "*Gute Nacht, mein Junge.*"

❋

October, and a Sunday, and Brydd had ridden north from the city, following the river as far as the Kahlenberg hills. It was not the first time he'd visited the vine-covered slopes or wandered among the groves of peach and apricot, the orchards of Vienna. The fruit had been harvested by now, and the summer haze had given way to a clear autumn light, clear enough for the rider to see the great country lodges and the river traffic and the open carriage that rattled out of a sidetrack and ran ahead of him through the trees.

He noticed the two occupants and thought the hat should be crimson, then remembered that Albany had ordered the same outfit in mauve.

There was a woman beside him in the coach. She turned to the heron, and as she did so she glimpsed the rider fifty yards behind. Before she could stop herself she'd turned further to look, then twisted forward again, the collar of her cloak pulled high around her ears.

The open carriage was of the type known as a landau, a fine-weather vehicle, but one equipped with a stiffened folding canopy. Keeping his pace, Brydd watched the ribbed hood swing up and forward, shielding the occupants from view.

The message was clear. Lord Albany d'Enville-Zurrant-Jevington did not wish to be recognised by his friend. And no wonder, when his companion was Annette von Kreutel.

❋

The young men had met from time to time throughout the summer, and continued to do so during the autumn and the onset of winter. Brydd had said nothing about finding the two horses tethered in the Wiener Wald, and he made no mention of his October visit to Kahlenberg. It was none of his business, though he hoped his eyes had failed him and mistaken Annette for someone else. If not, then the heron was playing a dangerous game, far more dangerous than dice.

Work progressed on the pinch-brakes, and the designer was expected to arrive early and stay late, overseeing his invention. As with the drawings, it went wrong, and wrong again, and it was not until late October that the shoes slammed tight against the wheel rims, locking the vehicle on the road.

It was only then that Brydd's fellow craftsmen shook his hand, nodded brusquely and went about their work. He'd done well, the foreigner, but it was expected of him as a member of the yard.

❊

The first letter to reach the address in the Bäckerstrasse was from Sophia and Joseph at Bristol. They congratulated him on having reached Vienna and found a job, then told him what he wanted to know, the news and scandal of the city port. Joseph's warehouses now dominated The Biss, and there was talk of buying shares in a trading vessel.

"Your brother-in-law thinks there's a future to be earned from the Americas," Sophia wrote. "He intends to offer a westbound passage to those who would settle in the colonies, then bring back tobacco from Virginia and hides from the Carolinas. I've told him I'll hand-stitch the sails for him, so long as he names the ship the *Sophia Biss*."

She delighted in recounting how, in the late spring, a fire had taken hold in a brothel near the port. Ten minutes ablaze, and it had smoked out a number of civic dignitaries, their faces masked by petticoats and lace-trimmed slips. "Justice was never more blind," she wrote cheerfully, "than on the night our magistrates fled."

The second letter came within days of the first. Brydd recognised Dr. Barrowcluffe's hand, settled himself in a chair and turned the envelope over and over before breaking the seal. He prayed that his parents were well, and the Darles and the Notts and Sam Gilmore. Time had passed, after all, and there might have been accidents, illnesses, even deaths in the Kennett Vale.

But all was well, thank God.

Ezra and Amalie were in full health, "though your father continues to strike sparks from the smithy, and your mother to make candles for half the county, so it seems. However, they thrive on their hard work, and I do believe it shakes the ague from the blood."

The Darles were well, George busy at Overhill Farm, Jed with an eye for the young ladies of Marlborough. "I, myself, have seen little of Elizabeth these past few months, though she continues to visit your parents and never fails to ask after you. I'm to tell you that she treasures the picture you sent of the Pont Neuf in Paris and cannot imagine that she will ever tire of the scene."

That's odd, Brydd thought, the drawing was for Ezra and Amalie, and I said so at the time. Why on earth should it have been passed on to Elizabeth? It was meant for the walls of Kennett, not Overhill.

He assumed there'd been a misunderstanding and shrugged the problem aside. He would send his parents a more recent example of his work; a view of the Danube, perhaps, or an aspect of the Wiener Wald.

The Notts were well, and Alfred had taken on a new apprentice. "The labourer Hach is the same as ever, so I'm told, and the valley has set itself the task of discovering where he gets his gin."

Sam Gilmore was well, "but talks of leading an expedition against the Cherhill gang. His livelihood has suffered this year, and any mention of the authorities provokes a furious response. I am doing what I can to stir those sluggardly gentlemen. Meanwhile, your father and George Darle and others have urged Sam to show restraint. The highwaymen would not stop short of murder, I fear, if he intruded upon them."

And then, toward the end of the letter, the doctor wrote, "Remember to use the castille soap whenever occasion demands."

Brydd's response to that was a wry grin, for he'd been celibate since his arrival in Vienna. It was not of his own choosing, but he'd been too well chained to the yard. Later, maybe, if the *Kutschemeister* gave him a few days off, then he might meet a woman. But it wouldn't happen between the Bäckerstrasse and the yard, the yard and the Bäckerstrasse . . . He was not at his best chewing a seeded roll in the morning, or stumbling wearily home at night . . .

❊

The air blew cold from the eastern marshes, and darkness squeezed the days. Snow invaded the city, occupying it as the

Turks had failed to do, cracking the roof tiles, then sliding down the pitch to land with a muffled thud in the streets, or on the carts and sledges, horses and riders.

One of Brydd's neighbours allowed him to wash and shave in an outhouse and supplied him with a jug of hot water—a favour beyond price. From there he plunged across the street to gulp the coffee or chocolate, collected his breakfast roll and made his way through the mud and snow toward the treacherous, swayback steps.

Ice was already forming along the banks of the Danube.

A few days before the westward approaches to the city were declared impassable, a letter arrived from William Cannaway. It was welcome, of course, the high point of the month, though it distressed Brydd to see how his brother's style of speech had been altered, his comments ironed flat. William had a fine head for figures, but he had never learned to write, save within the confines of an account book, and the letter was clearly the work of another, more pious mind. The vicar of Melksham, for a bet.

My dear brother,
I found your letter most acceptable, and hurry to reply. Sad news, however, for my master, the stonemason Andrew Cobbin, a good and religious man, has been taken from us, the victim of a falling lintel beam. God wills that I am to inherit the yard, and I shall do so with due humility and in the knowledge that, with the Lord's help, I shall protect those workers who have striven so long, yet with never a complaint.

Brydd tossed the letter aside, unable to finish it until he'd imagined how William would have told it, simple and straight.

Dear Brydd,
I'm glad to have your letter, and I envy your progress to Paris and down the river to Vienna. I remember the day you rode out to Melksham, and how courageous you thought yourself to have left the valley for the first time. You must now be as puffed as a toad!
It's a pity you never met Andrew Cobbin. He was killed in an accident the other day, tackling work that was beyond him.

He died in an instant, thank God, without undue suffering. I was very close to him, Brydd, and the yard's been a dismal place since then. He always said he'd leave the business to me and he's done so, and I intend to make it the best-run yard in Wiltshire. He'd have wanted that, and his men support me in it. I hope you're not wasting your money, but are learning all you can. The same day never returns, you know.

Yes, Brydd decided, it would have been a damn sight better, written like that.

He continued with the smoothed-out version, but it added nothing to what had been said. It was now the Cannaway yard, and Brydd was sure his brother would make the best of it. "I wish it so," he murmured, then shivered as the cold seeped down through the roof.

❈

The serving maids knew what to expect, and twisted nimbly as the young men attempted to encircle their waists and draw them close for a kiss. "You behave yourself, sir. There's places for that sort of thing down the street."

"Oh, don't be so drab," the customers cajoled. "A pretty girl like you, and a handsome fellow like me. The snow's outside, and there's a flagon of wine on the table, and—"

"Yes, and you've not yet paid for it."

"Paid for what, *mein Liebchen?* You set the price, and I'll be more than willing—"

"For the wine, sir. The other attractions are down the street, I've already told you."

That was usually enough, and the flirtation ended with a shrug of regret, the young man paying what he owed, the girl smiling tolerantly because they were all alike, with more arms than a windmill. But they were easy company, and if they occasionally cupped a breast or patted a bottom, there was no need for a fuss. Deny them that and they'd find another tavern, where the girls were less prim.

It was December now, and Brydd had been invited to join Albany Jevington and a score of his friends in an inn near the river. It occurred to him that he was the only one without silver buttons, doeskin gloves, a hat with a feather, a plume, a cockade. He was certainly the only one who worked for a living and paid his way kreutzer by kreutzer counting out the coins. The rest of them tossed florins on the tray, winked at the girls and made assignations they knew they wouldn't keep.

They entertained themselves with stories; a few truthful anecdotes at first, and then an embellishment, a wild exaggeration, a downright lie.

There was the young man who said he'd tamed a wild boar. He rode it around his estate, the reins attached to its tusks. "And, so long as it doesn't stop short, without warning . . ."

Howls of merriment for that one.

There was the young man who claimed to have swum the Danube, and in boots and gloves and greatcoat. He waited for the shouted denials to die down, offered a hefty wager in support of his story, then announced that he'd done so at Geisingen, near the source of the river, where it was less than ten yards wide.

Groans of disgust for that one, for he'd tricked them with the truth.

There was the young man who told them he'd bought a parrot in the Neuer Markt, taught it to speak, then successfully mated it with an eagle. "The offspring not only swoops on unsuspecting travellers, but demands they hand over their money!"

The listeners drummed the floor at that one, for it had the foolish flavour they were after.

The party was still in full sway at midnight, with the men chorusing sentimental ballads, patriotic marches, tavern songs too bawdy to have ever been written down. They danced between the tables, then *on* the tables, then fell *off* the tables, too drunk to know if they'd hurt themselves. ". . . so long as it doesn't stop short, without warning . . . not only swooping on them, but asking for their money . . . and crossing at Geisingen, the cunning bastard . . ."

The party was still in progress at dawn, though movement was slower, the wine more freely split. Albany had murmured something to one of the maidservants, and neither of them had been seen for an hour. But he was back now, gangling his way around the room, then nodding approval because Brydd was still awake.

"I've an idea," the heron said. "Tell me what you think of it." He ranged his skeletal frame on a bench, against a table, across the back of a chair. Then he leaned forward, seemingly none the worse for drink. "The party needs enlivening. Something active is called for. We'll have a sledge race."

"Oh? And where will we have it?"

"On the river. It's been iced over for weeks, as you know. You must have seen the traffic on it. It's as firm as the Graben."

"And when's it to be, need I ask?"

"Now, my dear chap, now! Before the city's up and about. I know where we can get the sledges and horses, leave it to me. Well, what do you say?"

"I say it's madness. Look around you. We are all stupefied. Look at that fellow there, dropping coins in his glass to see the splash."

"He'll come awake, don't you worry. They all will, when they hear what's to do. The Viennese love a challenge—watch." He flattened a hand, slapped a noisy tattoo on the table and indicated that those who were awake should rouse their friends. "We are going to leave here now," he announced, "and take part in a sledge race on the river. I offer a hundred florins as prize money, and I'd like to see it improved."

There were slurred murmurs of a hundred here, a hundred there, enough to total a thousand. The call had a miraculous effect on the young men, and all but a few hauled themselves to their feet, delighted that a fresh proposal had been made. It would be just the thing, a slide on the river; a perfect appetiser before returning to the inn for breakfast and a glass of *Schnaps*.

❊

They were off to a smooth start, Brydd and Albany and the two young Austrians who'd agreed to make up the team. There were four teams in all, each black-painted *Schlitten* drawn by a pair of sturdy, long-maned horses, their ridged shoes biting into the ice, the air around the single lantern clouded by the heat of their bodies.

It was Brydd's job to drive, Albany's to hold the lantern and watch for obstacles ahead. The other two men had as important a task, and a more dangerous one, for they were hunched over the sides of the sledge, sweeping the ice from the runners. Unless they did so, the flakes of ice would become impacted around the struts. However, if they were too zealous in their work, there was the chance that the sledge would jump and the runners slice across their fingers like so much *Rohwurst* in a shop. It was a demanding task for men who'd been drinking all night . . .

They cleared the point of Leopoldstadt and were out on the wide northern approach. The guide lights showed that the other sledges were still in the race, one almost level, two falling back. Albany was no fool to have chosen Brydd as his driver, for who else in the party had as much experience of ungainly vehicles, be it on the Danube or the wintry roads of Wiltshire? If they kept going like this, drawing ahead now, they'd be the first to reach the finish line, the promontory at Kahlenberg.

Then Albany was yelling, "Go left, Brydd, drag left!" And they avoided an ice-trapped log by no more than inches.

A moment later they heard a shout from the back of the sledge and glanced around to see one of their teammates pointing across the river. A lantern was spinning in the air, up and over and exploding as it hit the ice. The distant horses must have lost their footing, or collided, or dragged the *Schlitten* against some imprisoned driftwood. The leaders would return to it later, but there was nothing they could do at present, for the sledges were not designed to be dragged at speed and there was no way of braking.

Another lantern was extinguished and the two remaining sledges hissed and crackled along the river toward the dawn-grey hump of Kahlenberg.

Brydd snatched a glance at the rival. "We're well up on it, Albany. If we hold our lead—"

"There's something—"

"—we should—what?"

"There's something ahead in the ice, it's a boat, God, it's a boat stuck fast! How could it be this far—?"

"I can't swerve! *I can't get us by!*"

Nor could he, though the horses had seen for themselves the dull, immovable hulk. They sprawled and collapsed, swinging the *Schlitten* around and against the bulwarks, the four men cart-wheeling across the trapped vessel and out on to the ice.

It was a painful and sobering manner in which to greet the day. Their arms and shoulders were skinned, belts broken, buttons lost, hats sent skimming. But it was worse to see a lantern wink at them as it passed, and to hear the bray of victory from the surviving team.

❋

It seemed a long way back to the city. No one had been seriously injured and, by common consent, most of the prize money was given to the man who'd hired out the sledges and would now need a week in which to repair the damage.

The victors commiserated with their friends, and then the driver asked, "Who was in charge of that other tray, the one that hit the boat? Ah, so it was you, was it, Herr Cannaway? A good attempt. You will join us when we next make up a party?"

"With pleasure, *mein Herr.*" And with surprise, he told himself, aware that the young aristocrats were not in the habit of inviting a foreigner along, least of all if he was of common stock and earned his money in a yard.

Albany had been inspecting the damage to his new mauve suit. "Somebody's in for a find," he commented sourly. "I lost three gold snail-shells out there."

NINE

There were stretches along which the reeds and marsh grass leaned inward, as if threatening to entwine and block the road. It was spring now, the rushes tall and peppered with flowers, the air heavy and somnolent. A mysterious place at any time, it was now all but impenetrable, and the high-standing reeds concealed the spongy islands and placid backwaters that webbed the Marchfeld.

The reed cutters of Vienna could count on two crops a year, slicing diagonally through the stems, then splitting them with billhooks to make blinds and awnings. The leaves were bundled and sold to the basket makers, who would also weave them into panniers and boxes, cribs and matting, hats and belts and shoes. There was almost no limit to the uses one could make of the versatile marsh reed, and it waved in inexhaustible supply, free to anyone with a good sharp knife.

But it was no longer safe to work there, that was the problem, for it was now the province of the mercenaries.

These dregs of the Turkish invasion had made their nests in the Marchfeld, and they discouraged visitors by murdering any they found. They had stolen or hollowed out canoes, built squalid huts that defied discovery, learned the ways of wildfowl and the gathering pools of fish. It was estimated that at least three hundred of them were still at large in the great eastern marshes, and that they had recently turned to cannibalism. True or not, bones and skulls had been found, with the flesh burned away.

Small wonder that the narrow tracks through the Marchfeld were overgrown . . .

And yet there were those who had made the journey in safety, those who thought the risk and the route worth taking. No track or path or coaching road was entirely free of danger, and who was to say that a few hours spent crossing the Marchfeld was more hazardous than several days on the open road?

Among those who had chosen the direct, marshland approach to Vienna were the Hungarian architect Janos Czaky, his wife and daughter, their household maid and the driver he had hired in Györ. For the Czaky family it was not only worth the risk, but essential if they were ever to escape the terrors and memories of the past.

For twenty years the frail Janos had followed and led his profession, making the city of Györ his own. If one saw a building for the first time and nodded approval, it was probably a Czaky design. If one saw it for the hundredth time and nodded again, it was sure to be by Janos.

But then the Turks had invaded the city and commandeered his house, breaking his wrists on the doorstep because he had dared to stand in their way. His wife and daughter had been out that morning, and they'd returned to find him writhing in the street like a cruelly treated dog, his body beaten raw, the cobblestones littered with his savaged drawings and delicate, broken rules. They had found him crying, though not just with the pain.

He had never worked again, his injuries too great an impediment to his skills. The evicted family had sought refuge with friends, and prayed they might one day leave Györ and—risking the Marchfeld—find sanctuary and a future in Vienna. Even though Janos could no longer hold a pen or draw a line, his reputation was unimpaired. He'd be welcome in the Austrian capital, respected for his achievements and consulted by those who admired his style. He'd been a creative force in his day, Janos Czaky, and there was no reason to suppose the day was yet over.

And so they had left their homeland and crossed the border,

and were now within two hours' reach of the city. The reeds and grasses drooped across the road, but there was no sign of the mercenaries, and the worst they had to contend with was the insects that buzzed and hovered in the heat. Janos and his wife were seated together on a crossbench, and the angle of their heads showed that they were both asleep. Behind them, on another bench, their daughter and the maid exchanged a grin, then chatted quietly as the rushes brushed the sides of the cart. Alone on the driving bench the carter yawned, flexed his shoulders and indulged in the same repetitive daydream, in which he and the maid were in an isolated barn, the girl smiling as he untied the drawstring of her bodice, the drawstring of her skirt . . .

But no such luck for those at the picnic.

It was an ideal setting, on an island that lay between Leopold-stadt and the eastern bank of the Danube. The air was as listless as on the marshes, the grass dappled with the shadows of beech and chestnut, the river bubbling past. A fine place for daydreams and for easing the drawstring of a calico dress.

But not with the chaperones about, twirling their parasols and asking idiotic questions. "Tell me, Lord Jevington, which, in your opinion, is the most—ah, how shall I phrase it?—the most worthy building in Paris? The one you'd visit first, so to speak?"

Bored to distraction, he managed a weary smile and said, "No question of it, my lady. It'd be the hotel in which I intended to spend the night."

A tinkling, well-trained laugh, and the chaperone turned away to address a less difficult customer.

A dozen young men attended the picnic, along with half as many young ladies and a number of chaperones and servants. Whoever had catered the affair had done a dismal job, for the servants dispensed wine in a thin, halting stream, explaining that this was the last bottle and must be made to go around.

Brydd was there, press-ganged by Albany. "I don't say you'll enjoy yourself, my dear chap; indeed, you won't. It would take an alchemist to turn such a leaden outing into something with fire and sparkle, but I'm damned if I'll suffer alone. I've been invited, and I want someone to protect me from the matchmakers, and I've measured you to fit."

So there they were, sprawled on the grass, the chaperones alert to every twitch of an eyelid, wondering if *that* was the secret message, the planned assignation, a marriage on the cards. The desultory small talk was an advocate for silence. Those men who were already engaged had no choice but to smile and ladle out compliments, as though from a bowl. Of the others, two had been netted in conversation, whilst a third was being asked which building he thought the most, ah, worthy in the city of Munich?

"It's no good," Albany muttered, "I'm becoming insensate, paralysed. I'm as stiff as a broom." He twisted to his feet, indicated that Brydd was to go with him, then approached their hostess. "You must excuse our foreign ways, my lady, but a meal as delicious as the one we've been served is somewhat rich for the English tract. It would be best digested on the move."

The hostess hesitated, found the explanation plausible—the English were always different, or liked to think so—and smiled graciously. "Digest away, Lord Jevington. But don't forget to return to us. There's a young lady I'd like you to meet. She's spent a month at least in Paris, so there's a topic ready-made for you both."

Four of the unattached Austrians had already seized their chance, and the six deserters strode toward the tethering line, their progress envied by the friends they'd left behind. The chaperones sighed discreetly and let them go. It was only to be expected that some fish would bite and others wriggle free.

The cart squeaked on through the marshes. Janos and his wife were still asleep, their daughter and the maid discussing how best to cook pheasant, the carter enjoying his daydream for the umpteenth time. The Marchfeld seemed to draw the heat, and there was the occasional glimpse of water, with the air shimmering above it. He flexed his shoulders again, then took the maid into the isolated barn, leading her unprotesting toward a bed of warm, dry hay . . .

❋

The deserters from the picnic rode in silence as far as the bridge, then turned east, grinning and whooping because they'd made good their escape.

This narrow stone span was the last link between the three parallel islands and the eastern bank of the Danube—the final outpost of civilised Vienna. As such, it was guarded by a detachment of the city garrison, the soldiers grey with boredom, the parapet strewn with cards and dice and some pornographic etchings, all of them too well thumbed to retain any fresh appeal.

Surprised by the shouts and yells, the soldiers scooped up their games, buttoned their uniforms and did their best to come alert. The captain hurried to meet the riders, raised an arm in the air and recited the warning he was duty-bound to give. "We cannot guarantee your safety beyond this point, *meine Herren*, for you will be entering the Marchfeld, the known haunt of robbers and murderers. You are advised to turn back, though I am not empowered to arrest your progress."

One of the six deserters said, "We take note of your warning, *Herr Hauptmann*. But I assure you, a greater danger lies in wait for us around the picnic cloth. Unmarried ladies, *Herr Hauptmann*? And their chaperones?"

"I wish you well," he told them, stepping smartly aside to let them pass. He doffed his hat, timing it to perfection so that it caught the coins as they fell. Brydd inadvertently parted with a florin, cursed himself for his ignorance and spurred on across the bridge.

Without knowing why they were there, or what they would do, the young men trotted two abreast, following the paths as they appeared. They continued east and then south, the reeds as high as their shoulders, level with their hat brims, higher than their crowns. They were some way in when they heard the bang of a musket. Then the bark of a pistol. And another. And another.

They reined in and listened. Two of them drew pistols from their holsters, loaded and primed them, then held them level, so the powder wouldn't spill. Another leaned forward to ease his sabre in its scabbard. Albany fiddled with the contents of his pockets, unwrapping whatever was in them. Brydd was unarmed, without even his sword stick, but he was the countryman amongst them, and they looked to him to point.

"*Da drüben,*" he breathed. "Over there."

❄

The carter had turned to speak to the family, and to smile at the maid, and then the back of his jerkin had been distended by the passage of the musket ball as it passed clean through his body from the front. The sound of the shot came with it, and he brought his arm down with such force that it broke the bone and dented the frontboard. And then he was gone, thrown from the cart by the impact and sent flopping in the reeds.

Janos Czaky and his wife came awake, blinked and saw the bench was empty and did not know why. The architect lurched forward and upright, still clumsy with sleep, and the first pistol shot tore a hole in his shoulder. The second was higher and worse.

The wife's name was Katya, and the shock was so great that she ignored her fallen husband and reached forward to take the reins. They must get on to Vienna as they'd planned. That's what they'd talked about during the evenings and the years, and they must let nothing stand in their way.

Another bark, and Katya Czaky toppled forward across the bench, the reins not quite in reach.

Her daughter, Vitar, saw her mother fall, made a desperate grab to save her and was left holding a scrap of Katya's cloak. The maid had turned pale, gasped involuntarily and slipped to the floor of the cart. She lay in a grotesque posture, one hand cupped to catch the blood that ran from Janos's wounds.

It was the middle of the afternoon and in the full blossom of spring, and it did not seem possible that the driver had been killed and that Janos had been killed and that Katya had been killed, though they had.

And then the horses stumped to a halt and Vitar Czaky was left standing in the cart, a perfect target, and there was nothing to be heard but the hum of insects and the creak and rattle of the reeds.

She folded the fragment of her mother's cloak, over and inward, pinching the edges between finger and thumb. It seemed important to make a good job of it, as with sheets or napkins, over and inward, with the edges pressed flat.

And when it was done she did nothing, holding reality at bay . . .

She was eighteen years old, a woman who'd not flinch at the sight of a spider, nor stop if a bully said halt. There were many things about Vitar Czaky that one could admire or envy, though the most obvious was the most dangerous to possess. She was arrestingly beautiful, dark-eyed and dark-skinned, and it was for this that the mercenaries had spared her, preferring to keep her alive. For the while.

※

The path ended abruptly, forcing the riders to retrace their steps. They were no longer sure which way they should go, and even Brydd could only hazard a guess. They'd changed direction too often, skirted too many grass-fringed inlets, each like the last one, a mirror of the next. The echo of the gunshots had died away and there was nothing to guide them, no vantage point from which they might catch a glint of metal or espy a telltale feather of smoke.

They returned to the fork, continuing along another path, then reined in, convinced they were wrong.

They were still there, undecided, when they heard a woman scream; no pretty seductive squeal, but a shriek of terror that made the skin crawl and the young men flinch. It was all the more terrible because it was so loud, as though coming from the next reeded room. They turned toward the sound and plunged forward, trampling a fresh path in the Marchfeld.

※

The girl had regained her senses and seen a pool of blood in her hand. For an instant she'd imagined it to be her own, but then she'd moved her head and caught sight of her master, moved again to see the mercenaries grouped around the cart, and all control had fled. It was she who had screamed, clawing her way to her feet, then stumbling across the bags and cases in an effort to reach the tailboard and flee along the road. She was not to know that her shrieks concealed the drum of hoofbeats, the splintering of reeds, nor that her frantic bid to escape had drawn the attention of the mercenaries at exactly the right moment, as the riders emerged on the track. They'd arrived too late to save Janos or Katya or the driver, but they were not yet altogether too late.

The mercenaries turned, fumbled with their weapons. There were seven of them, but those who had murdered the travellers had not troubled to reload, knowing they were safe in the swamp. The others fired in haste, and the crack of the pistols brought Vitar to her senses. She knelt on the floor of the cart, aware that the maid was screaming and that horses were pounding past on either side. But it was a distant awareness, the sounds that stalk the perimeter of bad dreams. More immediate was the realisation that her parents were dead and that it was left to her to complete the journey they'd begun. But, before all else, she wanted time in which to bow her head and pray for them and weep . . .

The brigands had been about to scatter, then saw that not all the young riders were armed. The two with pistols had already let fly, one shot taking a mercenary in the throat, the other lost in the reeds. There was the sabre to watch for, and the charging horses, but the men were evenly matched now, six against six, and the day would never come when striplings from the city scored a victory in the Marchfeld.

The mercenaries regrouped on the track, skinning-knives at the ready, the blades winking obscenely in the sun.

And then the heron said, "Sit tight, my dear chaps," and fished in his pockets. The riders glanced at him, unwilling to think him hesitant. Lord Albany d'Enville-Zurrant-Jevington? Surely he wasn't the type to shy off when the enemy was less than fifty feet away?

"Now," he said, "this should announce us nice and clear," and produced a brace of pistols unlike any they'd ever seen. Small and flat and with scrolled metal butts, they were nevertheless equipped with four barrels apiece, double triggers, a double set of hammers and lidded pans that kept the powder from spilling out.

"Always like to have them loaded and primed," Albany murmured. "Ruins a good suit if it's bulging with flasks and shot. Villainous-looking fellows, aren't they?"

It was not clear if he meant the pistols or the brigands, but by the time he'd finished talking he had raised the lids and eased back the hammers.

Aware that there would be no headlong charge, the mercenaries advanced. Albany extended a bony arm, squeezed the forward trigger, slipped his finger back to squeeze the second, then handed the pistol to Brydd. "Rotate the block, would you, and uncover the other pans, there's a good chap." He levelled his second pistol, fired it once, then again, then exchanged pieces with Brydd.

The mercenaries had faltered, three of them hit, but now they stormed forward, convinced the pistols were empty. They'd seen double-barrelled weapons before; there was nothing new in that.

Meanwhile, the two armed Austrians had reloaded and, whilst Albany loosed off his fifth and sixth shots, his seventh and eighth, they sent their own heavier bullets into the astonished group.

The attack collapsed. Those brigands who were still uninjured made a run for it, leaving their wounded companions to die or be hanged. The air was full of gunsmoke and the smell of powder, the sound of snapping rushes, the groans of the wounded, the snorts and pawing of the nervous mounts.

It was time to take stock and withdraw.

❋

The cart that emerged from the Marchfeld resembled nothing so much as a *Pestwagen,* a plague wagon. It bore the bodies of Janos and Katya and their driver, two dead mercenaries and a third who would die on the way. Two more of the brigands had been roped behind the cart, their injuries dismissed as superficial, their pleas for mercy ignored. What else did they expect after what they had done and tried to do?

Brydd Cannaway was in charge of the cart, sharing the bench with one of the young Austrians. This allowed Vitar and the maid to be escorted on horseback and kept well ahead of the *Pestwagen.* The women were both exhausted, the maid slumped in the saddle, gabbling mindlessly to herself, Vitar expressionless and silent, the tears drying on her cheeks.

The two armed aristocrats had reloaded their pistols and stationed themselves at the rear of the column, one guarding the tethered brigands, the other alert for sound or sign of pursuit. No one spoke until they had reached the riverbank and followed it north to the bridge. There was not much to say that could not now be said better by a judge, or a priest.

❄

A week later, the worst of it was over. The funeral had been attended by all those who'd deserted the picnic and ridden—not altogether too late—to the rescue. The captured brigands had been summarily tried and hanged. The maid had been taken to hospital and thence, unhappily, to a home for the insane.

Vitar Czaky had been offered lodgings with a gentle, matronly woman who ran a *Gasthaus* near the Graben, and Brydd had called there every day—only to be turned away at the door.

"Fräulein Czaky is not well enough to receive visitors, Herr Cannaway. Another time, perhaps."

But his visits were not entirely wasted, for he brought sprigs of heather and bunches of late-flowering violet, and the woman could see that his concern was genuine and that he'd polished his boots to a shine.

On his eighth visit she invited him in and gave him sugared bread and coffee. When he had finished she cleared the table and said, "I shall leave the door open, Herr Cannaway." And then, with a smile, "Fräulein Czaky speaks English, you know. I do not, more's the pity. She will be down before long."

He had helped her from the cart and on to his horse, glimpsed her during the ride back from the Marchfeld, seen her again at the funeral service and, lastly, beside the graves. He'd murmured his condolences and she had thanked him for his part in the rescue. Then she'd been driven away to the *Gasthaus* and he had not seen her again. Not until now, as she turned at the foot of the stairs and entered the lace-lapped room.

But nothing had changed for Brydd Cannaway. It had been love at first sight, that most overpowering of emotions; an untried mixture of hope and ignorance, desire and conviction, the wildest folly stirred in with the firmest of resolves. He'd been in love with

her before he had heard her speak, before her tears of anguish had
dried. He had only learned her name from someone else, and felt
jealous because he had not been the first of the rescuers to know
it.

Even so, it was well within her power to make a fool of the
uninvited young caller, for he had never before taken the reins of
Cupid's Golden Carriage—a phrase he'd remembered from a popular romance—and any clumsiness would show.

He came to his feet and bowed. "Fräulein Czaky. May I intro-
duce myself? My name is Brydd Cannaway." He realised he'd
started in English and waited to see if Vitar would reply in his
language.

"Well, Herr Cannaway—Master Cannaway—I hope you live
nearby, else you'll have been somewhat inconvenienced, riding
back and forth all week."

"But I wasn't. Not at all."

"Then you do live nearby."

"No, Fräulein. In fact, my room's on the other side of the city.
But I would not regret the journeys, whatever the distance. May I
offer you these?" He scooped up a bunch of sulphur-yellow roses
and held them out to her. "I don't know if you've received the
others—"

"I have—"

"—then I hope—"

"—and they're in my room—"

"—they brought you—"

"—in innumerable vases—"

"—some cheer."

"—where they thrive. They did, Master Cannaway. They do."

They gazed at each other. And then emboldened by the exchange, Brydd risked a grin. "I understand it's best to flatten the
lowest inch of the stems."

"Is that how it's done in England?"

"As for that"—he shrugged—"but where I come from, the Kennett Vale in Wiltshire, yes, that's how it's done."

She nodded. "Then we've already something in common, for so
it is in Győr."

Brydd gestured to one of the lace-trimmed chairs. "Would you care to be seated, Fräulein Czaky?"

She hesitated a decent time, then said, "For the moment. Why not?"

"For the moment," he echoed. "Yes, of course."

The matron passed the open door, busied herself in the kitchen, made a second sortie, returned to feed the stove, prepared another batch of sugared bread and coffee. The young couple were chatting as she took it through to them, still chatting as the pot grew cold. Then, when Brydd asked her if he might visit Fräulein Czaky again, tomorrow, it was Vitar who inclined her head before the matron could reply.

※

They met regularly, at first bound by convention to the *Gasthaus*, then allowed to walk together in the evenings, with the matron dogging their steps.

She kept pace with them for a week, then gave it up. Fräulein Czaky and Herr Cannaway were obviously well suited, and she was content—more, relieved—to let them be. She had been asked to take care of the orphaned Vitar and she'd done so. But no one had said she must chaperone the young lady and get blisters in the process. Anyway, they were foreigners, and what did Vienna care if a Hungarian girl linked arms with an Englishman and strolled about the Am Hof square or along the Graben?

※

Even so, they were not yet alone, and Brydd asked the girl if she'd accompany him on an outing to the Wiener Wald. "I can borrow a horse-and-trap from the *Kutschemeister*. We could take some food and wine and spend the day—" He stopped, seeing the shadow of doubt cross her brow. He'd half expected a rejection, and waited for her to tell him it would be unseemly, improper, unbecoming.

Instead, she murmured, "The Wiener Wald? Is the countryside there—? It's not like the Marchfeld, is it?"

Relieved that he'd misunderstood, Brydd hastened to reassure her. "There's all the difference in the world between them, let

alone the city itself. I know a place—I discovered it by accident—
a glade that's almost completely floored with flowers. At the far
end of it there's a stream—"

"And that's where you'll take me? To this glade you found by
chance?" The shadow had passed and she was teasing him with a
smile. "It's not something you came upon with another woman?
It's not been a favourite haunt of yours, this floor of flowers?"

"No, Fräulein, it has not!" He wanted Vitar to know how
much she mattered to him, but he realised the words sounded stiff
and indignant. Lowering his voice, he repeated, "No, and you'll
not find the flowers trampled flat."

She decided he had made a nice recovery and said, "Then you'd
best borrow the trap, Master Cannaway, before the colours fade."

Next day, having tethered the horse around the corner from the
Gasthaus, Brydd collected Vitar, escorted her along the street, then
nodded in the direction of the gig. Grinning at their subterfuge,
they climbed aboard and went rattling westward, out of the city
and into the Wiener Wald.

Brydd had packed a picnic basket with wine and meat and
bread, a dozen small sugared cakes and a few stalks of twisted pastry, inset with almonds. They followed the road for a mile, turned
along a track, then huddled together as it narrowed and the trees
brushed against them.

Well, Vitar thought, he may be serious-minded and unpractised
at banter, but he knows the routes that'll bring a woman close
against him.

They emerged, as Brydd had promised, in a glade carpeted with
pink and purple flowers. Again, as he'd promised, a tributary of
the Danube washed the southern edge of the clearing. There were
no other carriages, no fishermen, no trodden paths or startled
lovers. Only the horseshoe of trees and the warm air and the
splashing of fish in the river . . .

Brydd left Vitar to decide where they'd eat, then broke the seal
on the wine jar and filled the glasses he'd brought from the
Bäckerstrasse. They chinked the glasses and he said, "This is the
twentieth time we've been together. Do you think it odd that a
man should remember such things?"

"I think it exceptional, Master Brydd. And accurate. It is, as

you say, the twentieth time." She smiled at him, saw the way he
gazed at her, then turned slowly to look at the river. Yes, she
mused, serious-minded though he is, there's much about him
that's exceptional. His disciplined behaviour in the Marchfeld,
when he loaded and primed the pistols for his friend Albany Jevington. His depth of concern at the funeral. His daily visits to the
Gasthaus, filling the place with flowers. He needs lessons in
banter, and he'd not be a man to cross; but he's not a dullard, nor
is he a drone. I already like Brydd Cannaway. I might well feel
more for him—in time.

As for Brydd, he continued to gaze at the girl. He studied the
fine dark sweep of her hair, stole a glance at her breasts and the
slimness of her arms and the curve of her legs, revealed below the
hem of her embroidered skirt. He was in love with her, and he
prayed that she might feel the same toward him—in time.

They reduced the picnic to crumbs. They were relaxed yet nervous, eager to learn what they could from each other, hesitant to
intrude too far, too soon. The returned the empty platters to the
basket, balanced their glasses on the wickerwork lid, then
sprawled contented near the river's edge. Brydd waited for Vitar
to look elsewhere and, when she did so, stared at her again. He
pretended to yawn and lay back, his hand within reach of her
waist . . . He wondered how she'd react if he leaned across and
touched her . . . If he said the things he wanted to say . . . If he
dared to hold her and—

"I noticed a satchel in the trap. Does it contain your drawings?"

"A few of them, yes." He did not tell her how long it had taken
him to select them, nor that they represented the very best of his
work.

"May I look at them?"

He managed an eloquent shrug. "If you'd care to, of course. I'd
welcome your opinion, your being the daughter of an architect."

His tone might have been just a little too languid, his modesty
ringing a little too false. Whatever it was, Vitar said sharply,
"More than that, Master Brydd. He was more than just an architect. Janos was the best there was of his time. Come to Györ one
day and you'll see."

Brydd nodded, his amorous mood in shreds. "Go ahead then. Look at them. I'm sure you'll find plenty that's wrong."

His nervousness had taken command. He pushed himself to his feet and went to stare at the river, fishing with his eyes. He could see silvered trout in the shadows of the bank, still and silent then gone in a flash, the water rippling on the surface. He remembered the swell of Vitar's breasts and the darkness of her limbs. He refused to watch her as she removed the sheaf of sketches. He could see her just as clearly in his mind, the woman he'd fallen in love with at first sight.

He prowled the bank, turned and gave in to temptation, glancing across to see her kneeling among the flowers, his sketches spread out on the satchel. He continued his patrol, his shadow on the water startling the fish. Damn it all, he thought, can't she nod or sneer or do something? It's worse than a lesson with Dr. Barrowcluffe. At least he'd have settled his wig or tutted or crossed things out with a pen. At least I'd have known his direction, known what to expect at the finish.

He heard the rustle of paper, the tap of Vitar's palm as she squared the sheets, the squeak of leather as the drawings were replaced in the satchel. He found a stone on the bank, wiped away the mud and prepared to send it skimming across the river. Damn it all, her opinion matters to me. I'd no idea how much.

The stone skidded, damn it all, damn it all, damn it all . . .

Vitar came toward him. Without waiting to see if the stone would sink or land, Brydd turned to her, searching her face for an opinion.

"You should have stayed in the grass," she told him. "I'm sure my breasts are the rival of fish and hopping stones."

He managed to say, "Yes. Yes, they are," then smothered his embarrassment by asking what she'd thought of the drawings.

"Those?" she said airily. "Oh, those are near perfect, my dear Brydd. You've a rare and outstanding talent. The world will tell you so one day. You must continue to design your coaches no matter what, then build them and be the first to drive them from the yard. I'm sorry I kept you waiting—sorrier still that you strayed—but I wished to study them in detail, to see how you'd balanced the line and wash, to understand why you'd used this colour in preference to that. I'll say again: my father was no ordinary architect. I spent as much time at his drawing board as I ever did in the nursery. He was willing to teach me, do you see, to show me why this shape was better than that, why this design for a building could be dictated by the space around it, or the natural folds of the ground. He taught me a lot, did Janos. Enough to see that you share his special skills. Enough to learn something about you, and come close to you, like this . . ."

She slipped into his embrace and they kissed, Vitar sharing the kiss to the full. They sank to the ground and kissed again, Brydd's hands around her waist, then on the flatness of her stomach, the swell of her breasts, the smoothness of her neck. Vitar curled her fingers in his hair, murmuring as she felt the more urgent movement of his desire.

She eased herself away, leaned over to kiss him again, then said, "In time, my dear Byrdd. In not too long a time. When I'm as certain of things as you are. We'll know the day, we both will, when it comes . . ."

❋

The *Kutschemeister* was pleased with Brydd's work, and the pinch-brakes he'd developed had been fitted to several new coaches. Other yards showed their respect by hastily copying the design, and it amused Brydd to learn that the wheels of the rival coaches often locked tight, leaving the furious passengers stranded until the blocks had been prised from the rims. Serves them right, he thought. They should have come to us in the first place.

He introduced Vitar to Albany, then wondered if he'd been wise to do so. The heron had met the girl briefly at the funeral, but this was the first time the three of them had sat together at a coffeehouse table, the first time Vitar had been at the mercy of Lord Jevington's charm.

He had a new outfit, of course, in sunrise pink, with maroon turn-top boots, matching gloves, matching hatband, matching feather, everything matching to the pin in his cravat. Once again the passing strollers faltered and stared, the women at Albany, the men at the beautiful Vitar. Since the death of her parents she had lived on the money Janos had carried in his purse—enough to see her housed and fed, but no more than that. She had no fine gowns or petticoats, no tippets or lace scarves, no damask shoes or fans or doeskin gloves. She had never had them, and saw no reason to suppose she ever would.

And yet the men who passed invariably glanced across at her, the husbands waiting until their wives had looked elsewhere, the single men smiling and dawdling. They guessed she was a country girl, and a foreigner by her dark complexion. But they could not begin to guess what she was doing in the company of a gaudy, long-legged heron and a drab-dressed crow.

Not to be outdone, the ladies cast their own subtle glances at Albany and wondered why such a gentleman would be seen in public with a gypsy and a servant.

Ignoring the strollers, Albany flourished his gloves, made the feather ripple in his hat and continued to work his considerable charms on Vitar. She had already decided that no young woman in her right mind would fall beneath his spell. If she'd any sense at all, she would jump.

Brydd found it hard to keep pace. If Albany had smiled like that at a girl in the Kennett Vale, he'd have found himself engaged to be married, or with a bloodied nose. And, if a girl played along as Vitar was doing, and laughed so huskily at his jokes, she'd be thought a trollop or an actress—it was all the same in the valley.

But this was not the valley of the Kennett. This was the Am Hof square in Vienna-on-the-Danube, and Brydd acknowledged that the rules were different. It was no good glowering, or drumming the table. He'd do better to make an attempt at—what was it?—banter, and stamp down hard on his jealousy.

No sooner had he decided than a group of Albany's friends approached the table. A few of them remembered Brydd from the ice race—remembered and then promptly forgot as they drew their chairs around Vitar. Their compliments were elaborate, their manner self-assured. They learned the girl was Hungarian, and two of them addressed her in her own language. They discovered she'd been born and raised in Györ, the daughter of Janos Czaky, and one of the young men declared that he, too, was an architect, then gave an accurate description of Janos's best-known designs.

Vitar said something that set them nodding, something else that made them laugh.

"We're going on to a party," they told her. "It'd be all the more festive for your presence, Fräulein Czaky." Then, addressing Albany, "Bring the lady along, won't you? There's some mad fellow who promises to eat fire and swords and heaven knows what else." And then, to Brydd, "You, too, Herr Cannaway. We might need you for a coach race later, who knows?"

He had not done well at banter, and he now kept his hands below the table, so they'd not see his fists balled tight. Albany looked at him, but before either of them could speak, Vitar said, "I hope you have more success at the card tables, *meine Herren*, for your judgement's badly off at this one. Albany Jevington is a newfound friend, but my more immediate companion is Brydd Cannaway. It's a pity you didn't address your invitation correctly, before marking him down as a driver."

There was some coughing and scraping of chairs, the muttering of apologies, the settling of hats. Too much the gentleman to take sides, Albany waved a casual farewell to his friends, then beckoned the waiter for another bottle of Kahlenberg.

He paid the man, toyed with his glass and said, "I wish they'd been right, of course. Your young lady is as gifted in her head as in her looks, my dear chap. I really do wish she was mine to take about." Then, smiling wryly at both of them, he raised his glass and added, "Reluctant though I am to admit it, I can understand your preference for each other. You've really no need of feathered hats, or fellows who chew knives. You're driving—if I may use the word—on a far better road than that." In case they thought him maudlin, he climbed to his feet and said, "Time for hard dice and soft women. Though the rolling of the one depends much upon—" Then he shrugged and gangled away across the square.

They watched him go, and Brydd said, "You spoke out damn well on my behalf."

"Yes, I did." Vitar nodded. "But not just for you, my dear Brydd. As I think you must know."

✸

He had been cheered by her opinions of his drawings, excited by her embrace, impressed by her knowledge and wit and the way she'd spoken out for him—for herself—for the two of them. They had walked and talked through the summer evenings, shared a thousand kisses, some gentle, some passionate, some the final cure for a quarrel. They'd eaten in the taverns that honeycombed the Wollzeile and the Bäckerstrasse, and Brydd felt he had come to know her, at least outside the bed.

But he was soon to witness another aspect of the remarkable Vitar Czaky—the rainbow of her wrath.

They'd enjoyed a stroll in the evening, their route taking them to a riverside inn. They had been there before, and now they nodded a greeting at the landlord and found themselves a table with a view of the Danube. Fishermen came in, and sailors, and merchants with their wives. Plates rattled on trays. Candles burned down and were replaced. The air was blurred by tobacco smoke, the steam of food, the soot from guttering wicks. The noise increased. Stories were thought worth retelling. Laughter turned to a bray. It was a fine raucous atmosphere, and no one noticed the five men who found a table near the door.

Brydd and Vitar were planning another outing to the Wiener Wald. "Where we went that first time," Vitar requested. "To that glade beside the stream?"

Brydd said, "It's probably as secret now as ever it—" then broke off to exclaim, "Now there's a youngster I've seen before!" He directed Vitar's gaze toward an odd, lopsided young boy who'd entered the tavern and was flinching at the noise. "I came down on the raft with him from Passau. Look, there's his father. He plays the most melancholy pipe you ever heard." Without hesitation, he raised his arm in greeting. The boy recognised Brydd as the man who'd found time to smile at him. His head jerking with the spasms of his affliction, he edged eagerly between the tables.

He was carrying a small open box, a begging box, but it hindered what he wanted to do. Instinctively, Vitar held out a hand and took it from him, allowing the boy to hook his fingers in his mouth and pull his lips in a grin. Brydd nodded at him. "I'm pleased to see you again. Have things gone well for you here? Does your father still play his pipe?"

The boy grimaced and dodged, his mind unable to grasp the words. He knew only that the lean young man was his friend and that he must reclaim the box and hold it out, as he'd been taught.

He took his fingers from his mouth, then turned his attention to
the box, not daring to look at Vitar. But she already understood
his concern and handed it to him. As she did so, Brydd leaned
across, laid some coins inside it, then ruffled the boy's hair. He
was rewarded with a stumbling attempt at a bow, and then the
boy made off between the tables. Brydd could already hear the
warble of the pipe and the sounds of chatter diminishing as the
diners turned to listen.

The boy zigzagged from table to table, the box sometimes echoing with the rattle of coins, sometimes not. He approached the
five men who'd taken their place near the door, his mind comforted by the sound of his father's pipe.

The men grinned and nodded together, and then one of them
emptied the leavings from his plate into the box.

The piper saw it and stopped playing. Most of the diners saw it,
though they kept their seats. Brydd Cannaway saw it and started
to rise, then felt Vitar go past him, her chair rocking empty on its
heels.

There'd been men like this in Györ. There were men like this
in every town and city, petty bullies who sniggered together and
weighed their chances by the width of their shoulders. They were
wonderfully strong when bunched together, like briars in a hedge;
but they were always at the mercy of a rake, if found alone.

She reserved her gaze for the man who'd emptied his plate.
Standing opposite him, she nodded at the boy, then took away
the box. He ran distraught to his father, who crooned to him in a
strange sibilant tongue.

A more obvious tongue for Vitar, though she'd not waste her
words. Elbowing aside his companions, she leaned toward the
ringleader and upended the box on his plate. Coins and bones and
the slop of his food spilled over, some of it running on the table,
some of it on his clothes. "Now fish out the coins, *mein Herr*, and
clean out the box. You may think yourself amusing, but let me
tell you this. Your behaviour shows you're more crippled than the
piper, and with far less knowledge than the boy." She heard a
snort of contempt from her left, swung the box and slammed it
down on the table. "If you also find it amusing, then you can also
pay for the fun. And you, *mein Herr*. And you. And you. And
you, as the last."

The men had hesitated, not wishing to be schooled by a woman. But they now wished they'd given in with more grace, for Brydd was standing over them, as were the fishermen and the sailors and the landlord, a knotted towel in his fist. By the time the box had gone all around the table, it was inches deep in coins.

Vitar took it to the boy. He waited for Brydd to appear before pulling aside his lips, though he kept his eyes on the woman, sensing he'd made another friend. The troublemakers paid their bill and left, and the piper talked with Brydd and his lady, the boy huddled in the crook of his arm. From then on the evening was set to music, the sound of the pipe still audible as Brydd took Vitar along the riverbank and into the city.

"Once again," he said, "you spoke out damn well."

"So I did," she replied. "But only in the knowledge that you were there."

❊

These were the best times, the days of spring and summer.

Brydd was deeply in love, the girl drawing closer to him, step by cautious step. She would not yet be intimate with him, not until she was sure that by giving herself she could also give her heart. But that day was coming, she believed. A little while more . . . Time enough to be certain . . . Another few weeks perhaps, another few days . . .

And then, beyond anything Vitar Czaky or Brydd Cannaway could do to prevent it, the situation shattered and collapsed. The best times were over. It was autumn now, and their happiness was snatched away like leaves in the wind.

❊

On this particular evening he had seen her home and was alone in his room when he heard footsteps on the unlit spiral stairs. It was after midnight, and the intrusion gave him the chance to dry the pens he'd been using and return them to their box.

He guessed the caller was a drunkard who'd lost his way—it had happened before—and he sprinkled sand over the still wet drawing, collected a lantern, then went to wait at the head of the stairs. His mind was still on the complicated tight-lock system that would, if it worked, allow a coach to turn in a narrower circle than before. It all had to do with the height of the foreperch and the way the springs straddled the axle. There was still much to be done on it, but by the end of the year—

"Sorry about this, my dear chap. My own damn fault, of course. I'll need a hand, if you'd care to."

It was the words that identified him, not the ruined suit or his blood-smeared face, nor even his voice, dry and rasping. It was Albany Jevington, but only just, by God, only just.

Brydd reached forward and caught him, almost lifted him clear of the steps, then helped him into the room.

"Most inconvenient for you, I'm sure, and I'm sincerely—"

"It's all right. Keep quiet. Lie out on the bed." He found a towel, dipped it in a basin of water and took it across to his friend. "Is anything broken, can you tell? There's a doctor who lives not far from here. He's a good man and he'll come if you—"

"No. They gave me the devil's own crack on the head, but they mostly applied their fists and . . ." His voice trailed off and he lay for a moment, his face hidden by the towel. Brydd gazed down at him, suddenly aware that every snail-shell button had been cut from his outfit, from chest and stomach and sleeves. A valuable haul for the bastards who'd waylaid him, thirty blobs of gold.

Leaving Albany to rest, he dusted a glass, poured a generous measure of brandy, then waited until he saw the heron stir and dab the blood from his face.

"Can you move?"

Albany grimaced, caught his strength at the flow and hauled himself upright against the headboard. He took the glass, frowned as he noticed that his knuckles were skinned and swollen, then winced with pain as the liquid filled the cuts around his mouth. "Thorough fellows. Ah, yes, and they've set a tooth rattling at the back."

"When did it happen?" Brydd asked. "Some of the blood's dry in places. That crack on the head; did they knock you senseless and leave you in an alley somewhere?"

"Pour another measure," Albany advised. "No, not for me. For you. Then find a seat and stay there, if you can, though I daresay you'll wish to complete what those fellows started, once you've heard the tale."

"You've jumped beyond me. I don't know what you mean. Are you safe here now? The street door can be locked, though I've never bothered with it, but if they're still after you—"

"No, my dear chap. I've been given a few hours' grace."

"Then they *are* still after you. Christ, Albany, yes or no?"

"Find a seat, Brydd Cannaway. And prepare yourself for the worst, for that's what I've brought you." He sighed and shifted and, by doing so, caught sight of his buttonless suit. "Well"—he nodded—"there's the thing. The ritual of dishonour, the insignia torn away."

Meanwhile, Brydd had taken his place at the table and instinctively blew the sand from his drawing. Then he shrugged an apology and waited for Albany to speak.

"I was sent a note this morning. From Johann von Kreutel. I was asked to present myself at his house on the island of Leopoldstadt. The one we visited together, do you remember? The appointment was for eight o'clock— Has it gone midnight yet? Yes, well then, for eight o'clock last evening. I knew the reason for it, of course. It was long overdue."

And I, too, know the reason for it, God help us both.

"Johann was not in the house, I'd not expected him to be, but outside the gates." He sipped his brandy, shuddered as it coursed its way down, then dabbed his swollen mouth. "The perfect gentleman, Johann von Kreutel. He'd dispatched his gatekeeper on some errand or other, allowing the two of us to talk. And, my dear Brydd, I think you can guess what was said, the gist of it at least."

Oh, yes, I can guess it to the letter.

"Perhaps. But tell it anyway."

"You recollect the day you were taking a broken cart through the Wiener Wald? You found two horses tethered in a clearing. You never saw the riders, but we saw you, and we knew we'd been discovered. And then there was the other time, and it *was* us in the landau, raising the hood in the hopes that you'd not yet recognised us. Vain hopes, eh, my friend? You knew then what you'd formerly suspected, that Albany Jevington and Annette von Kreutel were engaged in a fervid and deceitful affair."

Brydd took a pen from its box, rocked it between his fingers, twisted it aimlessly this way and that. He knew now that his career in Vienna was over, that there would no longer be a place in the yards of Vienna for the friend of a seducer. He granted himself a brief, humourless smile, remembering how Albany had recommended him to Johann, and Johann to the *Kutschemeister*, each accepting a degree of responsibility for the untried foreigner. If Brydd had failed it would have reflected badly on Lord Jevington, embarrassed Johann von Kreutel and convinced the coachmaster that he too should have said *leider nicht*, we regret.

But he had not failed. It was simply that Lord Albany d'Enville-Zurrant-Jevington had succeeded too damn well—with another man's wife.

He tossed the pen on the table. "And so? What's to happen now?"

"I've been called out. There'll be a bit of shooting tomorrow. Or rather today."

"You've been challenged to a duel, is that what you're saying?"

"That's the way of it. Four o'clock this afternoon, on the island."

"And the attack? Surely Johann was not a part of that? I can't believe—"

"No, no, though from what little was said, I imagine they were friends of the household, or servants who wished to show their disapproval. No one likes cats near the birdcage, though I think it shameful of them to have stolen my buttons."

"What *did* they say?"

"That's a curious question, young Brydd. You have every right to manifest your disgust with me; you've been sadly let down. But do you really wish to hear the insults that accompanied their blows?"

"Not for the pleasure of it, no. But it's too convenient that the servants should be laying for you. How many were there?"

"I counted six, though it felt like sixty."

"How did they know you were meeting Johann, and where and when? It's not the thing he'd confide to members of his household. Tell me what they said, as best you can remember."

Albany managed a weary, cut-about smile. " 'Take that for a libertine, that for a tempter, that for staining a Schoenholz, that for stinking betrayer, that for—' Hell, Brydd, what do angry men say?"

"They say 'von Kreutel,' " he answered, leaning forward in his chair. "They don't say 'Schoenholz.' Why would they? Why the lady's maiden name? Why would they speak of her as a Schoenholz when she's been a von Kreutel for years?"

"Why, indeed?" Albany murmured. "I seem to have supplied a curious answer to your curious question. But that's what they said: 'staining a Schoenholz.' "

Brydd gazed at his friend; still his friend, for it was not easy to condemn the heron, not with the scent of Vitar in the room. Albany and Annette had engaged in a—what was it?—a fervid and deceitful affair. But Brydd was just as ardent in his love for Vitar, and if deceit was needed to allow them together, then that's what he'd employ.

"I don't believe they *were* members of the household. Nor allies of the von Kreutels. I believe they were hired bunchers, paid for by the lady's brother, Carl-Maria Schoenholz! *He* could have known about the appointment, and it sits with his character to have you savaged and frightened off. It's bad enough that you're to duel with his brother-in-law, but what if you were to kill Johann? For all we know, Annette von Kreutel despises Carl-Maria—"

"Coming and going," Albany affirmed. "She thinks he ought to be turned loose during the boar-hunting season. Yes, my dear chap, the attack bears Carl-Maria's stamp. I'm convinced of it. He'd be lost without the tolerant Johann, and Annette would not hesitate to see him off."

"Do you wish me to visit the von Kreutels? You've been beaten about, after all; look at your hands. Johann's not the type to take unfair advantage—"

"As I did of him? No, Brydd, he's not. But I think it best to keep the appointment."

They were silent for a while, and then Brydd said, "I'm not up in these things. We don't have duels in the Kennett Vale. But you will need someone to assist you, to take you out there—"

"And bring me back, alive or dead?"

"You're a bloody fool!" Brydd erupted, slamming his fist on the table. "Getting yourself into this! A bloody fool!"

"And you as deep as I."

"Christ, that's not the concern."

"I know it's not," Albany said gently. "But be clear about it— I've put your career on the rocks, at least in Vienna. I could tell you I was in love with Annette, and perhaps make you believe it, though even I would be reluctant to offer so parboiled a morsel. We've enjoyed each other's company, in the bed and out, but we were really no more than performing players, appreciative of our skills. If we've shared anything in common beyond carnality, it was probably a knowledge of materials and a fondness for mirrors. And for that I've put you on the rocks." He shook his head, perhaps genuinely bewildered that it had come to this.

"You have," Brydd acknowledged, "and I don't much care for it. But it's done now, bottled and corked. I imagine there are certain proprieties to be observed when one goes duelling. You'd better tell me what they are."

TEN

The meeting place was near the southern end of the island, far from prying eyes. It was against the law to settle one's differences with powder and ball, and should the outcome prove fatal to one or other of the parties, the survivor might find himself arraigned for murder. He was unlikely to be hanged for his crime, but he'd do well to leave the district without delay. His friends would let him know when it was safe to return—when memories had faded and the investigation gathered dust.

But Albany Jevington would be leaving anyway, win or lose. He had already paid his bills, purchased a berline and, with Brydd's help, roped his luggage to the rack. His four o'clock appointment with Johann was merely his final act before departure, though how final remained to be seen.

They were met at the bridge by one of Johann's stewards, and the rider conducted them along a series of forest tracks, scarcely wide enough for the berline. Brydd sat alone on the hammercloth bench, Albany alone in the carriage.

"I don't know if I'll be praying, or what," he'd said, "but I shall need a few moments to myself. Oh, yes, and I've scrawled a note; you'll find it in one of the cases. It bequeaths my stuff to you, should the worst occur. Pity we're not of a size, eh, my dear friend? You'd look the cat's whiskers in crimson. The money's in one of the smaller cases, though I've rather gone through it, I'm afraid. Still, there should be enough to pull you off the rocks and see you settled in Munich or Paris, or wherever it is they make good coaches. You'll find some other letters, intended for my banks and estates and suchlike. See they get to the posthouse, would you?

"Now then," he continued, "there'll be fellows waiting for us at the ground, so let's say our good-byes. You've been the most loyal of friends, Master Cannaway, and not well enough served by me. But I think you'll forgive me. I think you'll have to, when you're so clearly in love with Vitar Czaky and can see how it tips us over. Love? Passion? Lust? Inextricable, wouldn't you say? Or would *you* have saved *me* from the rocks, as I suspect?"

"Had I been in your place and Vitar in Annette's? God knows, Lord Jevington, I wouldn't have spared you a thought. And I've forgiven you already, there being nothing to forgive."

"That's the way," Albany had told him. "Let's have some nice fat lies. Here's my hand, Master Cannaway. Tap on the roof when we get there."

❊

And now it was time, and the berline entered a triangular clearing, and Brydd could see Johann and Carl-Maria, a surgeon and his assistant, a priest who stood with his eyes downcast and the coachman who had brought the distinguished von Kreutel and the box-faced Schoenholz. There, too, was the Regulator, the man who would take charge of the proceedings.

More often than not the arrangements would be shared by the seconds—Brydd and Carl-Maria—but it was necessary that the seconds be of equal rank in society, and Herr Schoenholz had no intention of sharing his duties with a foreign coachmaker. So they'd engaged the services of a Regulator, and would abide by the rules he set.

The steward indicated a corner of the clearing. Brydd knuckled the roof, then took the berline alongside the other, more elegant carriage. He left space for Albany to alight from whichever door he chose—and for his body to be lifted in again, if that was the way things went.

The heron emerged immediately, and Brydd was aware that he'd powdered his face, rouged his lips, concealed his swollen hands with a pair of thin silk gloves. There was a stiffness to his walk, but he pressed his hands to the small of his back and made out that he'd been discomforted by the journey.

Brydd lifted the tether-weights from beneath the bench, carried them forward and looped the traces through the rings.

Johann von Kreutel crossed the grass to greet his opponent. They removed their hats and bowed to each other. Albany nodded at Carl-Maria, who frowned and stared at him. Yes, Brydd thought, look hard, you bastard, and wonder why your bunchers let you down.

"This is a sad business, Lord Jevington."

"It is, indeed, Herr von Kreutel."

"I wish it could be settled with an apology, a show of contrition. I wish I could ask for that."

"There'd be no need to ask, for it's volunteered, though I know it will not suffice. You took me on trust, Herr von Kreutel, and I've betrayed that trust, and for that I am deeply sorry."

"But not for misleading my wife."

"No, sir. Your wife is a fine lady, and doubtless she *was* misled. However, if I say I regret things now, that would surely compound my deceit."

"So it would, Lord Jevington, so it would." He expelled his breath in a sigh and said, "It is of little comfort to either of us, but this is not the first time my wife has been—misled."

Albany said nothing, his expression unchanged. He had offered an apology, at least for betraying Johann's trust, and the Austrian had also apologised, indirectly. It made no difference, of course; they would still take to the field, level their pistols and hope to score a hit. It was not enough to seduce a man's wife, then say, "Sorry." But neither was it enough to challenge the seducer without telling him the truth. They'd owed that much to each other before sparking the powder.

"You may wish to question the Regulator, Lord Jevington."

"Is he known to you, Herr von Kreutel?"

"No, sir, he is not."

"Then, sir, he will do."

They bowed again and moved apart. Johann knelt before the priest, whilst Albany walked about, flexing his fingers. Grim and helpless, Brydd Cannaway directed his gaze at Carl-Maria. The surgeon and his assistant busied themselves with salves and bandages, then fitted together a clumsy bamboo stretcher. The steward and coachman stood at a distance, passing a pipe from mouth to mouth.

And then the Regulator took charge.

❅

"Will you step forward, *meine Herren*, and be identified? You are Johann Franz Lothar von Kreutel?"

"I am."

"And you are Lord Albany d'Enville-Zurrant-Jevington?"

"I am."

"Very well. I shall now ask you this. Will you be reconciled with an embrace in full view of the assembly and put aside all thoughts or mention of this affair? It must be spontaneous, and I shall count to three beneath my breath. I begin now."

Carl-Maria was still frowning, the priest mumbling to himself, the surgeon wiping a scalpel on a dry, blotched rag. The coachman tapped his pipe against his bootheel. Brydd watched the Regulator, knowing he must now have counted to three.

"So you will pursue the matter. Very well. I shall now show you a brace of pistols, made in Brescia and bearing the signature of Bonomini. They are, to the best of my knowledge, identical in every respect. However, I shall load and prime them in full view of your seconds, lay the weapons in evidence on a cloth, then ask the challenger—Herr von Kreutel, I believe—to call the coin I shall spin. Is that agreeable to you, *meine Herren*?"

Johann nodded.

"Yes," Albany said. "Quite."

"You will then take the field, stand shoulder to shoulder and, on my command, turn away and step out fifteen paces. That done, you will face each other. I shall ask you to cock your pieces by calling 'Make ready.' I shall then call 'Fire!' and you will be at liberty to conclude the affair. Should either of you fail to register a hit, yet reconciliation still be beyond you, I shall ask you to hold your ground whilst the pistols are again made ready. A misfire shall be deemed equivalent to a shot. Any swaying or bending will be regarded as an attempt to flee. The calling of oaths or insults is severely discouraged, though a stricken man may say what he pleases, God granting him the time. Are the rules understood, *meine Herren?* Very well. I call on the seconds to observe the pack and prime."

These were twist-off pistols, and Brydd watched as the barrels were unscrewed, the chambers filled with powder, the lead balls thumbed in place. The barrels were then screwed tight, more powder sprinkled in the pan, the triggers brushed with doeskin to rid them of grease or sweat. The Regulator laid them on the cloth, produced a florin and held it up for inspection. The seconds withdrew and he spun the coin, inviting Johann to anticipate the face.

He called correctly, chose the pistol to his left and took it with him on to the field. Albany collected the other, made his way to the centre of the clearing, then stood side by side with his opponent. Then he winked at the young Cannaway.

Oh, yes, Brydd thought, that's right, that's how he'd treat it, as an afternoon's sport in high summer. Nothing must be too serious for the heron, until the ball raps for entry on his skull.

"I shall say 'Turn' and then count the paces. If you are ready, *meine Herren*—Turn! One, two, three, four, five . . . nine, ten, eleven . . . thirteen, fourteen, fifteen. Halt! Face off! Make ready!"

The onlookers were silent, the surgeon not daring to drop the rag from his hand, the priest soundlessly mouthing his prayers. Brydd heard his teeth grind together and cushioned them with his tongue. Thirty paces wasn't far. They were both tall men, and when they turned side on and extended their arms, and one added the length of the pistol barrels—

"Fire!"

The arms were raised, held out straight, Bonomini's impartial fingers pointing across the glade. The puffs of smoke emerged together from the pans, and more smoke erupted from the barrels, and Johann von Kreutel was turned and sent spinning. Albany looked at him for an instant, moved forward as though to help, then buckled and fell to the grass and spilled forward on his face.

The Regulator snapped. "Where are you, surgeon? Let's have you out there, sir! The worse-wounded first, if you please. Herr Schoenholz! Herr Cannaway! You may attend the principals."

The men ran forward. There was no doubt as to which of the opponents was worse wounded, for Johann had already regained his balance and was squinting in disbelief at the foot-long rent in his sleeve. Albany's shot had somehow tucked itself under the coat cuff, seared along Johann's forearm, then emerged to tear the sleeve from elbow to shoulder. The impact had been enough to unsettle him, and he'd remember the engagement every time he removed his shirt. But he'd think himself fortunate, and he did so now, whilst the assistant bandaged his arm.

Less fortunate was Albany Jevington, his rib cage shattered, the ball deflecting upward and outward through his chest. There had been duels in which a man had been saved by the coins in his pocket, the position of his buttons, even by the buckle on his hat. But none of these had availed the heron, for the ball had passed through unresisting cloth in its attempt to skewer his frame.

But he was still alive, and the surgeon crouched over him, cutting away the fine dark material and staunching the wounds with linen, then binding them tight to plug the holes. As he worked, his scowl of concentration deepened and he said, "Why was this man here today, will someone tell me? His body's the colour of plums. He's been beaten raw. And his face; d'you see how the powder and rouge come away to show bruises and scrapes? And even his hands; look, where the glove's peeled down." He finished what he was doing, glared up at Brydd and Johann, at Carl-Maria and the Regulator, then said, "There's been little honour in *this* exchange. I'd not have come out for *this*, had I known."

"No," Johann murmured, aghast at the condition of his adversary. "No more would I, by God." He covered his arm, as though ashamed that the wound was so slight, then said, "Herr Cannaway? Can you furnish an explanation for this? I shall want to know why I've been given such advantage—when all the world knows I would not have taken it, not if I'd known!" He shuddered with anger, an honourable man who had now been twice deceived.

"You're quite blameless," Brydd told him. "Lord Jevington was fit enough for the meeting. There's no cause for reproach, sir. It was well regulated and—yes, well enough performed."

Johann fought for control, turned away for a moment, then swung back to repeat his question. "You've done your best to soften the blow, Herr Cannaway, but I shall still have an explanation from you. Why was Lord Jevington so beaten before he ever took the field?"

"He had an appointment with you yesterday, at eight o'clock in the evening."

"He did, and kept it."

"And then he left you, and was ambushed on his way home."

"In the city? Are you saying he was caught—?"

"No, sir, on the island. He counted six of his attackers"—and now, still addressing Johann, Brydd gazed at Carl-Maria—"and heard one of them say 'that for staining a Schoenholz.' I questioned him about it, but that's what he heard."

Carl-Maria shrugged. "You're turning coincidence to profit, Herr Cannaway. The island has its share of brigands, like anywhere else."

"Maybe so," Brydd retorted, "though do they all make use of your name?"

"Lord Jevington was unlucky. Some of our neighbours must have learned of his misdeeds and—"

"Then they were not brigands?"

"Who can say, Herr Cannaway? Who knows?"

"You, for one, Herr Schoenholz. I say *you* know who they were. I say those bunchers were in *your* employ, and that all your talk of brigands and neighbours is so much spittle in the wind! I say you learned of the appointment and set the thing up, and that it's *you* who footed the bill! The Regulator is still here, Herr Schoenholz, and the sun is still up, so if you'd care to choose a pistol—"

"And you, Herr Cannaway, are still wonderfully righteous. But it'll be a distant day when I'm forced along by the blatherings of a tradesman." And with that he turned on his heel and strode away, leaving Johann and Brydd and the surgeon to avoid each other's glance.

With help from the assistant they lifted Albany on to the stretcher and carried him to the berline. The surgeon said, "There's a reliable doctor at Kahlenberg. Take him there. He's a skinny fellow, this Lord Jevington, but it may yet save him. The ball would never have passed through had he been more fleshy on the ribs."

Brydd thanked him, then looked at Johann. "I trust Kahlenberg is far enough away to satisfy you, Herr von Kreutel?"

"It is, Herr Cannaway. Take him along gently. I shall hope to hear that he's up and about again in a few days, and fully recovered."

"I too, sir. And now, if I may ask, how do I stand in this? Am I also to be banished from Vienna?"

"I'd intended it so." Johann nodded. "However, I'd made no provision for the assault on Lord Jevington; that was quite unexpected. You may therefore remain in the city as long as you like."

"And continue my work in the yard?"

"Ah, well, as to that . . ." A twitch of regret, a shake of the head. "I am sorry, Herr Cannaway, but no. You are too well linked with Lord Jevington. You may find other work, of course, but the yards will be closed to you. I'm sure you understand." He bowed correctly, couched his seared arm and withdrew. Brydd gazed after him for a moment, then turned abruptly and went to collect the tether-weights.

Yes, I understand, God damn him, his wife an adultress, and I linked with the heron, and his brother-in-law all but identified as the one who paid the bunchers. Oh, yes, I understand.

He looked in on Albany, then climbed aboard the bench and took the berline across the clearing. As he followed the steward toward the first of the forest tracks, he glanced back to see the Regulator cleaning his pistols, the priest eager to speak with Johann, the surgeon wrapping his instruments, Carl-Maria near the door of the von Kreutel coach. No one turned to watch the foreigners depart, and Brydd acknowledged that he would never again see the Austrians; not the beautiful Annette, nor the disciplined Johann, nor the treacherous Carl-Maria. Even so, he could not feel sorry that he'd guided them down the Cherhill slope in the dark and the rain, for how else would he have learned about Vienna and come across the map?

�֍

He stopped once on the island, again in the city, twice more on the riverside road to Kahlenberg. The stretcher had been placed in the well of the carriage and Albany seemed content to ride like that, the bamboo cradle helping to absorb the discomfort. He'd lost blood to the bandage, but during the final stop he had opened his eyes and said, "You'll tell them these buttons are worthless, won't you, dear chap? I'd rather they didn't snatch at them again. Every time I go down I lose buttons, on the ice or in the road . . ."

"They've not touched them, Albany. Your buttons are intact."

"And you'll see they're kept in place?"

"Yes. I shall see they're kept in place."

"That's the way. That's . . ." And then his senses left him again, and Brydd took him on beside the river.

The doctor in Kahlenberg was as bald as a stone and proved equal to his task, neither bustling for the sake of efficiency nor dawdling with indecision. He produced clean dressings, a jar of sulphur powder and an array of fishbone needles. He then treated the patient to a hefty dose of laudanum, slapped his face to make sure he was senseless and hummed cheerfully as he packed and stitched the wounds. "I'd say this man has been shot, though you've no need to agree, and most probably with a pistol at the range of some twenty or thirty paces, though you've no need to agree. I would furthermore guess that he's been duelling, and there's enough blood seeped out from him to suggest that you brought him from Vienna, though you've no need to admit it. I'm bound to report any injuries sustained in a duel; that's the law. The trouble is, I can never find time to record my opinions, so God knows when the authorities will hear about it. Come back in a week or so. Your companion should be up in bed by then. Or else we'll visit the graveyard."

Brydd trusted the doctor and asked if he would safeguard Albany's possessions.

"There's a coach house at the far end of the yard. Lead the team in there. You can leave the cases aboard. And don't look so doubtful, young man. This is Kahlenberg, not the jackdaws' nest of Vienna."

※

It took him two hours to walk back to the city, and by then the light was fading. He stopped near the church of Maria am Gestade—St. Mary at the Waterside—uncertain as to which way he should go. He knew which way he'd prefer to go: south through the Am Hof square, east along the Graben, then south again to the *Gasthaus* and Vitar Czaky. But he also knew he should first visit the yard, if only to explain his absence.

But there was more to it than that. It was necessary to find out if word had yet reached the *Kutschemeister*, instructing him that Herr Cannaway was no longer to be admitted. In short, Brydd was anxious to learn if he still had a job.

He continued due east, then along the Fleischmarkt, the street slippery with blood and offal, the walls and windowsills crawling with flies. The butchers had almost finished for the day and ignored the dogs that fought and snarled in the gutters.

Brydd reached the yard, to be met by the *Kutschemeister*. The man had seen him come through the gate and had lifted a sailcloth bag from beneath a table in the workshop. Now he placed it on the cobbles and said, "You have always been fair with me, Herr Cannaway. And I with you, I think."

"Always," Brydd agreed.

"Then I'll be brief. I have been told certain things—things you already know. They are not my concern, and I'd prefer to be deaf to them. But they will soon be widespread, the way such things invariably are. I believe you saw Herr von Kreutel today."

"I did, and I was warned that the yards would be closed to me. Are those my tools?"

The coachmaster nodded. "And the money you're owed. It's a damn waste, Herr Cannaway, but perhaps, in time, Herr von Kreutel will reconsider."

"He might," Brydd allowed without conviction. "Anyway, it has been a privilege to work in your yard, and I shall boast of it."

"I hope so, *mein Junge.* Good luck to you." The men shook hands. And then Brydd collected the bag and made his way to the street and that was that.

He had been fourteen months in the yard and, although he had little to show for it—a set of tools and measuring instruments and a sheaf of designs—he'd gained a wealth of experience, beyond anything he could have hoped to find among the coachmakers of England. He was shocked and dispirited that it had come so abruptly to an end, but at least he had *had* the fourteen months and made good use of them.

Even so, he must now tell Vitar he was finished in the city, unless he chose to work in the Fleischmarkt, or drive a carriage, or sell his sketches on the street. That was the worst of it, for leaving Vienna would mean leaving the woman with whom he was in love, with whom he had always been in love since that day in the Marchfeld.

※

They crossed the city and climbed the spiral stairs to his room, where he lit candles and a lantern. Then he took her in his arms and kissed her and was not surprised when she eased away.

"What's wrong, Brydd? Your expression's been clouded from the start. I must have asked ten questions on the way here, and they're still swirling, unanswered, in the street. Will you tell me what concerns you? I'd rather know the bad of it than imagine the worst."

"Yes"—he nodded—"though the bad is bad enough." He put glasses and a wine flask on the table, motioned Vitar to a chair, then twisted the cork from the bottle. He did not yet sit across from her, but paced the room, from bed to door, from door to southern window. He looked out at the smudges of yellow on the river, then returned to the table and said, "I had a visitor last evening—no, by God, it was after midnight—a visitor today . . ." Then he told her what had happened, of Albany's affair with Annette, of how the heron had been attacked, of the duel on the island. She did not once interrupt him, allowing the monologue to unfold and, perhaps in the telling, Brydd himself to find relief.

He was no actor, his abstracted kiss had proved that, but Vitar was terrified by the intensity of his dislike for Carl-Maria, then brought to tears by Brydd's description of his friend, lying bloodied in the well of the coach and asking that the buttons on his coat be left in place.

"It's the second time he's been forced to leave a city. Do you remember, I told you how we had to flee from Paris? It makes me wonder if he was on the run from London, and glad to leave Dover behind. Maybe he's always been like that, though I'm sorry to have seen him brought down. It jars with his style." He cuffed the edge of the table, paced the room again, then gazed directly at Vitar. "I warned you the bad is bad enough, and it is."

"Because you are so implicated? If so, I am not surprised, my love. Herr von Kreutel could hardly be expected to ignore you when you've been Albany's closest friend. You never did tell me what was in the bag you were carrying; that's one of my questions left scattered in the street, though I daresay it's your work tools and the like. You've lost your job now; is that how they've shown their displeasure?"

"You save me saying it." He tried a smile, but it was stillborn and he turned toward the window.

"No," Vitar told him. "I want you to look at me. That's it. That's what I want. Now tell me what you see."

"A beautiful woman. The most beautiful woman I ever . . . What would you have me say?"

She held his gaze in silence, aware that at first he'd be embarrassed and awkward, but that he must manage it for himself and go beyond it and find the honesty to tell her what she hoped it was within him to say. Later, she would help him in everything, but she would not lead or follow him in this. It had to be Brydd Cannaway's declaration, sincere and uninhibited, or guarded and grey, as he chose. But they both had to know what he saw in her, and what better time than now, when the yards were closed to him and they were just foreigners in the city? Vitar had to know, but so did he, for there was all the world beyond the ramparts of Vienna, and what if they should wish to travel it together?

"Well? What *would* you have me say? You *are* a beautiful woman, and I'm in love with you. If that's what you'd care to hear, then yes, I'll say it and be as fulsome as you like. You've a wonderful command of my language, and you're the only woman I ever met who made me laugh. Women have a different sense of humour, I think; no less than men, perhaps, but different. And you are considerate of others, and you've compassion for them. And you know about drawings and I can discuss them with you, and where else could I share that pleasure, with man or woman? Say something, Vitar. No? You won't? Then at least fill my glass."

She did so and smiled at him and decided he was doing very well.

"I was in love with you from the first, you know. That may sound a terrible thing to say to you, talking of love when your parents were— Well, terrible or not, I could not avoid seeing you, and my senses were quickened, and that's how it was. How else do we fall to liking or loving, if not tipped off balance at a glance?"

He meant to sip his wine, but his hand was unsteady and he was forced to wipe his lips. He looked at Vitar again to see if she'd noticed, but she had chosen that moment to drink from her own thick-stemmed glass.

"I want to say, my dear Vitar—I want to say that things are not finished for me, not by a long run. And you're not to suppose they are, not at all. I've learned a lot from my time in the yard, but Vienna is not the only place where I can find instruction. I'm a damn good coachmaker! I am, you know! And I'll be one of the best! And there's nothing to stop me—" Then he stopped himself, hearing his voice roar the length and breadth of the room. "Nothing," he repeated, careful to keep himself in check. "No reason at all why I should not go on. But the thought's been with me, my dear Vitar . . ."

She nodded yes, but would not yet say it.

". . . The thought's been with me that we should both go on." He hesitated, gripped the glass in his fist, then gave himself full rein. "I want us to be married, Vitar, though I don't know what's correct, how best I should ask it. How is it done in Györ? How *should* it be done?" He placed his glass on the table, thought it necessary to smooth his sleeves and brush the pockets of his thornproof suit, then reached out to guide Vitar from the table. "No matter how it's done in Györ," he said gently, "it's done here by the asking. And I ask you to marry me, Vitar Czaky, in the understanding that I have loved you from the start and that although your parents would doubtless have disapproved, they might yet have understood. I *do* love you, woman, and that's the hub of it, let life spin how it may."

He held her hands in his.

"Yes," Vitar said, "to your asking. And yes, my parents would have understood. And yes, that *is* the hub of it, love within the spinning of life. Yes, my dear Brydd, we'll be married, and I am already very glad." She reached up and kissed him, then slowly disengaged from his grasp and slipped off her shoes and unbuttoned the flower-trimmed bodice of her gown. She let the garment fall from her shoulders, untied the waist bows of her skirt, then moved her hips to free them from the matching flowered damask. She wore nothing now but a pale cambric shift, virginal in its simplicity, yet laced immodestly low across her breasts.

There was no coyness about her, no empty smile or the loll of practised abandon. Instead, there was the simple confidence of a woman who knew she was beautiful, or was made so by seeing it mirrored in the man she loved. That was all that mattered, whoever the woman, whoever the man . . .

They lay side by side in the bed, the warmth of their bodies helping to dispel their nervousness. Brydd remembered Mariette, the girl who had schooled him in the crimson-lit room above the gaming house in Paris. He remembered the other women he'd enjoyed on the way to Vienna and was grateful for what they'd taught him, then found it easy to herd them from his mind.

He turned and gazed down at Vitar. "That's an attractive shift, but you've no need to keep it on, 'less you're cold."

She shook her head in agreement—when better to signify no and mean yes?—and guided his hand to her hem. He raised the garment along her leg and past the swell of her hip, then stopped to lay his hand on her stomach and to cup her breasts, one and the other, the nipples firm within the curve of his palm.

He removed the shift, drawing it over her head, seeing her dark arms raised in surrender. Then he leaned down and kissed her and let his hand again explore her breasts and venture across her stomach and touch the softness of her thighs in the slow, inexorable invasion on which a lover may embark.

Vitar touched him in turn, and traced her fingers along the full dry length of his manhood, delighted that by doing so she made him more urgent, then rising to kiss him and catch him around the neck and plead with him to enter her, wanting to feel the quick pain of it and, when that was done, the pleasure. She was aware that she would never—not for wealth, nor comfort, nor for all the promises the spinning world might make—never would she feel so secure as when the man she loved made his love known to her like this.

They were moaning and gasping for breath, and then Brydd charged against her, not caring for the instant who she was, but only that *he* must be satisfied, clasping her buttocks and her breasts, then with his hands on her thighs, against her face and tangled in her hair, pinning her to the pillow and the bed. He yelled at her and at the wall along which the candlelight crept by. And then he became spasmodic and subsided and began to care again, edging the damp strays of hair from her face.

"Vitar . . ."

"Yes, my love . . . Ah, yes, to our loving . . . To all of it, all of it . . ."

He crept out in the morning and came back with seeded rolls and a jug of black, viscous coffee and a bunch of flowers that had to wait their turn until the jug had been emptied and rinsed clean. Vitar crushed the stems—the way it was done in the Kennett Vale and in Györ—and they retired to bed to eat breakfast. They asked each other, but neither of them could remember when they'd last done that.

Brydd wrote to his parents, via "Doctor Barrowcluffe, His house in Marlborough," and to Sophia and Joseph Biss at Bristol, and to his brother, William, now master of the stonemason's yard at Melksham. He told them all that he had met a young lady, Vitar

Czaky, from the Hungarian city of Györ, and that he was in love
with her—"Both in love, I would say"—and had asked her to
marry him and been accepted.

"She would like the ceremony to be performed in Györ, where
she has lived most of her life, and we shall be going there before
the winter snows set in. There'll be no time for you to reply, so I
ask for your blessing and look forward to the day when I shall
bring my wife to England, when you'll see why I'm perched so
high."

The letters were dispatched in late August, and would reach
their destination sometime in October. But by then Brydd and
Vitar would be on their way, Or, better yet, married and going on
into the world.

❈

Exactly one week after the duel, the time specified by the stone-
bald doctor in Kahlenberg, the young couple rode out to see if Albany Jevington was on the mend.

The doctor met them at the door, diverted them into his office,
then said, "You've missed him by a full two days, Herr Cannaway. He's gone, and left no indication of his route, though he
asked me to hand you this. I'll be about if you need me. If not,
then may I say that Lord Jevington—yes, he did disclose his name
—that he was the most charming patient I ever strapped up. And,
whatever he may have done to upset the citizens of Vienna, I'd be
firmly inclined to let him off with a warning. He was very per-
suasive, your companion."

Byrdd nodded, took the packet the doctor handed him and
gazed at the doorway as though he might see the heron gangle
by.

The doctor bowed and left. Brydd shrugged at Vitar, opened
the packet and drew out four flat rows of coins, this one a louis
d'or, this one a Spanish pistole, this a Venetian sequin, this a
Bavarian ducat, this a double mark from Bremen, this a rix-dollar
from Hamburg, this a gold florin from Frankfurt, this an English
crown.

Each coin was of considerable value, and there were several
duplicates—forty coins in all. Brydd could only guess at their

collective worth, but a glance was enough to tell him he'd been left a small fortune.

Folded around them was a note.

You brought me to a good man, my dear chap. However, I've heard there are some fellows out looking for me, and I'm inclined to think they're the bunchers, hired to try again. If so, it would not be right to let them visit their wrath on the doctor, so I shall be trotting along.

I know you would not have accepted so much as a kreutzer from me, had I offered it, but you must use this selection to see your way about Europe. It's hard to know what currency to carry these days, with every city minting its own.

Who knows but that we'll meet again, one day? I may even visit the Kennett Vale and put up at the "Blazing Rag." Though I shall expect the landlord to keep a set of dice in the bar.

And now I bid you an affectionate farewell, and remain your forgiven friend, Albany Jevington.

❄

They left the house and rode back in silence to Vienna. There was nothing Brydd could do but hope that the heron had been stitched up tight and would not meet the bunchers on his way. As they neared the ramparts of the city he turned to Vitar and said, "Whatever else we do with the money—"

"—we must first buy the best set of dice we can find."

"And we'll keep them with us, and give them to Sam Gilmore when we see him, and tell him they're only to be rolled by Lord Albany d'Enville-Zurrant-Jevington—"

"—a friend of ours, who might be calling by."

The idea cheered them, imagining the scene.

ELEVEN

Elizabeth Darle was now sixteen and a summer, though whenever she met Jed's ladylove she was made to feel forty, and with the winter of her life set in.

There was no truth to this, and any number of young men asked permission to call at Overhill Farm, or escort her to the village fairs, or lead her in a dance. The blond-haired Elizabeth was one of the prettiest women in the district, tall and slender and with a clear complexion—rare enough when so many disfiguring diseases went unchecked. As a companion she could be unnervingly quiet, though she was quick enough to let braggarts know what she thought of them and deflate those she found conceited or patronising.

All except Clare Halley, the girl Jed Darle had chosen as his bride-to-be.

But Elizabeth believed even that was incorrect: it was Clare who'd done the choosing.

Jed had met the girl in Marlborough early in the year, been much taken by her vivid good looks, then suffered months of torment as she'd blown alternately hot and cold. Elizabeth had seen her brother in tears more than once, counselled him as best she could and had her advice thrown back at her. "What would *you*

know about it?" Jed had raged. "Every man who's ever spent time
with *you* says you watch and listen like some damn cat, then
spring at their slightest mistake! They joke about it, all those
who've escorted you. They say they still bear the scratches!"

"Then they must have been rodents," Elizabeth retorted
calmly, and closed her eyes as Jed yelled, "There, d'you see!
You're as sharp as claws!"

"So you'll not heed my advice, is that it, brother?"

"What, and keep away from Clare? I should say I won't! She's
confused, that's all. She doesn't mean half the things she says, not
the bad ones, and she admits as much whenever we patch our
quarrels. No, I shall go down there and see her again and tell her
how sorry I am. The value of *your* advice is in my never taking
it."

"Sorry for what, Jed? What was the quarrel about this time?"

"Oh, something or other . . . I don't exactly . . ." And then, as
always, he had stamped off and saddled his horse and ridden
across the downs to Marlborough, never knowing why the wind
was blowing cold.

He'd even tried battling with his father, though George Darle
would have none of his outbursts, and merely told him to keep his
love at a distance, if it meant bringing hate into the house. "It's
your business, Jedediah, so you go about it. When it's running
more smoothly I shall be pleased to meet Mistress Halley. Meanwhile, you'll behave yourself or be off."

And then, suddenly, a few weeks ago, the turbulent winds of
the relationship had dropped, and Jed had become overbearingly
patient with his sister. He forgave her for the sharpness of her
comments and said he understood how she felt.

"You do? Well, that's perfect. Then I shall come to you for advice."

He smiled tolerantly and asked his father if he might bring
Clare Halley to the farm. "We've resolved all our problems, and I
know you'll make her welcome. But you will sheath your claws,
won't you, Elizabeth? My sweet Clare is no match for you, none
at all."

"I'll file them to the quick," she assured him, then gazed in disbelief as he wagged a playful, admonishing finger. Good God, she

thought, is this my brother, who's not yet twenty, or some pompous merchant in his middle years? Nevertheless, she nodded dutifully, if only to rid him of his complacent smile, and it was agreed that Clare would visit the farm on Sunday.

That first meeting had set the pattern, and a discouraging one it was. George remained in character, polite and steadfast, determined that his son should find no fault with his manners. He had even pinned a cravat for the occasion and pulled on his best, tight-fitting boots.

Jed was insufferable, nodding along with whatever Clare said, then laughing too soon and too loud. He was obviously besotted by her, his world ending at her fingertips, and he scowled at his sister when he found the chocolate pot empty and Clare fiddling with her cup.

Elizabeth had taken an immediate dislike to the girl, blamed herself for it and made a halfhearted attempt to reform. It was only to be expected that, as Jed's sister, she'd be critical of any girl he chose. They'd lived their lives together, Jed and Elizabeth, and there was no one—no one she'd admit to—for whom she had a deeper affection. He said he understood her, though he did not, but it was true she was prejudiced and difficult to please, and she owed it to him to take a long, fresh look at Clare Halley.

But it made not a scrap of difference. She still disliked the girl, and now not only the sight of her, but the sounds she made.

She was certainly attractive, with brick red hair and imprisoned breasts, startling shallow-river eyes and a mouth that Elizabeth thought generous to the point of philanthropy. Clare had powdered her face, awarded herself a beauty patch and rubbed enough ointment into her hands to make the lifting of her cup a hazardous pastime. She was certainly well gowned, though Elizabeth could see a number of faults in the sewing and an off-colour triangle inset at the waist. Well, no matter. The needle had probably slipped from sweet Clare's lotioned hands.

"It's most kind of you to have invited me out here, Master Darle. I've not been this far into the countryside for years."

"Is that to say you've not been out of Marlborough?" George asked.

"Oh, I'm not from Marlborough. I've only spent this year in that quaint little town. I thought you might have guessed by my voice; I'm from London, do you know of it?"

"We've heard tell it's the capital," Elizabeth murmured. "Is that still the case?"

"I think Clare means do we know of it from a visit," Jed hurried. "I told her we had never been there, but would be delighted to hear stories and—"

"Then, if Mistress Halley already knows we've not been there—"

"I'd quite forgotten, Mistress Darle. I still tend to assume that *everybody* has been to London, if only the once."

"Of course." Elizabeth nodded. "It's the assumption we hold about those who live in Marlborough. Everybody there has ventured into the countryside, at least the once."

"I suppose so, yes. Though one must choose the day carefully. When there's something to see."

There was so much smiling done, it made them ache. George kept out of it, easing his feet in his boots, then surreptitiously fingering the strangle knot of his cravat. Jed accepted that his sister was being difficult, and prayed that she would soon find someone who could sheath her claws, or enjoy being scratched. Clare and Elizabeth smiled and saw each other's way about things, smiled and exchanged compliments, smiled and circled, the mistress of Overhill and her rival come down from the city and out from the quaint little town.

"I'd never have dreamed of asking," Clare murmured, "but I'm so glad you stayed in to greet me, Mistress Darle, Sundays being what they are, so precious to us. I trust your young man will make allowance for it. From the district, is he? The fortunate young man?"

Elizabeth looked at her brother, set her expression to trap him, then asked, "Why are you so secretive with Mistress Halley? Surely you're not ashamed of your family?"

"No. Why should I be? And I've never held secrets from Clare."

"So you must have told her I'm hard to please."

"Oh, don't worry," he laughed, "she knows all about—"

"But you'd quite forgotten," Elizabeth purred at her rival, "is that it? Or was it just a gentle tease, knowing all the time there was no one, no fortunate young man?"

"In fact," Clare smiled, "it was neither. It was simply that you'd not come up in conversation for a while, and I'd supposed that someone had called by. Why not, when you've kept your looks to perfection through the years—"

"And hope to retain them for a short time yet."

"As I'm sure you will. And I'm convinced a man *will* come along to take you out of the house of a Sunday."

"You're adding colour to my dreams, Mistress Halley, though you're far in advance of me."

"With a fine man like Jed here, yes, I confess I am."

"And with your knowledge of city life, coming from London and all."

"I admit, I was glad to live there when I did."

"And with the time God has granted you, far longer than I've enjoyed."

"Oh? Would you say you were younger than I, Mistress Darle? I thought the reverse."

"What's age but numbers, Mistress Halley? You had probably quite forgotten."

❊

Some twenty miles to the west, another man had met a woman who'd taken his fancy, though there was nothing fancy about William Cannaway or the lady he admired.

Now owner of the stoneyard at Melksham, the big, easygoing William had at last found a quarry that could supply most of his needs. He'd overlooked it at first, and it was not until one of his stonecutters had spoken well of the place that William had ridden to the nearby village and down into the deep, terraced pit. He'd looked and listened during that first winding descent, remembering the day when he'd been blown off his feet and deafened by a premature blast.

But there was nothing slipshod about the quarrymaster, Nathan Reed. Within the course of the year they'd become good friends, both solid, shambling men, the breed of Wiltshire, their hands and faces weathered by their work. They were not the type to roar with laughter or pound the table, preferring to smile where others would have howled, their favourite stories going against themselves. They were men in the mould of George Darle, or the landlord Sam Gilmore, or William's father, Ezra Cannaway; quiet man, gentle men, yet men who could see sharp practice at a clear, cold mile, and were rarely taken for fools.

William learned that Nathan had a sister, Margaret, and was invited to dine with them. "Though I warn you, William, she's uncommonly shy. *You'll* have to make the running."

"Then it may be a slow-going evening, though I'll be pleased to attend."

He was still living in his damp two-room house near the yard at Melksham, still taking his meals in the tavern and, more often than not, alone. He was somewhat old to be single, twenty-seven, though in appearance more than ten years on. And it was this that went against him, for the women he met would eventually ask his age, then refuse to believe the truth. If a man looked forty, as did William Cannaway, he could scarcely hope to shed thirteen years and expect his story to be swallowed. The women thought him not only old, but a liar, and a clumsy one at that, and they left him to eat alone.

He wondered what to tell Margaret Reed, if she bothered to ask.

The quarrymaster was right about his sister, she *was* uncommonly shy. But so was Nathan, and so too was William Cannaway, and the three of them stretched the silence deep and wide. They had none of the skills of small talk, none of the easy laughter that could whip the evening along. Instead, they twitched a smile and nodded a comment and ate with the minimum of fuss. And then they repeated what little they'd said, in the hopes of mining something extra from the seams.

Margaret excused herself to the kitchen, and William beckoned to Nathan across the table. "I hope you won't think it presumptuous," he said hesitantly, "my being merely a guest here—"

"Nonsense, man, you're a friend. Say what you will."

"Yes, well, it occurred to me that—that you might wish to check the sheds in the quarry."

"It's all been taken care of," Nathan dismissed. "I checked them before we— Oh, I see. You mean—"

"Just for a while."

"And leave the two of you— Now, that's a damn good idea, William." He raised his head and called toward the kitchen, "There's some things to be seen to in the quarry. I'll not be long. Half the hour." He glanced at William, who nodded his thanks. Then he struggled into his greatcoat, lifted a ring of keys from their hook beside the door, jammed on his hat and was gone.

Margaret returned from the kitchen, almost as though she'd been waiting, and invited William to take a seat at the fire. "He's always in and out, is Nathan, though it's not often he sets time on his ventures. Now, Master Cannaway, all we have to offer is some Portugal sherry. Will you take a glass of that?"

"With pleasure, Mistress Reed. Personally, I have always thought the Portugal better than the Spain." He was not sure why he'd said that, for he was no authority on either, but the gentle Margaret said yes, she too would take the Portugal for preference. She handed him the glass and he came to his feet until she was seated at the other side of the fire. Then he said, "May I commend you on the meal, Mistress Reed? It was one of the best I've— One of the best in years."

"Nathan said you'd have an appetite, being a well-built— Like him. Although the Portugal's all we have, there's plenty of it. It was in settlement of a debt. Do people ever pay you like that?"

"Half the time, it seems. Let me see, what was the last thing, a mule I think it was, and the second day I had it it gave me the very hell of a—" He smiled apologetically.

"Do go on, Master Cannaway. The very hell of a kick?"

True to his word, Nathan roamed his quarry for half the hour, then came back to find his sister giggling quietly at something William had said and William chuckling to see her so amused. They invited Nathan to join them, but he'd practised his yawn to perfection, and bade them an unintelligible good-night. The last thing they needed was company, now that they'd found their own.

❄

Ezra and Amalie were at a loss as to what they should do: keep the news from Elizabeth—but for how long?—or break it to her as gently as possible and hope the pain would ease with time. They talked it over for almost a week, realised that the girl would be down to see them at Kennett in a day or so and decided to tell her the truth. Better she should hear it from them, in the privacy of their home, than from the friend of a friend in the marketplace at Marlborough, or in some barn, swept out for a dance.

However, when Elizabeth next visited the elderly Cannaways it was with news of her own, and bad news at that.

She had already told them about Clare Halley, and how Jed had turned from a distraught and lovelorn swain into a puffed-up toad, all weary patience and wagging fingers. "Well, now we know the reason for it. She's with child, our sweet Clare. My brother has done what he wanted with her, and what *she* wanted, I've no doubt of that. And now they're to be married, after which they will live with us at Overhill." She sighed, attempted a smile that showed its wounds, then said, "I know I should be glad for him, and I am, some of the time. I'm truly fond of my brother, and I daresay I'm more difficult to get along with than ever he was. But what can I say of Clare Hally?

"I don't like her. I don't *trust* her. I believe she has Jed on a leash, and that she did the choosing, *and* the bedding—excuse me, Amalie, but that's what's happened—and I think she could make a list this very moment of everything my father owns at Overhill, and the size of the rooms and where the pastures begin and end."

She smiled again, with a little more success, and said, "You'll regret this visit by the time I've finished. Am I growing bitter, do you think? Is Jed right to say I'm as sharp as claws? I can certainly find faults that were never apparent before, and I lose patience the way others lose pins. Am I jealous of Mistress Halley? I can't believe it. And if Jed proclaims himself in love, then it's not what I understand by the—what I imagine it to be. Anyway, I've complained enough for today. Tell me how you two have been this week. I suppose you've not heard from Brydd, else you'd have mentioned it. Has William been over, perhaps, or Sophia and Joseph? Now *there's* a marriage that could make me jealous. A wife as elegant as Sophia and a husband as amiable—"

"Yes," Ezra muttered, "we have."

"—as Joseph Biss. I could never think of Sophia as being avaricious or— Master Cannaway?"

"We have heard from him. From Brydd." He said nothing more, and both he and Amalie knew they would have to share the burden of it, passing it back and forth. It was too much for them to carry alone, and neither wished to be singled out by Elizabeth's haunting gaze.

"And he's well?"

"Oh, yes," Amalie told her, "so he says. And he's met all kinds of people."

"You can imagine," Ezra told her, "in a city the size of Vienna, maybe ten times larger than Marlborough. And he's been to all kinds of gatherings. And I suppose it was there he met Vitar."

"Vitar? That's an odd name. Is that a man's name, or—?"

"It's a girl," Amalie told her. "A young woman from a place called Györ, somewhere in Hungary. They've been friends for quite a while, so he says."

"Aye, and they seem to have grown close," Ezra told her, "during the months. Brydd and Vitar."

"And he talks of getting married," Amalie told her, "though who's to know how serious he is, an impetuous fellow like Brydd? It's most likely the sort of thing that's said and then—"

"But he's not impetuous, not really. He wouldn't say—that— not unless it was true." Elizabeth kept talking, and all the time the tears were brimming and spilling over and she was reminding them that she had always loved him, though that was not the only reason she visited them, they mustn't think so, no, but she had loved him, and still did of course and, although life was filled with coincidence, it was rather odd, wasn't it, that Jed should be marrying Mistress Halley whilst, far away in Vienna, Brydd had spoken of the some thing, of marriage, no less, to this—this Vitar . . .

"I knew he'd have to go there, he spoke of nothing else after seeing that coach, but I never believed he'd go so far as to get married, really I didn't, no, not so far as that . . ."

She found her way to the door, then turned and screamed at them, not blaming them because Brydd Cannaway was their son, nor for having let him go from the valley; not blaming them for anything, but wanting to tell them, and through them, perhaps, tell Brydd, that all was not yet lost.

"I can prevent this, you know! I can nudge the devil and have it stopped! I know where he sleeps and how to raise him! You know it too, and it's worked for others, and they were less determined than I! He'll stir for me, *you see if he does not!*" Her face was distorted, her eyes wide and swollen, the frame of hair caught in tendrils by her tears. Then she twisted away, leaving the door to swing shut and the elderly couple to gaze at each other and wonder if the devil could be aroused. He very well might, with Elizabeth offering herself as his prey.

❊

The time to do it was now, before fear hobbled her steps. Now was when the devil would listen and scratch his scabrous body and churn in his lair. If he chose to respond, he would claw his way to the surface, black froth around his mouth, his breath like poisonous steam. His emergence would ensure that the girl's wish was granted, though that was only half the compact, for he would then stalk her, or hunch in wait, his scales overlapping tighter and tighter until he seemed no larger than a huddled boar. A scented liquid would run from ducts in his neck, masking the foetid stench of his body, and he would still his breathing to nothing, the poisonous vapours giving way to the trickling scent of flower and hedgerow. And then he would be as part of the ground itself, with only the redness of his eyes showing like fresh stabbed knife wounds in the horror of his face.

He would take her if he could and drag her down beneath the earth, then do what he wanted with her, then devour her, skin and hair and bone. That was the other half of the compact, if one chose to seek help from the devil.

It was evening when Elizabeth left the Cannaways and turned westward along the coaching road, toward Beckhampton and the "Blazing Rag." But there was to be no welcome from Sam Gilmore today, for she had set her sights on the hill that stood between the two villages, the ancient pagan hill of Silbury. More than a hundred and twenty feet high, the vast cone of earth loomed above the northern edge of the road, its presence and purpose unexplained.

There were those who thought it the burial mound of chieftains, and had dug into it and found nothing. There were those who had scrambled up the escarpment, among them King Charles II and his brother, the future King James II, attended by the writer and naturalist, John Aubrey. They'd found snails at the top, and Aubrey had pocketed a few for later investigation. And then one of the royal guards had mentioned the devil who lived in the base of the hill, and that the weight of earth was there to keep him down. King Charles and his brother had laughed about it until their laughter withered, then skidded down the slope, pretending it was a race to the bottom.

The locals had never doubted that the devil was there, and the sight of King Charles and his brother going down on their backsides had only served to confirm their belief. It was not the only devil in the country, but the one allotted to Wiltshire, the Devil of Silbury Hill.

The devil to whom Elizabeth Darle must appeal.

And this was his lair, the grass-covered cone around which she must run, not once, nor twice, but five times without pause. There was no indication of where the devil would emerge, though there were plenty who claimed to have seen him, several who'd made the run and gone mad, others who'd set out for the hill, never to be seen again.

The mound was encircled by a ditch, thirty feet deep, and Elizabeth walked along the verge, peering down for signs of—what? Claw marks? Poisoned bracken? A place where the earth had been disturbed?

She could no longer see the road, her view blocked by the hill. There were flecks of grey in the sky now, and the numbness of fear was already slowing her steps. She must descend, or desert the field, knowing she would never find the courage to return.

She scrambled over the lip and ran, windmilling, to the bed of the ditch.

She sensed the ground shift underfoot. No, not yet, surely not. He'd wait until he'd heard her make her wish.

She wrapped her mantle around her, knelt in the dampness and whispered at the ground. It was not a curse against Vitar, nor yet a prayer, for Elizabeth would not pray to the devil, not even for this. It was simply a hurried, trembling plea that the man she loved might never marry this other girl, but would one day return to the Kennett Vale, his heart his own.

And then she began to run.

The first circuit was easy, though the light was fading. She could not tell how long it took, five minutes, maybe more, but she ran it well, keeping to the base of the hill, dodging the thorns and bracken as they appeared.

The sky was ageing fast, with more grey in it now.

She forced herself to count as she ran, numbers at first, then the contents of the kitchen at Overhill Farm, then the names of those she knew, had met, had heard of. She completed the second circuit and felt a sudden chill of fear, not because the earth had been disturbed, not yet, but because she had failed to gauge the distance and was already short of breath.

The ditch was filling with shadows.

She tried to vault a low thornbush, snagged the toe of a shoe and came down heavily, wincing with pain. She'd not broken the shoe or twisted her ankle, but there were specks of blood on her hands where she'd fallen against other strands of briars. And with that came the thought— *Can he smell blood?*

She stumbled around the hill to where she'd started, bent forward to catch her breath—*but keep moving, keep moving, it must be done without pause*—then plunged forward again, aware that the ditch was now flooded by the dark.

And it was then that the terror took hold, for the devil had had enough time to dig his way clear, and yet there were still two circuits of the hill to complete, and she could no longer see which were the bushes, which the snare of his claws.

She made her way around the eastern curve, and the southern, and most of the west. Then she imagined she saw him and cried out and kicked with her shoes—as though her puny efforts could ever keep the devil at bay. She had heard such vile things about him, such indescribable things, those things he would most enjoy. But she was no longer protected by the counting of cutlery, the

listing of those in the Kennett Vale. It was too dark, too long
since he'd been alerted, exactly the time he would choose in
which to emerge from hiding and rise up, not at all like a wild
boar, but as something—yes, vile and indescribable—standing
twice the height of a man. He'd had long enough, and it was his
time now.

She recognised a hump on the verge of the ditch, just darker
than the sky, and set out on the last, long round.

She was blind to the route, weaving erratically across the bed of
the ditch, her mantle torn by the briars. And then, when the garment had been shredded, her stockings were torn, and her legs.

She felt the ground move, and there was no doubt about it this
time, it *was* moving . . .

She edged against the outer bank, not yet prepared to cringe or
cower, but with her fists curled tight, her pale hair tangled across
her face. She could *feel* the trembling underfoot . . .

And then, ahead of her, she could see the limpid yellow eyes,
winking, then closed, then wide open and staring. They were not
the blood-red slits she'd expected, but they drained the strength
from her, and she felt the numbness scatter through her body.

She saw what it was, this monster, and ran toward it, dashing
after it as the rumble of the coach and its winking lanterns swept
past on the way toward Beckhampton. They lit the upper slopes
of the hill, but that was enough to encourage her, and she staggered in pursuit, rounding the southern curve before the last yellow smudge had vanished. And then there was only half the circuit to complete and she trudged forward, pulling aside the
brambles and daring the devil to catch her when he had so far
failed. She'd seen her father lay bets on the dogs and the hares
and the horses, and if the devil couldn't catch her in four clear
rounds—and the half she'd just completed—what chance that
he'd catch her now?

She was no longer running, but forcing her way along the
ditch and mouthing over and over to herself the name of the man
she loved, the man for whom she had dared arouse the Devil of
Silbury Hill.

She was sure she'd completed the circuit, and so all five of
them, and kept her part of the bargain. Nevertheless, she went on

for a few more yards, in case the devil had moved the bushes in a final attempt to mislead her. Then she stumbled away from the hill and across the ditch and started the thirty-foot climb to the rim. *Is it over yet? Or will he cheat and drag me down, if he can? What a question, will the devil cheat!*

But at last the ground fell away in front of her and she crawled from the verge. Her clothes were in tatters, her arms and legs scratched by the thorns, her hands pricked and swollen, her face smeared with blood, her pale hair lank and entangled—no longer an appetising sight, even for the devil.

She pushed herself to her feet. And then, because she was Elizabeth Darle, she did not immediately run onward, but turned and looked down into the night-filled ditch. She swayed there for a moment, almost daring him to come after her, then nodded slowly, in triumph, and began the three-mile walk across the downs to Overhill Farm.

❄

George had already hooked lanthorns on the fence, stringing his property with light so that his children might see them and be guided home.

Fortunately, perhaps, Jed had not yet returned from Marlborough, where he'd spent the day with Clare Halley and her parents. They were a lazy, sharp-eyed couple who'd failed as grocers in London, and now seemed set to fail in the wool-town.

They'd shown sympathy toward Jed during the first stormy months of his relationship with their daughter, and there'd been much talk of clearer skies ahead. They'd learned that Jed would one day inherit Overhill, and that there was no one to challenge the inheritance. They'd also learned about Elizabeth and her touchy ways, and nodded in solemn agreement as Jed voiced the hope that she would soon find someone, anyone, and make a life for herself beyond the farm.

Then Clare had announced she was pregnant, and her parents had clucked and tutted at Jed, inquiring as to his intentions in the matter. He'd told them he wished to marry their daughter, and the tutting had stopped. There'd been talk of the hot-blooded ways of young lovers and how, if the truth be known, half the children in the world were, well, need they say more? They'd been wonderfully understanding, Master Halley and his wife, and they saw no reason to tell Jed Darle that the family had already discussed the likelihood of Clare becoming pregnant . . .

They knew a hundred ways to flatter the young farmer, and he stayed late at Marlborough, as taken in by them as washing from a line.

So only George was at home when Elizabeth returned.

The realisation of what she'd done had now caught up with her and she was shivering uncontrollably, rattling the door-catch, then letting the door itself slam back against the wall. Her father had been out twice to look for her and was, at this moment, adding oil to a lantern. There was not much that could shake George Darle, but the sight of his daughter sent the black oil slopping on the table.

He came toward her and caught her in his arms and let her loll against him, gazing past her at the open doorway, half expecting her assailant to appear. "That's it," he growled gently, "you're all right now, Beth, it's all right now. You've been followed along, have you? Well, don't you worry, they'll not be coming in. Here, I'll close the door, that's the way. That's it, my Beth, now you'll be fine as lace, you will. You'd best sit in my chair, it was always the most comfortable, I made sure of that. There, now. You've got some good wood around you, and a big old man in their way." He looked at the web of cuts and scratches on her arms, the thorn pricks in her hands, the gown and mantle ripped by briars and still festooned with pieces of the stem.

He warmed some cider and gave it to her, found a clean cloth and dipped it in the pan of water that simmered day and night on the range. He growled on, calming her, telling her she was safe, and never moving too far away, lest she thought herself alone.

They were there for an hour, the two of them, and although he never pressed her to speak, she eventually told him that Brydd Cannaway was to marry a foreign girl named Vitar, and that she'd done what she could to prevent it by going around the hill.

"Did he see you?"

"The devil?"

"Aye."

"I think so, yes. I think he snatched at me once, but I got away unmarked."

"And you made the rounds?"

"All five. And a few steps more, to be certain."

"Well, well, Beth, if you're not a girl to be prized . . ."

"Then you'll not be angry about it? I never prayed to the devil, I didn't do that."

"I'm sure you didn't. And no, I'll not be angry. I just hope the scratches heal quick, that's all, else I can see the young Cannaway lifted up from wherever he is in Vienna and dumped on his arse in the yard here, and all before you're ready to greet him! Ah, that's better, a bit of a smile."

※

There were, as yet, no signs of demonic possession in the room above the Bäckerstrasse, though the place *was* in an unholy mess. But this was only to be expected, since Brydd and Vitar would be leaving in the morning for Györ.

He had already purchased a sturdy gig, complete with an iron-framed baggage net, then collected Vitar and her belongings from the *Gasthaus*. The matron had been sorry to see the young foreigners depart, though she'd bubbled with delight when Brydd presented her with an armload of flowers—flowers for her, at last, and not the fortunate Fräulein Czaky.

And now they were back in the room, the floor littered with Brydd's valise and sailcloth tool bag, two bulging satchels, a column of books strapped around with a leather belt, an assortment of shoes and boots, a half-empty bottle of brandy. His hat and thornproof suit were draped across the bed, the table still covered with pens and chalks, corked jars of ink, a box of sand and a foot-high stack of drawings. He nodded grimly at them and said, "I should have bought a third satchel."

"No," Vitar corrected, "you should have bought a sea chest."

In fact, he'd bought very little during his time in Vienna, beyond the requirements of his work. But there was one thing he *had* bought—the first, as he'd promised—with the money Albany Jevington had left him. This was a set of perfectly balanced ivory dice, each engraved with the image of a palace, a musket, a mitre, a wig, a coronet and a crown—the markings of the heron's favourite game, *Locataires*. The six dice were cushioned in a velvet-lined box, its crimson leather lid inscribed, so as not to embarrass him, A.d'E.Z.J. Even so, when Brydd handed the box to Sam Gilmore, as he hoped one day to do, there'd be a few eyebrows raised in the bar of the "Blazing Rag."

"Looks like a word in itself; that it does. Couldn't your friend 'ave been satisfied with just the two names, same as the rest of us? I'd not want more than the two, myself, lest I forgot what the others were!"

The box was in a pocket of Brydd's greatcoat, and he left it there, more concerned to find space for his sketches and charcoals. His work, after all, was more important than the heron's game . . .

Eventually it was finished, and they went to bed and made love as though this was to be the last time, after which they'd be parted. But it was not that they feared being parted from each other. It was the knowledge that they would now be parted from the city, from these few streets, the Bäckerstrasse and the Wollzeile, and from the people they'd met there, and from the taverns in which they'd spent the hours they'd not spent walking, or in the street-noisy room above the arch. They were clinging to each other, and that was the best of it. But they were also clinging to the city in which Brydd had worked and made a name for himself, the city in which they had learned about each other and, in their own time, come to call it love. They would remember Vienna-on-the-Danube with affection, and hold it up as an example to the other cities they visited, in the days beyond Györ.

And then they awoke and stirred and saw the windows pale to grey. They sat on opposite sides of the bed to pull on their shifts, Vitar her simple travelling gown, Brydd his breeches and waistcoat, Vitar her stockings and shoes, Brydd his well-waxed boots.

There was no one to see them—not that they'd have cared— and they stood for a moment in the open doorway, Brydd bowing with gratitude to the first proper room he'd ever had, whilst Vitar also nodded her thanks. Then they collected the satchels and cases, books and sword stick and other belongings and Brydd flinted a lantern to light the way downstairs. He'd shaved the previous evening, and that would have to do until he found an innkeeper who'd supply a basin of hot water, but not charge the price of mulled wine.

There were, as yet, no signs of the devil's handiwork. And how would he know where to look once they'd left the confines of the city?

❊

Brydd took the gig south, then eastward, skirting wide of the Marchfeld. They were both aware of the flat, desolate expanse in which Janos and Katya Czaky had been murdered, but they were determined to ignore it, for the past was past, whilst the future unrolled ahead of them, bleak though it appeared in the early October light.

They kept warm with blankets and scarves and an occasional sip of brandy. A few hours more and the winter sun was turning the dull grey sky to gold.

"Which reminds me," Brydd said, "I've yet to buy you a ring."

"And I for you, my love."

"Is that the custom?"

"Does it worry you?"

"Not at all. It's an attractive idea, the exchange of rings."

"And a practical one," she grinned. "All the pretty young women you meet will know you for a husband, and reserve their glances."

"So they will," he said. Then, after a moment, as though the subject had been changed, "There is something else I must buy."

"Hmm?"

"Gloves. For every occasion."

❊

They reached the border, shared their brandy with the Austrian customs official and were waved onward into Hungary. Almost immediately they were stopped again, though just long enough for the Hungarian customs official to upend the bottle, slap his chest and welcome them to his country. Brydd remembered the shed at

Calais and wondered how the *douaniers* would have reacted if he'd offered *them* the bottle. Most likely they'd have broken it over his head.

They crossed a number of rivers, some by bridge, others by ferry. They forded several of the shallower streams and a few that were no longer shallow and would soon be impassable. "It's the eastern shoulder of the Alps," Vitar said knowledgeably. "The rain spills down from there. Another few weeks, a few days if there've been storms in the mountains, and the way back to Vienna will be closed until spring. You'd best jump out now, if you've a mind to. It'll save you buying all those gloves."

They were poled across the Fischa and stayed the first night in the riverside village of Fischamend, where the happily inquisitive landlord soon discovered that they were on their way to Györ, to be married. He gave orders to the maidservant, and bricks were lifted from the oven and dropped into slings and carried to their bed, to heat it for the lovers. Meanwhile, Vitar was plied with herbal biscuits and Brydd taken aside to gulp a thick, colourless liquid—very good, he was assured, for a man. He asked what was in it, and the question was flagged aside. But he insisted on knowing, so the landlord showed him a shelf along which were ranged a dozen bottles, each containing a fully grown snake.

"We catch them, then push them into the flasks. They are still alive, and so naturally they seek the way out. We wait until they raise their heads through the neck of the bottle and then—" He produced an invisible cord, made an invisible loop in it and went through the motions of strangling an invisible snake. "After that they drop back and we pour in the fermented juice of plums and other fruits, and their venom mingles with it and—as I say, sir, very good for a man." He gestured cheerfully with fist and forearm. Brydd nodded, and felt his stomach churn.

The landlord might well have been right, though neither Brydd Cannaway nor Vitar Czaky were in need of herbal biscuits or the venomous liqueur.

❋

Next morning they continued eastward, again rattling across some of the rivers and splashing through others. Brydd guided the vehi-

cle along one of the rickety bridges, and Vitar asked if she could
take the reins for a while, through the next stretch of woods. He
passed them to her, watched as she urged the horses up the steep
path from the river, then grunted as she dared a narrow passage
between two fallen branches and made it without a jolt.

"Is that the best you can offer, a wordless grunt?"

He shrugged equably. "I could say you drive well. I could say
you have a good, anticipating grasp of the reins and a nice eye for
the width of the cart. I could admit I'd not have done better myself. Shall I say all that, or will you be content with a grunt, as
one driver to another?"

She smiled with delight and clicked the horse on through the
leafless woods.

They reached the brow of the hill and then a wide avenue, cut
through the trees to the south. At the far end of the swathe and
arresting in its isolation stood a gaunt mediaeval castle, the slates
fallen from its turrets, the battlements crumbled, its towers like
rotted teeth. But the gloomy entrance was still intact, perhaps
concealing a fanged portcullis that would one day, without warning, slide down from the vaulted roof. One could imagine things
living there that were not quite human.

"God, what a sinister place," Brydd murmured. "But why do
the foresters keep the trees cut back? Surely not for the view?"

"It may not be them," Vitar said, then pointed dramatically at
the castle. "It may be done from *there!* By werewolves or vam-
pires! Maybe *they* keep the avenue clear, to have *us* in view!" She
shuddered, enjoying her invented fears, then flicked the reins and
sent the horse on down the long shadowed slope. "Watch out for
them, my love. Listen for their baying, or the rattle of their
wings!"

Half amused, yet disquieted by the mention of werewolves,
Brydd turned and looked back.

The horse trampled fast down the hill.

And then Vitar was shouting again, no longer inventing horrors
from which to flee, but with an urgency that was real. Brydd
swung forward on the bench and they saw together that a few dis-
creet boards had been nailed to the trees. The meaning of the
signs was lost on him—*Arviz! Az ut jarhatatlan! Lassan! Behajtani*

tilos!—but he understood what she was shouting. "It's in flood!
Impassable! That one, it says Slow! And those, Stop! Stop! Stop!
But it's too steep, it's—Brydd!"

The horse stampeded from the trees and across a riverside track
and into the river. Churning and splashing, it streamed across
their path, and there was just time enough to see that it was wide
and angry, too wide and too angry to let them pass. And then, although Brydd had the reins and they were cutting into his hands,
there was nothing to be done. The animal was immediately swept
away to the north, toward the Danube, to be drowned. The shafts
of the gig twisted and snapped. The vehicle rocked forward, came
level again with the weight of baggage, then flipped backward, its
wheels already splintered by the stones and the undertow. Vitar
was thrown sideways with the swirl of the river, Brydd sent
crashing on to the cases and into the water, the gig coming down
on top of him. He felt the edge of something thud against his
skull, and then he was being pressed down and held there, his
back flayed by the stones of the bed.

He suddenly thought of the day Abram Hach had cornered him
in the hut, long ago, but now startlingly clear, and how the
labourer had pounded him—"You're done in, chalker, you're done
in, my friend"—the monster's knuckles thudding like this against
his skull. A strange, random thought, but enough to make Brydd
resist the sinking vessel and find the sense to urge it ahead of him,
downstream. Then he tore himself free and clawed his way upward, convinced that the river was a hundred feet deep and that
his strength would leak into the water, like the venom from a
snake.

He broke surface, spat and coughed, then sucked air from the
sky as though to draw down the clouds. He croaked Vitar's name,
and twisted left and right for a glimpse of her, but there was no
hand or head to be seen.

He was carried along, not knowing how to swim, yet still power-
ful enough to stay afloat. He'd been close to panic on the
riverbed, but he'd seen dogs paddle across the Kennett and he
imitated them, discovering that, for a while at least, he could keep
his head above water. Taken on by the current, he passed the

wallowing gig, upside down and with its spokes and wheel strakes broken. There was still no sign of Vitar.

He saw the water bubbling ahead of him and was dragged under before he could take breath. Once again he struggled upward, but now his strength was truly leaking away. His clothes were like sponges, the water sluicing through his nostrils and down into his throat. His ears were blocked and dinning, his eyes swollen, his mouth taking in more river than sky. He no longer paddled, but thrashed like a snap-winged bird, then rolled exhausted, each respite longer than the last. His limbs were numbed by the coldness of the river and he acknowledged that he was drowning, and was surprised that the determination he'd shown in life could be so quickly turned to lethargy, to a deadening weariness in which he became cold and heavy, not even incensed by the loss of the woman . . . the woman, and all his possessions . . . all his sketches and drawings, his measured inventions . . . all the work he'd ever done . . . his sketches and . . . all his work . . . and the woman . . .

His face was scratched and torn, and he thought Hach had struck him again and used the last of his strength in a feeble retaliatory blow. He spiked his hands on broken reeds, felt mud squelch beneath him, touched a slippery root with his fingers, then caught it and clung to it and found there was something in him beyond mere strength—a final, God-given burst of energy that the desperate and the dying may use.

Not much, and not for long. But enough to take hold of the root and draw forward against it, a crab come ashore for the night.

And all the while the river swirled past, taking the gig on toward the Danube and scattering the bed with cases and satchels, books and clothes and whatever else it judged too heavy to be carried . . .

※

He coughed, arched his back involuntarily and vomited a mass of brackish water. Then he coughed up more of it and fought for breath, convinced that he still might drown.

He was festooned with slime and riverweed, his back skinned and bloody from its initial flaying, his hands torn by the edges of the reeds. He did not know how far he'd been swept downriver, but the memory of what had happened came flapping back to its perch, to caw a reminder.

Brydd dragged himself to his knees, rocked back and howled her name. "Vitar!"

Then, stumbling to his feet, he howled it louder, the word ringing across the damp river stems. "Vi-tar . . ."

And a final time, though he feared that it was anyway too late. "*Vitar Czaky* . . ."

The words echoed among the trees and were caught by the rushes and came back to him from the far side of the river. Then they fell away, or were carried along on the water, light enough to be borne to the Danube, where they'd be taken eastward, past the city of Györ . . .

He waited, stooped over, until he felt strong enough to move. Then he waded back into the river and sluiced the mud from his face, returning to the bank and wondering where best to start his search, upriver or down. His breath was ugly and rasping, water still trickling from his mouth.

He went north, following the current. There was no riverside path, and he was once again forced into the water, battling his way through the reeds and past the straddled roots of the trees. He fell against the bank, went on and fell again, seeing nothing but the flotsam brushed from the shoulder of the Alps.

What little strength had returned was already threadbare, and this time when he fell he lay still, gone in the fabric and the seams. His boots were swollen and filled with mud, half the coins washed from his money belt, the set of dice undisturbed in his pocket, though with the gold inscription curling from the leather and the velvet running to dye.

And that was all there was of him now. That and the soundless crying of his fears.

❊

Without a murmur of regret for their lost day's fishing, the two men laid aside their rods and nets, touched the body to see if its owner was alive, then nodded at the movement of a hand. They asked no questions, but abandoned their equipment and carried him a mile upstream to where a group of men and women were standing in silence around a cart. The back of the cart was filled with hay and covered by a blanket, the body of Vitar Czaky laid out on the coverlet, her gown arranged and her dark hair combed, a spray of wild flowers tucked beneath her hands.

The fishermen helped Brydd to his feet, then nodded as he shrugged them away. Someone asked quietly, first in Hungarian, then in German, "Was it you who called out?" and Brydd gazed down at the woman who'd known the secrets of their happiness and said, "Yes. Do you think she might have heard?"

"There was a breath in her when we found her. For a while."

"Then I'm bound to believe she heard me. Am I not?" He gripped the edge of the cart and looked down at her until her face and hair and the colours of the flowers and gown became blurred. Then the fishermen came forward to catch him.

❋

He awoke to find he'd been stripped of his boots and clothes and money belt—though not for profit, not in this impoverished village. His belongings had been put where he could see them, his clothes scrubbed and left to dry in front of the fire, his boots pulled down on a shaping post, the belt and dice on a table, well within reach.

He'd been washed and shaved, dressed in a woollen shift, then put to bed with the fire for warmth and a lantern left glowing on a shelf.

He realised immediately that he had lost the will to speak. He could move, sit up in bed, lift back the goose-down quilt. He could remember the sequence of events, the gig overturning and the pounding of the river, and how he'd been washed ashore and then discovered and carried to the cart. He understood that Vitar Czaky was dead, but there was no need to speak of it, nor of anything else in the world.

His injuries had been swabbed, and a dark green powder sprinkled on the cuts. He was grateful to the fishermen for what they'd done, and to the villagers who'd respected Vitar's body, and to

those who had taken him in. But he had no wish to address them.
He shook his head and thought to say, "None at all," but his lips
moved in silence and he knew then that he'd lost both the will
and the power of speech.

He pulled on his clothes, took the remaining coins from his belt
and the dice from their case, then threw the ruined leather on the
fire. He was still enough of a countryman to know that the villagers would not accept payment for their kindness, but he turned
down the lantern, to conserve its oil.

He'd slept half a day since the accident, and all the following
night. It was now morning, and he was made to sit near the door
of the cottage and drink a strange, fortifying brew. The woman
who served him was joined by her husband, and Brydd guessed by
the smothered yawns that they'd taken it in turn to stay awake
throughout the night. They asked him nothing, and he did not
utter a word.

Then the husband led him to a barn, where he found two more
women seated beside the cart. They collected the wool they'd
been carding through the long dark hours and edged their way
out. The husband indicated that the cart was his, accepting the
coins Brydd gave him as payment for the vehicle and a horse. The
man waited to see if he'd be needed to harness the animal, then
bowed and clenched his fist and held it out for Brydd to rap in
the custom of the district. And then he, too, left the foreigners
alone.

✳

Brydd took the cart eastward, in the direction of Györ, guiding his
woman home as he had promised. He changed horses in the evening, but saw no reason to stop. Seemingly unaware that it was
winter, he continued on toward the city, feeding the horse in the
dark, then climbing aboard the bench again, content to be drawing nearer to her home. He never spoke aloud, though he believed
he was speaking, and that Vitar was speaking, the two of them
discussing the things they'd seen and done, laughing at this occur-
rence, infuriated by that. It did not seem at all strange to him
that he was a tongue-tied man and she a drowned woman, not

whilst he could still hear the sound of her voice and be made to smile by the memory of her laugh.

A day and a night and a day, and he crossed the Rabnitz River and turned north into the fortified city of Györ. He knew nothing of the language, but recognised the streets from the way she'd described them. He noted this as one of her father's buildings, and those towers, and that long, corrugated wall. It was just as Vitar had said—Janos had made the city his own—and Brydd felt a strange welling of pride and respect, as the maker of coaches for the architect of such fine buildings, as the man who'd have been his son-in-law, had Janos and Vitar survived.

He drew up at the steps of the church; *their* church, when the family had lived in Györ. It was late afternoon, and the stocky, thick-girthed priest was on the steps, bidding good-bye to some elderly women. He glanced at Brydd, smiled at the ladies, then escorted them down the steps. They hobbled off along the street and he returned to pass the cart. When he spoke it was in his own language, but the gruff meaning was clear—Are you lost, sir? Can I be of help? Then, thinking of markets and where the driver might be headed, he glanced down and saw Vitar's body and knew immediately who she was.

His show of recognition was enough for Brydd, who clambered from the bench, gazed across at the priest for a moment, then quite simply walked away. He left behind him half the coins he possessed, sufficient for a hundred burials, a thousand choristers, a hundred thousand flowers.

And he kept walking, out of the city and back across the Rabnitz River and westward now, knowing the way must eventually lead to England and Wiltshire and Kennett, however long it might take . . .

PART FOUR

ELIZABETH

1700–1701

TWELVE

The winter had come mild-mannered at this, the end of the century, causing less disruption than many a summer storm. The coaching road had been blocked by snow near Chippenham, and the downs encrusted, though the weather had turned suddenly warm in January, as though determined to start the new century aright. A drying wind had then hardened the mud on the tracks and in the farmyards, and the inhabitants of the valley accepted that winter was over.

Suspicious of their good fortune, they'd waited to see if the slates and thatching would fly with the spring.

But the gales had been infrequent and short-lived, the rain content to water the crops, then drain obediently into the river. Colour had come to the fields and downs and hedgerows, to the kitchen gardens and the banks of the Kennett, and the worst the villagers could expect was a long, scorching summer.

It was now the first week of April, Easter week, and a lazy afternoon in the valley. The wheelwright's yard at Lockeridge was deserted, Alfred Nott and his wife in their cottage near the gate, the craftsman John Stallard visiting relatives in Pewsey. The young apprentice Alfred had taken on was in Marlborough, enjoying himself at the Eastertide Fair, whilst the labourer Abram

Hach was—well, no one was ever sure of Hach's destination, though it might have been a magic cave in the hillside, its walls lined with bottles of gin.

Although it was a holiday—and there were few enough of those in the year—the elderly wheelwright was once again wrestling with pen and ink and ledger, bending the nib and spilling the ink and tearing yet another ruined page from the book. "The damn thing'll drive me mad, it will! How many times have I said it? I can *remember* what's loss and what's profit, what we're owed and who owes it, those who've paid up and those who— Just ask me, Mary. Name a name, then bet a penny I can't remember how he stands with us."

His wife smiled at him from the kitchen, seeing her gentle husband hunched at his desk in the tiny end room, the pages crumpled at his feet. "Very well, Alfred, why not leave it for today? Come and talk to me while I finish the baking."

He was out of the room with the alacrity of a schoolboy from class, his hands rusty with the colour of the ink. He scrubbed them at the pump, left the cottage door open and lowered himself into his deep wing chair. He was still there an hour later, discussing the things they'd do that year, when he saw Abram Hach zigzag his way unsteadily across the yard.

Alfred noticed that the labourer was carrying three bottles of gin, each equivalent to a lost day's work. "By God," he muttered, "I'd like to know where he gets it. And what he does to earn it, when there's next to nothing he can do." He turned away to light a taper at the fire, and was drawing on his pipe as Mary glanced out through the doorway. She saw Hach stumble; fail to correct his balance and go down with a crash, at least one of the bottles splintering on the ground. There were few people Mary Nott had ever disliked in life, fewer still for whom she felt an abiding disgust; but the drunken, work-shy Hach was one of them. Yet she now heard herself say, "He's fallen, Alfred, and may have cut himself on the glass. Perhaps you should see to him."

"If he could only manage to cut his throat," Alfred said sourly, then went out to do what he could.

He passed the sawpit then called to the labourer, waiting for the man to balance himself on his hands and knees, like a massive, lank-haired dog. The ground sparkled with shards of glass. There were two bottles smashed, not one, and Alfred peered down at them, realising immediately that not all of it was glass . . .

The late afternoon sun was also reflected from a gold watch, *two* gold watches, and from several cravat pins and a shoe buckle, another, four of them, and a lady's brooch and a thin silver necklace; a mass of jewellery, most of it wet with gin.

The wheelwright then knew what Hach had been up to all these years, and guessed that whatever was scattered here, on the ground, was but a fraction of the man's accumulated wealth. "Where did you get the trinkets?" he demanded. "From the Cherhill gang? Is that it, Abram? Are you their spy in the valley, meeting them by arrangement to tell them when there are passengers staying over at the 'Blazing Rag'? A short walk to the foot of the Cherhill slope and a few words of warning, so they'll know who's coming along? Is that the way of it, Abram? A nod from you, and a supply of gin from the highwaymen? And a share of the trinkets, eh, taken from those they catch? It fits like a dovetail, though I'll admit I was fooled until now. But now I can see it, now I can see you crouched in the inn, then slinking out to meet the brigands to tell them who's stopped by. *You're* the one, Abram Hach. And as much the murderer as they."

But by then the labourer was on his feet and with the last, unbroken bottle in his hand.

❀

It was as lazy an afternoon in Kennett, and a family reunion at the smithy. There was now a welcome addition to the Cannaway family, for the unworldly William had found the courage to tell his friend, the quarrymaster Nathan Reed, that he'd be asking for the hand of Nathan's sister, Margaret. "If you've no strong objections."

"None where you're concerned," Nathan assured him, "though it'll mean my finding someone else to cook and keep house for me. I don't know what I'll do about that."

"You might marry," William said helpfully. "You're a well-set man. There's bound to be somebody who'll have you."

"Aye, somebody might, I suppose. If they don't expect too much from me in the way of talk." He frowned at the struggles that lay ahead of him, then decided he was being selfish and said, "You go on and ask her, William. I know for a fact she'll marry you; she's already told me so." Returning to his own problems, he mused, "There *is* a woman, lives on the outskirts of Devizes. Maybe I'll ride over there one day. When I've thought up something to say."

"Say anything," William grinned. "It all leads on."

For William and Margaret it had led to marriage and a new house he'd had built near his stoneyard at Melksham. Ezra and Amalie had made the sixteen-mile journey to attend the wedding —the first time either of them had ever left the Kennett Vale. They'd thought Melksham attractive enough, in its way, and had admired the newlyweds' house, as durable as William himself. But they were quite content to return home and remain in the valley for the rest of their days. Why look around corners if one is no longer curious?

And now they were at the smithy for Easter; Ezra and Amalie, William and Margaret, Sophia and Joseph Biss. Nathan Reed was there, and, a fugitive from Overhill Farm, the unhappy Elizabeth Darle.

Amalie Cannaway was delighted with her daughter-in-law, Margaret thrilled at the way she'd been accepted by the family. The two women were deep in conversation near the range.

"I used to prepare a concoction," Amalie said, "oh, many years ago, of course. A mixture of thyme and sage, rosemary and marjoram, and some wine I'd steal from my father's cupboard. It was called The Queen of Persia's Fountain, and I used to wash in it whenever the moon was at its rind. It was supposed to keep me both beautiful and healthy, though the recipe said nothing about getting caught by one's father for tipping off his wine." She smiled at the memory, and they went on to discuss the merits of this cosmetic, the extravagant claims of that. Neither of them could remember when they'd last indulged in such a welcome, frivolous chat. Not for months, that was certain, and perhaps not for years.

In the yard at Lockeridge, it was over before Mary had time to move. Alfred had started toward her, foolishly turning his back on Abram Hach, and the labourer had swung the bottle across and down with such force that it had shattered against the wheelwright's skull. The blow killed him instantly and he fell, small and limp.

Too shocked to call or scream, Mary reached behind her, took a knife from the drawer and ran out of the cottage, her eyes only for Hach. He did not seem to notice her until she was almost upon him. But it made no difference, for he struck her with a stonehard fist, leaving her sprawled among the glittering shards. He collected the scattered jewellery and the knife she had brought him, then stood swaying in drunken debate as to what his next move would be.

In the main body of the room were Ezra and William, Joseph and Nathan, their feet stretched toward the fire. Ezra was in quiet conversation with his son, regretting that they'd not heard from Brydd in half a year. They lied to each other, agreeing that he was probably married to the Hungarian girl and working as a coachmaker in some distant European city. And soon to be a father, why not? An important man now, young Brydd, and much in demand by those who wanted the best carriages—a Cannaway carriage.

They did not suggest that he might be in prison, or making his way as a beggar, or dead, and buried in an unmarked grave. They'd imagine the best for him, until they heard otherwise.

Joseph Biss and Nathan Reed were engaged in a stop-start game of dominoes, not quite sure who was winning or whose turn it was to go. They'd eaten well, and were content to let the day and the game amble on.

The two who were absent, Sophia and Elizabeth, had gone for a walk in the direction of the grassy Roman Hill. The excursion had been Elizabeth's idea, though Sophia was happy to accompany her, aware that the young mistress of Overhill—if she was still mistress at the farm—had no one else in whom to confide. They walked in silence through the village, exchanging small talk as they crossed the meadow to the south, then saved their breath for the ascent of Roman Hill. It was only when they had reached the top and were lit by the sunset that Elizabeth said, "Your brother has found a fine woman in Margaret."

Sophia nodded. "Indeed he has." Then she watched Elizabeth brush nervously at the hem of her mantle. "I believe," Sophia prompted gently, "that things have not gone so well for your own brother, Jed. What is the name of his young lady? Clare?"

Elizabeth combined a shrug with a lift of her chin, as if to show her complete indifference to the name. But she was far from indifferent, and when she spoke it was with a growing rhythm, her voice at once weary and desperate, her fingers flicking the mantle or sweeping aside her hair. "You could not tell *him* that things have gone badly, thought he must know it by now. He's changed beyond recognition. In his behaviour most of all, but even in the way he moves, and most especially in his sneers; I detest the way he sneers." She glanced at Sophia, then said, "It was such an obvious trap, the one they set for him, sweet Clare and her parents. He's never been remarkable for his shrewdness, but I thought he'd see the snare in time and avoid it. I thought he'd have that much sense at least."

"I heard she was carrying his child."

"How better to bait the trap?" Elizabeth retorted. "Yes, she's carrying his child. And will be, for a few days yet. They're married now, her parents saw to that. William and Margaret? Jed and Clare? It's becoming quite the thing to do."

Sophia said nothing, letting Elizabeth's words gather pace, the loss and pain spilling out, though only to bring momentary relief. The slender, pale-haired girl had lost the two men she loved, Brydd and her brother, the one to a woman she'd never seen, the other to a woman who'd lain in wait, quite literally so, for the unwitting Jedediah.

"And as for the Halleys—that's their name, her parents—well, they've fulfilled their promise and failed in Marlborough, as they've already failed in London. They sold their grocery shop a month ago, and now they've moved into Overhill and driven my father into a corner and all but taken the farm for themselves. Did you know that Amalie offered to help as midwife, but was rejected by Clare and her mother? Who would ever have thought it, Amalie Cannaway turned down." She again snatched at innocent strands of hair, and Sophia moved forward to hold the younger woman in her arms.

Then she looked past Elizabeth to the west and said, "Do you see there? Where I'm pointing? Do you see smoke and flames?"

Elizabeth turned, dismissing the village of Kennett, marking the village of Lockeridge. The darkness was closing in now, though there was light enough to show that the church was safe, and the mill beside the river, and the houses clustered between. Once they'd been excluded it was easy to identify the source of the fire—the wheelwright's yard, beyond the shadow of a doubt.

They ran together down the hill and back to the smithy, banging in through the door to disturb the men seated at the fire, and the women discussing cosmetics, at the range.

Sophia left it to Elizabeth to say, "I think Alfred Nott's place is on fire. I'm sure of it. I know it from—from when Brydd was there. And it's burning up, by the look of it."

❋

There was a way to these things, a man to be chosen as leader, a team to be formed, each with a job to do. It took no more than the turning of heads, and then Ezra Cannaway was telling Nathan to harness a horse and cart, telling William and Joseph to collect buckets and a hay rake from the yard, telling the women to fill lanterns, whilst he, himself, went in search of axes and a length of rope.

Within a matter of moments the blacksmith and stonemason, merchant and quarrymaster had loaded the equipment and were driving as firemen to the fire. William and Nathan took the bench, Joseph divesting himself of his tailored greatcoat, Ezra coiling the rope and standing the lanterns inside the coil. He wanted everything to be right, so his old friend Alfred would have no cause to complain.

❊

There were seven or eight huts around the perimeter of the yard and half of them were burning, the others beckoning the flames. But none were blazing as fiercely as the cottage itself, where part of the roof had collapsed, drowning the desk and ledger in a shower of sparks.

The villagers of Lockeridge had been the first on the scene. They'd already forced their way inside the building, discovered Alfred and Mary on the floor and carried them out, Alfred dead and with the side of his skull caved in, Mary still alive, her face purpled by a bruise.

The undernourished Reverend Swayle arrived, knelt beside her and put his thin, pinched ear to her lips. Then, with commendable speed, he gave her into the care of the neighbouring women and told the men, "Mistress Nott says it's the doing of Abram Hach. She asked if anyone found a knife on the ground. . . . No? Then Hach may have taken it, so go cautiously in the shadows. He's most likely run off, but—" The clergyman hunched his shoulders in perplexity. He wasn't much up on drunkenness or murder, or the setting of fires. His wife even rationed the kindling at home, and told him to blow harder to raise a flame.

More villagers ran in, and farmers on horseback, and then the Cannaways, though Joseph Biss was the first from the cart. He snatched a bucket and ran toward what he mistook for a trough, seeing the flicker of firelight as the ripple of water. The pail banged his leg as he ran; his fine, Sophia-made shirt billowing at the sleeves.

Then he realised his mistake, saw men drawing water from the pump and turned to edge past a pile of sap-sprung timber. As he did so, Abram Hach loomed from between the wood stack and a low, tarred shed, his drunken senses telling him that the man in shirt sleeves had come to ferret him out.

He took Joseph by surprise, raised a small, brassbound box and struck out with it. The flat of the box caught the merchant on the shoulder and sent him staggering, though he managed to swing the pail in retaliation, missing his target. And then Hach was run-

ning with the shadows, whilst Joseph yelled against the crackle of
the flames.

Thirty yards behind, William Cannaway glimpsed the attack.
Ezra was already crouched beside the body of Alfred Nott,
Nathan lifting the rope and rake from the cart. There were other
carts in the yard, blocking the way, and William realised the
chase would be on foot. He shouted something at Nathan, hoped
the message was clear and jumped from the frontboard.

He was no runner, almost comically clumsy, his feet flapping
the ground, his hands at his sides, his mouth wide open to
breathe. A sprinter would have outpaced him by ten yards in
twenty. But then, Hach was no sprinter. He was of a size with
William, but drunk and confused, and slowed by the brassbound
box. So he, too, was lumbering and gasping as he led the way
from the yard.

William shed his greatcoat. He tore the Easter cravat from his
neck. He discarded his jerkin and followed the labourer up the
first steep slope.

It was dark, though not yet too dark to see. They toiled on,
Hach turning left along a sheep path, then south again, then
along a rutted downland track. William plodded after him, his
heart hammering at his ribs.

The gap closed as Hach climbed another hill, opened as he ran
level or stampeded down a slope. They were now among great
grey columns, another forest of stones that dotted the Wiltshire
hills. Both men veered and staggered in their attempts to avoid
them.

Another few moments and there was only moonlight to guide
the labourer. William lost sight of his quarry, then grunted with
satisfaction and went forward again—hearing the telltale rattle of
whatever was in the box.

They continued across the grass and around the stones. And
then, quite suddenly, the rattling ceased and William peered
about him and listened, his mouth shut to smother his breath. He
was encircled by stones, the ground level on the left, humped on
the right, ahead of him the pale scar of a cart track. But there was
no sign of Hach, no sound of him, only the certainty that he was
there . . .

He came with terrible swiftness, Mary Nott's kitchen knife held high in his grasp, its blade silvered by the moon. He'd abandoned his box, but only whilst he dealt with his pursuer, fearing that William would otherwise dog him clear across the county.

The easygoing Cannaway had never been called to fight. As a child he had been too big for the bullies, and after that a gentle giant of a man. And even now he was slow to react, needing the slash of the knife and the warmth of blood on his arm before he'd let anger take the reins.

They could have stood in turn on a weighing platform and been pound for pound the same. They could have stirred their hair on the lintel of the same high door, exchanged gloves and boots and been comfortable, swapped belts and fixed the buckles to the same frayed holes.

They were an even match, at least in this, and they might have traded blows through the night.

But they did not, because Hach struck again, cutting William to the hipbone, and then William piled against him and drove him back into the darkness, wishing only to overpower him, but slamming him back against one of the upright stones, and doing so with such force that it broke the man's neck and disjointed his spine.

And that was the end of it for Abram Hach. As some would say, too quick and clean an end.

But it was not over for William, for he was left to clamber to his feet and look down at the body, hoping that, whatever kind of monster Hach might be, he'd survive to be hanged. He spoke to the man, lifted him and felt the limpness of him, the roll of his head, then stood back and trembled, sorry for what he had done.

The beam of a lantern picked him out and he started with alarm. Shielding his eyes, he could make out the shape of a cart on the track ahead, and two travellers on the bench.

Then Nathan Reed identified himself. "And I brought the Reverend Swayle along. By God, William, you've been cut!"

"Not deep," William mouthed, then felt the need to say, "but I've killed Abram Hach, throwing him back against this rock. He came at me with a knife and I put my weight against him, and in falling he—"

"Utter nonsense," said the other voice, the well-kept tones of the Reverend Swayle. "We've not just arrived, you know. Have we, Master Reed?"

There was a pause, and then Nathan measured, "No. We've not just arrived."

The clergyman said, "He went back of his own accord, Master Cannaway—"

"But no, sir, he didn't."

"And I say yes, sir, he did. Of his own accord. He cut you and retreated, and that's how he came to grief. Master Reed?"

Not such a long pause now. "That's it," Nathan responded. "That's how he came to grief."

The Reverend Swayle nodded. "Quite so. Clear as day to the two of us, sat up here."

They helped William to the cart, searched the base of the stones for the brassbound box, then dumped it on Hach's body whilst they lifted it aboard.

"Best let me do the driving," the clergyman announced. "I know this part of the country." Then he touched William gently on the shoulder and said, "And best let me do the talking, if you will."

❆

They attended the magistrate's bench. The Reverend Swayle steepled his skinny fingers and reported what had happened— what he and Master Reed had *seen* happen, as clear as in the day. The magistrate gazed at the witnesses, stroked the feather of his pen cross his lips, then said, "I'll admit it, I'm envious. There are some happenings I'd enjoy watching, if I'd your keenness of vision. Certain young ladies who—" Then he signed the document that declared William Cannaway innocent.

Sam Gilmore had been brought from the "Blazing Rag" to identify the contents of the brassbound box. No problems there, since he'd seen much of it strung around the throats of attractive female passengers, or pinned enticingly close to their breasts. Couldn't help noticing, he'd remarked, whilst the magistrate nodded and the Reverend Swayle turned his steepled fingers into churches, and made spires of his thumbs.

Alfred Nott was buried with care and solemnity, the farms and villages emptied for the occasion. Mary was offered shelter by a score of her neighbours. She could no longer afford to employ the craftsman John Stallard or the young apprentice, and it was decided that, come the summer, she would sell off her husband's tools and the salvaged timber. Somebody might make a bid for them, for they were of the best quality, every plank and spokeshave bearing the imprint of Alfred Nott.

❄

And after that, there was a lull in the valley. Life continued as usual, though the villagers needed time to absorb the horror. Alfred murdered and his wife struck down, then left in the hopes that she'd be burned alive. The yard set on fire, and Hach discovered as a spy for the Cherhill gang. William Cannaway stabbed by the murderer, John Stallard and the apprentice out of work, the cottage at Lockeridge charred to the shell, the wheelwright's establishment lost forever.

There might be a murder a day in London or Bristol, a fire in every street. But such events were not yet commonplace, thank God, in the hard-worked valleys of Wiltshire, and the villagers were not so heartless as to shrug and toss them aside.

In the third week of April, Clare Darle gave birth to a daughter. The days before had been filled with screams, her sullen father in conflict with George, Jedediah blaming the pain on his sister, Clare's mother weeping on the stairs and deciding now that they ought to have had Amalie Cannaway as the midwife, she'd always said they should, right from the start!

Elizabeth listened as Jed told her that all Clare's agony was "all your doing! You never made her welcome! I'm sickened to think what spells you've put upon her, so the pain will be unbearable! Just because your man's gone from you and married a foreigner, and no doubt some harlot who'd lift her skirts beneath a bridge, there's no cause—"

And then, with a power beyond her looks, Elizabeth had slapped him across the face and left him smarting whilst she climbed the stairs for the fiftieth time, to see why Clare thought discomfort worth a scream.

It had been an unwanted outing to hell for George and

Elizabeth, in those days before the birth. But then the screams had faded, and Jed and Clare were closeted in their room, crooning over the child.

The Halleys, who'd failed in this as in everything, had also retreated to their room, and it was left to George and Elizabeth to patrol the kitchen and cook the meals, then answer when a heel rapped the floor above their heads.

On one occasion the farmer said, "I could turn the Halleys out. But where would they go? And how would Jed and his wife view that?"

"It's strange," Elizabeth murmured. "I was worried about the trap they'd set for Jed. I never thought they'd make it large enough to catch you and me. You can't turn them out; it's far too late. Unless you'll turn Jed out as well."

"No," George said, "not that. Not my son."

And a short while later came the thunder of heels. The family were ready to eat.

❊

Away from the disturbances at Overhill, it was a slowly turning April, the start of a fair-weather May.

If anything good had come from the tragedy at Lockeridge, it was that the Cherill gang had lost their favourite spy and failed to recruit another. As a result, the coaches that had once kept clear of the "Blazing Rag" now rattled through the archways. Sam Gilmore could again serve the gentlemen and their ladies in the comfort of The Private, again light their way upstairs to the dormitories, again count a score of elbows on his plank-and-barrel bar. He regarded the death of the murderous Abram Hach as the best thing to have happened in years.

In a wild, sentimental moment, he loaded a keg of brandy aboard a stage wagon bound for Melksham and told the driver to deliver it to the house of William Cannaway. "But don't say who sent it. Just say it's from a well-wisher in Beckhampton."

"Don't you think he'd guess it was you? There's no other tavern around, and who else would send brandy from here?"

"That's true," Sam admitted. "Then don't say anything. Just leave it on his step."

Margaret found it there, called to her husband to help her carry

it indoors, then pointed to the shipper's mark, lettered on the side
Gil/Rag/Beck.

"Business must be looking up." William nodded. "Good old
Sam."

❈

So, a fair-weather May . . .

In the middle of the month an elderly ditcher looked up from
the roadside, south of the Beckhampton crossing, to see a thin,
unkempt rider approach from the direction of Devizes. The old
man squinted because he always squinted, his vision milky with
age. He nodded politely, but the rider ignored him, too graceless
to return the greeting. So the ditcher made a point of putting his
back to the stranger, and it was only later that he eased himself
erect and squinted toward the crossing and wondered if he'd been
wrong to take offence.

The rider dismissed the "Blazing Rag" with a glance and
turned his horse eastward, into the valley. Sam Gilmore saw him
go past, marked him as a catchpenny tinker and went back to raking the straw and manure from the yard. He had almost finished
when he leaned on the rake and considered where he'd met the
man before.

The rider went on along the road, leaning aside to cough, then
wiped his mouth on his sleeve. He reached the dreaded Silbury
Hill, but it failed to impress him and he let his mount keep its
own plodding pace. He was seen by shepherds, who gazed at him
from the slopes of the downs; and by farmers, who looked and
went on with their work; and by their wives, who paused before
ramming another peg on the line. He ignored them all, his tricorn
hat tipped forward and pulled down after every bout of coughing.

He reached Kennett, and let the reins droop on the neck of his
horse. The animal stopped in the centre of the road, at the entrance to the narrow village street. The emaciated rider sat quiet
for a moment, as though in doubt as to why he was there. Then
he shuddered and coughed, wiped his lips and took the horse
along the street, as far as a small thatched house. He slipped
from the saddle, the animal indifferent to the loss of weight, and
tied the reins to an iron ring in the wall. Then he breathed in

deeply, as though the air would improve his appearance, and rapped one-two-three on the door.

There was no immediate response, but then the latch was lifted and Ezra Cannaway swung the door open. "Yes, sir? May I help you?" The man said nothing, but by then Ezra was frowning up at him and the word already forming on his tongue. "Brydd . . ." He stared at the hollowed, sunken features of his son, the face almost unrecognisable, even at this small distance. But it *was* his son, in spite of the scarred and pallid skin and the way his body had shrunk to the frame. Ezra nodded, his expression betraying none of the alarm or concern he felt welling inside him. "I'm pleased to see you home, my boy. It's been a long while. In you come." He held the door open and Brydd entered the room with all the uncertainty of a stranger.

❊

He slept for twenty hours without waking, unaware that he coughed and shivered, churned the bedclothes to rope, muttered threateningly in his sleep. Time and again Amalie or Ezra untangled the covers and wiped the perpetual beads of sweat from his face. They said little to each other during their vigil, for the shock of his appearance—not so much at Kennett, but the way he looked—was heightened when they saw the scars that laced his body. What was he now, they wondered; still a coachmaker, or someone beyond the law?

They sent for Dr. Barrowcluffe. When he arived from Marlborough it was to find his patient listless, but awake. The elderly Cannaways waited downstairs, and then the doctor joined them, took a jar of cider and pushed back his ill-fitting wig.

"He'll survive. The young fool's half starved himself, and he's got the cough of a dying horse. But there's no blood in his spittle, and his breath doesn't smell of infection. He'll let you know when he's hungry; otherwise leave him to sleep. We may never discover a better cure-all than sleep." He crisscrossed his chest with a finger and asked, "Those injuries, did he tell you how he came by them?"

"He's not said a word to us," Amalie murmured. "We thought he might have told you."

"No. Nor did he mention the woman Vitar—his wife, perhaps —simply closing his eyes when I asked. However, he did say something; not about her, but about the contents of his bag. Maybe you already know what's in it?"

They shook their heads, mildly affronted. "His possessions are his own," Ezra said firmly, and the doctor smiled. "So they are, so they are."

Amalie waited, then said, "Well, what *is* in this mysterious bag?"

"Coins, Mistress Cannaway. Several hundred of them. Young Brydd may look impoverished, though in truth he's a very rich man. I'd say he's worth two or three hundred guineas, at the least."

Amalie gasped, and Ezra frowned at the doctor. The news went too well with their earlier fears. It was a great deal of money for a coachmaker to have earned, but a possible haul for a robber, who'd chosen his victims with care.

"And did he say how he—?"

"No," the doctor told them. "I regret, he did not."

❋

Brydd ate and slept, drank mugs of honeyed water, ventured no further than the smithy. Each long sleep was more restful than the last, but he was not yet ready to talk.

And then, five days after his arrival, his father stood by the bed, lifted the brown leather bag and set it down again unopened. "Dr. Barrowcluffe has told us of the money. How you came by it's your affair, but no one knows you're here, so—"

"So if I stole it you'll hide me out?"

A brusque, "God knows I will."

Brydd reached up and held Ezra's arm. "Don't torment yourself," he said. "I never earned it, but neither was it stolen. I won it, and half the scars I'm carrying came from those who hated to lose. I won it at dice and cards, and at the rails of cockpits and bearpits, and in half the dens between Györ and Calais. I don't expect your approval, my dear father, but I won it fair and square. Not a pennyworth's been stolen." He smiled and added, "Though you might think so, the way some men laid their bets."

Ezra looked down at him, nodded, satisfied, then asked, "Is that what you've become, a gambler?"

"It's what I was for a while. But now—" He shrugged and lay back against the firm grey bolster, shutting his eyes to Ezra's, "What happened to your lady, to Mistress Vitar?"

❋

His strength returned and he was no longer cadaverous, no longer coughing and sweating through the nights. He waited until the moment was right, then sat with his parents around the fire and told them how Vitar Czaky had been taken from him by the river, and how he had not much cared for life since then.

They knew better than to badger him with questions. Instead, they let him dwell on the memory for a decent length of time, then recounted news of those in the Kennett Vale and beyond.

Unsure how he'd take it, they mentioned that William had met a fine young woman, Margaret Reed, and were relieved to see Brydd show an immediate interest in his brother's welfare. "They're married now," Amalie told him, and he listened eagerly as they took it in turns to describe Margaret, and the quarrymaster Nathan Reed, and the new Cannaway house at Melksham.

"I'll visit them in a day or so," he said. "Then I'll go on to Bristol, to see Sophia and Joseph. It seems odd now, after all the places I've been to, but it'll be the first time I ever saw Bristol."

They were forced to balance their good news with bad, telling him first about the Darles and the Halleys. "There's been another wedding in your absence," Ezra informed him. "Your friend Jedediah is a husband and father. But by all accounts he's changed from the springy young fellow *you* remember, and there's talk that Overhill Farm's in disrepair and that George sits cheerless in a corner." He explained about Clare and her parents, and then Amalie took over to say, "Elizabeth feels driven out, and who's to blame her? Add her to your visiting list, if you can. She never failed to ask about you, not even when you and Vitar seemed—" She stopped herself, then added, "Never."

"As soon as I've seen William and his wife. And got myself back from Bristol. Oh, yes, and had a talk with Dr. Barrowcluffe;

I was a surly patient the day he came to see me. After that, I'll go up there and see if Jed's changed as you say, and if the Halleys are as bad as they sound."

Amalie had no choice but to settle for that. Nevertheless, she asked, "What if Elizabeth visits us whilst you're away in Bristol? Shall I tell her you've returned?"

"By all means. And say I look forward to paying them a call."

I'll do better than that, Amalie decided. I'll say Brydd's home, and that his marriage to Vitar was prevented, and that one of the first things he asked was, "How's Elizabeth Darle these days?"

There was more bad news—had things really been so turbulent in the valley?—as they told him of the fire at Lockeridge and of the deaths of Alfred Nott and Abram Hach.

Brydd pounded a fist against his knee and spoke ill of the dead. "That bloody, monstrous man! I wish to God I'd followed him on one of his secret jaunts! Then we'd have had him tried and hanged, and Alfred would still be alive. And a good few passengers who've been murdered by the Cherhill gang!"

"There are many that might have followed him," Ezra said. "We all harboured suspicions, though we never linked Hach with the gang. We can all share the blame, you no more than others. Less, perhaps, for remember this: you were away for two years and two months, yet in all that time we did nothing. We suspected that he was up to no good, but we misjudged his cunning, thinking that his crimes would be as stupid and petty as he. There's a slice of blame for all of us, and I, for one, can taste it."

However, if there was anything to set against the loss of Alfred Nott, it was William's lumbering heroism. Brydd made his parents recount the story step by step, as it had been pieced together by Ezra and Nathan and the Reverend Swayle. True to his character, William Cannaway had kept silent on the subject, shifting with embarrassment when, at the wheelwright's funeral, half the valley had insisted on shaking him by the hand.

❋

Now that he'd heard the story, Brydd did not go first to Melksham. Instead, he went to see Mary Nott, and sat with her throughout a long summer morning, talking of Alfred and the way he had spent his life, to end it in credit.

"That's nicely said," she told him, "and I believe he did. Though God might doubt it, if He ever saw the ledger. You know how Alfred hated putting pen to ink to paper." She smiled, seeing him in her mind's eye, grousing as the rust-red ink splashed his hands and the ledger and the floor. Then, when the image became painful, reminding her too clearly of the man, she straightened in her chair and said, "Now then, Master Cannaway, tell me this. What's to become of your life, may I ask? Will you remain in the valley, or are you bound abroad again, before long?"

"That I don't know," he admitted. "I'm not yet resolved. But there's something I'd ask you, if I may. Was it quite burned up, the yard and its timber?"

❊

He continued his rounds, visiting William and Margaret at Melksham, but stopping on the way to see Sam Gilmore at the "Blazing Rag." The inn was a hive of activity, and Brydd waited until Sam had passed a dozen earthenware mugs beneath the cider tap before stepping forward to rap on the bar.

"Can a man ever get served in this place?" He'd already been recognised by several of the locals, but they played along, grinning behind Sam's back and agreeing that what the "Rag" needed was a fleet-footed landlord.

"Aye, and less water in the brew."

"He goes round at night, topping up the barrels."

"Having filled the jug from a ditch."

Sam turned to defend himself, saw Brydd and said, "So that's where the trouble stems. He's been spoiled, my lads. How can a modest place like this compare with the taverns of Vienna?" He came forward to embrace the young traveller and pound him on the back. Then he called to one of the locals, put him in charge of the bar and led the way through to the kitchen, where he and Brydd Cannaway could fill in the gaps of time.

They talked for an hour or more, Sam confirming that Overhill Farm was indeed going to rack and ruin. "George carries on as best he can, but Jed has not done a hand's turn in months. And as for the Halleys, they'd think it work to shake a pillow. God knows what'll become of them up there, once they've eaten their way through the larders."

Before he left to ride on to Melksham, Brydd asked, "Are there any new yards in the valley, now that Alfred's is done with?"

"None, and we're in sore need of one. Why, is there a chance you'll—?"

"Maybe," Brydd demurred, "maybe not."

✻

He visited William and his wife, admired his brother's foursquare house and felt immediately at ease with Margaret. They talked through the evening and half the night, and William said, "When can I take delivery of that gig you promised me?"

"You shall have it," Brydd told him, "as soon as I know my mind."

William covered Margaret's hand with his. "At the end of the year? That should give you time enough. It'd be just the thing for a baby to ride in, on his way to be christened. His or her, which-ever."

✻

He left at dawn and rode the twenty miles to Bristol.

For the first time since his departure from Györ he was able to enjoy the journey, stopping at a tavern at midday, tipping his hat to those he passed on the road, smiling at the farm girls who cared to give him a glance. He thought nothing of the distance, though he could well remember the days when he'd have shied at ever leaving the Kennett Vale. Twenty miles in his own country was as nothing compared to the hundreds he'd travelled abroad, and it occurred to him that Melksham was not so far from Bristol. Come to think of it, neither was Kennett.

In the early afternoon, he reached the city, trotted through the Castle Gate and along The Shambles, then around a crescent to the river frontage of The Key and The Biss.

Joseph was out when Brydd arrived, but Sophia was there in the elegant ten-room house, and she hummed with delight as the vinegary butler announced in his own mannered style, "There is a Master Brydd Cannaway at the *door*, my lady. Says he's your *brother*. Would that be the gentleman as works in *bricks*, or the one as went abroad to make *conveyances?*"

She hurried down to greet him, whirled him around on the mosaic tiles, then took him on a tour of the house. "It might not compare with Paris or Vienna, but look, you can see the Cathedral. And look, there's a view of the slipways. And do you know what vessel's been hauled up there? The *Sophia Biss!* Joseph promised that if he ever took shares in a trader he'd name it after me. As soon as it's been scraped and tarred, it'll sail for the Carolinas."

He stayed three days with Sophia and Joseph. Then, throughout the last night, he sat awake in his room, realising that without Vitar he'd lost all taste for city life. Sophia and her husband had been the easiest of company, but it was simply that cities reminded him of Vitar, and that memory was too painful, even now. Better, perhaps, the place he knew above all others, and which Vitar had never seen . . .

❊

He rode eastward, in the direction of London, but stopping short at Marlborough. He knocked at the door of Dr. Barrowcluffe's house and was met by the housekeeper, Mistress Cable, who beamed a welcome, then checked that he'd scraped his boots.

The doctor was in his office—part ransacked library, part alchemist's den—and he asked Brydd all the questions he had not dared ask in Kennett. "Did you stay free of the pox? . . . That's good. So you used the castille soap I gave you. And what are they like, the women? Not in their performance, I don't mean that, they're all alike in that. But in their knowledge of things. Superstitious, are they? Start with the French, and then you can tell me about the Germans and all the others. Take your time."

❊

And, finally, he crossed the downs to Overhill Farm, to see George and Jed and Elizabeth Darle, and Jed's wife, Clare, and the Halleys, famous for the way they'd failed.

George was in the yard behind the house, Elizabeth in the scullery, sorting husks from the flour. The Halleys were upstairs with their grandchild, Jed sprawled in front of the fire, his wife gazing morosely out of the window, bored with marriage and motherhood and the isolated house.

So it sparked her to see a rider cross the horizon and trot down toward the gate.

"Someone's approaching," she said, then went to rap her husband on the arm. "I said, someone's approaching the farm. If he wants to see my parents, tell him they're in Chippenham. There's no one they want to see." She rapped him again for good measure, and he yawned and wiped his face with his hands and shuffled out to the yard.

Elizabeth emerged from the scullery. She knew that Brydd was back, and that his woman had drowned in some far-off river, and now she brushed the dark grey flour from her hands, in case, God willing, it was him. He was leaner than ever, so she'd heard, and looking ten years older than his age. But how else was he supposed to look if he'd lost his woman and come alone across the map? It didn't matter at all how he looked. Just so long as he came.

Clare glanced at her, then turned to the window again, and Elizabeth took the opportunity to slip the bow of her apron and shake the flour dust from her hair. She tossed the apron out of sight, then stood quiet at the back of the kitchen, willing God as she'd once braved the devil.

And outside Jed was yawning and blinking the fumes of the fire from his eyes. There was something familiar about the rider . . . The way he held the reins, perhaps . . . The forward tilt of his hat . . .

And then his vision cleared and he smirked to split his cheeks, seeing the famous young Cannaway on his slap-hoofed horse, and with his clothes smeared and stained; not one bit the returning hero, not one ounce the ambitious young wheelwright who'd gone to make a name for himself, not one pennyweight the victor.

Brydd raised a hand in greeting, then let it hang again at his side. He entered the yard, stopped short of the doorway and gazed at the man who had once been his friend, but who now preferred to smirk and loll, as if paid to do so.

"Jed."

"Thought you'd have come by coach to see us. I'd have wagered you'd be dressed in velvet, and would hand me down your gloves." He sighed with feigned disappointment. "Well, no matter. Tie your horse. We all want to hear your adventures." He imagined himself more awake than he was, turned and misjudged his step and stumbled into the room. He cursed viciously, and Brydd thought how far Jed had come from his simple "damn me" days. He tethered the horse, removed his weatherworn tricorn and followed the slovenly Darle inside.

"Now then," Jed yawned, "here's my wife. Clare Halley, as she was. And this, my sweet Clare, this is Master Brydd Cannaway, come home from his travels. Well, come along, Brydd! Let's see some bowing!"

But Brydd had already seen past the vivid, self-confident Clare. He was looking now at Elizabeth, two years more the woman than when he had left. She was still slender, still pale-eyed, her blond hair in a tangled mane about her shoulders. Her eyes would have been the nicest thing about her, if it were not for her hair and her smile, the push of her breasts and the nip of her waist, the swing of her hips as she stepped forward and the tone of her voice as she spoke. "No need to bow to me, Master Cannaway. It's greeting enough that you're here."

"I make it a rule," he said, "never to bow when I'm told. Only when it suits." He levelled the remark at Jed, then looked at Elizabeth again and added, "Such as now." He employed all the flourish he'd learned from Albany Jevington—"The right toe down, the left knee bent, the right arm sweeping, the left hand pressed to the spine, thumb out wide, that's the way, dear chap" —and Jed smirked to move his ears.

Clare was also amused, but Elizabeth watched from the far side of the kitchen, knowing just what it had cost him to do it. He had risked being thought a fool, and he had been thought a fool by her besotted brother and his vulgar wife. But he had done it anyway, partly, as he had said, because it suited him to do so and partly, Elizabeth believed, because he had known she'd not smile or smirk.

George Darle came in through the scullery. He managed a weary greeting for Brydd and said, "I told Elizabeth you'd be brought back, the night she made the rounds of Sil—" Then he caught himself, mumbled something about another hour's work before dark and went out again, armed with a hammer and rosehead nails.

Clare was meanwhile itching with displeasure. Her husband had introduced her in an offhand manner; the Cannaway caller had all but ignored her in favour of Elizabeth; the lumpen George had talked of work and glowered at his son as he did so. And as for Elizabeth, there was enough sparkle in her eyes to sell them off as jewellery.

It was time to recruit some help.

"I do trust you'll stay and meet my parents, Master Cannaway."

"The moment they appear, Mistress Darle."

"Well, that's excellent. That's quite perfect then. I shall ask them to come down." She smiled, decided not to curtsey—one fool's flourish was enough—and went upstairs to summon her parents.

Brydd saw that Jed had sunk into a chair, and he made his way past the table to Elizabeth. There were already sounds of activity in the room above, but there was time enough for Brydd to say, "I thought to have found you married by now, my dear Elizabeth."

She hesitated, then murmured, "No. Not so far. Not yet." She'd said that much with her eyes downcast, but now she raised them and looked at him with a strange mixture of guilt and defiance. "I heard that your lady Vitar was—I'd not intended that —I mean, I am truly sorry that it happened, Master Cannaway." The thing she knew she must one day tell him was as yet beyond her to admit.

"It's Brydd, if you please. I'm not master of much, at present."

"Oh, but you will be, I think. I think you'll be master of whatever you choose. Will you stay in the valley?"

"It's not yet resolved. But there's the chance that I will."

They heard footsteps on the stairs, and irritable whispers.

"Then we're bound to meet," Elizabeth hurried. "If you stay."

"Bound to," Brydd told her, then was forced to give his attention to Clare's parents, who wanted to know all about Paris and Vienna. "We are from London, ourselves; city people, as you might say. Does Paris have a river, same as London? . . . It does? And Vienna? . . . There, too? Well, then, are the streets of Paris paved at all? And do they have fine parks in Vienna, same as London? . . . Good God, Master Cannaway, one would think those cities as splendid as ours, the way you defend them so!"

❉

He returned that evening to the "Blazing Rag." He beckoned Sam Gilmore from the bar, marched him through to the kitchen and demanded, "What do you know of properties for sale? A house with some yards and stables, a derelict farm, something I can turn to account?"

Sam puzzled over it for a while, then said, "There's a place down the road from here, a mile or two toward Devizes. You've probably passed it, though it's been empty for years. It used to belong to a man named Fax. Lazy swine, he was. Upped and left without settling his debts. The place was awarded to old Ben Royton. Not that he wanted it, for he's got a farm of his own."

"Royton." Brydd nodded. "And what's the place called?"

"Well, it was Fax Farm until the owner defaulted and made off. I'm sure Ben Royton never changed it."

"I'll go there tomorrow. And can you then bring us together?"

"You'll be together if you're in the bar at midday." He smiled and added, "If you decide to buy the place, you'll have to drink here; it's the nearest place for miles, dishwater brew or not."

"Tomorrow," Brydd repeated, "around midday."

THIRTEEN

It took two hours to rebuild the place in his mind.

As a farm it was no great catch. The spring-fed pond was too far from the house, the soil too thin, the three-sided yard too extensive for the property. The arms of the yard were roofed over, walled at the back and open at the front. Between these arms was a tiled building, rising in the centre to form a massive, windowless barn, its entrance wide enough to admit a herd of cattle at the trot.

Or the passage of a wagon. Or a gig. Or a coach.

The farmhouse itself was locked and shuttered, but Brydd could guess from the position of the windows that it contained five or six rooms, two on the ground floor, three or four above.

He found a pump in the overgrown garden, worked the fishtail handle until the flakes of rust broke free, then levered it up and down until filthy water, clouded water, clear cold water gushed from the dolphin mouth.

He was drawn back to the yard again. He paced it from side to side, from front to back, then stood square in the middle, twisting his bootheel on the moss. It took him no time at all to build wagons and gigs and coaches, swaying as they rattled past, noisy in his mind.

He knew he would need to combine the wheelwright's yard at

Lockeridge with his father's smithy at Kennett—installing a bellows forge and an anvil, tyring rings and a grindstone, timber lofts and nail stores, stables and granaries and seasoning sheds, a tack room and sawpit, a paint-and-varnish house, a lathe and an inspection ramp and all the tubs and barrels, chests and boxes he could find.

But first he had to see Ben Royton.

They met in the inn at noon, and the cautious farmer said, "Sam told me you've been looking at Fax's place. Have you an eye to buying it, Master Cannaway?"

Brydd wanted to tell him that he'd also a heart and a mind for the place. But he knew Royton would lose respect for him if he did more than shrug the question.

"It's possible. I'll need to see others. I'm in no special hurry."

"That's it," Ben Royton told him, enjoying the haggle. "You look around, and take your time. Maybe those fellows from Pewsey won't want it, after all."

"To be honest with you, Master Royton, I cannot see who would. A tumbledown place like that. Still, it has a certain appeal. I heard you took it as an unpaid debt. Would you care to say what you were owed at the time?"

"I'll tell you what it's worth today." He did, and Brydd smiled at the humour of it and offered half the sum. The farmer then groaned at the ways of youth, adjusted the figure and waited for Brydd to counter it. There were more good-natured smiles, more groans, more glances of appeal at the rafters, and gradually the farmer's price was lowered, as Brydd's was raised to meet it.

Then they shouted in unison, "Done and done!" and slapped palms with a ferocious crack, letting all within hearing know that a contract had been made.

It was Brydd's duty to buy the cider, and he invited Sam to join them. Then he raised his mug in salute to the farmer and asked, "Those people from Pewsey?"

"Cousins of mine," Ben Royton chuckled. "I always trot 'em out when I've something to sell."

※

And then Brydd Cannaway went to work. He'd lost the better part of a year since Vitar's death, and not for more than a year had he put chalk to paper, or shaped a wheel spoke, or sawed plank along its tricky, twisting grain. Yet had he not as good as promised his brother a gig by Christmas?

He visited Alfred's widow at Lockeridge and asked if she'd be willing to sell his tools and timber. "It's to start me in a place I've bought, just south of the Beckhampton crossing. It's to be known as Faxforge." He smiled and forestalled her questions. "I like the sound of it, that's all."

"And I like better the sound of what you're doing," Mary told him. "And so, I believe, would Alfred. Go ahead and take what you want, Master Brydd. The yard wagon was also saved from the fire. You'll need it to haul the wood." She shrugged aside any talk of payment, but Brydd insisted on valuing every plank and block according to its quality, the bulk of it ten years seasoned. He priced the tools and the wagon, ladders and sawhorses and other equipment, then asked her if the figure seemed fair.

She made him repeat it, for although she'd bullied Alfred into keeping his ledger up to date, she had not imagined that the stock was worth much. "It's far more than I'd expected. But it won't do, you know, if there's charity involved."

"Well, let's see," he told her with mock severity. "I could take you around and let you question me on the subject of elm and ash, beech and oak; on the casting of bark and the splitting of grain; on why some woods dry quick, but distorted, whilst others seep for years. Or, as I'd prefer, you could regard me as a businessman who would never pay a penny for a halfpenny bolt. Now, my dear Mistress Nott, here's my hand. Smack down on it and we've a deal. I'll come and collect you soon, and drive you across to Faxforge. Though, of course," he grinned, "I may have to levy a penny for the trip."

A few days later he called on the elderly John Stallard to ask if the craftsman would help put Faxforge into shape. Stallard lived alone, and had found little to occupy him since the closure of the yard. He'd always thought well of the young Cannaway and was glad of the chance to work again, but his pride forbade him to look eager. "I might manage a day here and there, when there's nothing else doing."

"Whenever it suits you, Master Stallard. I would anyway welcome your advice."

"Ah, now that I can give you by the armload. I'm a regular compendium when it comes to telling others what to do."

"Then come and tell me when you will. There'll be enough problems for a dozen pair of arms."

❈

After that, he only had time for Faxforge. He moved from Kennett and slept on a straw-filled sack, sometimes in the great barn, sometimes in what had once been the kitchen—would again be the kitchen before long. He travelled to Marlborough and Pewsey and Devizes, using the yard wagon to bring back tiles and glass, barrels of pitch and paint. He set the ladders against the house, then balanced on the topmost rungs, his mouth serrated with nails, his wrists aching from the weight and bounce of the hammer. He longed to be working in the coach yard—he was already calling it that—but he had the sense to replace the weakened rafters in the house and smear pitch along the angles of the roof.

He remembered a rhyme Alfred Nott had taught him, when he'd first gone to Lockeridge as a nervous stripling of twelve. "First things first, though slow and dull; For then the rest and best won't fall."

On the third morning, early, John Stallard arrived, bringing his own personal tools in a tipcart. He had come, it seemed, intending to offer more than just advice. Brydd took him on a tour of inspection, saw him glance quizzically at what had so far been achieved, then nodded when Stallard said, "That flooring's got the damp in it. I'll change a board or two whilst I'm here."

By the end of the week he had replanked an entire room and was laying seasoned boards along the landing.

Ezra and Amalie came over, and Sam Gilmore strolled down from the inn. Ben Royton arrived at the reins of a large haycart. He drove it past the pond and into the yard, then dismounted, strangely ill at ease.

"What's the matter?" Brydd asked him. "Did your cousins from Pewsey *really* want the place, after all?"

The farmer shook his head, then jerked a thumb at the cart and growled, "Doors and benches and—well, they belong here. I took 'em away last year, but I never got round to sawing 'em up. They've been kept in the dry, so— You'd best have 'em back."

There were no visits from George or Jed. However, during the second week Brydd turned from setting in a window frame at the side of the house to see Elizabeth Darle squinting up at him, a hand raised to shield her eyes. "It's gone noon," she said. "I brought some meat and apple cake. Have you time to eat it?"

The invitation reminded him that he'd not eaten since yesterday morning, and then only stale bread and cheese one could build with. "My eyes play tricks," he called down to her. "Have you been sent from heaven?"

"I'd rather say I've escaped from the kitchens of hell. Anyway, finish what you're doing. I'll set the things out here, on the bank." She heard sounds from inside the house and, with an urgency that surprised him, she asked, "Who is that, Brydd?"

"John Stallard, the craftsman from Lockeridge." He frowned, amused and uncomprehending. "Who did you suppose it was?"

Elizabeth shook her head, dismissing the matter, then said, "Ask him to join us, there's enough for us all." She put the split-reed basket on the ground, lifted out a dish of sliced red beef and the apple cake, then leaned forward to tie back her hair.

Brydd had meanwhile clambered down the ladder, strode to the front door of the house and called inside to Stallard. The craftsman appeared, slapping sawdust from his clothes. He blinked in the sunlight, recognised George Darle's daughter and mumbled to himself, "Not before time."

Thinking the man had addressed him, Brydd queried, "Master Stallard?"

"Nothing, Master Cannaway." He followed the weed-covered path around a neglected vegetable plot to the bank. Then he nodded cordially at Elizabeth and was handed his share of the meal. Brydd sprawled against the bank, his legs trembling from the hours he'd spent balanced on the ladder. But Stallard said, "It's a difficult bit I'm on at the moment. If you'll forgive me, Mistress Darle, I'll take the food inside with me. Wouldn't want to forget the measurements and, uh—"

"By all means," she smiled. "I shall be down again." Then she glanced at Brydd, waiting for him to confirm it if he would.

"Indeed," he said, "I hope so. Whenever you like. This is the best-cooked meat I've had in a long time."

Stallard disappeared indoors. He thought Brydd Cannaway an

intelligent young man and a damn good worker. But in the matter of Elizabeth Darle, the new master of Faxforge was the next best thing to a fool. Oh, yes, there'd been the tragedy with the Hungarian woman, what was her name, but it was long since over, and time he came to his senses.

Stallard shook his head, then smiled approvingly at the way Elizabeth had brought the food and tied back her hair and dressed in the plainest of gowns. The young Cannaway would have no time for idle visitors, but if the girl was prepared to put a few hours' work into the place . . .

And, outside in the sunlight, she was coming around to just that. "Have you a name for it yet?"

He was daydreaming, seeing coaches in the yard. "Here? Yes. Faxforge." He explained about the former owner, then said, "There'll be a forge, of course, though the real work will be with carts and wagons, coaches and—whatever people want."

"I'd rather stay clear of Overhill, for a while. Clare was screaming fit to bring down the roof when I left. I thought I'd weed the path, or rake the leaves from the pond, or sweep out the house."

"There's no need, you know. I wouldn't ask it of you."

No, she thought, you wouldn't, would you; more's the pity. "Well, you haven't asked. I have."

He turned his face to the sun and murmured, "You do enough of it at Overhill."

"There's a difference. I'd enjoy helping you. Helping you with Faxforge."

He grinned and put a hand on her arm. "Then my eyes weren't playing tricks, after all. What's it to be then, the pond or the path?"

※

She came down again, and more often, and throughout the stretch of the day. She did not always bring food, for the shelves at Overhill were already depleted. But it was Elizabeth who stood knee-deep in the pond, raking out the mat of leaves and twigs. And it was she who traced the overgrown paths and wiped the grime from the windows and scoured the dolphin pump until the fish looked ready to leap.

However, if the morning sky was overcast or the clouds scudded past to the north, the girl was reminded of the night she'd braved the Silbury Devil, of the demon that had failed to catch her, of the ghost that must still be laid. She would have to tell Brydd of her part in Vitar's death, for although she had never wished it, never once voiced it during the terrifying circuits of the hill, she had come to believe that the desire had been there and that the awakening devil had sensed it for himself.

But her fears outstripped her courage. She would tell him today, she decided. She would tell him now. And then she would stand with him under one of the trees, sheltering from a shower, or sit with him in the kitchen, and the words would form in her head and cling to her tongue, unwilling to be spoken. How could she tell him that the girl he had known since childhood, the woman who worked alongside him at Faxforge, was the very one who had helped send Vitar to her death? What would the man she loved think of her then, blighting the past and the future with her admission of murder?

So the thoughts formed and the words dissolved, and Elizabeth was left with the knowledge that one day she must tell him—whatever the consequence, whatever the cost. One day, she faltered, but not just yet. Soon, perhaps, but not now.

Meanwhile Stallard had floored the upper level of the house and, together with Brydd, laid dark red tiles in the kitchen, and what would one day be the parlour. Jealous of his coach yard, Brydd had cleaned out the sheds, rehung the doors that Ben Royton had so honestly returned, then stored the timber, plank by plank and block by block, the ash away from the elm.

By the end of July there had been two remarkable changes at Faxforge, though the one more obvious than the other.

The first—important enough to bring villagers and farmers the length of the Kennnett Vale—was the installation of a bellows forge, an anvil and shoeing shed, and the announcement that John Stallard had agreed to stay on, full time, at the yard. He had already moved into a small one-room cottage behind the house and sold his place at Lockeridge. "I hope you'll not regret it," Brydd told him, and the craftsman retorted, "I hope I'll not have cause to, eh, Master Cannaway?"

Ezra was one of the first to inspect the layout of the yard. Three times in an hour he muttered, "I see you've done it like at

Kennett," and only then would he give it his nod and accept a mug of ale. They stood near the forge, Ezra and Amalie, their son and the invaluable John Stallard, and Amalie said, "I want this place to last as long for you, Brydd, as the smithy has for us." Then she shyly raised her mug and the men tapped it, aware that however gentle they had been, Amalie would worry that one of the containers had been cracked.

The second and less obvious change was in Brydd himself. His time was still given to Faxforge, though he now looked forward to Elizabeth's visits. If he saw her in time, he went to meet her at the gate, helped her dismount, then led her pony to the cleaned-out stables. He'd not thought himself an insensitive man, but he realised that, in all the visits she'd made to Faxforge, she had never angled for compliments, nor sought for favours.

No trace in Elizabeth of the tiresome Georgina Warneford . . .

None of the practised allure of Annette von Kreutel . . .

Not so much as a shadow of the vulgar, painted Clare . . .

And yet, though her hair was pale where the other had been dark, and she was quiet where the other had been vivacious, and she was tall and slender, where the other had been diminutive . . . Yet, for all their differences, they seemed to Brydd to have much in common, Elizabeth Darle and Vitar Czaky . . .

But that was the very hurdle in her path. She was not Vitar, whatever strengths or failings they might have shared. She was Elizabeth Darle, daughter of George Darle, widower of Overhill Farm; sister of Jedediah Darle, and now, though she tried to forget it, sister-in-law of Clare Darle, who could always find powder for her face, it seemed, though never flour for the pastry. That's who she was, and who she wanted to be for Brydd Cannaway, her strengths and her failings her own.

❋

She went down to Faxforge in August, to find Brydd harnessing his team to the yard wagon. "I need some furniture for the house," he told her. "I thought I'd see what's going in Devizes. Would you care to come along? I'm quite likely to purchase the chairs and tables, then overlook the— Well, there you are. What else do you think I'll need?"

Elizabeth left her pony chewing from its nose bag, waved at

Stallard and greeted a farmer who'd brought in a plough, to have
the blade resharpened. Then she climbed aboard the wagon and
said, "Dressers. Benches to go with the table. Pots and pans.
Hooks for the larder. I'll recite a list on the way. I've never been
to Devizes; can you imagine that? I should have dressed for the
occasion."

"You're dressed well enough for Devizes. And for me. Hold on
now, here we go."

On the way there they talked of Faxforge; of the orchard he'd
plant and the things he should buy for the house. He told her
about the gig he'd be making for William and Margaret, and how
he'd base the design in part on a French *cabriolet*, in part on a
curricle. And then matter-of-factly he added, "But with my own
improvements, of course. When it's finished it'll be the best in
Wiltshire, if not in the whole of England." He turned to her and
grinned. "Is that not the most puffed-up boast you've ever heard?"

"I'll wait and see the gig. If the wheels come off at the first jolt
of the road . . ."

It took them three hours to reach Devizes, another four to
make a tinker's cart of the wagon. Once again Brydd realised that
Elizabeth had weathered the lurching journey without complaint,
walked the length and breadth of Devizes, helped him choose
benches and a dresser, tables and chairs, cooking pans and platters, enough clinking, jangling articles to give warning of their approach.

"We passed a tavern on the way into town," he said. "Shall we
see what they can offer us in the way of a meal?"

She nodded gratefully. "I'll admit, my appetite's been sharpened by the sight of all these plates and knives we've bought.
But I've enjoyed it. And now I've been to Devizes."

They made their noisy way through town and along the road to
the low, thatched inn. The landlord believed in rationing the candles, and they sat in a dark, oak-walled booth, a tallow stub between them on the table. The other occupants of the inn had enjoyed the arrival of the furnished wagon, but they were now
clustered at the far end of the room, leaving Brydd and Elizabeth
alone. The landlord found time to serve them soup and then a
stew of rabbit, carrots, onions and herbs, and let them pour their

own ale from a hefty half-gallon jug. "Shout out when you're ready for the pie. Berries of some kind. D'you want me to ask?"

"No," Brydd told him, "so long as they're not from holly or poison yew."

"Can't say." The man shrugged. "It's my wife who does the picking."

They waited for him to leave, then laughed and did their best to stifle it. Brydd splashed ale into the mugs, glanced around at the dim-lit tavern and said, "It reminds me of places in the Bäckerstrasse and the Wollzeile, where Vitar and I . . . Well . . ."

Elizabeth nodded and knew how to scale the hurdle. It might go against her, but it seemed the only way to do it if she was to cause the least hurt to Brydd Cannaway. And to the memory of Vitar Czaky. And to herself.

She inquired, "Where else did you go in Vienna, the two of you?"

And then, when he had answered at length . . .

"Could she speak more than her own language?"

And then, when he'd answered . . .

"You must have valued her opinions of your drawings, the daughter of Janos the architect."

And then . . .

"She was an exceptional woman. I'd have been timid of her perhaps, though I believe I'd have liked her if we'd ever met. But that can never happen now. Unless you bring the ghost of her to Faxforge." Conscripting the remnants of her courage, Elizabeth blurted, "I would rather you did not do that, my dear Brydd. I would rather you could look across at *me*, and see *me*, and think how I could be for you, though I'm not as exceptional as she. I've been in love with you most of my life, Brydd Cannaway, and I am deeply in love with you now. Yet I'm sorry for the loss of Vitar and— Well, there's something more I must tell you, something you may never forgive."

"I'm sure there's nothing you could do that's beyond forgiveness," Brydd started, then stopped abruptly as Elizabeth said, "But there is! There is!" She entwined her fingers, twisting them in desperation, staring at him as though to witness his fury and suffer the full penalty for her sins. "I never intended that she should come to harm. You were there, with her in Vienna, and I knew I would lose you to her, so I— Oh, God, Brydd, so I went around Silbury Hill and dared the devil, and he must have acted in his own vile way, he must have, for I never wished her harm, it was just—just to have you back . . ." Her voice was failing as she murmured, "That's all it was for . . . I never asked . . . It was only for that . . ." She could no longer face him, and sank back, sobbing behind the mask of her hands.

He gazed in astonishment, reached out as though to touch her, then thought better of it. He knew all about Silbury Hill. He knew of the superstitions that swirled like mist around its base, and he could imagine how it had been for the girl. She'd have gone at night, of course. And, knowing Elizabeth Darle, she'd have completed the five long circuits. The briars would have torn at her legs and tripped her, and all the while she'd have sensed the devil's eyes, heard the dry scrape of talons, felt the sudden gust of foetid breath. It must have been the most terrible experience of her life. And she'd suffered the grim ordeal for what? Yes, as she'd told him, just to have him back.

He was suddenly reminded of his own private fear—his horror of werewolves—and thought of the evening when he and Albany Jevington had fled across the gloomy plain beyond Essenbach. No power on earth would have made Brydd enter the nearby forest; not as a dare, nor in pursuit of an enemy, nor for love. Yet that was what Elizabeth had done, her forest the ditch at Silbury, her werewolf the devil in the hill.

Brydd reached out again and this time placed a hand on her workaday sleeve. "I'll not bring Vitar to Faxforge," he said gently. "But you'll come there. I hope and pray you will. I'm not so far back in my feelings for you, my dear Elizabeth, though I grant you it's time I gave them full rein. You will come, will you not? And not just to work there. Things will be more as you'd wish them to be from now on. As I would wish them to be. As they should already have been."

She slowly uncovered her face and saw Brydd turn his hand, the rough palm uppermost. She wanted to take it, but could not do so until the question had been answered: "But what of Silbury?"

His voice quiet and even, he said, "Now, listen to me, Mistress Darle. When I was a boy I used to go in the evenings and dig flints from the Silbury ditch. As a youth I'd go there with some fellows from Lockeridge and Kennett—never with Jed, he was far too frightened—and we'd drink an entire jar of whatever it was we'd scrounged, then shout, 'Demon, demon, can't you see me?' all around the hill. Oh, no, my courageous Elizabeth, you did nothing to harm Vitar. The devil moved out of Silbury Hill more than fifty years ago. Found a cave somewhere on the far side of Chippenham. Dr. Barrowcluffe told me."

He took her hand in his, leaned forward and kissed her gently at the edge of her lips. And again, on the fullness of them, sensing the kiss returned.

"Please," she asked him, "do as you said. Give your feelings full rein from now on." She managed a smile. "I'll go as slow as you like, Master Cannaway. Until you've caught me up." Then she sat back on the bench and suggested, "Shall we brave the landlord's pie? I don't think I'd be poisoned, whatever it contained."

Clare had plenty to scream about in the weeks that followed. Elizabeth held a quiet conversation with her father, embraced him and cried with happiness on his neck, then showed her sister-in-law and the Halleys that she, too, could be greedy and selfish and leave the pans piled high in the sink.

She was greedy for time and selfish of the days, and the Halleys now made their leaden-footed way to the kitchen, only to discover that their meals were still in the bins that lined the larder.

It was Jed who had to rake the stove and light the fire, then feed it with wood. It was Clare who winced and contorted her face as she filled the lanterns and saw the smoke curl from the greasy wicks. It was the Halleys who fetched and carried, scoured the dishes and filled endless buckets at the pump. They dared ask nothing of George, for he was already seeing to the sheep and mending the fences and doing his best to keep Overhill alive.

Elizabeth left early in the mornings and did not return until dusk. She was sometimes escorted home by Brydd, though more often than not she made the journey alone, stabled her pony and set her lips in a smile before entering the kitchen.

"My, my, you look worn to the fabric, Mistress Clare. Have your parents retreated to bed already? Retired, should I say? And what's happened to the range? It's as cold as a gravestone. Will you wake your husband, or shall I?"

She behaved with cheerful contempt toward the Halleys and their daughter, aware that they were no harder pressed than any family, on any farm, in any part of the country. It'd do them good to get soot in their eyes and an ache in their bones. And it might encourage them to go back to London and make a better job of their grocery shop, where the most they'd have to lift would be a scoop or the weights for the scales.

At Faxforge, Brydd and Stallard began work on the gig, interrupting it to shoe horses, mend carts and wagons, braze the hoops of a barrel, bolt this together, or nail that firm, or fix one thing to another.

Elizabeth whitewashed the barns, prepared vegetable soups on the stove, turned and tilled the garden. An area was fenced off for the orchard, and the three of them worked together, preparing the ground and lowering in the fruit trees. When the final row had been planted and the tactful Stallard had found things to do in the yard, Brydd and Elizabeth walked among the saplings, nodding at the apples he'd get from these, the yellowish plums from those. Small and fragile though they were, the trees seemed to offer them a sense of privacy. They were more at ease with each other, Elizabeth listening as Brydd gave voice to his dreams. She smiled and thought, He really can conjure a coach with words. I can almost believe it's rattling past us down the rows.

Time and again, Brydd found himself referring to the girl, seeking her opinion of things, then nodding in agreement. He had not noticed until now the cautious way she spoke of *his* orchard, *his* coaching yard, *his* house. They were all his, of course, and his alone until such time as he chose to share them . . . Until, for example, he found himself a wife . . .

Excited by his own description of how a proper passenger-carrying coach should be balanced, he held Elizabeth by the arm, using his free hand to show that if the springs were set right and not brought too close together there was no reason why the body of the vehicle should not ride—

"I think," she said shrewdly, "you've put a pinch-brake on my arm. I don't at all mind, my dear Brydd, though I'd rather be held for myself than as a wheel."

"What? Oh, I'm sorry."

There was no one to hear her, no one to think her forward. "For myself," she murmured. "I'd much rather that."

Whatever it was—the beauty of the young woman, the courage she'd shown at Silbury Hill, the uncomplaining way she'd helped at Faxforge, the words she'd used just now—whatever it was, it set the cornerstone on his feelings. He continued to hold her, but more gently, his hands on her arms, then around her waist as he drew her forward and kissed her. In this, too, he was gentle, but only at first. They were not in the tavern near Devizes today. There was no need for compassion here, in the orchard. This was the time and place for a kiss without special reason, beyond its being the most eloquent declaration of love.

They were a long time in embrace, a long time walking between the rows of slender plants. Not that it seemed long to Brydd and Elizabeth when there was so much to murmur, and the greater eloquence to share . . .

※

It was something of a ritual; the banging of fists on benches and the slapping of boarded walls. The retorts were always the same, as though the elderly Stallard and the young Cannaway were rehearsing their parts for a play.

"I'll thank you not to tell me how wood should be shaped, Master Brydd! Damn it, sir, I was expert at this before you were ever in the world! You'll not tell *me* how it's done! And you'll be favoured if I tell *you!*"

And then more banging and slapping, and it was Brydd's turn to shout.

"These are new ways, Master Stallard! It's how it's done in the rest of Europe, and how I want it here! Wheels are no longer sliced from logs, sir! There's more to springs than plaited rope!"

And that called for more pounding of benches and hacking of

heels, after which they glared at each other, let their anger fade and agreed that if they studied the problem again a solution might possibly be found.

They loved every moment of it, and were confident that the gig would run for ever.

❈

The young couple walked beyond the orchard. John Stallard could see them of an evening, pacing out the perimeter of Faxforge, and could hear them laughing and shouting in the August air.

Elizabeth Darle was less cautious now, for she knew Brydd loved her. Even so, she would not mention marriage, nor speak of the place as anything but his. It was for Brydd to do that, when the wounds of his life with Vitar had healed and the scars no longer showed.

However, seeing him stride ahead of her, or hearing him tell his dreams, or being lifted in his arms and swung and set gently down again—these were times when she wished the scars could be magically erased.

In late August they were seated on one of the grassy hillocks above Faxforge. Brydd extended his arm, pointed to where a narrow strip of ground ran between the orchard and the vegetable garden and queried, "What can we make of that, do you think? It's odd, perhaps, but although I love the open country, I'd hate to see our own ground wasted. Another row of fruit trees? A flagged path to the pond?"

What can we make of it, she thought, to stop our own ground going to waste? Oh, I'm sure we'll thinking of something, he and I.

❈

". . . And I'm telling you, Master Cannaway, well travelled though you are, the way to set an axle at ease is like this!"

"Yes." Brydd nodded equably. "As you say, Master Stallard."

The elderly craftsman stared at him, then shook his head and went on with the work. There was little pleasure to be derived from an argument if all Brydd Cannaway could do was say yes, as you wish, do it the way you think best. And then gaze along the

road, waiting for Mistress Elizabeth to appear. There was no question of it; Brydd was a man in love, and sinking deeper by the
day. For all he cared, the wheels of the gig could be square . . .

❊

In the first week of September they walked to a clump of trees
known as The Bellringers. It was Ben Royton who'd passed on
the name, though he'd no idea why they were called that—"Except they're bowed down like men tugging on bell ropes." As soon
as he'd mentioned it, it seemed to fit, and Brydd was content to
keep the name.

The trees were in the northeast corner of the property, one of
the few places they had not yet ventured. Elizabeth was chattering about something as they climbed the slope, then glanced away
to the north and let the words fade on her lips. Brydd glanced at
her, then followed the direction of her gaze. There was nothing to
be seen but the folds of hills, the cluster of dwellings at Beckhampton, a glimpse of Kennett to the east. And then he realised
she was looking between the villages and across the distant ridge
to the summit of Silbury Hill.

"Forgive me," she said. "I'm being foolish. I didn't know we
had a view of the hill from here, that's all."

"But you must have seen it a hundred times since—that night."

"Yes, and thought nothing of it. I said I was being foolish."

"We can go down again if you wish."

She shook her head, moved forward a few paces and gazed
again at the smooth, rounded summit. Then, when she'd murmured something under her breath, she lifted her chin in a nice
show of defiance and waited to see what would happen.

A moment later she turned away to join Brydd near the trees.
"You must be right," she told him, "you and Dr. Barrowcluffe, or
my insults would have brought the devil out."

Brydd grinned and kissed her. "You're a rare young woman,
and that's the truth. What did you say to him?"

"Ah, no," she refused. "They're not the kind of words to be
aired." She nodded to where one of The Bellringers formed a canopy of branches. They walked around the base of the trees and
settled themselves in the shade. They could see Faxforge and hear

the tap of John Stallard's hammer, light on a nailhead, heavier on a spring bar.

Brydd plucked a grass, knotted it two or three times, then threw it aside. He drummed the heel of his right boot against the instep of his left. He brushed his hands together, shifted, fidgeted, swung suddenly to his feet. Elizabeth looked up at him, her expression amused and quizzical. "Is Master Stallard shaming you with his sounds?"

"No, it's not that. There's something I wish to ask you."

The girl said nothing now, sharing his nervousness. The hammer taps seemed to fade away, the day itself halting to listen. Please, God, she thought, please, God . . .

"My feelings," he started, "well, they've long since caught up with yours, as I'm sure you must know. Most likely they were always there, though I see now that I held the reins tight for my own purpose. To break free of the valley. To learn what I could elsewhere. But now that's done with. No matter that I lost the satchels in the river, I've brought back the knowledge, and that's what counts. I've achieved what I set out to do, at least abroad, and I'm content to be here at Faxforge, and—I ask you to marry me, my dear Elizabeth, and live with me here and know that the reins are cast aside. Together we can turn things to great advantage, you and I, and I pray I can make you happy. I believe I can. Do you share that belief? Will you take me on? Will you be my wife, Mistress Darle?" Then he said, "I should have been on my knees."

"You should," she agreed, then ran toward him, forgetting for the moment to say yes.

❋

He rode to Overhill, to ask George Darle for the hand of his daughter in marriage. George led him around the side of the house, past the sheep pens, past the hay barn, past the untended kitchen garden. Then the weary farmer burrowed a hand beneath a pile of rotting sacks and produced a flask of sweet French brandy. "We'll take it in turns," he cautioned. "I'll watch for the Halleys; you drink the toast."

"Then you give your permission?"

"I gave it years ago," George told him. "It's just taken you time to hear it, wouldn't you say?" He reached for the earth-smeared flask. "Now you watch, and I'll drink." He did so, buried it again, then shook Brydd's hand. "Marry her soon," he requested. "I'm anxious that she be part of Faxforge before—well, before things go too wrong here." Then he grinned what must have been his most mischievous grin in years, fringed though it was by despair. "Come on, Master Brydd. I want to barge indoors and bring them all down, Clare and her city folk, then tell them that the worst of their fears have come true. My darling Elizabeth is saved, after all, and the stove is theirs, and the sink and the larder, and the scrubbing of the floors. Come along and enjoy it. You'll see their faces fall like damp plaster!"

❊

The wedding was set for the eighteenth of the month. Written or spoken invitations were relayed to Sophia and Joseph at Bristol, William and Margaret at Melksham, Dr. Barrowcluffe and Mistress Cable at Marlborough, Sam Gilmore at the "Blazing Rag," John Stallard at Faxforge, Ben Royton and his wife at their farm, Mary Nott at Lockeridge, Nathan Reed in his quarry, George and Jed, Clare and her parents at Overhill and—before all others— Ezra and Amalie at Kennett. Amalie wept for joy and was comforted by Elizabeth, whilst Ezra shook his son by the hand, then abandoned such formalities and embraced him. "We'd always hoped for this . . . You and Elizabeth . . . It's just the thing, that's what it is, just the right damn thing . . ."

The service would be at Lockeridge, conducted by the half-starved Reverend Swayle. Afterward, the guests would be invited to the yard at Faxforge, comestibles on the table and a variety of drinks on tap. A number of sheds would be furnished with straw-filled mattresses and sheepskins in case any of the wedding guests were too—how should one put it?—pot-valiant to drive home in the dark.

The Halleys declined the invitation. They claimed that they'd be needed at the farm to look after their granddaughter, keep the stove alight and make sure there were lanterns on the fences for when George returned with Jedediah and sweet Clare. But they sent their blessings, "To the enchanting Mistress Elizabeth and the well-travelled Master Cannaway. May God, in His mercy, grant you the good fortune He has seen fit to deny us, His humble servants."

"Don't spit," Elizabeth told Brydd. "I did so twice on the way over, once for each of us."

Now that they could forget about the Halleys, the Cannaways went ahead with preparations for the wedding. Amalie stole the girl, gave her Brydd's old room at Kennett, then made her stand for an hour at a time whilst she pinned and tucked, hemmed and stitched, and gradually turned a white satin dress into a lace-trimmed gown that seemed to ebb and flow with the draught. Mary Nott came to help, though she was far too wise to do more than hold the pins. September 18, 1700, would belong to Elizabeth. But the week before was Amalie's, and heaven help anyone, including lifelong friends like Mary, who dared to interfere.

Sophia and Joseph hired a special express rider and sent him galloping from Bristol with a beaded purse. Had he known his jewels, he'd have recognised that the purse was sewn with pearls from Sumatra. But he was content to get Ezra's mark on the bill of receipt, ensuring he'd get his shilling when he trotted back to Bristol.

Margaret worked feverishly to make an embroidered shawl, and this, too, was sent by messenger to Kennett.

Brydd and the craftsman postponed further work on the gig. They locked the door of the coach house and spent the next four days making something that was far more essential—a bed for the bride and groom. This was one of the few things he had not brought back from Devizes, and he made a secret appeal to Amalie, asking for a feather mattress and whatever she could spare in the way of bolsters, pillows and coverlets. The plea was relayed to Mary Nott, who returned to Lockeridge and went to work with needle and thread.

Brydd purchased a slate-grey outfit in Marlborough, topped it off with an expensive moleskin tricorn, and added boots, gloves, shirt and cravat.

Then he visited a goldsmith's shop near the Market Hall and made the man parade his stock. The goldsmith's own daughter offered her hand, smiling as she wore this ring and that for his inspection. In the end his choice was plain and simple, and she said, "If only one of you young gentlemen would mean it. I'm sure that when I get married I shall take off the ring again and wrap it in paper, by force of habit."

"Now that," Brydd told her, "I very much doubt."

"So do I," she agreed. "It'll be a grave robber that gets it from me."

The spacious oak bed was completed, taken upstairs in sections, then jointed together and nailed firm. The room was at the western end of the house, one window looking south toward the orchard, the other across the kitchen garden and in the direction of the gate and the tree-flanked pond. Newly floored, and with a table, chair and wardrobe, the whitewashed bedroom would be airy in the daytime, intimate at night. At least, Brydd thought, that's the intention.

Mary Nott had the mattress and bedclothes carted across from Lockeridge, and Brydd was astonished to see that Alfred's widow had found time—made time, more likely—to embroider the letter C on the pillow cases and oatmeal-coloured sheets.

The day before the wedding, Sophia and Joseph arrived from Bristol. They insisted on a full tour of Faxforge, though Sophia refused to enter the bedroom. "It's unlucky for a sister to see where her brother and his bride—"

"And you a lady of Bristol!" Brydd exclaimed. "You sound as though you'd never left the Kennett Vale."

"There are some things," she told him, with a nice, haughty air, "that would be deemed unlucky in heaven. Now show me the orchard, for we must then get on to Kennett." She waited for Joseph to precede her from the house, then turned and kissed her brother and said, "I'm so happy for you both, you know. There's a strength of character about Elizabeth that's, well, that's matched I think by yours. But tell me, why Faxforge? Why not The-Brydd-Cannaway-Coach-and-Wagon-Making-Establishment?"

"Because," he retorted, "there are some things that would be deemed unmemorable, even in Wiltshire."

Sophia and Joseph were leaving as William and Margaret arrived, accompanied by Nathan, and the driveway was blocked for an hour. Then Sam Gilmore came down from the "Blazing Rag," bringing a wagonload of kegs and bottles, an assortment of roasted meats and a box of taps and bungs for the barrels. He stood on the frontboard of the dray and yelled lustily, "There may be a wedding, but there'll be no party 'less the family clear the way!"

It was William who'd escort the groom to the church at Lockeridge, so he and Margaret and Nathan would stay the night, sleeping in the range-warmed kitchen. They helped Sam set up the benches, hung the meat from hooks in the larder, then uncorked one of the flagons. Brydd sat with them for a while, content to be the victim of their banter. Then he accompanied the innkeeper to the gate and waited in the gathering darkness as Sam said, "You'll be a married man tomorrow, and I'm pleased for you, for you both. But I'm best pleased to have you as neighbours. You'll bring this end of the valley wide awake, and there's a need for that. Here's my hand, Master Brydd. Now then, let me know if the hubs will clear the gateposts."

He walked around the pond and between the spindly young trees in the orchard and into the yard, the barrels and bottles stacked ready, the planks set out on their trestles. He thought about Elizabeth and the ruinous state of Overhill, then of the gig he was building for William and the proudly pregnant Margaret. He thought of the von Kreutel coach that he'd helped bring down the slope from Cherhill, and of the heron in a hat, and of the worldly Mariette in the crimson-lit room in Paris. And of the werewolves of Essenbach and the race down the Danube and the duel between Johann and Albany. He thought of the murderous Hach, and of Elizabeth again and the promising state of Faxforge.

And he thought of Vitar, but looked slowly around the yard and saw no ghost of her, none at all.

Time to sleep, if he was to be at his best tomorrow. And life had certainly encouraged him to be so by providing Elizabeth Darle.

❋

Sam Gilmore returned at midday to drive Brydd, William, Margaret, Nathan and John Stallard to the church. However, at the last moment the craftsman muttered something to the innkeeper, then told Brydd he'd follow on horseback. The groom nodded equably. "As you wish, Master Stallard, though it *is* a wedding cart, you know. We're not going off to prison."

At about the same time, another wagon was leaving from the smithy at Kennett, this one carrying the bride and the elderly Cannaways, Sophia and Joseph Biss.

The doctor and Mistress Cable would come in a gig from Marlborough, the Darles in a cart from Overhill, Ben Royton on a shire horse, with his wife clinging tight around his waist.

The Faxforge wagon arrived at Lockeridge, where William and Nathan promptly abandoned the groom to the care of Margaret, whilst they stood in grinning conversation with the skeletal Reverend Swayle. The talk was of that night on the downs, when William had lumbered in pursuit of Abram Hach and Nathan and the clergyman had followed along the moonlit track.

Linking her arm in Brydd's, Margaret said, "Let's hope the villagers don't imagine we're the ones to be married." Then she pulled a face, as though their guilt had been discovered, and laid a hand on her belly, seven months rounded with child.

More nervous than he'd expected, Brydd was grateful for any distraction, and walked his sister-in-law unhurriedly toward the porch.

The Reverend Swayle greeted him, nodded Nathan and Margaret inside, then made sure the Cannaway brothers knew what they should do, and when, and that there'd be no unseemly fumbling for the ring.

They took their places at the front of the pews. "Your hat," William hissed. "It never rains in church." Brydd winced a smile, bared his head and wondered if the service would ever start, if the bride would bother to arrive, if his boots would squeak as he knelt.

The guests filed in, nodding and saluting and edging along the pews. Hired musicians, well practised in these affairs, tuned up, looked to the clergyman for a lead, then serenaded the guests with a medley of popular tunes.

And then there was an outburst of applause, not for the musicians, there was nothing special about them, but because Elizabeth Darle was being escorted along the aisle on her father's arm.

Brydd glanced across at her and thought her more beautiful

than even— Yes, he could think it, than even the chased golden
cross on the altar . . .

❋

Had he been a farmer, they'd have scattered grass on the path to
the lych-gate. Scraps of leather would have served for a cobbler or
tanner, sheepskins for a butcher or shepherd, rushes for a basket
maker, a line of pans for a smith. But for a carpenter, or wheelwright, or coachmaker-to-be the guests strewed the path with
wood shavings, though they were careful not to shower the bridal
pair.

There were several who wanted to be the first to say it, but it
was Amalie who insisted on holding open the gate and murmuring, "Master Cannaway. Mistress Cannaway." Brydd leaned down
to kiss her, and then Elizabeth kissed her, and the guests roared
and shouted and set off for the party.

The yard wagon had been decorated with flowers, and the newlyweds were expected to stand throughout the five-mile journey
home. This was only fair if the occupants of the villages and vale
were to see them as they passed. It was a triumphal procession,
after all, though worse than balancing on a ladder to mend windows.

Brydd kissed his wife, and Elizabeth kissed her husband, and he
could tell her now how beautiful she looked, and she had time to
study the ring and compliment him on his suit and tricorn hat.
They saw John Stallard canter past; but whatever his mission,
he'd only time to wave a greeting before disappearing around the
next bend in the road. It was drawing toward evening now, the
sun red beyond Beckhampton, the chalk still white on the out-
crops, or turned pink above the purple of the valleys.

Their driver, Sam Gilmore, gestured at the "Blazing Rag." "I
left someone in charge there tonight. First time I've done so in
years. Hope the place isn't wrecked when I get back."

"How could it be?" Brydd queried. "Most of your customers are
on their way to Faxforge. The fellow you put in charge will spend
the hours tossing cheese at the mice."

"Oh, that's the way," Sam laboured. "The humour of a newly-wed. Tossing cheese at the mice." He cracked the whip harmlessly in the air and reserved his grin for the horses.

❋

They reached the yard and could see why the craftsman had raced ahead. In the precious few moments he'd gained, he had flinted several dozen candles, lit every available lantern and started a small, safe bonfire near the gate. As the wagon rolled in, Elizabeth hung her arms around Brydd's neck and leaned against him, her eyes brightened by the lights.

Sam Gilmore—who else?—played landlord. He stood mugs beneath the ale barrel, mugs beneath the cider, then turned away to uncork the brandy or run sherry from its keg, swinging back in time to close the taps and lift the mugs on the table, the froth climbing to the brim. Not much one could teach Sam Gilmore when it came to serving drinks.

Jed and Clare rode in, having left George to follow with Ezra and the others. It was the first time Jed had been to Faxforge, though not the first time he'd been at the bottle. Whooping noisily, he attempted to circle the yard, and Sam was forced to heave aside one of the unopened barrels, to avoid it catching the wheel.

"That's enough of that, Master Darle. Get yourself down from there before you tip the damn thing over." John Stallard had already taken the bridle, and Jed shrugged and clambered to the ground. Clare squealed that he'd left her stranded, seemed to enjoy the sound she was making and squealed again.

There were carts at the gate now, and along the drive, and turning to find space in the yard.

Several villagers had been asked to the party, and a number of them had brought their cousins and friends and neighbours. But they were decent people, and Brydd was in no mood to close the gate. He and Elizabeth strolled from group to group, then went their separate ways, the bride to be surrounded by the younger women, who insisted she turn to let the lace ebb and flow, then show off her beaded purse, her shawl, most especially her ring. Brydd was cornered by men who wished to talk business—the repair of a haycart, the need for a barrow—and by those who had jokes to tell about the bridal bed and how the innocent young maiden had seen for the first time what he'd brought her, and had grumbled, "It's supposed to be pleasure, not work. You should have left the hoe in the garden."

The Reverend Swayle had managed to shed his robes, don a long black frock coat and hitch a lift to the party. He kissed Elizabeth, shook hands with Brydd, then moved from end to end of the food table, loading down his platter. The guests made room for him, fearful that he'd spill his hoard.

He approached Amalie Cannaway, who said, "What a pity, sir. I'd already prepared you a plate."

"And I'll see it's not wasted," he assured her. "I'll be finished with these morsels in no time."

Dr. Barrowcluffe arrived, escorting his housekeeper and impervious to gossip. Even Sam ran short of hands and fingers, and John Stallard offered his services. "Though don't you rush me, Master Gilmore, or the yard'll be awash."

The guests discovered, to their stifled amusement, that the doctor loved to dance. His wish was granted, for the musicians had been brought along from the church, and they played to make one leap or weep, according to the tune. It was one of the sights to be treasured, Dr. Barrowcluffe with a hand on his ill-fitting wig, his knees thrown out and his heels kicked up, his free hand curled in a fist against the waistband of his coat. Not much, it seemed, one could teach Dr. Barrowcluffe when it came to the jig and jaunter.

There was, inevitably, a certain amount of stumbling and groaning as the drink found its way through the body. Nathan prevented a skirmish between Jed and a man from Beckhampton and, sometime later, Ezra Cannaway used his authority to stop a neighbour from Kennett taking a swing at— "Hell, Jedediah, there are men recruiting for the militia, if you've an appetite to fight!"

And then, as the level of the bottles was lowered and the candles burned down, the bride and groom were invited to dance together, alone, in the centre of the yard. The musicians played a favourite tune, "Trotting the Downs," and the young couple turned in a circle about the yard, the bride's gown set off nicely by her husband's sober grey. The music filled the air and was caught by the candlelight and lifted up and sent spilling beyond the long, tiled roofs. Another sight to be treasured, no question of that.

They danced to the fading echo of the tune, and then Brydd bowed and Elizabeth curtseyed, and they waved their farewells to family and friends. Brydd thought then, and not for the first time, of the angular gentleman with whom he'd crossed half of Europe. If anyone was missing from the party it was the heron, for no one could make a party go better than Albany d'Enville Zurrant Jevington. Who on earth had attended more parties, or been the more welcome guest?

It would have been nice had he been there, but it was enough for Brydd to think of him at this moment and imagine he was somewhere in the crowd.

Amalie wished to kiss the bride, as did Margaret and Sophia. But Ezra and William and Joseph were content to raise their hands in salute, then see if the musicians could play something a bit more lively.

❄

On their way from the yard the newlyweds each took a lantern, though it was easy enough to follow the path between Stallard's cottage and the garden. But the house itself was in darkness, and they needed the lights to see their way indoors. Brydd checked that none of the guests had taken refuge in the kitchen or parlour, closed the door and swung the bar in place. Elizabeth waited, then lifted the hem of her gown and climbed the stairs. Brydd followed, the lanterns showing how well the old craftsman had laid and levelled the boards.

She waited again, not knowing which of the three small rooms would be theirs. Brydd said, "Shall I—?" and edged past her, opening the door. Then they stayed where they were for a moment, on the landing, and gazed at each other and kissed, the lanterns held away from their clothes.

They entered the bedroom, where Brydd tilted the glass of his lantern and touched four candles to the flame. Elizabeth glanced at the furnishings and the bed and the windows, this one overlooking the orchard, this one giving a view of the garden, now tilled and planted, and of the trees around the pond. Views for to-morrow.

Brydd placed the candles in holders around the room, then ex-tinguished the lanterns. He could see Elizabeth was nervous—he, himself was nervous—though not as wide-eyed, or trembling. "Now," he murmured, and took her in his arms and kissed her again. "Will you like the room, do you think?"

"Everything about it," she whispered. "I shall like every-thing—"

A barrage of pebbles clattered against a window. It was the one that gave a view of the garden; only now the view was of Jed Darle, stamping back and forth to keep his balance, then digging for another handful of stones. He shouted up at them. "Shadows on the glass! You're giving yourselves away!" Then he changed his tune, and there was a whine in his voice as he complained, "More people here than when I got wed! And I never went away!"

Brydd turned from the window. "I'll see him back to the party. He's too drunk to know what he's doing, but he'll be there half the night—"

"No, wait." Elizabeth nodded toward where her brother was rooting for stones. "Someone's coming to collect him."

Jed was shouting again. "Sleep well, dear Elizabeth, if he'll let you! Sleep well, old Brydd, if you've nothing better to do! Don't be concerned for me! I've made all manner of friends, more than when I got—" And then the watchers saw George Darle clamp a hand around the back of Jed's neck and heard snatches of what he said. "No son of mine . . . his own sister . . . last public display or I'll have you out of Overhill, you and the rest of them . . . to the yard and stay there . . . and without a bottle in your hand . . ." Then he propelled his son away from the garden, his fingers like a horseshoe around Jedediah's neck.

"Well, well." Brydd nodded. "Your father seems to have taken charge again."

"Since you've equipped the place with shutters," Elizabeth said, "won't you close them?"

He did so, at both the windows, and then there was nothing more to disturb them.

He undressed her slowly, without fumbling, and she wondered

—no—and put the thought from her mind. No matter who else—no—it was enough that she felt at ease with him, and was excited by what he was doing and that it was he who was doing it after the years of his ignorance, the years of his absence, the too many years of regret . . .

She laid the light satin gown across the foot of the bed, noticed the initial that was embroidered on the sheet and pillows, smiled as he lifted her up and drew back the coverlet and leaned down to kiss her again. She'd expected him to put the room in darkness, but was glad he had not.

And then he was with her and leading her, stroking her fine pale hair and showing her how *she* could lead *him*, and she was startled by the force of him, though not frightened, nothing he'd do would frighten her, not even this and, making her cry out, this . . .

"I used to touch . . . But only in the dark, I used to touch myself . . . I used to touch my breasts, yes, like that . . . And there, like that . . . But you were the one who was . . . It was you, Brydd, it was . . . But it was never really like . . . It was never— Oh, my love—Brydd . . ." He drove himself into her, and when he shouted, it was a shout redoubled, part for the surging pleasure of the act and in part because he was shouting, "Elizabeth—Elizabeth!"

"Sleep well," had Jedediah said, "if he'll let you?" "Sleep well," had he said, "if you've nothing better to do?" But, no, they didn't care to. Nor try to. Not tonight.

FOURTEEN

More so in the towns than the cities, but most of all in the villages and hamlets and isolated farmsteads, they were at the mercy of the weather. Townsfolk might huddle indoors from the rain, or raise a protective awning above their stalls. The wind might loosen a few roof tiles, or sweep a pedestrian off his feet. A bolt of lightning might shatter a chimney stack, or strike the stirrups of a horse. But it was the snow that inflicted the greatest hardships, for it placed a curfew on the land.

The first snowfall came in the final days of October, and it continued to fall for the next eleven weeks.

At Faxforge, Brydd and Elizabeth counted eight days in eighty during which the clouds rearmed, but otherwise the snow swirled and tumbled and settled, levelling the ground and blocking the road between Devizes and the "Blazing Rag." And not only that road, but all the others, and every farm track and downland path for twenty miles around.

Brydd had delivered the gig to William and Margaret just in time, for it was still October when he drove the vehicle to Melksham. Even so, he was forced to lead the horse the last half mile, with the snow clinging to the wheel spokes. His brother had invited him to stay the night, then agreed, "Yes, it might be bet-

ter if you get back whilst you can." He put his arm around the ra-
diant Margaret, nodded unnecessarily at the size of her belly and
told Brydd they'd send word the very day the child was born,
sometime in late November. "And then there'll be the baptism.
We must get Ezra and Amalie over for that. And then there'll be
the family reunion at Kennett for Christmas. We'll have had
more celebrations this year than ever before."

"We will"—Brydd nodded—"if the snow's gone by then."

"Take my word for it," William told him. "I've a nose for these
things. The winter will be as good as over by the time my son is
born. Our son. Son or daughter, whichever."

Brydd left them standing by the gig. They'd said it for him, of
course, but he would say it himself—it was a damn fine piece of
work, with its special springs and triple-varnished body, its cane
and leather hood, bow-back shafts and, to please them most of all,
a crest painted on the doors, depicting a fluted column heaped
around with bricks. What better for Master William Cannaway,
Stonemason?

By the time he'd reached Faxforge, the snow had covered the
middle bar of the gate. Elizabeth had done her best to clear the
garden path, and Stallard had wrapped the dolphin pump in
straw. Brydd told him William's views on the weather, then
asked, "Do you think it's an early winter and that we'll soon be
free of it?"

"I'll tell you if it's a Monday," Stallard growled, "on a Monday."

❄

By the third week the roads were impassable.

Those farmers who had intended to bring their carts and
wagons for repair could no longer do so.

Those who had already brought them were forced to leave them
at Faxforge until the downland tracks were clear.

Those vehicles that were too badly damaged to be brought
from the farmyards would remain in their sheds until Brydd or
Stallard could get to them, again when the tracks were clear.

The master of Faxforge had made no provision for this over-
whelming assault, this undeclared war by the weather. He'd

counted on at least another month of work and payment, as had everyone else. Now was the time for settling bills, but what good was that when the snow had already done the settling?

The yard at Faxforge was filled, not only with snow, but with tipcarts and wagons, the sheds were lined with water butts, wheels, row upon row of spades and pitchforks, rakes and hoes, all with new shafts and handles. And all repaired, at least for the moment, at Brydd Cannaway's expense.

But why should this matter? He still had his leather bag, ajingle with coins, did he not? Why should the onetime gambler care if it snowed until Easter? He'd given his wife enough money with which to purchase food and stock the larder, had he not? He'd made sure of that, as a priority. Or had he not?

The truth was, he hadn't. And no, the bag was not ajingle with coins. They'd gone to buy Faxforge, and the timber from Mary Nott, and the tiles and planks and glass he'd needed to put the place in shape. And on the horses he'd purchased. And on the making of William's gig. And on fifty special bolts he'd had made up in Bristol. And on leathers he'd had cured and sent from Chippenham. And on expensive chalks and paper. And on the wedding. And on the coachmaking tools that were far in advance of anything Alfred Nott had owned, but that Brydd had decided he must have.

There was some food in the larder, though not much. And, as for the bag, the only thing ajingle was the fastening on the strap.

And then came the fifth week of snow, and the seventh, and the ninth. The young Cannaways were imprisoned for Christmas, not knowing if Margaret's child was alive and healthy, nor how the mother had fared. They saw nothing of Ezra and Amalie, who must have spent the time fretting for news of their son and daughter-in-law and their late-November child. They saw nothing of Sam Gilmore, who probably *was* tossing cheese at the mice, nor of anyone else, save John Stallard, who'd agreed to desert his cottage and sleep in the kitchen.

The only mark of cheer, though it was enough to make Brydd yell for joy, was when, in the seclusion of their bedroom, Elizabeth said, "There are things that are supposed to happen to a woman. They happen every month of the year. But they haven't happened, not for two months now, and I think, well, I believe I have your child." She saw the smile scatter along his lips and heard him laugh, then blinked as he yelled to clear the snow from the roof. "Oh, that'll do nicely as a piece of news! That'll see out the winter, by God, yes, it will!" He caught her up in his arms and kissed her and said, "Does your condition allow—?"

"What, allow us to make sure and certain? Oh, for quite a while yet."

❊

It snowed for the tenth continuous week, and the eleventh, and a day or two of the twelfth. And even when it no longer fell, it was there on the ground, well used to Wiltshire and reluctant to leave.

Elizabeth had already been slicing the meat thin, and then thinner. But now she kept the skin and bones and gristle, and boiled them once for their nourishment, then again, just for the taste. She baked stale bread three times over, and used it to give some body to the ever weaker soups. She watered the cider, to make it last, and attempted a brew of fruit and herbs, so Brydd and Stallard would have something warm to drink. It was a miserable concoction, but the men drank it and gazed at each other, then managed a smile for the brewer. The next time Elizabeth was alone, she sipped the stuff, grimaced with distaste and poured it away, outside the kitchen.

It was not until mid-February that the snow surrendered its hold on the county, or rather turned it to mud. The coaching roads remained impassable, though a horseman could now follow the ridges of the hills and make contact with his family and friends.

This was how William travelled, to bring news of his son, Waylen. The birth had been quick and easy, and Margaret was— "Well, as you'd expect her to be, the most perfect of mothers."

Brydd told his brother that Elizabeth, too, would soon bear a child. "In June or July, that is, though I think of it as soon! It was never hard to imagine you as a father. You'll also be most perfect, William, though I wonder if I'll have the patience for it."

"You will," Elizabeth smiled. "For the first, and the others."

They took their good news to Kennett, approaching the village by way of Roman Hill. The elderly Cannaways had spent a trapped and cheerless winter, though they had allowed themselves a drink on Christmas Eve, another on Christmas Day, a third at the start of the year. However, with their sons come over from Melksham and Faxforge, Ezra and Amalie saw nothing wrong in a mug of cider or a smallish measure of sherry.

And then, in March, another rider travelled the ridge of the hills, though the news he brought was not the kind to raise a smile or a glass. It was Jedediah Darle, weeping much of the way.

He reached Faxforge, reined in near the gate, then hesitantly walked his horse along the path to the yard. The mud was still inches deep, but he stayed where he was as Brydd floundered toward him, for the sight of the garden reminded Jed of the wedding night, and of his drunken performance with the pebbles.

"Jed."

"Master Brydd."

"Brydd's what it's always been between us, so far as I'm aware. You look damn dismal, Jed. What's to do?"

"I was hoping I might—I'd care to speak with my sister, if I may. I'll not say a word in her disfavour, you've my promise on that. She'll be free to call on you—"

"Yes, she will."

"—and I'll leave the door open, if you like. But I would care to speak with her. I must do that, and you must let me, if only for a moment." He was weeping again, his hands describing gestures that he could not yet match with words. Brydd felt a sudden surge of pity for him, and his mind was filled with shards of remembered outings, of discussions they'd had together, resolving the ways of the world. He'd been a good friend, the younger Jed, with his loyalty and wild-flung punches, and it hurt to see him like this.

"Elizabeth is in the kitchen. If you follow the path around . . ." He went forward again to take Jed's horse, then turned away, as though not to notice the tears. Jed mumbled too many thanks—for taking the horse, and allowing him in, and letting it still be just Brydd—then tramped along the path, but never once on the garden.

He wiped his face dry on the way to the kitchen, rapped on the doorpost and assembled a grin for Elizabeth. It was never a more meaningless grin, but he kept it in place whilst she greeted him and hugged him and told him to sit at the table.

"Shall you drink something?"

"No, not today."

"It's well watered, I assure you."

"Even so." He'd sat so close to the end of the bench that it had started to tip. Then he edged along it, his hands in front of him, his fingers whitened at the knuckles.

"I'd not blame you if it made you happy . . ."

Elizabeth watched in silence.

"I'd not blame you if you told me it would happen. They did their best to make you miserable, we all did, I know, and I'd not blame you if—"

"What is it, Jedediah?"

He sighed and shuddered, assembled another grin, then let it fall. "I led the horse into ditches all the way here, and I'm doing the same with words. But the truth is—the truth is— It's that the Halleys have left us. They've packed their bags, stolen what food they need and left us. They were gone two days ago, but it's taken me a while to— Well, they're gone, that's the thing."

Elizabeth sat across from him, on the other bench. "And what does your wife think about it?" she asked gently.

He stared at her as though she was making mockery of him, then pounded down on the table and said, "Oh, no, you've not understood! I mean all of them! I mean the Halleys and the Halleys-cum-Darles! They've all left, parents and daughter and child! My wife, she's gone! And my daughter, oh, yes; oh, yes, oh, she's been snatched away! I meant to be clear about it! They have all left us! All!"

The pounding had brought Brydd to the doorway, but he could see that Elizabeth was safe and stayed outside. Jed was hunched forward, mouthing something about theft, not just from the scullery, but the cot.

He remained with his sister for an hour, then left as quietly as he'd come. Elizabeth had offered him what comfort she could, though her sympathy ran dry at every thought or mention of the

Halleys. She was naturally concerned for Jed and her father. But she could not fully accept that the Halleys had gone for good. They might make their way to a nearby town or another county, but where would they go when they'd finished the food from Overhill? Who would give shelter to such a miserable band as they? There was every likelihood that they'd come crawling back to the farm.

Jed himself might welcome Clare and would certainly welcome the baby. But George would once again be forced to support the good-for-nothing parents—and in the knowledge that they would never put their foot on a spade, nor turn a forkful of earth.

Sorry though she was for Jed, Elizabeth admitted to herself that the Darles were well rid of the Halleys. She tapped absently at the table. A fine way for her to think, being glad that her brother's wife had taken their child and run off . . .

✵

Elizabeth asked her husband for money, so that she might replenish the larder. "I've no wish to squabble with you, but I was cutting at the very bone this winter, then digging the marrow from it. I'm not here for the comfort of it, Brydd, but I've seen the tools you've bought, and those fancy bolts, and the leathers strung on poles in the sheds. Leather enough to shoe an army, but not enough food for us. I really don't see why you're secretive about it—"

"Why should you when I'm not?"

"Very well, you're not. There's the money you won as a gambler, and I'm simply asking you—"

"There is no money. Not in the bag. We'll have to wait and be paid for the repairs."

"There's no money at all, save what we're owed?" She turned away in confusion, then swung back to ask, "But—if you say this now, you must have known it months ago, when we were first caught by the snow! But you said nothing about it, not a word about it! And yet you bought paints and varnishes, foreign woods and the greatest array of tools ever seen in a country workshop. You knew we had no money, yet were in ignorance of what winter would bring—"

"Word's gone around. There'll be those that want good coaches."

"—and you thought not to tell me, confident that— What was that claim? Word's gone around? Well, yes, Brydd Cannaway, it might have gone around, but who has ever heard it? Or is that another secret?"

"The weather's clearing," he said grimly. "There'll be squires and townsfolk coming along, and prepared to pay ahead."

"I pray they do," she said, matching his tone, "for the weather may be clearing, but the shelves in the larder are already clear!"

It was the first time in their marriage that she turned away from him in bed, and it made things worse that he let her do so.

❄

A number of farmers arrived to collect their rehandled tools or their mended wagons or their greased and sharpened ploughs. They were proud and decent men, and they made it clear to Brydd that, in the wake of such a destructive winter, they would not be able to settle their bills for quite a while. Would he prefer to keep the wagons or implements, or would he allow them to be used until the crops had been harvested, the fruit gathered, the sheep sent to market?

"Of course you must use them. But find a place for me, fairly high on your list. My crop's inedible."

Elizabeth felt herself cast, as though in a village play, but badly cast, miscast, a long way out of character. She did not wish to chant for pennies, or tell the man she loved that it was no good to wait until harvest time, or market time, or any other time but now. She did not wish to badger him or nag, or, worst of all, turn away in the bed. But how else could she bring the truth to his attention? How else could she feed her husband, and the innocent craftsman, unless she reminded him that flour made bread but that coins purchased flour?

❄

And never in March did a squire trot along to order a coach, or a townsman arrange for a gig.

Night after night Brydd closeted himself in the parlour, redrawing the entire range of vehicles that had once been housed in his satchels, until they and all the rest had been drowned.

Day after day he carried out mundane repairs, taking money from those who could pay it, then handing it over to his wife. It allowed Elizabeth to buy coarse salt, but no sugar; the cheapest vegetables, but not even the cheapest meat; dark, verminous flour, in which weevils and roaches burrowed or lay dead.

In need of sympathy, she approached John Stallard and said, "With all this fine wood in store, and the tools and strapping and suchlike, why don't you just make an ordinary wagon? There's farmers who might buy a wagon, though they'd never buy a gig."

"Master Cannaway has other ideas."

"I see. And what do you think, Master Stallard?"

"I think," he murmured, "that the world is short of ideas, Mistress Cannaway, and that I could live forever on dark bread and cabbage."

She gazed at him, then grinned and asked, "Have I been admonished?"

"Not at all. You've been complimented on the way you run your house."

Well, she thought later, what a cunning old devil he is. He's left me no choice but to go on scraping the leaves and picking out the roaches.

❊

And never in April did a gentleman call at Faxforge to slap down money for a curricle, or a merchant come asking for something elegant, with a certain swish about it, a certain polished air.

❊

But, in May, Sam Gilmore came down from the "Blazing Rag" and asked Brydd to walk with him around the pond. Then when they were out of sight of the house, the innkeeper said, "I want no credit for this, whatever it is, and by God, I want no blame. But I found it nailed to the beacon post, and thought you could make some sense of it." He then produced a poster, and waited to see if his two-mile journey had been wasted.

What had appealed to the illiterate Sam was the woodcut of a coach that rushed across the paper. However, what appealed to Brydd Cannaway were the words beneath. Holding it away from the shadowing trees, he read the contents of the poster slowly and carefully, and his blood began to sing.

CONTEST

It is put at Public Notice that, on April Twenty-Fifth in the Year Seventeen Hundred and One, the Well-Known Merchant Edward Flowerdewe—at present residing in the Fragrant and Harmonious City of Swindon—did offer a tender for the Services of a Coach!

BUT NO ORDINARY COACH!

The Aforenamed Edward Flowerdewe, much Concerned by the Lack of a Service through the Wool-Towns, wishes to Set Up such a Service between the Stations of Swindon, Marlborough, Pewsey, Devizes, Melksham, Chippenham and—again—Swindon. He therefore offers to the Coachmakers of Wiltshire the Chance to Manufacture a Suitable Conveyance, to the Acclaim of Passengers and in the Expectation of a Very Reasonable Reward.

HOW THE COACH MUST PERFORM

This Coach must Complete a Sixty-Mile Circuit, Commencing at Swindon and Passing Through All and Each of the Aforenamed Towns, and Stopping Over at Their Designated Stations for One Quarter of an Hour. The Circuit—Swindon to Swindon—must be Completed within Two Clear Days. The Overnight Stop shall be at Devizes. Each Coach shall Transport Fourteen Passengers, Six of whom shall be Insiders, Eight of whom shall be Outsiders, their Luggage to be weighed at the Finish. Of these Passengers, All but Two shall be Adults, or Above Four-feet-and-six-inches in Height.

REWARD!

Stewards and Time-Keepers being posted at all the Designated Stations, the Circuit shall be deemed Open at the First Stroke of Six O'Clock in the Morning on August First, in the year Seventeen Hundred and One. The First Coach to Complete the Circuit and Comply with the Rules shall be Declared the Winner. The Owner of the Winning Coach shall receive One Hundred Guineas. The Next-to-Winner shall receive Twenty Guineas. The Aforenamed Edward Flowerdewe shall present the Monetary Prizes and Award a Contract for Two Such Coaches, According to his Discretion.

GOOD LUCK TO WILTSHIRE!

Brydd stared hard at Sam Gilmore. "Do you know the gist of this? Has anyone explained it to you?"

"No. I told you; I found it posted up and thought, from the picture—" He shrugged. "Does it say something as might be of advantage?"

"By God, it does, Sam!" He rapped the paper with his fist. "It might have been made to measure."

"Glad to hear it. Now tell *me* what it says."

❊

He read the notice aloud to Elizabeth and John Stallard. When he'd finished there was silence for a moment. Then Elizabeth said, "The garden's recovered better than I'd expected from the winter. So long as you gentlemen will accept a diet of vegetables, you'd best turn your hands to the coach."

He went forward and kissed her, not minding that Stallard was there. "A hundred guineas." She nodded. "Now that would improve the diet."

"It would, but it's not the money I'm after. It's this—where is it?—yes, the 'Two Such Coaches.' That's the prize I'm after!" He turned to the craftsman. "Well, Master Stallard? Can you and I make a winning coach in less than three whole months?"

"I doubt it," Stallard said promptly. "I doubt it to the hilt. But I've been wrong once or twice in my life."

❊

By June, the mistress of Faxforge had grown heavy in the belly. She was less rotund than Margaret had been and continued to tend the garden until the snatches of pain became more frequent and sent her to sit or stand by the fire.

She was rarely alone, for news of her forthcoming child and, for all Stallard's doubts, of the forthcoming coach had brought friends and neighbours to comfort the wife and spur along the husband. They were quite straightforward about it; they wished to see the mistress growing fatter and the master growing thin. They understood that no one would be allowed inside the yard. After all, that, too, was a womb, in which the coach was taking shape. The spokes and felloes would be brought together to form the wheels, the bones of the bed attached to the axles, the body shaped and the limblike shafts secured in place. It was an inanimate object, though it, too, was growing and moving within the protective walls of Faxforge.

Nevertheless, it worried Brydd to learn that there were at least four other entrants in the contest, all from established yards in the surrounding wool-towns. It was rumoured that two of these coaches were almost ready to take the road, and that the third had been designed by the Frenchman, Linon, hastily brought over from Paris.

On the last day of June, and with Dr. Barrowcluffe and Amalie in attendance, Elizabeth Cannaway gave birth to a son. She was not helped by her slender hips, but she chose to take a wadded glove between her teeth and scream into the coarse grey linen. The child was small, though Elizabeth was heartened by Amalie's assurance that the lumbering William had been not much bigger. "And, as for Brydd, he was the puniest thing I ever saw. Scarcely worth the trouble."

"Oh, yes," Elizabeth whispered, "I think so."

She presented her husband with their son, as Margaret had done for William, and joked feebly that the Cannaways were siring workers for their yards. They had already agreed on a name—Jarvis—and that was the name Brydd murmured, "Elizabeth . . . I never was so happy . . . Unless on the day we were wed . . ."

"That'll do nicely," she remembered. "That'll see me up from the bed, so it will. Now, my love. Welcome young Jarvis, then crack mugs with Dr. Barrowcluffe and Master Stallard. There's a bottle hidden behind the flour bin. *Unwatered* cider, for the occasion."

❊

He had travelled from Calais to Paris, but never from Swindon to Marlborough. He'd fled eastward with Albany toward Strasbourg and Stuttgart, though he had yet to ride from Marlborough to Pewsey. He'd braved the werewolves of Essenbach, but not the country road between Pewsey and Devizes. The wooded *Vorstädte* around Vienna, yes, but not the track that linked Devizes with Melksham. He knew the way to Györ, but was ignorant of the way north from his brother's town to Chippenham, and thence across to the finish at Swindon.

Brydd Cannaway could claim a certain knowledge of Europe, but none at all of the Sixty-Mile Circuit.

He would anyway require a second driver, someone experienced in handling a coach-and-four. And, God willing, someone who knew his way around. One name sprang immediately to mind, though Brydd had no idea if the man was still in the district. He might be, though he might also have been hired to drive one of the other coaches.

Nevertheless, Brydd left word with Sam Gilmore at the "Blazing Rag," then returned to Faxforge and the last, shrinking month.

On July tenth the men hitched up the coach and, whilst John Stallard walked beside it, Brydd drove the vehicle slowly around the yard. One of the wheels was chafing against the bodywork; the harness traces needed adjusting; a lynchpin was working loose; the pivot of the splinter bar needed attention. More work, and they'd try it again.

Two days later Elizabeth came to see what her husband had poetically named the "Cannaway Carrier." She considered it the most elegant vehicle she had ever seen, then amended her opinion. It was elegant, though it was more than that—it'd need to be—and a better word was arrogant. Quite in character, she smiled, with its designer.

The front wheels were of average size, the rear wheels half the height again. The hubs had been painted a cornflower blue, the spokes and rims as black as a burnished stove. There was a high driving bench, another bench behind it, another behind that that faced the rear of the coach and shared common foot space with a final railed seat. There was room up there for the two drivers and nine outside passengers, one more than Edward Flowerdewe demanded.

Below the two middle benches was the enclosed body of the coach, again with two full-width seats, though these had been covered and backed with leather. Six inside passengers could ride in comfort, seven or eight at a pinch. The baggage would be carried in two wickerwork baskets, one below the driving bench, one at the rear. Each was protected by a waxed leather lid, to keep the spatter of mud from the cases.

There were four lanterns, on a level with the upper edge of the doors. It was these door panels that boasted the words "Cannaway Carrier." Above the panels were square glassed-in windows.

It *was* elegant, *and* arrogant, and Elizabeth insisted that Brydd take her on two jaunts around the yard. She travelled first as an inside passenger, then beside him on the driving bench. When the joyrides were over he asked, "Was it worth the waiting?"

"For a coach like this? I should say it was, my love. Though there's still the race."

"There's still the road," he admitted. "It's not yet been out of the yard."

He took it out next morning, with Stallard clinging unhappily to the high swaying bench. Brydd was content to let the horses get used to the weight and the myriad creaks and rattles of wood and leather, metal and glass.

"I shan't be coming with you around the circuit," Stallard warned him. "I hope that's understood. I can handle my tipcart, the seat's near the ground. But we must be ten feet up on this thing."

"Near enough," Brydd agreed. "But don't worry, I've another driver in mind." Yes, he thought, in mind, though not yet in sight . . .

Whey-faced and miserable, the craftsman accompanied Brydd on another dozen testing runs, each at a smarter pace than the last. They worked on by the light of the coach lanterns, making further adjustments, and Elizabeth abandoned serving food in the kitchen, bringing it out to them, spoon and bowl, in the yard. Vegetable broth, or vegetable stew, or vegetable soup, for they'd now scarcely enough money to keep the lanterns in oil.

❋

They heard that George and Jedediah had been seen working together in the sheep pens near Overhill. There'd been no word of the Halleys, nor of Clare and the child she'd taken with her, though they were probably in a distant part of the country, failing again. It was small comfort, but better than nothing, to learn that father and son had made peace and might yet save their farm from ruin.

❋

The inhabitants of Faxforge pooled their pennies. It seemed clear to Brydd that he would not find the driver he wanted in time. He would therefore take the Carrier to Swindon and hire whoever he could get in the marketplace. Anyone he could get.

And then, three days before he was due to leave, a wiry figure came stumping in at the gate. He still bore the scar of the bullet that had turned along his cheekbone, but it had narrowed and darkened with the years and he looked quite dashing, did the impish Step Cotter.

He grinned and winked at Elizabeth, who took an instinctive liking to him, and there was much talk of the von Kreutel coach and that slab-faced creature, what was his name, Carl-Maria Show-and-Hold?

"I was over beyond Chippenham," Step explained. "There's a young woman there who— Well, never mind, I was tiring of her anyway. Not half as pretty as you, Mistress Cannaway. Not a quarter. Where was I?"

"Over beyond Chippenham."

"That's it, yes, and I was in conversation with this stage-wagon driver, and he said he'd come through Beckhampton, and that old Sam Gilmore had said that Master Brydd Cannaway of Faxforge —nice name, that—had said he, you, wanted to see me. Wouldn't have nothing to do with the race, I suppose?"

"The coach is out in the yard. And harnessed up."

"See it, could I?"

John Stallard joined them and they waited in silence as Step Cotter studied it, inspected it, explored it, and all to the ceaseless accompaniment of clicks and grunts, hums and whistles, the sucking of air through his teeth.

He clearly enjoyed the suspense, and Stallard growled, "Is he hoping to buy it, or what?" Then Step clambered on to the bench and took it five times around the yard.

No fool the young Elizabeth, who smiled up at him and said, "That's the smoothest I've seen it run, Master Cotter. The race would be assured if you were up there with my husband."

"Just what I was thinking." He nodded. "Cotter and Cannaway. Well—Cannaway and Cotter."

❋

He slept in the kitchen, and quickly resigned himself to a diet of vegetables.

When Brydd was sure his wiry old friend had all but fallen in love with the Carrier, he admitted that he could only pay Step in pennies. "I'll understand if you turn the job down. A man should be paid for his work. On the other hand, whoever drives the winning coach will be something of a hero in the county. But you might, I suppose, value coins above fame. There are such people, so I've heard."

"And all the time," Step told him, "I thought deceit belonged to Herr Show-and-Hold. But you, old Brydd, you could give lessons."

"We'll be setting off at dawn. You'd best drive, to get the feel of it. And, Step? I put word out for you. No one else."

"Thank you," Step grinned. "But who else is there?"

❋

Elizabeth and Stallard insisted on coming to the gate. True to his word, the craftsman was a compendium of advice, and eventually Step Cotter growled from the driving bench, "Is he the owner, or what?"

Elizabeth reached up and Brydd down and he kissed her hand and said, "Three days and we'll be back. My parents—"

"Yes, they're coming over today." She blinked and said, "I

know you'll win. I always knew you'd win." And he told her, "I've
done so already, don't you know, in all but the race."

✻

They travelled the twelve miles to Swindon in three hours flat. It
was faster than they'd expected, for the road was appalling,
though they did not yet have their fourteen passengers or the baggage.

They met Edward Flowerdewe, his face as rosy as his name
suggested, his hands as pink as petals. He was a cheerful, easygoing man, who seemed both surprised and excited that his offer
had been taken seriously. "Five coaches!" he enthused, and then,
with tactful impartiality, "and all of them magnificent. Shall I
have someone, ah, show you the agreement, Master Cannaway?"

"By all means, Master Flowerdewe, though they'll not need to
read it to me."

"Very good. A scholarly entrant. Sets a perfect tone for the
affair. Now then," he bustled, "you and Master, ah, Cotter, yes,
that's the name—with so many entrants it's hard to remember—
you two will stay the night at the 'Black Horse.' At my expense,
of course. A meal, bed, ale in the morning, it's all been arranged.
You'll set off, well, you all will, all five of you, from the milepost
just along the road there. One-minute intervals. I thought that
should suffice. And you, which is to say the 'Cannaway Carrier,'
you will be the last to leave. Nothing untoward in that, I assure
you. I put all the names in a hat—there's witnesses if you'd care
to question them—all in a hat, yes, and that's the way it came
out. Shall you mind being the last?"

"Yes, Master Flowerdewe. But only at the finish."

The successful merchant of Swindon patted his thighs at that
one. "Only at the finish! Well, there's a scholar's wit, if ever I
heard it! Only at the— Oh, my lord— Oh, dear."

"Do you think he's good for the money?" Cotter hissed. "He's
not just some mad old fool, is he?"

Brydd elbowed him silent, read his copy of the agreement,
signed it with a pen held ready by Flowerdewe's clerk, then doffed
his hat to the merchant and took the Carrier around the marketplace to the "Black Horse."

Had the innocent Edward Flowerdewe known the darker ways

of men, he need not have reserved the five tavern rooms. This was
the night before the race, when strange things tended to happen
to an opponent's coach; when it was most advisable to stand
guard and carry a hefty stick. The prize was a hundred guineas or
twenty guineas, and the contract for "Two Such Coaches," and
only a fool would take to his bed—then find a wheel sawed
through in the morning.

Brydd and Step had their share of visitors, self-styled friends
who had come to see the Carrier.

"We'll not be in town for the start tomorrow, so we wondered
if we might—?"

"You might do as you wish," Brydd told them, "at a distance of
fifty feet. There's enough light in the yard to show you the Carrier. Those are the seats, and that's the door, and the wheels are
front and back. But come much closer, gentlemen, and I shall
brain you with this bar."

A few of the self-styled friends continued to act the part.
"There's no call for such incivility, sir. We only thought to admire the vehicle. And wish you the best of luck." They huffed and
puffed and strode away, as though terribly insulted, leaving Cotter
to call down from his perch on the driving bench, "They had saws
and chisels, did you see?"

But most of the self-styled friends abandoned all pretence, cursing the vehicle and its drivers, and hoping the damn thing turned
over, crushing everyone on it to a pulp.

"Did you notice," Cotter said, "an axe and some rope and a
lever?"

It was a long night. And then, suddenly, less than an hour to
the start.

❋

It seemed as if half the inhabitants of Swindon had volunteered
to ride as passengers, and that all of Swindon had turned out to
watch the start. The knowledgeable Step Cotter thrust his way
into the yard, choosing husband and wife, mother and daughter,
the two permitted children and anyone else who shouted, "Step!"
The best passengers were those who'd sit quiet, or those he knew,
or those who'd be willing to help lift the Carrier from a ditch.

Flowerdewe was there, flapping and bustling, enjoying the time of his life. All these magnificent coaches! All here at his invitation! Dare he say it, at his command? Oh, lord. Oh, dear . . .

There were similarities in the vehicles, though one designer had placed the baggage on the roof and the outside passengers on a fenced-in platform at the rear. Another had harnessed his coach to six horses. Another vehicle had three drivers. Another had wheels the size of a merry-go-round.

Cotter and Cannaway—Cannaway and Cotter—heard the tolling of a town clock and saw the first coach race for Marlborough, its three drivers hunched forward on the bench.

One minute more, the minute that Flowerdewe had thought would suffice, and then the merry-go-round was turning.

Another minute, and the coach-and-six were off.

A longer moment, it seemed, before the passenger-platform went lurching on its way.

And then an interminable time, Brydd and Step grinning without humour, their passengers settling, inside and out. "Come on, come on," Step muttered. "Come on, you mad old fool!"

"Away!" Flowerdewe shouted, a fine silk handkerchief fluttering from his hand. "Away you go! Away!"

Brydd flicked the reins. The horses twitched and pulled forward. The traces came taut. The Carrier moved, rolled past the milepost, rattled south from Swindon, swayed and rocked on the road. They were already minutes behind the leader, the four minutes lost forever.

❈

They might have been in procession, most of the way to Marlborough. The triple-driven coach kept its lead, though the merry-go-round was already discovering that the larger its wheels, the more the mud tended to stick.

It was eleven miles between Swindon and Marlborough, and the coach-and-six might have gained a mile on the run. Even so, the merry-go-round stayed ahead of it by the simple tactic of taking the width of the road.

Behind the coach-and-six came the passenger-platform, its weight so much in the rear that the front wheels tended to lift. But it, too, held its position and blocked the "Cannaway Carrier."

They were timed at Marlborough, where it was nine in the morning. Then after the statutory fifteen-minute stop, the race continued to Pewsey.

There were several sharp bends on the way, and it was at one of these that the merry-go-round came to grief. Its massive wheels failed to navigate the turn, plastered as they were with mud, and the horses ran one way, the vehicle another. There were spills and shouts, though no one was injured, and the coach-and-six went past, then the passenger-platform, then the Carrier, all of them witness to what Step Cotter promptly termed "The mis'ry-go-round."

The triple-driven vehicle was leading into Pewsey, the coach-and-six thundering behind it. And then there was a gap, as the passenger-platform swung and swayed, making certain that the Carrier came in last. The scarred and wiry Step could be seen standing on the bench, howling imprecations at the wagon that blocked his path. "That's what it is, a wagon! Get it aside! Put it in the ditch! Damned wagon, I'd not use it to haul stones! Pull over, you—"

"Come on down," Brydd told him. "We'll take him on the way to Devizes."

It was ten minutes past eleven in Pewsey; almost half past the hour before the Carrier raced off.

And now they were faced with their longest run of the day— the longest single run the Carrier had ever made. Apart from the journey to Swindon in order to enter the race, the Carrier had travelled eleven from Swindon to Marlborough, and a further six to Pewsey. But now there was almost fourteen miles to be covered before Devizes, a road that Step Cotter ominously described as "Perfect for cattle."

The triple-driven coach held its lead, though it was never lost from sight by the storming coach-and-six. The passenger-platform was still in the race, though its once willing volunteers were now crying to be abandoned, the platform dipping and yawing like a ketch in a storm. They clawed their way across the roof of the coach, intent on arresting the drivers, but they were punched and elbowed, their only virtue now being in the weight of their bodies and the number of their heads. Edward Flowerdewe had demanded eight outside passengers, and eight outside passengers would arrive in Devizes. Too bad if they didn't like their perch.

A hundred yards behind, and with his hands on the reins, Brydd said, "I'm going past; what do you think, Step, quick, what do you think?"

"It'll get no smoother, that's for sure." He turned back and shouted, "Aren't you tired of trailing that sickly lot? Hang on tight then, and Master Cannaway will see us by!" He winked at the ladies, punched a fist in the air for the men, then faced forward again and said, "Now, old Brydd, or we'll be smashed between some nice chalk banks."

Brydd lifted his back from the rails, his buttocks from the seat and crouched like a jockey, snarling at the team and leading them wide of the wallowing platform.

He ran it so close that the sickened passengers aboard the platform reached out to change coaches. For a few thundering seconds there was less than a foot between hub and hub, lantern and lantern, the passengers' imploring hands and the rails of the "Cannaway Carrier." But then Step Cotter was grinning in triumph at the other angry drivers and the Carrier was clear and running between the banks.

And all the time the triple-driven coach retained its lead, arriving in Devizes eight minutes ahead of the coach-and-six, and a good half hour before the Carrier.

"It's win and lose," Brydd told the stalwart Cotter. "We've overtaken two of the coaches, but we're now further behind than when we started. Four minutes in Swindon, do you remember? And thirty here."

"Never put your money on a race," Step told him. "Things turn out odd."

Once again, they ignored the rooms the well-meaning Flowerdewe had reserved for them and took it in turns to sit guard on the bench, or sleep like inside passengers, in the coach. The real passengers had a marvellous time, their meals and dormitories paid for by the organiser of the Sixty-Mile Circuit.

❈

In the kitchen at Faxforge, Elizabeth Cannaway crooned her child asleep, then glanced around at Ezra and Amalie and the patient John Stallard. She hoped they could not see her trembling, nor that Jarvis would sense it and awake. "I think they must have done well, don't you, with such an arrogant—Carrier—as that? Wouldn't you say they'd done quite well today?"

Amalie smiled and Ezra nodded thoughtfully and Stallard said, "Best workmanship. Best drivers."

❀

The leaders were allowed their advantage of time, and the triple-driven coach was released at six in the morning.

Eight minutes later the coach-and-six sprang forward on its way to Melksham, though a further twenty minutes elapsed before the Carrier was allowed to leave. The passengers fretted, some of them determined that their coach should win, and annoyed that the drivers had let it fall behind.

"I saw plenty of places—*plenty of places*—where you could have overtaken that platform. I told you so at the time. I was shouting—didn't you hear me?—plenty of places, *way* beyond Pewsey, and *way* before—"

Step Cotter rose on the bench, and Brydd pushed him down again and leaned on the backing rail and said, "It's not the time to ask you, sir, since I've never seen you drive. But be assured, sir, I shall seek you out at the end of this race and take you by the turn of your collar and sit you here beside me, and then, sir, you shall have your chance! Or if you are not a driver out of work, then sit tight and keep quiet and let us choose the places you always seem to see!" He slapped the rail to make the metal ring and resumed his place on the bench.

"'Cannaway Carrier'! Seeing you off! Five down to four down to three down to two—and away you go!"

Eight miles to Melksham, with an angry Brydd at the reins.

❀

Maybe the all-knowing passenger had helped, or maybe Brydd was fully aware that he couldn't afford to lose. Maybe it was the knowledge that Elizabeth and the young Jarvis and his elderly parents and the splendid Stallard were expecting him to win that drove him on. Or maybe, and most likely, it was Brydd himself,

refusing to believe that anyone, Frenchman or Austrian, Englishman or German, could design a better coach than this.

Melksham was the one town he knew, thank God for brother
William, and he entered it wheel-to-wheel with the coach-and-
six.

There was the regulation halt, and the entire coach shook as
William lumbered forward and slapped the lettered door. Margaret was with him, and they both wanted to know about
Elizabeth and young Jarvis, and why the "Cannaway Carrier"
wasn't first in the race—"Hello, Step, how are you? You're just
the fellow he needs,"—and if Ezra and Amalie were well, and
what a grim winter it had been—"I had stones that split with the
frost!"

And then there was only time to embrace and shake hands and
be helped along by the cloud of good wishes. "The Carrier's as
good as the gig!" William bellowed. "Can't see how you'll fail!"

❊

The timekeeper at Melksham had decided that, though the coach-
and-six had arrived wheel-to-wheel with the Carrier, it should be
the coach that left first, since it had left first from Swindon. Step
Cotter was up from the bench again, but Brydd eased him down
and they planned to overtake the coach before Chippenham.

In the event, they had no need to swerve and go wide of it, for
one of the six-strong team collapsed on the way, bringing down
its matcher and one of the leaders and leaving the coach in
confusion by the road.

So now there was only the triple-driven coach, the one designed
by Linon the Frenchman, the one that was half an hour ahead.

But by the time the Carrier reached Chippenham, the gap had
been narrowed to twenty-seven minutes, and the longest stretch
to come.

Brydd and Cotter cleared Chippenham at noon, with forty-two
miles of the circuit completed and an interrupted eighteen miles
to go. Times and figures, miles and minutes, though it boiled
down to this. The "Cannaway Carrier" would have to make up
the twenty-seven minutes in the eighteen miles—plus a horse's
neck for good measure. In short, they would have to go faster
than they'd gone.

Step knew the way, and Brydd asked him to shout it out. Four miles without sight of the leading coach. Then a glimpse of it, disappearing over the hill the Carrier had yet to climb. Six miles, and it was still a mile ahead. Step Cotter took the reins, whilst Brydd asked the passengers to stay in their seats. "It's no help if you make things sway."

The know-it-all muttered, "Plenty of places where you might have spurred ahead. I could see them coming. Plenty of them. We'll never win it now."

However, several of the outside passengers had the grace to encourage the drivers. "I'm sure you're doing your best, Master Cannaway, Master Cotter. If it was up to me, you'd win."

Brydd winced his gratitude and at the eight-mile mark took back the reins.

The leading coach was still almost a mile ahead.

There was no change at the ten-mile mark, nor at the twelve.

By the time Step Cotter said, "Fourteen; four to go," the gap had shrunk to less than five hundred yards. But what was that, compared to a horse's neck?

Brydd took over, and thought himself gaining. And then he could see he was gaining, and that something was wrong with the triple-driven coach. Two miles to go, and the Carrier was gaining, not a feather of doubt about that!

He stamped and shouted, urging the team onward, and Step shouted with him, and the passengers disobeyed and crowded forward in their seats. A mile to go—only a mile—and the "Cannaway Carrier" was charging the other coach, charging it down to the ground!

"We shan't make it!" Cotter shouted. "Damn me if we shan't!" And the approach to Swindon was wide enough to take two coaches, running as best they could . . .

And then it was over, and they had passed the decorated finish post and the "Cannaway Carrier" had lost by sixty yards. By sixty yards. Sixty dismal yards in sixty miles.

❊

Edward Flowerdewe awarded the first prize of one hundred guineas to the owner of the triple-driven coach. He awarded the second prize of twenty guineas to Brydd Cannaway. The arrangement was that Flowerdewe would then be taken on a short, triumphal run aboard the winning coach. The drivers conferred with the owner, who then told Flowerdewe that the horses needed time to recover their wind. The drivers had meanwhile evicted their passengers and were keeping the crowd at a distance from the machine.

Step Cotter stood on the driving bench of the Carrier and yelled something at Flowerdewe. Then he snapped, "By God, I know their game!" Without further ado, he clambered to the ground and elbowed his way alongside the "Successful Merchant of Swindon." Dulled by his defeat, Brydd gazed emptily at where Step and the winning owner were competing for Flowerdewe's attention. He imagined he could hear the man saying, "Oh, my lord. Oh, dear."

Then Step returned and called up to him, "He wants us to wait with the Carrier over there."

"Why's that?" Brydd asked tonelessly. "Why?"

"Just for a while," Step told him. "And we must both be on the bench, where he can see us."

❋

Next morning they brought the Carrier back to Faxforge. As Brydd turned the horses in through the gate, he could see Ezra and Amalie waiting for him on the path. John Stallard was there, and Sam Gilmore, mugs and a small keg of brandy at his feet. And a little way off was Elizabeth, her hair combed neat, one hand resting lightly on a wooden cot—property of Jarvis Cannaway.

They'd agreed that Stallard should do the asking. He could read nothing in Step Cotter's expression, nor in Brydd's weary features. He waited until the last chink and rattle of the coach had died away, then said, "Well, Master Brydd? Were you first around the circuit?"

Brydd gazed down at him, at the innkeeper, at his parents, at his wife and child. Then he shook his head slowly and said, "No, we came in second." He said it again—"Second,"—but this time he was grinning and holding up the bag full of coins.

"Second across the line, Master Stallard, so I can't say we won the race. There was sixty yards in it at the end, though the winner was done for, run into the cobbles, coming apart at the seams. Its axles were breaking, its springs sunk flat, half its bolts sheared through. You ask Step what *wasn't* wrong with it."

"Doors were still on," Step said generously.

And then Brydd again took up the story. "There should have been a victory run for Flowerdewe, but the winner couldn't have travelled to the end of the street and back. He told us later, when he'd inspected it, that he wouldn't have had it as a barrow for his leaves!"

There was something in his son's voice that made Ezra Cannaway start forward. "But he does want the Carrier," Brydd shouted. "And two more as soon as we can make them, and maybe another two for the future. Ezra? Amalie? Sam? Master Stallard? You're witness to the first of a fleet!" And then, looking directly at Elizabeth, he repeated quietly, as though for her ears alone, "The first of a fleet, my love. The first, 'Cannaway Carrier.'"

He handed the reins to Step and swung himself to the ground. Sam Gilmore lifted the brandy keg and prepared to fill the mugs. The men shook hands and then Step Cotter launched into a mile-by-mile account of the race. Leaving him to it, Brydd embraced his mother, then joined Elizabeth beside the cot. She put her arms around his neck and he lifted her to him. Their kiss was unabashed, though he felt her tremble and knew she was on the brink of tears. "Now," he murmured, "weeping's a poor welcome. I leave such squalls to Jarvis." He gazed down at his son, smiled, then led Elizabeth gently away, so they might walk and talk in the warm summer air.

"It was worth it, I think," he said. "If you think so."

"It always was," she told him. And then with a fine finality, "It always will be." They walked on along the path and through the orchard. The new Carriers could stay as planks until tomorrow.